D0436543

THE SECULAR WIZARD

BY CHRISTOPHER STASHEFF
Published by Ballantine Books:

A Wizard in Rhyme:

HER MAJESTY'S WIZARD

THE OATHBOUND WIZARD

THE WITCH DOCTOR

THE SECULAR WIZARD

Starship Troupers:

A COMPANY OF STARS

WE OPEN ON VENUS

A SLIGHT DETOUR

Christopher Stasheff

>>>>>>>>>>>>>>>>>>>>>>>>>>>>>>>>

THE
SECULAR
WIZARD

Book IV of
A Wizard in Rhyme

>>>>>>>>>>>>>>>>>>>>>>>>>>>>>>>>

A DEL REY® BOOK · BALLANTINE BOOKS
NEW YORK

A Del Rey® Book
Published by Ballantine Books

Copyright © 1994 by Christopher Stasheff

All rights reserved under International and Pan-American Copyright
Conventions. Published in the United States by Ballantine Books,
a division of Random House, Inc., New York, and simultaneously
in Canada by Random House of Canada Limited, Toronto.

Library of Congress Cataloging-in-Publication Data
Stasheff, Christopher.
A Wizard in rhyme / Christopher Stasheff.
    p.   cm. — (The secular wizard ; bk. 4)
"A Del Rey book."
ISBN 0-345-37600-5
I. Title. II. Series: Stasheff, Christopher.
Secular wizard ; bk. 4.
PS3569.T3363W59   1995
813'.54—dc20   94-22480
CIP

Manufactured in the United States of America

First Edition: January 1995

10 9 8 7 6 5 4 3 2 1

THE SECULAR WIZARD

Prologue

The tall roan stallion looked up and nickered. The other horses crowded to the doors of their stalls to watch Accerese the groom as he came into the barn with the bag of oats over his shoulder.

A smile banished his moroseness for a few minutes. "Well! At least *someone*'s glad to see me!" He poured a measure of grain into the trough on the stallion's door. "At least *you* eat well, my friends!" He moved on down the line, pouring grain into each manger. "And well-dressed you are, too, not like we who—"

Accerese bit his tongue, remembering that the king or his sorcerers might hear anything, anywhere. "Well, we all have our work to do in this world—though some of us have far less than—" Again he bit his tongue—but on his way out of the third stall he paused, to trace the raw red line on the horse's flank with his finger. "Then again, when you *do* work, your tasks are even more painful than mine, eh? No, my friends, forgive my complaining." He opened the door to the fourth stall. "But you, Fandalpi, you are—" He stopped, puzzled.

Fandalpi was crowded against the back wall, nostrils flared, the whites showing all around its eyes. "Nay, my friend, what—"

Then Accerese saw the body lying on the floor.

He stood frozen in shock for a few minutes, his eyes as wide and white as the horse's. Then he whirled to the door, panic moving his heels—until he froze with a new fear. Whether he fled or not, he was a dead man—but he might live longer if he reported the death as he should. Galtese the steward's man would testify that Accerese had taken his load of grain only a few minutes before—so there was always the chance that no one would blame him for the prince's death.

But his stomach felt hollow with fear as he hurried back across the courtyard to the guardroom. There was a chance, yes, but when the corpse was that of the heir apparent, it was a very slim chance indeed.

King Maledicto tore his hair, howling in rage. "What cursed fiend has rent my son!"

But everyone could see that this was not the work of a fiend, or any other of Hell's minions. The body was not burned or defiled; the prince's devotion to God had won him that much protection, at least. The only sign of the Satanic was the obscene carving on the handle of the knife that stuck out of his chest—but every one of the king's sorcerers had such a knife, and many of the guards besides. Anybody could have stolen one, though not easily.

"Foolish boy!" the king bellowed at the corpse. "Did you think your Lord would save you from Hell's blade? See what all your praying has won you! See what your hymn-singing and charities and forgiveness have brought you! Who will inherit my kingdom now? Who will rule, if I should die? Nay, I'll be a thousand times more wicked yet! The Devil will keep me alive, if only to bring misery and despair upon this Earth!"

Accerese quaked in his sandals, knowing who was the most likely candidate for despair. He reflected ruefully that no matter how the king had stormed and threatened his son to try to make him forsake his pious ways, the prince had been his assurance that the Devil would make him live—for only if the old king lived could the kingdom of Latruria be held against the wave of goodness that would have flowed from Prince Casudo's charity.

"What do I have left now?" the old king ranted. "Only a single grandson, a puling boy, not even a stripling; a child, an infant! Nay, I must rear him well and wisely in the worship of Satan, or this land will fall to the rule of Virtue!"

What he didn't dare say, of course, was that if his demonic master knew he was raising little Prince Boncorro any other way, the Devil would rack the king with tortures that Accerese could only imagine—but imagine he did; he shuddered at the very thought.

"Fool! Coward! Milksop!" the king raged, and went on and on, ranting and raving at the poor dead body as if by sheer rage he could force it to obey and come alive again. Finally, though, Accerese caught an undertone to the tirade that he thought impossible, then realized was really there:

The king was afraid!

At that, Accerese's nerve broke. Whatever was bad enough to scare a king who had been a lifelong sorcerer, devoted to Evil and to wickedness that was only whispered abroad, never spoken openly—whatever was so horrible as to scare such a king could blast the mind of a poor man who strove to be honest and live rightly in the midst of the cruelty and treachery of a royal court devoted to Evil! Slowly, ever so slowly, Accerese began to edge toward the stable door. No one saw, for everyone was watching the king, pressing away from his royal wrath as much as they dared. Even Chancellor Rebozo cowered, he who had endured King Maledicto's whims and rages for fifty years. No one noticed the poor humble groom edge his way out of the door, no one noticed him turn away and pace quickly to the postern gate, no one saw him leap into the water and swim the moat, for even the sentries on the wall were watching the stables with fear and apprehension.

But one did notice his swimming—one of the monsters who lived in the moat. A huge slaty bulge broke the surface, oily waters sliding off it; eyes the size of helmets opening, gaze flicking here and there until they saw the churning figure. Then the bulge began to move, faster and faster, a V-shaped wake pointing toward the fleeing man.

Accerese did not even look behind to see if it was coming; he knew it would, knew also that, fearsome as the monster was, he was terrified more of the king and his master.

The bulge swelled as it came up behind the man. Accerese could hear the wash of breaking waters and redoubled his efforts with a last frantic burst of thrashing. The shoreline came closer, closer . . .

But the huge bulge came closer, too, splitting apart to show huge dripping yellow fangs in a maw as dark as midnight.

Accerese's flailing foot struck mud; he threw himself onto the bank and rolled away just as saw-edged teeth clashed shut behind him. He rolled again and again, heart beating loud in his ears, aching to scream but daring not, because of the sentries on the walls. Finally he pushed himself up to his feet and saw the moat, twenty feet behind him, and two huge baleful eyes glaring at him over its brim. Accerese breathed a shuddering gasp of relief, and a prayer of thanks surged upward within him—but he caught it in time, held it back from forming into words, lest the Devil hear him and know he was fleeing. He turned away, scrambling over the brow of the hill and down the talus slope, hoping that God had heard his unvoiced prayer, but that the Hell spawn had not. Heaven preserved him, or perhaps simply good luck, for he reached the base of the plain and raced toward the cover of the woods.

Just as Accerese came in under the trees, King Maledicto finally ran out of venom and stood trembling over the corpse of his son, tears of frustration in his eyes. Yes, surely they must have been of frustration.

Then, slowly, he turned to his chancellor. "Find the murderer, Rebozo."

"But Majesty!" Rebozo shrank away. "It might be a demon out of Hell . . ."

"Would a demon use a knife, fool?" Maledicto roared. "Would a demon leave the body whole? Aye, whole and undefiled? Nay! It is a mortal man you seek, no spawn of Hell! Find him, seek him! Bring the groom who found my son, question him over what he saw!"

"Surely, Majesty!" Rebozo bent in a quick servile bow and turned away. "Let the groom stand forth!"

Everyone was silent, staring about them, wide-eyed. "He was here, against the stall door . . ." a guardsman ventured.

"And you let him flee? Fool! Idiot!" Maledicto roared. He whirled to the other soldiers, pointing at the one who had spoken. "Cut off his head! Not later, *now*!"

The other guardsmen glanced at their mate, taken aback, hesitant.

"Will no one obey?" Maledicto bellowed. "Does my weak-kneed son still slacken your loyalty, even in his death? Here, give me!" He snatched a halberd from the nearest guardsman and swung it high. The other soldiers shouted and dodged even as the blade fell. The luckless man who had seen the groom tried to dodge, but too late— the blade cut through his chest. He screamed once, in terror and in blood; then his eyes rolled up, and his soul was gone where went all those souls who served King Maledicto willingly.

"Stupid ass," Maledicto hissed, glaring at the body. He looked up at the remaining, quaking guardsmen. "When I command, you *obey*! Now *bring me that groom*!"

They fled to chase after Accerese.

It was the chancellor who found and followed the fugitive's trail to the postern and down to the water's edge, the company of guardsmen in his wake.

"Thus it ends," sighed the Captain of the Guard. "None could swim that moat and live."

But Rebozo glanced back fearfully at the keep, as if hearing some command that the others could not. "Take the hound into the boat," he ordered. "Search the other bank."

They went, quaking, and the dog had to be held tightly, its muzzle bound, for it squirmed and writhed, fearing the smell of the monsters. Several of them lifted huge eyes above the water, but Rebozo muttered a charm and pointed at each with his wand. The great eyes closed, the slaty bulges slid beneath the oily, stagnant fluid—and the boat came to shore.

Wild-eyed, the dog sprang free and would have fled, but the soldiers cuffed it quiet and, as it whined, cringing, made it smell again the feed bag that held Accerese's scent. It began to quest here and there about the bank, gaining vigor as it moved farther from the water. Its keeper cursed and raised a fist to club it, but Rebozo stayed his hand. "Let it course," he said. "Give it time."

Even as he finished, the dog lifted its head with a howl of triumph. Off it went after the scent, nearly jerking the keeper's arm out of its socket, so eager was it to get away from that fell and foul moat. Rebozo shouted commands, and half a dozen soldiers ran off after the hound and its keeper, while a dozen more came riding across the drawbridge with the rest of the pack, led by a minor sorcerer in charcoal robes.

Down the talus slope they thundered, away over the plain, catching up with the lead hound, and the whole pack belled as they followed the trace into the woods.

They searched all that day and into the night, Rebozo ordering their efforts, Rebozo calling for the dogs, Rebozo leading the guardsmen. It was a long chase and a dark one, for Accerese had the good sense to keep moving, to resist the urge to sleep—or perhaps it was fear itself that kept him going. He doubled back, he waded a hundred yards through a stream, he took to trees and went from branch to branch—but where the hounds could not find his scent, sorcery could, and in the end they brought Accerese, bruised and bleeding, back to the chancellor, who nodded, eyes glowing even as he said, "Put him to the question!"

"No, no!" Accerese screamed, and went on screaming even as they hauled him down to the torture chamber, even as they strapped him to the rack—where the screaming turned quickly into hoarse bellows of agony and fear.

Rebozo stood there behind his king, watching and trembling as Maledicto shouted, "Why did you slay my son?"

"I did not! I did never!"

"More," King Maledicto snapped, and Rebozo, trembling and wide-eyed, nodded to the torturer, who grinned and pressed down with the glowing iron. Accerese screamed and screamed, and finally could turn the sound into words. "I only found him there, I did not kill . . . AIEEEE!"

"Confess!" the king roared. "We know you did it—why do you deny it?"

"Confess," Rebozo pleaded, "and the agony will end."

"But I did not do it!" Accerese wailed. "I only found him . . . YAAHHHH!"

So it went, on and on, until finally, exhausted and spent, Accerese told them what they wanted to hear. "Yes, yes! I did it, I stole the dagger and slew him, anything, anything! Only let the pain stop!"

"Let the torture continue," Maledicto commanded, and watched with grim satisfaction as the groom howled and bucked and writhed, listened with glowing eyes as the screams alternated with begging and pleading, shivered with pleasure as the cracked and fading voice still tried to shriek its agony—but when the broken, bleeding body began to gibber and call upon the name of God, Maledicto snarled, "Kill it!"

The blade swung down, and Accerese's agony was over.

King Maledicto stood, glaring down at the remains with fierce elation—then suddenly turned somber. His brows drew down, his face wrinkled into lines of gloom. He turned away, thunderous and brooding. Rebozo stared after him, astounded, then hurried after.

When he had seen his royal master slam the door of his private chamber behind him, when his loud-voiced queries brought forth only snarls of rage and demands to go away, Rebozo turned and went with a sigh. There was still another member of the royal family who had to be told about all this. Not Maledicto's wife, for she had been slain for an adultery she had never committed; not the prince's wife, for she had died in childbirth; but the prince's son, Maledicto's grandson, who was now the heir apparent.

Rebozo went to his chambers in a wing on the far side of the castle. There he composed himself, steadying his breathing and striving for the proper combination of sympathy and sternness, of gentleness and gravity. When he thought he had the tone and expression right, he went to tell the boy that he was an orphan.

Prince Boncorro wept, of course. He was only ten and could not understand. "But why? Why? Why would God take my father? He was so good, he tried so hard to do what God wanted!"

Rebozo winced, but found words anyway. "There was work for him in Heaven."

"But there is work for him here, too! Big work, lots of work, and surely it is work that is important to God! Didn't God think he could do it? Didn't he try hard enough?"

What could Rebozo say? "Perhaps not, your Highness. Kings must do many things that would be sins, if common folk did them."

"What manner of things!" The tears dried on the instant, and the little prince glared up at Rebozo as if the man himself were guilty.

"Why . . . killing," said Rebozo. "Executing, I mean. Executing men who have done horrible, vicious things, such as murdering other people—and who might do them again, if the king let them live. And killing other men, in battle. A king must command such things, Highness, even if he does not do them himself."

"So." Boncorro fixed the chancellor with a stare that the old man found very disconcerting. "You mean that my father was too good, too kind, too gentle to be a king?"

Rebozo shrugged and waved a hand in a futile gesture. "I cannot say, Highness. No man can understand these matters—they are beyond us."

The look on the little prince's face plainly denied the idea—denied it with scorn, too. Rebozo hurried on. "For now, though, your grandfather is in a horrible temper. He has punished the man who murdered your father . . ."

"Punished?" Prince Boncorro stared. "They caught the man? Why did he do it?"

"Who knows, Highness?" Rebozo said, like a man near the end of his fortitude. "Envy, passion, madness—your grandfather did not wait to hear the reason. The murderer is dead. What else matters?"

"A great deal," Boncorro said, "to a prince who wishes to live."

There was something chilling about the way he said it—he seemed so mature, so far beyond his years. But then, an experience like this *would* mature a boy—instantly.

"If you wish to live, Highness," Rebozo said softly, "it were better if you were not in the castle for some months. Your grandfather has been in a ferocious temper, and now is suddenly sunken in gloom. I cannot guess what he may do next."

"You do not mean that he is mad!"

"I do not *think* so," Rebozo said slowly, "but I do not *know*. I would feel far safer, your Highness, if you were to go into hiding."

"But . . . where?" Boncorro looked about him, suddenly helpless and vulnerable. "Where could I go?"

In spite of it all, Rebozo could not help a smile. "Not in the wardrobe, Highness, nor beneath your bed. I mean to hide you outside the castle—outside this royal town of Venarra, even. I know a country baron who is kindly and loyal, who would never dream of hurting a prince, and who would see you safely spirited away even if his Majesty were to command your presence. But he will not, for I will see to it that the king does not know where you are."

Boncorro frowned. "How will you do that?"

"I will lie, your Highness. No, do not look so darkly at me—it will be a lie in a good cause, and is far better than letting you stay here, where your grandfather might lash out at you in his passion."

Boncorro shuddered; he had seen King Maledicto in a rage. "But he is a sorcerer! Can he not find me whenever he wishes?"

"I am a sorcerer, too," Rebozo said evenly, "and shall cloud your trail by my arts, so that even he cannot find it. It is my duty to you—and to him."

"Yes, it is, is it not?" Boncorro nodded judiciously. "How strange that to be loyal, you must lie to him!"

"He will thank me for it one day," Rebozo assured him. "But come, now, your Highness—there is little time for talk. No one can tell when your grandfather will pass into another fit of rage. We must be away, and quickly, before his thoughts turn to you."

Prince Boncorro's eyes widened in fright. "Yes, we must! How, Rebozo?"

"Like this." Rebozo shook out a voluminous dark cloak he had been carrying and draped it around the boy's shoulders. "Pull up the cowl now."

Boncorro pulled the hood over his head and as far forward as it would go. He could only see straight in front of him, but he realized that it would be very hard for others to see his face.

Rebozo was donning a cloak very much like his. He, too, pulled the cowl over his head. "There, now! Two fugitives dressed alike, eh? And who is to say you are a prince, not the son of a woodcutter wrapped against the night's chill? Away now, lad! To the postern!"

They crossed out over the moat in a small boat that was moored just outside the little gate. Boncorro huddled in on himself, staring at the huge luminous eyes that seemed to appear out of the very darkness itself—but Rebozo muttered a spell and pointed his wand, making those huge eyes flutter closed in sleep and sink away. The little boat glided across the oil-slick water with no oars or sail, and Boncorro wondered how the chancellor was making it go.

Magic, of course.

Boncorro decided he must learn magic, or he would forever be at others' mercy. But not black magic, no—he would never let Satan have a hold on him, as the Devil did on his grandfather! He would never be so vile, so wicked—for he knew what Rebozo seemed not to: that no matter who had thrust the knife between his father's ribs, it was King Maledicto who had given the order. Boncorro had no proof, but he didn't need any—he had heard their fights, heard the old man ranting and raving at the heir, had heard Prince Casudo's calm, measured answers that sent the king into veritable paroxysms. He had heard Grandfather's threats and seen him lash out at Casudo in anger. No, he had no need of proof. He had always feared his grandfather and never liked him—but now he hated him, too, and was bound and determined never to be like him.

On the other hand, he was determined never to be like his father, either—not now. Prince Casudo had been a good man, a very good man, even saintly—but it was as Chancellor Rebozo had said: that very goodness had made him unfit to be king. It had made him unfit to live, for that matter—unsuspecting, he had been struck down from behind. Boncorro wanted to be a good king, when his time came—but more than anything else, he wanted to live.

And second only to that, he wanted revenge—on his grandfather.

The boat grounded on the bank and Rebozo stepped out, turning back to hold out a hand to steady the prince. There were horses in waiting, tied to a tree branch: black horses that faded into the night. Rebozo boosted the boy into the saddle, then mounted himself and took the reins of Boncorro's horse. He slapped his own horse's flank with a small whip, and they moved off quietly into the night, down the slope and across the darkened plain. Only when they came under the leaves did Prince Boncorro feel safe enough to talk again. "Why are you loyal to King Maledicto, Rebozo? Why do you obey him? Do you think the things he commands you to do are right?"

"No," Rebozo said with a shudder. "He is an evil man, your Highness, and commands me to do wicked deeds. I shall tell you truly that some of them disgust me, even though I can see they are necessary to keep order in the kingdom. But there are other tasks he sets me that frankly horrify me, and in which I can see no use."

"Then why do you do them? Why do you carry them out?"

"Because I am afraid," Rebozo said frankly, "afraid of his wrath and his anger, afraid of the tortures he might make me suffer if he found that I had disobeyed him—but more than anything else, afraid of the horrors of his evil magic."

"Can you not become good, as Father was? Will not . . . no, of course Goodness will not protect you," Prince Boncorro said bitterly. "It did not protect Father, did it? In the next life, perhaps, but not in this."

"Even if it did," Rebozo said quickly, to divert the boy from such somber thoughts, "it would not protect me—for I have committed many sins, your Highness, in the service of your grandfather—many sins indeed, and most of them vile."

"But you had no choice!"

"Oh, I did," Rebozo said softly, "and worse, I knew it, too. I could have said no, I could have refused."

"If you had, Grandfather would have had you killed! Tortured and killed!"

"He would indeed," Rebozo confirmed, "and I did not have the courage to face that. No, in my cowardice, I trembled and obeyed him—and doomed my soul to Hell thereby."

"But Father did not." Boncorro straightened, eyes wide with sudden understanding. "Father refused to commit an evil act, and Grandfather killed him for it!"

"Highness, what matter?" Rebozo pleaded. "Dead is dead!"

"It matters," Prince Boncorro said, "because Father's courage has saved him from Hell—and yours could, too, Rebozo, even now!"

There was something in the way he said it that made Rebozo shiver—but he was shivering anyway, at the thought of the fate the king could visit upon him. Instead, he said, "Your father has gone to a far better place than this, Prince Boncorro."

"That may be true," the prince agreed, "but *I* do not wish to go there any sooner than I must. Why did Father not learn magic?"

"Because there is no magic but evil magic, your Highness."

"I do not believe that," Prince Boncorro said flatly. "Father told me of saints who could work miracles."

"Miracles, yes—and I don't doubt that your father can work them now, or will soon. But miracles are not magic, your Highness, and it is not the Saints who work them, but the One they worship, who acts through them. Mere goodness is not enough—a man must be truly holy to become such a channel of power."

Prince Boncorro shook his head doggedly. "There must be a way, Chancellor Rebozo. There must be another sort of magic, good magic, or the whole world would have fallen to Evil long ago."

What makes you think it has not? Rebozo thought, but he bit back the words. Besides, even Prince Boncorro had heard of the good wizards in Merovence, and Chancellor Rebozo did not want him thinking too much about that. What quicker road to death could there be, than to study good magic in a kingdom of evil sorcery?

"Will Grandfather ever die?" Boncorro asked.

Rebozo shook his head. "Only two know that, Highness—and one of them is the Devil, who keeps the king alive."

The other, Prince Boncorro guessed, must be God—but he could understand why Rebozo would not want to say that Name aloud. Not here in Latruria—and not considering the current state of his soul.

It was half a year before Chancellor Rebozo came to Baron Garchi's gate again.

"Welcome, welcome, Lord Chancellor!" cried the bluff and hearty lord. "Come in and rest yourself! Take a cup of ale!"

"Ale will do."

The implication was clear, so Garchi sighed and said, "I have wine, if you'd rather."

"Why, yes," Rebozo said. "The cool white wine that your country is so famous for, perhaps?"

"The very stuff." Garchi reached up to clap him on the shoulder, but thought better of it. "Come in out of the sun!" He started to lead the way, then remembered himself and bowed the Lord Chancellor on before him.

Rebozo acknowledged the wisdom of the move with a nod, then asked, "How is your charge?"

"Oh, the lad thrives! Our country air is good for him—and it is also good for him to run and play with my own cubs."

Rebozo fixed him with a steely glare. "They do not mistreat him, I trust?"

"Not a bit," Garchi assured him. "Oh, there was the beginning round of fights, as there always is with boys . . ."

"You supervised it carefully, I trust!"

Garchi nodded, a little nettled. "Carefully, but without their knowing. When it got too rough, one of my knights just 'happened' to come by."

"*How* rough?" Rebozo snapped.

"Well, your little wolfling had my middle boy down and was setting in to beat him with a fierceness that took me quite aback, I can tell you. My youngest had already picked a fight with him and been soundly trounced—they're the same age, I'd guessed—and my eldest was standing by, looking as if he was going to jump in to help his brother, for all I'd told him not to. Lad's fourteen," he explained.

"But your knight stopped them?"

"Aye, and saved my middle boy a nasty beating, I fancy! Had to take your lad aside and explain to him that fights between boys don't need to be for life or death, that it's only a little more serious than a game."

"I'm surprised he believed you."

"Not sure he did, but he's been nowhere nearly so vicious since—and they've had their dustups, of course, for all they've been fast friends from that first day; boys will be boys, y'know."

"They will," Rebozo agreed, with the air of one who doesn't really understand. "Where are they now?"

"Oh, out rabbiting, I expect. Quite taken to hunting, the lad has, though he's so demmed serious about it that it makes me chill inside." He gave the chancellor a keen glance. "Is he really yours? Thought powerful sorcerers like you didn't indulge."

"We do not, but you need not concern yourself with whose bastard he truly is."

"Oh, I don't, I don't," Garchi said quickly. "Shall I send for him?"

"No, I've time enough to wait an hour or two—and refresh myself. You will have a bath drawn?"

"They're heating the water now," said Garchi, who didn't understand this obsession with washing. "I'll have the boy sent 'round to you as soon as he comes in, eh?"

"Oh, let him clean up first. After hunting, I expect he'll need it."

It was only an hour later that Boncorro stood before the chancellor—or the other way around, perhaps; Rebozo was amazed at the way the boy made him feel as if it were *he* who had been summoned. The lad was smiling, though. "It is so good to see you again, my Lord Chancellor!"

"I am sorry that it has been so long, Highness," Rebozo said. "I had to wait until your grandfather sent me on a tour of the provinces, to remind the lords of the tax they owe him."

"Of course. I knew I would have to wait long for news of home."

Rebozo took the hint. "Your grandfather continues in good health, and has somewhat emerged from his gloom. He still lapses into long periods of brooding, though, and gazes out the window at nothing."

"I should feel sorry for him," Boncorro conceded.

"Yes, perhaps," Rebozo said, a trifle disconcerted. "And how have you been faring, your Highness?"

"Oh, well enough, though it was somewhat rough at first. I have friends now, or acquaintances, at least."

"Yes, Lord Garchi tells me you have made companions of his sons, and that you were hunting even now."

"They are skilled at that." Actually, the boys had led Boncorro to a knothole they had discovered, where they could peek into the chambermaids' sleeping quarters. They had taken turns watching the strapping young women disrobe and slip into their beds. Boncorro had dutifully taken his turn, though he couldn't really understand why his playmates seemed so excited about the whole matter. Way down deep, he had felt some stirring within him as he watched a well-curved peasant lass go through her ablutions, and he had to admit it had been somewhat pleasant—but surely nothing to make such a fuss about.

"I remembered it was your birthday soon." Rebozo drew a package from beneath his robe. "I regret we cannot celebrate it more elaborately—but take this, as a token of good wishes."

Boncorro took the package, astonished. "Why, thank you, Chancellor! What is it?"

"Well, there would be no surprise if I told you." Rebozo smiled. "Go ahead, unwrap it."

Boncorro did, and held the book up, staring. "A book of spells!"

"You had said you meant to learn magic," Rebozo explained. "They are only simple spells, scarcely more than a village herb wife would use—but enough for a beginning."

"Yes indeed!" Boncorro stared at it, round-eyed. "Thank you, Chancellor! Thank you deeply!"

"Guard it well!" Rebozo raised an admonitory finger. "Simple or not, those spells could cause a great deal of trouble if everyone were to know and use them. Let no one else open it! The first charm inside is one that will keep any but you from opening that cover—learn it at once, and use it often!"

"Lord Chancellor, I will." Boncorro held the book close to his chest, almost hugging it, and looked up at Rebozo with shining eyes. "Thank you, oh, thank you deeply!"

It was almost a shame, Rebozo thought, that the lad had been born to be a prince. He would have made a fine sorcerer—if he were led down the path . . .

As Rebozo was leaving the next day, Garchi cleared his throat and said, "Understand the boys have been getting up to . . . to some mischief with the, ah, wenches. I'll see to it that there's no more of that sort of thing."

"You'll do nothing of the kind!" Rebozo turned to glare at him. "The lad must learn to be a man, Lord Garchi—in all ways!"

"Why, yes, Lord Chancellor," Garchi muttered, staring in surprise, and found himself wondering if the lad might not be Rebozo's own, after all.

Boncorro learned a great deal in the next few years—learned from watching through knotholes, and from reading the book of spells. Some of them seemed anything but harmless, and he recoiled naturally, but others he learned and practiced avidly. He stayed firmly away from any that invoked Satan, or worked magic by any other name—but that left a great many, and some of them afforded him views that surpassed anything he saw through a knothole. He began to be interested in that, after all. When Rebozo brought him a thicker book, he was ready for more direct activity in both spheres. As the years went by, he became quite skilled—in all aspects of manhood. Just as Rebozo wanted.

The king had lost heart. Oh, it wasn't in anything he said or did—he kept on extorting taxes from the merchants and noblemen, who respectively gouged their customers and robbed their serfs in order to pay. The king continued to encourage them, just as he kept the taxes low on the brothels and made sure the Watch never imprisoned a pimp; he subsidized the gambling dens and kept the tax high on malt and fruit and juice, but low on beer and wine and taverns. In a word, he did all he had ever done to encourage corruption and wickedness and poverty—but he did not think of anything new.

More than that—it wasn't what he did, so much as how he did it. He never ranted and raved any more, even if a courtier disobeyed or sneered. He would bark out a rebuke, yes, and signal to a guardsman to beat the foolish rogue, but he seemed too weary to do anything more. He would snarl at a messenger who brought bad news and signal for the whip, but he never killed one outright with his own hands anymore, nor flew into a towering rage. He seemed to be only a shell of the villain he had once been, and didn't even seem to listen to his chancellor any longer—he would only gaze into space, nodding automatically as Rebozo spoke. He spent hour after hour alone in his chambers, gazing out the window and sipping from a tankard. At first the tankard held brandywine, and he would be red-eyed and staggering at dinner—if Rebozo could talk him into coming to dinner. The chancellor was not too concerned, though he had to take more and more of the burden of running the kingdom upon his own shoulders. His only fear was that Maledicto would die before Boncorro came of age—or begin a campaign to ferret out the boy. Indeed, when he was deep in his cups, the king would ramble on about having to see his grandson, finding out where the boy had fled. Rebozo would have to remind him that Boncorro was dead, had died hunting the day after his father's death. But Maledicto waved him away irritably, as if he knew the truth, but did not particularly resent what the chancellor had done. The reason was clear when he was sober, for then he would drop occasional scathing remarks about what little monsters children were, especially ones who thought themselves royal, and how the world would be a better place if there were none of them—but in the evening, drunk and staggering, he would turn maudlin and querulous, wondering aloud if his grandson were well.

Then he turned to white wine, though, and his drunkenness lessened. That concerned Rebozo, though not too much—he merely made sure there was always a measure or two of brandywine mixed with the white in the king's jug.

But he nearly panicked when the king turned to a brew of herbs boiled in clear water.

He was right to be alarmed, for as the king's sobriety returned, so did his will—or, rather, his resolution. What he was resolved to do, though, he would not say, neither to Rebozo nor to anyone else. Finally, ten years after his son's death, King Maledicto sent Rebozo on his annual tour of the provincial barons, watched him out of sight, then turned to his court with grim resolution. He summoned Sir Sticchi and Sir Tchalico, ordered them to be ready to ride the next day before dawn, then retired to his bed, where he lay a long time gazing at the canopy—and trembling.

Cold or fear notwithstanding, the king arose in the darkness of predawn, dressed himself for a journey, buckled on breastplate and helm, and went out to meet his two knights. They mounted their chargers and rode out across the drawbridge in the eerie light of false dawn.

They rode for several hours without a word, but the king seemed never to doubt where he was going. Sir Sticchi and Sir Tchalico exchanged puzzled glances now and then, but neither could enlighten the other at all.

They came into a little village, scarcely more than a hamlet gathered around the ruins of a church, and the two knights moved together. "The king has heard of some priest who has gone into hiding," Sir Sticchi said to his companion, sotto voce. "No doubt he has come only to apprehend the rogue." But his face was taut and his voice quavered.

"If it were only apprehending, why would he come himself?" Sir Tchalico sounded angry in his fear. "He could have sent us alone!"

"We, the only two of his knights who are secretly pious? Oh, do not look so scandalized, Tchalico—I heard it from court gossip; it is widely known, just as I'm sure you must have heard about me."

"Well—I have," Tchalico admitted. "I wondered, now and again, why the king let us live, let alone keep our rank."

"Why, because he had some such use as this in mind for us, no doubt! What shall we do now, Tchalico? He must have brought us here as a test! No doubt he means to torture the poor monk to death, and force us to watch!"

"When he knows we shall not stand idly by," Sir Tchalico agreed, his face grim, "knows we shall leap to the priest's defense—whereupon we shall be unmasked, and he shall slay us with magical fire or some such torture." He felt a sudden cold clarity thrill through him, and straightened in his saddle. "It has come, Sticchi—the hour of our martyrdom."

Fear showed in Sticchi's eyes, cavernous fear—but it passed in a moment, and the fierce delight of battle burned in its place. "Then let us go to meet our deaths with joy, for tonight we'll dine in Heaven!"

"To Heaven let us sail," Sir Tchalico agreed, "and here is our boatman, though it is doubtless the last thing he intends."

They drew rein only a few feet behind the king, who had himself stopped in front of a hovel meaner than the rest, so ill-kempt one might think it was vacant, and tumbling with neglect. But the king sat straight and roared out, "Friar! Monk and shave-pate! Come out to meet your king!"

Eyes watched from huts all about, and a few burly peasant men emerged, fear evident in every line of their bodies, but their faces grim and determined, their fists clenched, sickles and flails in their hands. But the king paid no heed; he only called out again, "Man of the cloth! Man of the clergy! Come forth!"

Still the village sat in silence. The king took a deep breath to call again, but before he did, a peasant came out, one no cleaner than the rest, with a tunic just as patched and frayed as theirs, his hands just as callused from toil—but he wore a hat beneath the sun of June, where the rest of them did not.

"Uncover before your king!" Maledicto roared.

The peasant raised a trembling hand and took off his hat. The bald spot was too regular, too perfect a circle to be natural; it was a tonsure.

"Do you deny you are a priest?" Maledicto demanded.

Suddenly, the fear was gone, and the peasant straightened with pride. "Nay, I will boast of it! I am a priest of the Church, and I serve God and my fellow man!"

Why did the evil king not wince at the holy Name? Why did he not raise his whip to strike, or draw his sword?

And why was he kneeling in the dust before the peasant, hands clasped and head bowed, intoning, "Bless me, Father, for I have sinned!"

The peasants stared, flabbergasted.

"Turn away!" Sir Sticchi barked. "Have you never heard of the seal of the confessional?"

The peasants came to themselves with a start and turned away into their houses. In seconds the village seemed empty.

The words came pouring forth from the king's mouth, the tale and toll of a century of sins; the priest barely had time to whip a worn, threadbare stole from his pocket and yank it around his neck. As he listened to the list of horrors, his face grew haggard and his shoulders slumped. In a few minutes he was kneeling beside the king; in a few more he had clasped the old man's trembling hands and was listening, nodding, wide-eyed, in encouragement.

"It would seem we are not to be martyred after all," Sir Sticchi said, staring and numb.

"Do not believe it for a second," Sir Tchalico snapped. "I doubt not the Devil heard as soon as the king said 'Bless me,' and dispatched a demon before he'd said 'sinned.' Sell your life dearly, Brother Sticchi—for the king's sake, and for the kingdom's! We will pay with our lives, but we must buy him enough time to—"

Flame erupted not ten yards from them.

The priest cried out and shrank away, but King Maledicto held his hands with an iron grip and kept him near enough to hear as the sins poured out of him, so fast as to be scarcely intelligible.

It was no demon, but a horrible, glittering serpentine thing that stood on a dozen clawed feet while four more pawed the air. A saddle was fastened between those upper legs, a saddle for a man in a flame-red robe, masked and hooded, nothing showing but his eyes. In his hand swung a battle-axe two feet across, far too big for any mortal man to swing.

Sir Sticchi bellowed, "For God and Saint Mark!" and kicked his charger into a gallop.

"For the Saints and the Lord!" Sir Tchalico echoed, and came charging after.

They careened into the monstrosity before it could take two steps. It screamed and lashed out at them with steel-sharp claws; its rider bellowed rage in a voice that shook the village, and swung his sword. Sir Sticchi shouted in pain as the blade cut through his armor and into his shoulder, but he struck anyway, his sword thrusting into the monster's chest. It screamed in agony and anger, blasting him with breath that blackened and pitted his helmet. His horse screamed in fright, but the knight held it in place, hewing and hacking and madly singing a battle hymn. Sir Tchalico joined in, striking from the other side, and beast and rider alike howled in pain and rage. Sword and tooth and talon struck, and struck again. Sir Sticchi fell, blood fountaining from a torn throat; his horse screamed and ran. Sir Tchalico howled in agony as flame enveloped him; then he fell, and the monster stamped down, through his armor, through his chest, and the horse neighed in terror and wheeled to run. But the twisting sword cut it down, and the monster stepped over the bodies, reaching out for the king.

"*Ego te absolvo!*" the priest cried an instant before a huge battle-axe flashed before his face, and the king fell headless to the ground. A second later, the priest's head rolled beside it in the dust.

The monster screamed in terrible pain, and its rider howled in frustration—for the king was dead, as was the priest who had shriven him, but three souls had gone to Heaven, and one to Purgatory instead of Hell. Satan was cheated, and his minion suffered far more than the victims had. Fire exploded around them, and monster and rider were gone—but the peasants did not come out to bury the bodies until the smell of brimstone had faded away.

"So good to see you again, Lord Chancellor!" Garchi raised a hand to pound the chancellor on the back, then remembered and withdrew the slap. "Your lad does well, very well indeed."

"You have followed my instructions, then?"

"We have—but alas, it did no good," Garchi said with a sigh. "Oh, the lad can wench and swill with the best of them—but he doesn't. Not all that often, at least. He'll only bed one wench a night, and not even every night, at that. I've never heard one of them complain of his treatment, though."

Rebozo thought that he might be more reassured if the women had complained—but he had enough tact not to say so. "I regret to hear it; a boy his age ought to enjoy the leisure to play while he can. Should have, I should say—I fear that time is at an end."

"Oh?" Garchi looked up, alert, but neither sad nor glad. "You're taking him from us, then?"

"I fear so—he must begin his work in this world. Send him to me, Lord Garchi."

"When he's done with . . . the matter at hand, of course."

"Of course."

Garchi didn't mention that the task at hand was a book in Latin, about the lives of the old emperors. He wasn't sure Rebozo would be happy about it.

Consequently, Rebozo was rather surprised when the servant announced Sir Boncorro only fifteen minutes later. Rebozo did not have to rise, since he was still pacing. The prince came in right behind. "Your pardon for not dressing more elaborately, Lord Chancellor, but I did not wish to keep you waiting . . . What means this?"

The chancellor had sunk to one knee, bowing his head. "Long live the king!"

For a minute Boncorro stood frozen, as the meaning of the salutation sank in and he adjusted his mind to it. He seemed to stand a little taller, even straighter than he had. "So it has happened. The Devil has tired of my grandfather, has withdrawn the sorcery that kept him alive, and the king is dead."

"Long live the king," Rebozo returned.

Boncorro stood still a moment longer, to let the shock and numbness pass—and then came the first fierce elation of triumph. Grandfather was dead, and Boncorro was still alive!

Then he stepped forward to clasp Rebozo by the shoulders and lift him to his feet. "You must not kneel to me, old friend. You have ever been my companion in adversity, my shield in danger. You shall always stand in my presence, and may sit when I sit."

"I—I thank your Majesty for this high privilege," Rebozo stammered.

"You have earned it," Boncorro said simply.

The chancellor stood a moment, looking at him. Prince Boncorro had grown into a fine figure of a man—six feet tall, with broad, muscular shoulders and arms, legs that showed as pillars in his tights, but shapely pillars indeed, and a very handsome face, with straight nose, generous mouth, and large blue eyes, beneath a cap of golden hair. It was a face that seemed deceptively frank and open, but Rebozo knew that appearance was mostly illusion. He also knew that of the women who came to Boncorro's bed, few came reluctantly. ·

"You do not mourn, your Majesty?"

Boncorro permitted himself a smile of amusement. "I shall appear properly grief-stricken in public, Lord Chancellor—but you know better than any man that I rejoice at my grandfather's death. I feared him and hated him as much as I admired and loved my father—and I have no doubt it was he who gave the order to kill his own saintly son.

Indeed, I charge you with the task of finding the man who struck the blow."

Rebozo stared. "But—But—it was the groom! The man who found the body!"

Boncorro waved the idea away impatiently. "He discovered the corpse, that is all. There is no reason to believe he thrust the knife himself."

"He confessed!"

"Under torture. All his confession means is that he wanted the pain to stop."

Rebozo felt a cold chill enwrap him; the prince—no, king, now—was showing wisdom far beyond his years. "Then who could have done it?"

"Who gained by it?" King Boncorro fixed the chancellor with a piercing gaze. "Only me—and Hell. I know that *I* did not slay him. Now how did my grandfather die?"

"Why—beside two knights, his only guards; they were dead, too. And a peasant . . ."

"How was he slain? With what weapon?"

"His . . . his head was . . . he was beheaded, Majesty."

"Beheaded?" Boncorro frowned. "Were there any other wounds?"

Definitely, he saw too much for a youth of twenty. "There was a dagger—in his back, between the shoulder blades."

Boncorro's face lit with keen delight. "Describe the dagger!"

"It . . . it was—" Chancellor Rebozo paused to picture the dagger in his mind. "—double-edged, the blade sloping straight to the point on both sides . . . an oval for a hilt . . . The handle . . ."

"Say it, man!"

"I cannot!" Rebozo looked away. "It was sculpted, it was . . . obscene . . . evil."

"Like the dagger that slew my father!"

"Very like it," Rebozo said unwillingly. "A twin."

"Then the same man did it, or two assassins who served the same lord! Find me the murderer of my grandfather, Rebozo, and I doubt not you shall find me also the murderer of my father!"

The chancellor stared. "Then—you still wish me to serve you, your Majesty?"

"Of course. You saved my life when my father died, you served my grandfather from fear rather than desire, and you have always been gentle and kind to me. I can think of no man more capable, nor one I would more readily trust and wish to have by me. Now make ready for us to go to the capital."

"Surely, Majesty," the chancellor said, and turned away, a gleam of satisfaction in his eyes.

A local bandit was tortured until he confessed to the murder of the king and his knights. Unfortunately, Baron Garchi and his sons were overly zealous, killing the outlaw and his whole band on the spot.

None of them owned a dagger with an obscene and horrifying hilt. None of them rode a flame-skinned monster, or carried a battle-axe of any size; they were all archers and swordsmen. But Rebozo was satisfied and reported his results to the king.

The king was not convinced.

At least Boncorro didn't start making changes the instant he arrived at the royal castle. He waited until after his coronation—three weeks. That also gave him time to recruit his own bodyguard, and to lay protective spells against them. He also laid protective spells against everyone else, throughout the castle and all around it. They sent Rebozo into constant nervous agitation—wherever he went, the blasted things sent his blood tingling! It was unnerving to know that the king didn't really trust him—though the chancellor had to admit that Boncorro seemed to trust him more than anyone else. It was even more unnerving to Rebozo to know that the king had learned so much magic—so much that he didn't really need the protection of his chancellor's sorcery. That made Rebozo more nervous than anything else—not being needed. He felt as if he stood on sand, and the sands were constantly shifting beneath him.

They shifted even more because the young king spent an hour a day in the library, locking the door securely to make sure he would not be disturbed. There were a few old Greek and Roman manuscripts in there, but most of the shelves were filled with books of sorcery. The spells he actually used, though, were scarcely sorcerous at all, such as the ward that held the library doors constantly locked against even Rebozo's magic when the king was not there. Where had he learned such power? Some of his spells were actually based on Goodness, and gave Rebozo a real shock when he encountered them, a shock that had aftereffects of nausea and palpitations that went on for hours. At least, the chancellor consoled himself, none of them invoked the power of the Saints or their Master. But that was cold comfort indeed. Where had the son of a sorcerer learned such magic? Surely not in Baron Garchi's castle—though the country lord was far from the most sinister in the kingdom, too easygoing to be truly evil in any way, he was nonetheless fond of his pleasures, and most of them rather wicked; some were definitely corrupt. He had done his best to raise the boy in debauchery, even as he had raised his own sons—and now look what had happened! Had there been some secret priest among the baron's servants? Some copy of some holy book that the prince had found? Rebozo resolved to give Garchi and his castle a thorough housecleaning—as soon as King Boncorro allowed him time enough. If ever.

The demands were almost constant, first redecorating the castle to Boncorro's taste, then supervising the strengthening of the defenses of the town and the castle, as well as preparing for the coronation. It was while he was wrapped up in all of this that the king had laid his network of spells in and around the castle, giving Rebozo such a rude shock when he discovered them. He thought he would have some respite after the coronation was over, but Boncorro called him in the very next morning, not long after dawn—and the chancellor was dismayed to see that the young king had obviously been awake for at least an hour already!

He sat at a table in his solar, surrounded by books and papers. He looked up as the chancellor entered, and his face lit with a smile. "Ah! Rebozo, old friend!" He stood and came around the desk to clasp the chancellor by the shoulders. "And how are you this morning?"

"Quite well, thank you, your Majesty." Rebozo reflected sourly that he had felt better before having to confront the young king's energy and enthusiasm.

"Good, good! Then to work, eh?" Boncorro swung around behind the table and sat again. "We must begin new ways today, Rebozo!"

"New ways?" Rebozo felt a chill of apprehension. "What innovations have you planned, your Majesty?"

Boncorro looked down at his papers. "There is a law that any priests who are discovered are to be executed on the spot."

"Surely your Majesty will not repeal that law!"

"No—but I wish to see that it is no longer enforced." Boncorro looked up at him. "It is too easy for someone with a grudge against his rival to slay him out of hand, then claim he was a secret priest. Issue commands that no priests are to be slain, or even arrested."

"But your Majesty! That will mean that people will start flocking to Ma—their M-M-M—"

"To Mass," Boncorro finished for him. "It would seem I am not so far gone in sorcery as you yourself, Rebozo, for I can still say the word. Yes, people will go to the priests—but only those who wish to. If Grandfather did nothing else, he did at least free the common folk from fear of religion and the tyranny of the clergy—only those who truly believe, or wish to, will go."

"Satan will scourge the Earth of you!"

"No, he will not," Boncorro contradicted, "for I am scarcely a saint, Rebozo, and I am not abolishing the law that prohibits the priests, or their services. There is still room for the Devil to think I can be swayed to his service—and more grounds for that than I like to admit."

"More grounds indeed," Rebozo said heavily. "You are a young man, Majesty, with a young man's appetites, and a young king's lust for power."

"As I am even now showing," Boncorro agreed. "But I am not turning this country toward the powers of Heaven, Lord Chancellor—only toward my own."

And Rebozo realized that this was true. Somewhat reassured that his young king was not really trying to do good, but only to tighten his hold over his kingdom in a way his grandfather never had, the chancellor went out to give the necessary orders.

The king said, "Send word to all the noblemen that the taxes are being reduced to half of their income."

Rebozo stared. "To *half?*"

"Half." The king turned a sheet of foolscap around so that Rebozo could read it. "I have cast up accounts and found that we can easily maintain this great castle, all our army, and all our servants on half. Indeed, there will remain a substantial sum to squirrel away in the treasury." He sat back with a sigh, shaking his head. "It is quite empty. I was horrified to discover how Grandfather had spent it all."

Rebozo was horrified to discover that Boncorro did not approve of the old king's extravagances and pleasures. "Majesty, it is those luxuries and affairs of state that held the barons' loyalty!"

"Stuff and nonsense," said the young king. "It was fear of the royal army and the king's magic that held them in line, naught else—a royal army that will do quite well without a florin's worth of ale for each man, for each day. They will fight all the better for being sober."

"But these are merchants' tricks!" Rebozo cried. "Where did you learn such lowly notions?"

"From the traders in the fairs, while my foster brothers were learning how to be fleeced by tricksters," Boncorro replied. "I will not disdain any knowledge, if it is sound and will help me to hold my kingdom."

"But magic, your Majesty! Sorcery! Virgins cost dearly, and animals for slaughter, and dead bodies! There must be money for my sorcery!"

"My magic is far less expensive," King Boncorro assured him, "but nonetheless effective for all that. Indeed, I look forward to the first baron who seeks to rebel." His eyes glinted with anticipation. "Once I have settled with him, no others will dare."

Rebozo stared into the guileless blue eyes and felt his blood run cold.

"Tell the barons their taxes are lowered," Boncorro said softly. "That much of my message they will be glad to hear."

Rebozo recovered. "Majesty—is it not enough to tell only the dukes? Cannot they send word to their barons, as they always have?"

"They would not; they would continue to draw every groat of the old tax from their vassals, aye, even if it took thumbscrews to draw it. I wish to make sure that every lord knows of this news, every knight, every squire—for I also wish you to see to it that their own tax on their serfs is cut by at least a third!"

Rebozo stared, aghast. "Now they *will* rebel," he whispered.

Boncorro grinned like a wolf. "I await it with eagerness."

"But Majesty—*why?*"

"So that I can teach them that I am no less formidable than my grandfather, Rebozo, and my magic no weaker, though nowhere so twisted."

That, Rebozo doubted—and he had no wish to see the prince he had formed and nurtured drowned under a wave of greedy barons. "Majesty, in this world, you cannot balance yourself between the Deity and the Devil. You must choose one or the other, for every single action is either Good or Evil."

"Then I shall choose neither, but another source of power altogether."

"Your Majesty," Rebozo cried, exasperated, "you *cannot!* In another world, perhaps, but not in this one! And this is all the world you will ever know! Every single action in *this* world sends you either one step closer to Hell, or one step closer to Heaven! Every thought you cherish, every breath you draw!"

"Then I shall play one off against the other," King Boncorro told him, "as good statesmen have ever done with powers that they cannot conquer. Go send my word to the dukes, Chancellor—and to the earls, and the barons."

Rebozo knew a royal command when he heard one, especially since the young king had addressed him by his title, not his name. He bowed, resigning himself to the worst. "As your Majesty wills. Am I dismissed, or is there more you would tell me?"

"Oh, I think that is quite enough for one morning," Boncorro said, smiling. "Go do your work, Chancellor, while I think up more troubles for you."

Rebozo wished he could be sure the young man was joking.

Chapter
One

Matt fingered a turnip absently as he eavesdropped with all his might. It wasn't easy—the marketplace was alive with noise and color, particularly noise. Rickety booths draped in bright-hued cloth crowded every available inch of space; the fair's marshals kept having to order merchants to move their booths back to leave the mandated three yards of aisle space, especially where those pathways opened out into the small plazas where the acrobats and minstrels performed. There were even fiddlers and pipers, so the fair always had strains of music underlying its raucous clatter.

There was a surprising variety of produce for a town so far inland— but then, Fairmede had grown up around the merchants, for it sat right against the Alps, at the foot of a pass through the mountains, and beside a river, too—a small river, but one that ran northwest to join a larger, and the towns grew bigger as the river ran farther. Merchants came down on barges to meet other merchants coming in over the Alps, and peasants came flocking from the countryside on both sides of the mountains, to sell food to the merchants. There were vegetables and fruit, pork and poultry, cloth and furs, ribbons and thread, pots and pans and crockery—even spices and silks from the East. Those were being sold by the few professional merchants; most of the other vendors looked to be peasants, trying to turn a few pennies by selling the surplus the lords allowed them to keep. Matt knew that in Merovence, Queen Alisande insisted her lords leave their serfs at least a little for a cash crop; and the new King of Latruria, the kingdom to the south, seemed to have decided on the same policy—at least, to judge by the conversation Matt was working so hard at overhearing.

At the next booth the serf who was selling fruit was boasting a bit. "We have two cuttings of hay each summer now, and the harvests of wheat and barley have been rich these last three years, very rich."

"That may be so," said a goodwife, "but how much of it do you take home?"

"Half now! A full half! Ever since young King Boncorro came to the throne, we have paid to our lord only half of what we grow!"

"Truly?" asked a musclebound peasant. "Your young king made his noblemen give you that much?"

"Aye! And of our share, my wife and I live on three parts and sell one! She has copper pots now! I have an iron hoe, and our children wear shoes!"

"Shoes?" A third peasant stared, eyes huge. She was young, with a baby in her arms, and the hulking youth beside her was as amazed as she. "Real shoes, of leather?"

"Aye! No more of wrapping their poor little feet in rags to keep out the winter's chill! Real shoes, of soft leather, with hard soles!"

The girl turned to her husband. "Mayhap we should follow him home."

"'Tis not so far." The youth frowned, his gaze still on the fruit seller. "We could journey home easily enough, to pass the holidays with our parents."

"You do well enough here," the older woman protested.

"Well enough, but still we must give two parts in three to Sir Garlin!" said the girl. "'Twould be sweet indeed to have shoes for the little one, when she is old enough to walk."

"There's truth in that," the young husband admitted.

"We have built ourselves new houses," the fruit seller boasted. "No more of such tumbledown huts as we had seven years ago! We live behind walls of wattle and daub now, and new straw for the thatch every year!"

"A cottage," the girl murmured, eyes shining. "A true cottage!"

"Are you going to make love to that turnip, or buy it?" the peasant behind the vegetables growled.

Matt came out of his reverie with a start, realizing that he'd been squeezing the turnip for several minutes. "No, I guess not." He put it back. "Kind of soft on one side—I think it might be rotten."

"Rotten! Do you say my produce is bad?"

Matt surveyed the rest of the display with a jaundiced eye—rubbery carrots, sickly looking parsnips, and radishes that had a distinctly brown tinge to them. "I've seen sounder produce in a silo."

"THIIIEEEF!" the man yelled. "Ho! Watchmen! Here is a hedge sorcerer who steals!"

"Shhhh! Hush it up!" Matt glanced around frantically—this wasn't exactly the way to be inconspicuous when you were trying to gather information. "Shut up, will you? I'll buy it, then! I'll give you a real, genuine copper penny! A whole penny, for that one measly turnip!"

"THIIIEF!" the man called again. "HO! HO, THE WATCH!"

"Okay, forget it!" Matt turned away, meaning to walk fast—but before he'd gone two steps, a hand the size of a loaf clapped down on his shoulder and swung him around to confront the men of the Watch. "Where do you think you're going, peasant?"

Well, what was Matt supposed to say? "I'm not really a peasant, I'm just dressed like one because I wanted to wear something comfortable"? "Hi there, boys, I'm the Lord Wizard of Merovence, glad to see you're on the ball"? He was supposed to be gathering information in disguise, not starting a riot. How was he going to get out of this one, without letting them know who he really was? "I didn't steal anything, watchmen—I just refused to buy."

"Because he said the turnip was rotten!" the peasant shouted. "If it was, he must have turned it himself, because when I brought it, it was—" His eye lit with inspiration. "—it was sound! All my vegetables were good! Now look at them! Why he should hate me so much as to turn my produce bad, I can't think—I've never met him before in my life!"

"Or mine," Matt snarled. "What would I want your moldy vegetables for?"

"Moldy! Do you hear, watchmen? He has turned them to mold!"

"This is a serious charge, fellow," the beefy watchman said. "If what he says is true, you have practiced magic without leave from the count!"

"How about if I had leave from the queen?"

The watchman gave him a sour smile. "Oh, aye, and how if I had a gold sovereign for every word you've said? What would a ragtag road conjurer like you know of the queen?"

For a moment Matt was tempted to conjure up a dozen gold coins, just to prove the man wrong—tempted to reveal himself as really being the Lord Wizard of Merovence; but he reminded himself that if he did, he could forget about learning anything more in this market about the discontent that was brewing here by the southern border with Latruria. He improvised fast. "But I'm not even a conjurer! Just a packman looking for something to pack!"

The watchman frowned. "This man accuses you of turning his vegetables bad."

"And he did!" the peasant cried. "Would I have set out from Latruria with a cartful of vegetables that were not sound? What could I hope to get for them?"

The same as any con man hopes for, Matt thought, but aloud he said, "There! See? You've heard it yourself! His vegetables are sound!"

"*Were* sound!" the peasant brayed. "*Were* sound, until you came to finger each one and bewitch it!"

"That's nonsense!" Matt grabbed a turnip, muttering,

> "Here's old Penny, coming to town,
> With a whole load of veggies,
> Not one of them sound!
> But the rot shall be gone
> As each tuber I touch,
> And the healing shall run
> Through each leaf and each bunch!
> Hard times in the country,
> As we for pennies farm!"

It wasn't much of a verse, but improvisation had never been Matt's strong point. He had started it with a folk song, though, so it should have some effect.

And it did—the bad spot on the side of the turnip diminished and disappeared even as he thrust it under the watchman's nose. "There! See? No rot! And this one!" He put the turnip back and pulled out a dingy parsnip. As soon as he touched it, the root began to look distinctly healthier, and by the time it reached the watchman, it was positively glowing with vitamins. "Not a spot of decay! Try a carrot!" Matt turned back to the booth and noticed that the Vegetable Revivification Project was spreading out in a circular wave, just as he had ordered. He grabbed a limp carrot for show and held it up. "Fresh and crisp as if it had just been pulled." And sure enough, it was.

"It would seem that is not the only thing being pulled." The watchman shouldered past him, glaring at the vendor. "We've too much to do to have you wasting our time on pranks, peasant!"

"I beg your worships' pardon." The peasant bowed, trying to restrain a gleeful smile. "I must have been mistaken; no doubt it was just the one turnip he was fingering that was bad."

"Another false alarm, and we will be fingering *you*," the watchman promised, and turned away to join his mates, grumbling. Matt chose the course of prudence and followed them away from the booth before the peasant could try to blackmail him as a sorcerer—because the whole load of vegetables had been about as bad as you could get and still be marginally edible. Not that Matt had anything to fear, of course—he just couldn't retaliate without blowing his cover. So he followed the Watch, seething, because the man who had made trouble for him was going to make a lot more money than he would have if he hadn't gone picking on Matt. The Lord Wizard hated to see vice rewarded. No, be honest—he hated to lose. For a moment, he was tempted to recite another quick verse and turn all the peasant's produce to mold and mildew, but he resisted the temptation—petty revenge wasn't worth it. Besides, using magic for hurt, rather than benefit, was the first step on the road toward black magic, and Matt didn't dare go that route. The Devil had too many grudges to settle with him.

It was just lucky for him that magic in Merovence worked by verse. How else could an English major have made a living? Matt had been looking forward to a quiet, inoffensive, and unrewarding existence as an impoverished graduate student, about to graduate to an impoverished instructorship, when Saint Moncaire of Merovence had plucked him off his college campus and into an alternate universe where he was needed to help unseat a usurper and put the rightful queen back on the throne. It helped that he had fallen in love with that rightful queen and, after proving to her that marrying him was the best policy for her country, managed to take her to the altar. But it had been two years since the wedding, and they still didn't have any children. Matt couldn't help feeling that he must be doing something wrong—and in Merovence, doing something wrong could have very serious consequences.

Consequences such as going to the fair and being accused of witchcraft, for all the wrong reasons. Matt finally managed a smile as he saw the irony in getting out of a charge of black magic by working white magic—all magic in this universe worked by the power of Good, or the power of Evil. Somehow, Matt had a notion the peasant could appreciate the humor of it, too. He wondered how he had gotten himself into such a fix.

Of course, he hadn't, exactly—Queen Alisande had helped a lot.

She had received reports of discontent along the border between Merovence and its neighbor to the south, Latruria—discontent that seemed to have its roots in rumors of fine living in a country that had, only five years before, been mired in poverty. Matt remembered his frustration at trying to find something more substantial in the way of information.

"Isn't there anything a little more specific?" he asked Alisande. "A boost in the gross national product, maybe? An increase in capital investment? Subsidies and price supports, maybe?"

Alisande made an impatient gesture. "Speak clearly, Matthew. Terms such as these are only for wizards."

Matt was tempted to agree with her, but he tried to translate anyway. "Are Latruria's farmers having better harvests all of a sudden? Are her craftsmen making more carts and wagons? Are they building more new hovels?"

"I do not know," Alisande said, "nor do my informants. They speak only of rumors of better living—aye, even better than here in Merovence."

Matt frowned. "Thought you had done pretty well at boosting the standard of living, and in less than ten years, too."

"I had hoped so," Alisande admitted, "but these rumors do make me wonder. How have they come into Merovence? Has this new King Boncorro sent agents to spread discontent among my people?"

"I wouldn't put anything past a sorcerer-king. Of course," Matt amended, "we don't know that he *is* a sorcerer—but his grandfather was, and his father died from too much goodness, if your spies had the story right. So it would make sense for Boncorro to be a sorcerer, too."

"Certainly we have had no word that he is saintly," Alisande agreed, "and until we have such, we must assume he is a pawn of Hell, as was his grandfather before him. Certainly the fruits of these rumors are such as would please the Devil—our serfs are growing quarrelsome and fractious, and more indolent in their farming."

"Which makes for a smaller harvest, and *that* makes them grumble all the harder," Matt said dryly. "How is the nobility taking it?"

"The elders are only concerned, as of yet—but they are concerned even more about their children."

"The younger generation is getting rebellious, huh?"

Alisande frowned. "An odd notion—and no, I would not say they challenge their parents, though I hear they do become surly and contentious."

"How about 'insolent' and 'impertinent'?"

"Then you have heard these reports!"

"No, but I've worked with kids." For a moment, Matt felt a very irrational urge to go back to teaching college. Maybe if he founded the first University of Merovence . . . NO! Temptations were to be resisted! "I take it the young noblemen are becoming moody and defiant?"

"Aye, and the young noblewomen, too."

"Why not?" Matt reflected that discontent was very egalitarian—it was no respecter of rank or sex. "Any particular reason?"

"Nay." Alisande frowned, gazing out the high, narrow windows of her solar at the gardens below. "The only clear issue seems to be that they are cozening and wheedling and demanding that their parents send them to my court."

"Oh, so *that's* how you heard about all this! They made such pests of themselves that a dozen or so lords are petitioning you for posts for their offspring, eh?"

Alisande looked up at him in surprise. "Sometimes I despair of your density, husband, but at times like this, your perceptiveness amazes me. How did you guess?"

"Because fond but exasperated parents will do almost anything to get the high school graduates out of the house. I take it you can't find enough posts for them all?"

"I cannot," Alisande said slowly, "and I am not altogether certain that I want such surly young courtiers, especially not in such numbers. What else could I do with them, Matthew?"

"Found a university," Matt said promptly, "a place for higher learning. It keeps the monks out of trouble, too, at least the ones who like to spend their time hunting up old Greek and Latin texts and trying to find out more about how the universe works. Bring them here to the capital and build a cloister full of workrooms and lecture halls. Then tell some of your more enterprising citizens to build extra inns, and let the nobility know that you've found a great dumping ground for the kids, so they can get them out of their hair for their four most fractious years."

"That has a costly sound," Alisande said, frowning.

"You noticed that, huh? And we don't even have college-age kids yet! But don't worry, the younger folk will come flocking, to gather around the scholars and learn—or at least pretend to for a few hours every day, so they have an excuse to get down to the serious business of partying."

"What assurance would we have that the teachings of these scholars would be true and good?"

Matt shrugged. "That isn't a requirement, where I come from. Can't prove most of it, anyway. What matters is teaching the kids to think seriously about what they're doing and about the world around them—get them to make plans for the future, give them a chance to think over what they believe and how they should live those beliefs, before they actually have to go out and start making decisions that will affect the lives of thousands of people around them. It's a chance to build the foundation of their lives, dear—and hopefully, to find some bedrock to build it on. When they're actually out there dealing with the work of this world every day, they won't have time to think over what's right or wrong, or best and wisest for everybody. They have to do that before they start their lives' work."

"And they must be right," she said, with a jaundiced look, "and for that, I am not altogether certain I trust these teachers you would bring."

Matt shrugged. "Politicians never do. That's why they make the budget renewable every year."

"Still, there is merit in the notion." Alisande gazed out the window pensively, and Matt wondered if she was thinking about the children they didn't even have yet. "It is for the future, though," she said at last, "and we must deal with this matter in the present. I tell you frankly, Matthew, that I suspect subversion from the sorcerous kingdom of Latruria."

"Fair guess," Matt said judiciously. "Just because we chased the sorcerers out of your kingdom once, doesn't mean that they've given up on trying to win it back. So you think King Boncorro might be sending agents across the border to stir up discontent?"

"Yes, and to make the young folk of all classes yearn for a life of leisure and luxury."

Matt smiled. "Don't we all?"

"True, but those of us who are grown know that we must labor for it and earn it. Yet even for mature folk, if rumor says there is Heaven on Earth for free, many will flock to seek it."

"Or start agitating for you to provide it for them," Matt said, nodding, "carefully avoiding the issue of who is going to provide the food, or build the houses."

"I do not say that King Boncorro is doing that," Alisande said, "but only that he might." She turned to look at her husband. "Would you travel south to discover the answer for me, Matthew? I know you have been restive of late."

"Well, yes," Matt admitted. "I can take only so much of court life before I start going a little crazy from all the intrigue and backstabbing. I don't know how you can take it, darling."

"I glory in it." Alisande gave him a toothy smile. "There is a certain thrill and excitement in keeping these courtiers in line, and making them be productive for the land as a whole to boot."

"Yeah, and I'll bet you're the kind who tap-dances on crocodiles for fun. Okay, honey, I'll go hunting—my Chief Assistant Wizard, Ortho the Frank, should be able to handle anything routine."

"He did well for me, when we had need to follow you into Allustria," Alisande said. "You have trained him admirably."

"Not too well, I hope," Matt said, with a wary glance. "Still, he'll know how to get hold of me if anything really big comes up. Want me to leave today?"

"Soonest gone, soonest come back." Alisande caught his hand and tugged. "Do purge your restlessness and come back to me quickly, mine husband. The nights will be long till you've returned."

He followed the pull to zero in on her lips, and made it a very long kiss. After all, it was going to have to last him a while.

Matt shivered at the memory of that kiss, and of what had followed, then resolutely forced his mind back to the present and this southern fair. He had indeed left that afternoon, buying a pack and some trade goods in town, then strolled south, trading and swapping pots and pans and copper coins while he absorbed information. The farther south he went, the juicier the scandal. He'd found that Alisande was right—there were murmurs of discontent, and people were beginning to think that maybe Latruria was better run than Merovence. By all reports, people in Latruria seemed to live better, even the serfs—and everybody had at least some money. The commoners were believing every rumor they heard.

But those rumors weren't coming from government agents—they were coming from relatives. Matt was amazed to learn that there was no attempt to guard the border from anything except an invading army, and no one really thought that would come. Oh, the marcher barons guarded the roads, but mostly to collect taxes and tolls—they didn't seem to be particularly worried about invasion. And the peasants were traveling back and forth across the fields with a blithe disregard for the invisible line that presumably ran right across the pasture and down the middle of the river. Small boats crossed the river both ways, with no concern for any law but Nature's, and that only in regard to the current and the weather.

Not that there *was* any law, of course. The only one Matt could think of was that sorcerers were barred, along with armed bands. Everybody else was legal—if they paid a tax.

Some people didn't want to, of course. There was an inordinate amount of smuggling going on.

The marcher barons didn't seem to care, maybe because import taxes were supposed to go to the queen. Why should they care, if there was nothing in it for them? Oh, they sent out patrols, every few days, to ride through the pastures and fields along the invisible line— but they seemed far more interested in hunting small game than illegal immigrants. They made a lot of noise, too, playing pipes and joking and laughing; any peasants out to visit their in-laws on the other side had plenty of time to take cover and wait until the riders had passed out of sight.

Not that Matt objected to any of this, exactly, though it would have been nice to have the tax money. Still, he was the last person alive to try to keep relatives from visiting one another, or of taking up job opportunities—that was as apt to work in favor of the people of Merovence as those of Latruria.

His travels had led him to this market, almost on the border. He had seen the river traffic, bank to bank, for himself—no one seemed to find anything wrong in it, which was fair enough, if one overlooked the little matter of taxes; and Matt personally wouldn't really want half a bushel of turnips as a medium of exchange. The merchants seemed to be paying their import tariffs and grumbling about them as he would expect—but not grumbling with any real conviction, because the tariffs weren't that high. Of course, they did keep mentioning that when they were taking goods into Latruria, they didn't have to pay any tax at all . . .

He had heard peasants bragging about how well they lived, about having meat for dinner every other week, real meat—chicken! And fish three nights out of seven; about the repeal of the Forest Laws, and it being legal to hunt and fish as much as they wanted, provided they didn't kill too many animals, or fish the ponds empty. They bragged about their new cottages, about the woolen cloaks their wives wove with the wool they bartered for with the shepherds; about their new tunics, for they could keep more of the flax they grew—indeed, about all the things the people of Merovence had been looking down on them for lacking. Now it was the Latrurian relatives who could brag, and they were making up for lost time.

No wonder the peasants of Merovence were grumbling—and meaning it.

Matt decided he had just about had enough of this disguise. He was ready for something a bit more genteel, and a little smoother on the skin. Time to check up on the moods of the aristocracy.

Accordingly, he ambled out of the fair and the rudimentary town that had grown up around it—only a couple of blocks of houses and more permanent shops. The houses were long and low, built of field-stone, but large enough for four big rooms—more than your average peasant expected, but just about right for town dwellers. The shops were two-storied and half-timbered, with the living quarters upstairs and the shop downstairs—the pride of their owners, no doubt, until their cousins from Latruria had started bragging.

That was all there was to it; two blocks of that, and he was out of the town. No city wall or anything—this was a burg that hadn't really decided to be permanent yet. Of course, Matt could have taken the road, but he had reasons to want to avoid any undue amount of notice. He hiked across the fields, being careful where he stepped, heading for a barn he saw in the distance.

It turned out to be a communal barn—the townsfolk ran some live-stock of their own, at a guess. It was certainly big enough for a knight's estate. Fortunately, the cows were all out grazing at the moment, and the pigs were wallowing in the spring mud and the May sunshine. Matt ducked into a stall, found a patch of clean straw, and pulled a doublet and hose out of his pack. Okay, they were wrinkled—but what would you expect, for a minor lord who had been on the road for a week? Which was exactly what Matt planned to claim, and it was true enough, in its way.

He changed clothes, packed his peasant's tunic and leggings away, and sauntered out of the barn, feeling a bit more his old self, in spite of the pack slung over his shoulder. *Now* he wanted to meet the owner—or whoever was in charge.

There he was, or at least a likely source of information: a middle-aged peasant, chewing a stalk of hay while he leaned on his shovel, surveying the pasture and counting cows. Matt sauntered up to him. "Ho there, goodman!"

The man looked up, startled. "Ho yoursel—uh, good day, milord." But he darted a suspicious glance at the peddler's pack.

Matt swung it around to the ground. "I found an old packman hard up on his luck. I took pity on him and bought it all for three pieces of gold."

The herdsman stared; the sum was enough for retirement, if you didn't mind living skinny.

"However, I've no mind to go lugging it about," Matt said. "Would you store it for me? And if I don't come back for it by Christmas, give it to some deserving lad who wants an excuse to travel for a bit."

"To be sure, my lord." The gears were grinding inside the peasant's head; Matt could have sworn he could hear them. If this foolish lord had given three pieces of gold in charity, what might there be in that pack that could even begin to justify such a sum? Matt had a notion that if there were anything of real worth, it wouldn't make it to Midsummer, let alone Christmas.

"My horse went lame," Matt went on, "and someone told me I might be able to hire one here."

"Well, not hire," the man said slowly, "but Angle the cartwright has a colt he is willing to sell for five ducats."

"Five?" Matt stared. "What is it, a racehorse?"

"It is high, I know," the peasant said apologetically, "but the beast is still too young to discover if he will be worth anything as a warhorse, and Angle does not wish to chance losing money. Myself, if the colt were mine, I would bargain—but since it is not, I can only direct you to Angle's shop."

Matt sighed. "No, I've no wish to go hiking back to town." He really didn't, especially after that tangle with the Watch—having a peasant recognize him in lord's clothing would be bad enough, but having a watchman catch him at impersonating a lord could be a lot worse. Real trouble, in fact, with the upshot being him having to reveal his true identity—and he wasn't quite ready to do that. "Well, five ducats is far too much, but if I must pay it, I must. I've only the royals of Merovence, though. Will you take four of those?"

"Gladly!" the herdsman said, and watched with avid attention as Matt counted the golden coins into his hand. Well he might, Matt reflected sourly—the royal was worth almost two of the ducats; he was paying about seven ducats for a nag that couldn't be worth more than two!

It was significant, though, that the man had asked for the coins of Latruria, rather than those of Merovence. He hoped it indicated nothing more than Latruria's nearness. Surely the peasants of Merovence couldn't have more faith in a foreign king than in their own queen!

At least, when he saw the colt, he could see it was worth two ducats—though the distinction between a plow horse and a warhorse was a bit ambiguous, when the chargers had to be built to carry a full load of armor. This draft animal was testimony to the fact that a smart stallion, scenting a mare in heat, can outwit even the strongest stable and the smartest groom, for the colt was at least half Percheron. The other half wasn't much smaller or less massive, either—but the colt was a hand or two short of a Clydesdale and built a little more lightly; it wouldn't quite have blended in with a team of horses pulling a TV beer wagon. All in all, Matt didn't feel too badly about having been robbed, especially since the herdsman threw in a saddle and bridle. They were old and cracked, but they worked.

So, mounted as befitted the dignity of a wandering knight, Matt rode up to the local castle, braced for them to ask where his armor was.

Chapter
Two

The lords and ladies of King Boncorro's court laughed, clinked glasses, drank, and laughed some more. Here and there a man slipped a hand beneath the long table to stroke a lady's thigh; there and here the lady returned the gesture. Some were bolder and more open, kissing and caressing above the board, where all could see; in fact, there was as much fondling as conversation. The only rule seemed to be that the interplay had to be with someone else's spouse, but even this was not always followed to the letter. The *married* couples who kissed, though, did shock their neighbors.

A Puritan would have said that the surroundings encouraged such behavior, for King Boncorro's great hall was hung with tapestries depicting scenes from the newly rediscovered classics, ferreted out of moldering libraries by lapsed clerics. Here Venus cuddled within the circle of Adonis' arm; there she reached out to Mars, while Vulcan stood by, fuming. Danaë stood in her shower of gold; Europa rode off on the back of the white bull; Cupid gazed down at Psyche, asleep in the posture of a wanton. All of them, true to the spirit of the Classical statues that had been unearthed, were completely nude.

King Boncorro, though, seemed to be quite pleased with the overall effect. He leaned back in his chair at the high table, gazing at his court over the rim of his goblet with a feeling of satisfaction as he watched the high spirits below him. "It is good to watch my courtiers enjoy themselves, Rebozo."

"Yes, your Majesty—especially since their dallying here means they are not plotting rebellion on their estates in the provinces." The chancellor looked up at his king with a cracked smile. "Your tapestries are very well-chosen toward the encouragement of such vices."

"I know," Boncorro sighed. "I had meant them to be an inducement to education and culture. It seems I still overestimate human nature."

"Perhaps, though, they would be a bit more effective if your Roman gods and goddesses were being a bit more forthright in their play," the chancellor suggested, "or if your tapestries showed them in all the various stages of the game."

"No, I wish them to inspire my courtiers with the urge to cultivate their aesthetic senses," the king replied. "I will have the tapestries show nothing obscene—my lords and ladies do well enough at that as it is."

"Wherefore?" Rebozo spread his hands. "I had thought your Majesty's aim was to have them occupy their time with pleasure, to keep them from objecting to your plans for government."

King Boncorro looked up at the chancellor with pleased surprise. "You delight me with your insight—or am I so transparent as that?"

"Only to me, and I am used to the ways of intrigue," Rebozo assured him. "But why seek to stimulate their appreciation of the arts, Majesty? Why not merely encourage them to wallow in the pleasures of the flesh, as your grandfather did?"

"Because those pleasures pall, Rebozo," the king told him. "The proof of it is the increasing decadence of my grandfather's amusements, as he strove harder and harder to pique his interest in the flesh. His courtiers, too, found that sexual pleasure required greater and greater excesses to stimulate them, when it was pleasure of the flesh alone."

The words sent a thrill of alarm through Rebozo—new ways, always new ways!—so he tried to make light of it. "Greater excesses, and greater expenditures to buy living bodies for them to degrade and torture."

" 'Living bodies,' yes—not 'people,' " Boncorro said with irony. "Well, there is some truth to your claim, Rebozo—my courtiers are far less expensive than grandfather's depraved coterie. My lords and ladies provide one another's amusement and pleasure. Still, the cost of these nightly revels is substantial."

"What cost? The tapestries, which you bought once, and once only, whereas your grandfather had need to procure new toys every week, sometimes every night? The acrobats and jesters, the musicians who fill this room with lush strains and a sensuous rhythm? They are serfs, and glad indeed to have such light work, with better lodging and food than ever they might have had in their villages! The nightly banquets and the barrels of wine, all provided by your own farms and vineyards? The occasional troupe of strolling players, who are glad of a few ducats for a week's work? These cost only a fraction of your grandfather's expenditures on performers of decadent amusements and providers of perverse pleasures."

The king smiled. "Come, Rebozo! The cost is still considerable."

"Aye, but it yields a handsome profit, though it will never show on the ledgers you so assiduously scrutinize!"

King Boncorro laughed aloud, and the nearer aristocrats looked up, alert for a joke they should share. He only smiled indulgently and waved his cup at them. They raised their own in salute, then went back to their badinage.

"That must be half the reason I keep you by me, good Chancellor," Boncorro said, "to have one about who can appreciate my scheming."

"Your genius, you mean." Rebozo's smile fairly glowed with pride. "I rejoice that my risk in preserving your Majesty's life was so richly merited. But tell me—" A shadow of concern crossed his face. "—why do you not join in your courtiers' games? Why do you hold yourself aloof, and not disport yourself among them? You, too, must have your lighter moments, Majesty!"

"I must, and you know that, as you suggested, I maintain a dozen beautiful serving maids who have no work but to wait upon me in my private chambers," Boncorro answered. "As to the behavior of my aristocrats, I do not think it politic to impose my own morality on them—or my lack of morality; I have no objection to fornication, though I do not share their delight in adultery."

"Do you not?" The old chancellor cackled. "I think you long for it as much as any man, your Majesty! I have seen the way you look at Lord Amerhe's daughter!"

"Yes, and so has the rest of the court." Boncorro glanced at the lady in question and felt the fire of lust blaze as he let his glance linger on her flawless cheek, her full ruby lips, her swelling bosom more displayed than covered by the cut of her neckline. For a few minutes he devoured her with his eyes, enjoying the surge of desire she wakened in him—then he forced his eyes to look elsewhere. "The new Contessa of Corvo, you mean? Ah, Rebozo! You know I must not gratify my senses with such as her, no matter how I long to!"

Even as he spoke, Sir Pestilline, seated next to the countess, reached past her for a tidbit from a platter on her other side; as he was bringing it back, it "happened" to drop into her cleavage. The lady squealed, clapping a hand to her décolletage, while the gentleman laughed, leaning forward, reaching—and the lady shrank away, giggling, her hand slipping lower . . .

A hand clamped down on the man's shoulder and wrenched him about. He stared up in surprise—at the Conte of Corvo. With a single motion, the count loosed his hold and slapped the offender's cheek. Sir Pestilline's head rocked; then he was on his feet catching his dagger from the table. Corvo sneered and stepped back, drawing his sword. The ladies screamed, the men shouted, benches turned over as all sprang up and away. In seconds a circle had opened around the two men, even as the count lunged at Sir Pestilline.

The knight jumped aside, dagger flicking out to parry the count's lunge as he drew his own sword—but too slowly, for Corvo riposted, then shouted in anger as he lunged again. And again Pestilline dodged, but too slowly; Corvo's blade slit his doublet and came away with its edge reddened. Pestilline howled in anger and leaped in, thrusting and parrying in earnest now. Corvo gave back as good as he got, and there wasn't even the slightest sign of mercy in either of their faces.

"Enough!" Boncorro cried, but the two hotheads could not hear him over the clash and clang of their swords. The king's mouth tightened in disgust, and he waved to his guards, who plowed through the throng, halberds at the ready. But they were taking too long; one man might be dead before they came. Boncorro rolled his hands about one another, then pantomimed throwing as he rapped out an arresting verse in an archaic language.

A loud report shook the great hall, and smoke billowed up between the two fighters. Ladies screamed and clung to their men; the two fighters leaped back, covering their mouths and noses, already coughing.

Then the guardsmen were there; the king flung his hands up and out, and the smoke disappeared, leaving not a trace or a teary eye behind. Corvo and Sir Pestilline looked up, startled, to find crossed halberds separating them.

"Not within my great hall, lord and knight!" King Boncorro called. "My lords of L'Augustine and Benicci! Act for these two while they cool their heels outside my door! Conte Corvo! Sir Pestilline! Leave this hall at once! Do not return until you have settled your differences and can sit at the same table without seeking to murder one another!"

The two men turned to face him, drawing themselves up and

sheathing their weapons. They bowed, then turned and marched out. The guardsmen opened the door before them and shut it after.

L'Augustine and Benicci stepped forward to confer with one another as the courtiers turned to take their seats again with a buzz of avid conversation, everyone comparing notes on the incident. Even the young countess, the cause of the fracas, sat down and joined in the talk with a merry glint in her eye.

"They shall duel at sunrise tomorrow, I doubt not," the chancellor said, just as hungrily as any of the others.

"I do not doubt it," the king said, "and the outcome is forgone, unless Pestilline has some noteworthy surprise in store, for Corvo is the best swordsman among the young bloods, and has slain two in duels already."

"And wounded four more. But he has not contended against your Majesty, and I believe you are more skilled with the blade than any of them."

"That may be true," Boncorro said frankly, "but I shall have no chance to put it to the test—for kings do not duel with swords."

"Noblemen do not challenge kings," Rebozo returned. "Is this not reason enough for you to do as you please?"

"No, Rebozo, for though noblemen may not *challenge* kings, they may rise up against them," Boncorro said.

"Surely no lord would dare!"

"No *one* lord, perhaps," the king agreed, "but they might very well band together in twos or threes or tens, if all felt they had grievances against me that could not be answered in open court—grievances such as the seduction of a wife or daughter, or even of a sister or true love. Then would I have a civil war on my hands and watch my plans come to naught as battles ravaged the countryside and destroyed the prosperity that I labor so hard to achieve. *That* is why I must not seek the favors of this luscious young countess, or of any other woman of station."

"Surely a knight's leman would be fair game for you, Majesty, for no knight could stand against the might of a king!"

"No, but his lord might . . . What?"

A servant had come up behind his chair and murmured in his ear. The king nodded, satisfied, and the man bowed and went away.

"When and where?" asked the chancellor.

"Tomorrow at dawn," said Boncorro, "in the Summer Park, by the Royal Pavilion."

"More entertainment for your court," Rebozo mused. "How considerate of these two young men!"

"Yes, and if I have learned of their duel, it will not be long before word has spread to every man in this room, and not much longer before it has been heard by every woman. There are trees and hedges in plenty about the pavilion, and I doubt not each one will be hiding its dozen of secret witnesses tomorrow morning."

"Every man of your court," the chancellor agreed.

"Well, two out of three, at least—the third will be still dead drunk, or too lazy to rise. There will be quite a few of the ladies, too, I doubt not—the Contessa of Corvo first among them, though she will pretend she is incognito in her cloak and mask. Entertainment indeed, Rebozo—and those who do not watch in person will listen avidly to the reports. It will keep my court busy for another tedious day, and preserve them from mischief for three more as they review the details of the duel and the merits of the argument."

"Sound policy, your Majesty," Rebozo agreed.

"It is," the king mused, "so long as I do not become embroiled in such disputes myself. No, Rebozo—I must forbear the tour, and content myself with the view."

"Yes, I see." Rebozo shook his head sadly. "If a dalliance with a highborn lady did not lead to a battle with her father, it would be sure to bring a confrontation with her husband—or even with an alliance of noblemen who considered their honor impugned. Yes, Majesty, you are wise, though it must cost you dearly."

Boncorro nodded. "No matter the number of aristocratic beauties who parade their charms before me, wearing their décolletages as low as convention and natural philosophy permit—I must not touch them."

"Poor lad," Rebozo sighed. "Still, though you may not touch, you may look."

Boncorro did, his eye gleaming as his gaze caressed the beauties of his court. "There is no harm in that, and no cause for offense, if I do not let my enjoyment show too keenly."

"But the desire it raises, Majesty," Rebozo murmured, "surely that must be released."

"That is the task of my luscious serving girls, Rebozo. If my foster brothers taught me nothing else, they taught me that."

They had taught him quite a bit more, Rebozo knew—but as far as he was concerned, not enough, or not deeply enough. He felt a moment's burning anger at the country lord and his boys. Because of them, Boncorro would waste his youth on good governance!

Boncorro did not notice, but went on explaining. "Later, my doxies will satisfy the lust my ladies raise now. For the moment, though, the illusion that one of the young ladies might inflame me to the point of granting favors to her husband, if she has one, or even of proposing marriage, if she has not—such hope will keep my courtiers dancing attendance upon me, vying for my favor and thereby falling even further under my sway." It is one of the reasons why he was resolved never to marry, though he would not let even Rebozo know that.

The chancellor shook his head sadly. "A misspent youth, your Majesty! A lad your age should be riding to the hounds and rolling in the hay, not sealing himself away with parchment and ink until the blood in his veins has run dry!"

"Oh, I find exercise enough, I assure you," Boncorro said, eyeing a young countess fresh from the country and thinking of the newest of his personal maids. "Beyond that, I find delight enough in witnessing the pleasures of my courtiers."

He nodded to himself as he glanced about the great hall. It was no mere extravagance to maintain a lavish court, but a political necessity. "Yet I must find some other game to occupy their attention when their delight in the pleasures of the body slackens, so that they may vie with one another for some goal other than the bed of the most beautiful, or the attentions of the most dashing, so that they will not turn to intrigue out of sheer boredom."

"Your grandfather's courtiers were scarcely bored, Majesty," Rebozo grunted, but without much conviction, for he knew it was a lie—and worse, knew that the young king knew it, too.

Boncorro held his cup out, and a servant refilled it. He traced the sign of skull and bones over it as he murmured a verse, then lifted the cup to his lips . . .

The dark wine turned bright red—the red of blood.

King Boncorro dashed the wine to the floor with a curse. The courtiers fell silent, staring at him, wide-eyed.

"Majesty!" Trusty old Rebozo was by his side, hovering over him, anxious, solicitous. "Majesty, what was that foul brew?"

"Poisoned wine, of course!" Boncorro snapped, seething more with contempt than with anger. "Have you not found the assassin who set that gargoyle to fall on me, Rebozo?"

"Yes, Majesty, and he confessed. He died in agony!"

"He confessed under torture, you dolt! . . . No, I wrong you." The king throttled back his exasperation at the attentive old man, and his desire to throttle him, too. "But I have told you a hundred times that a confession under torture proves nothing! Now it is clear that the man was guiltless or, at the worst, only one of many—for the true assassin has struck again!"

"My apologies, Majesty!" Rebozo had turned ashen. "My most abject apologies! I would never have thought—"

"You should have," Boncorro snapped, "since this is the twelfth attempt in five years!" He reined in his temper again and forced his voice to be more gentle. "Though perhaps I wrong you—this one was far more clumsy than its predecessors. Poison in the wine, indeed! The work of a rank amateur, if ever I saw it! Any churl could slip poison in the wine—and I want the bottler and his servers all questioned, to discover who did it! Questioned, mind you, with no more torture than suffices for each to give you a name, not a confession!"

"Majesty," Rebozo protested, "that entails scarcely more than a beating—and how can you be sure of an answer gained with so little pain?"

"By comparing it to the other answers, of course! Those given by the other servants! I tell you again, Rebozo, that an answer given to stop pain proves only that the subject will say anything he thinks you wish him to! And as often as not, *that* will be a lie! Though I do not think this would-be murderer will prove to be the same one who has striven to slay me these five years past."

Rebozo stared. "How . . . how does your Majesty see that?"

"Because the other attempts required evil magic of a very difficult kind. To make a block of stone fall, when none were near it, and that at the exact moment I was passing beneath it? 'Twas only my own warding spell that made me hesitate in midstep, to see that block of granite smash the paving in front of me! And the gargoyle who came alive, the cat with teeth like scimitars, the sword that leaped from the scabbard even as I buckled it on—these all required a lifetime's knowledge of magic, or a pact with the Devil such as only a man of great importance could achieve!" His gaze strayed; his voice sank. "A man such as my grandfather, King Maledicto, reaching out from beyond the grave . . ."

"Come, Majesty!" the chancellor scoffed. "If the Devil was so displeased with your grandfather as to withdraw protection, why would he now give him power to reach out from Hell?"

"Why, because his disappointment with the grandson has become even greater than the lapses of the grandsire!" Boncorro snapped at him, then looked away again. "But I shall not yield! I shall not become what that wicked old man was—a murderer, a child slayer—"

"What a notion!" Rebozo cried. "You who have no children, to worry about slaying them! Come, Majesty, bolster your spirits! We shall find and defeat this sorcerer yet!"

King Boncorro lifted a brooding gaze to him. "See that you do, Lord Chancellor, see that you do! Begin with the servants, all of them—but not with torture, mind you! Take each into a separate chamber and question him or her closely, then compare their answers and see if there is any agreement! If there is, bring word of it to me before you take any action—simple consensus is no proof of truth! It could just as easily be a sign that one person is disliked by all, and since so many of them are left from my grandfather's court, dislike of one could mean that only he can be relied upon!"

"Majesty, it shall be done as you say." The chancellor bowed. "May I congratulate you on your courage in having the determination to persevere in your reforms in the face of such concerted effort by the power of Evil to destroy you."

Boncorro waved the compliment away. "There is little danger in it, Chancellor. The powers of Evil have little cause to be displeased with me, for whatever my purpose, it is certainly not the doing of good for its own sake. I attempt to gain power and riches, that is all."

"Aye—by making the whole country more rich."

"My wealth comes from the people, one way or another, Lord Chancellor. I saw that as I watched serfs plow and reap. If I would have greater riches, I must first inspire the people to produce greater wealth from which I may draw."

"Yes, you have explained that many times." Rebozo sighed. "That, however, does not explain your determination to see justice done, and to protect the innocent from punishment or abuse."

"Does it not? People will work harder when they feel they are safe, Chancellor, and can bend their minds to their tasks without the constant worry that the sword will fall on their necks, or their goods be plundered at a lord's whim. When they know they will keep a fair share of that which they grow, the farmers will work harder to grow more—and when serfs can be sure which efforts will *not* bring punishment, they will put more sweat into those that will be rewarded."

"Yes, you have explained that time and again," Rebozo said, "and that greater assurance of safety and greater wealth should lead people to use their newfound gains to buy pleasure."

"Why, so they do." Boncorro waved at his court. "Even here you can see it—they are better dressed than ever before, and come flocking to my castle to seek pleasure, the young most of all! For each of those you see here, Rebozo, there are a thousand serfs who are drinking more ale and buying the favors of wantons. Vice flourishes, so the Devil should be not only appeased, but even pleased."

"Then why should the same Devil give a sorcerer power against you?"

Boncorro shrugged. "The greater the worry and fear, the happier the Devil. Look for an extremist in sorcery, Rebozo—one who believes that any human happiness is wrong if it is not wrung from the pain and suffering of others. There shall we find my would-be killer."

"Majesty," said the chancellor, "I will."

"Then do." The king waved him away. "Be about your task, Rebozo—but remember, no torture! Well, not much," he amended.

"Only a little, Majesty," the chancellor agreed, "never fear—which, unfortunately, is what the servants and bottler and cooks shall say, no doubt. Still, I shall strive." He bowed and turned away.

Boncorro watched the old man leave the great hall, and frowned, still brooding, till he was out of sight. Then, with an effort of will, he threw off the mood, tested a whole pitcher of wine, then filled his own goblet and drank deeply. A duke's daughter came by below the table, fluttering her eyelashes at him. Boncorro laughed and sprang down off the dais, crying, "Fiddlers! A dance tune! We shall caper before we taste the next course!"

The fiddlers struck up a gay, lively tune, and Boncorro began to dance with the beautiful young lady, devouring her charms with his eyes. She blushed demurely, lowering her gaze, but glancing up at him through long lashes. All about them courtiers left their meat and came to dance, quick to ape their king, quick to join in the attempt to cheer him, ever quick to curry favor.

Rebozo slammed into his private exchequer, muttering darkly under his breath. LoClercchi, his secretary, looked up in surprise. "Good evening, Lord Chancellor."

"Not when some amateurish idiot seeks to poison our king," Rebozo snapped, "who commands me to find the culprit without delay."

"Ah." The secretary nodded in sympathy. "Not a good evening, indeed. I fear I must make it worse."

"Worse?" Rebozo swung about, glaring. "How is this?"

"A message." The secretary held up a scrap of parchment. "A carrier pigeon landed in the dovecote, just as the sun set."

"News from a spy?" Rebozo snatched the message and sat down to puzzle out the tiny letters. At last he threw it down on the desk. "Oh, a pox upon it! Your eyes are far younger than mine, LoClercchi—what does it say?"

The secretary took the tiny parchment, but did not look at it, so Rebozo knew that he had already read it. "It is from your peasant spy on the estates of the Duke of Riterra, my lord. He writes from a market in Merovence—though not very far into Merovence . . ."

"Far enough!" Rebozo's eyes kindled. "What does he find that is worthy of report?"

"He writes that a wizard is nosing about the market," the secretary said, "eavesdropping on conversations, and particularly interested in those who tout the virtues of Latruria. Our spy tested the man and thinks he may be the Lord Wizard himself."

Rebozo rubbed his hands, nodding vigorously. "I had thought he must take notice of the remaking our young king is doing!"

"Especially since our folk have been boasting and bragging of it whenever they cross the border," LoClercchi said with irony. "It is marvelous to have agents who work for free, my lord, and without even realizing they do our work. I do not know how you managed it."

"Bosh! You know well enough that I sent one man about the border farms, gloating on the bragging he would do in Merovence, on the next fair day! Does our peasant informer say what manner of test he gave the wizard?"

"No, my lord, there was no room on so small a parchment—and, frankly, I do not think he could write quickly enough. His letters are horribly clumsy, and his spelling atrocious."

"Still, it was worth the cost of a teacher, to gain this report! Well, we shall have to wait till the man comes home, for his reeve to question him more closely. If it is her Majesty's wizard, though, we shall not have long to wait till he seeks to cross the border and stop the unrest at its source!"

The secretary looked up in alarm. "He could set all of King Boncorro's plan awry, my lord, and your own as well!"

The chancellor waved a hand to dismiss the notion. "The king's plans are my plans, LoClercchi, no matter how I may caution him and plead the course of prudence."

"And your plans are his?" the secretary asked, amused.

But Rebozo shook his head. "I cannot claim that, for I would not of myself depart so quickly from the old king's ways. Indeed, I tremble for my young master, and hope that the Devil will not too quickly become so angry as to destroy him."

"And us with him." LoClercchi's voice trembled. "Let us hope our young king keeps his balance on the tightrope he has stretched for himself."

"Fences have their purposes," Rebozo agreed, "but serving as pathways was never one of them. Still, we have no choice but to resign or to follow him—and I am too old to seek new work, and too deeply steeped in sin to wish to reform." He looked up at his secretary. "You, however, are still young, LoClercchi. If you wish to go, you may."

LoClercchi stared at his employer, silently weighing the relative merits of a virtuous life of uncertain income and modest means, with the certainty of wealth and privilege that came from serving the chancellor. His decision was almost instantaneous, for he had fought the long battle against this temptation years before, and periodically since. Like many young men, he decided there would be time enough to work on salvation later—after he had made his fortune. "I am loyal to you, my lord."

Rebozo nodded, satisfied. "Good, good. Let us deal, then, with the problem of this Lord Wizard."

"Perhaps he shall not become a problem," LoClercchi said hopefully. "Perhaps he shall stay on his own side of the border."

"Perhaps, LoClercchi, but also perhaps not. Certainly he is nothing to worry about—yet. But I prefer to do my worrying in advance; it makes no sense to take undue chances—and it is my duty to King Boncorro *not* to wait until the man becomes a threat. Write for me."

The secretary seized parchment and ink. Rebozo began to pace as he dictated, "My dear young Camano—you are, I believe, currently in the castle of your father, the Count d'Arrete, hard by the Alps in Merovence. I suspect that a nobleman or knight may soon call at your gate for hospitality, claiming to be only a knight errant, or a messenger about the queen's business, or some such. Be not deceived—this man is a wizard, and may well be the Lord Wizard of Merovence."

He went on to detail exactly how the young lord should test the man, and how he should deal with him—in no uncertain terms. When the secretary had finished writing, Rebozo took the quill and signed the document. Then he took it to a separate table, sprinkled it with a powder that stank abominably, muttered a verse in an arcane language, and touched a candle's flame to a corner of the document. It went up in a flash that lit the whole chamber and was gone in less than a second.

The chancellor nodded, satisfied. "He will find that on his table when he comes to his chamber this night, a hundred miles to the north." He gathered his robe about him, shivering. "Glad I am that I do not have to suffer the rigors of that climate, so hard by the mountains! Well, we shall see what young Lord Camano may make of this wizard. In any case, we shall discover his purpose." he turned back to his secretary. "Now—issue orders that as soon as the cooks and scullery maids are done with their work, they be taken to my audience chamber. As the servers are released from their duties, let each be taken to join them. Then I shall question each one alone, and closely."

LoClercchi looked up with a frown. "What good is that? Whoever poisoned the wine, he shall already be fled!"

"He shall," the chancellor sighed, "if he was here at all, and not some sorcerer enchanting the wine from miles away—or a wizard; let us not forget that our young king has enemies in both camps now."

"What sorcerer has n—" But Rebozo's glare froze the words on his secretary's tongue, and he did not finish the sentence.

"Of course, there are his courtiers, too, any one of whom might have dropped poison in the wine when the server was ogling one of our oh-so-casual beauties," the chancellor went on, as if there had been no interruption, "but our good Boncorro would certainly never approve their questioning on so mere a suspicion. No, we shall go through the forms, LoClercchi, but we shall learn nothing. I would that we could torture a few of them as we did in the old days, so that we might at least gain a satisfying answer!"

"Even if it were not true," LoClercchi murmured.

"True!" cried the chancellor, exasperated. "What matters truth? Satisfying our master—*that* is everything!"

Chapter
Three

The Captain of the Guard gave Matt a jaundiced look. "A knight errant, without armor?"

"I lost it at the last tournament," Matt explained. "I know, I know, I'm a little old to be a knight bachelor—but what can you do? Some of us are just more talented than others."

"Well, you would not be the first knight to come to this door when he is in misfortune," the guard admitted. "Still, I can tell by your bearing and your raiment that you are indeed a knight."

That gave Matt a feeling of satisfaction. He'd worked at choosing upper-class clothing that looked just worn enough to be right for a knight with a string of bad tournaments behind him. The bearing, of course, came from actually having been knighted. That was the way things worked in this universe. "Thank you, Captain! Now, if you could send someone to guide me to your lord, I would like to pay my respects."

"Aye, and that is all you will pay," the soldier grumbled. "Ho! Page!"

A passing boy stopped passing and sprinted up to the captain, skidding to a halt that ended in a perfunctory bow.

"Escort this stranger to the count," the officer told him, "and be mindful that he is a guest!" Then he snapped his fingers, and a hostler came forward to take Matt's horse.

"Sir Matthew of Bath, you say?" The Count d'Arrete gazed up at the ceiling, stroking his beard. "Ah! Now I have it! 'Tis a town in Angland, is it not?"

Matt always marveled that England, Scotland, and Ireland had pretty much the same names in this universe as they did in his own—Angland, Scotia, and Eire. All the other countries had names he scarcely recognized, though he could pick out their sources. On the other hand, the English language that he knew and loved didn't exist here—everyone in Angland spoke the same language spoken in Merovence, and throughout Europe, for that matter. There was no English Channel in this version of Earth, so Hardishane, this world's counterpart to Charlemagne, had conquered the Anglo-Saxons, Welsh, and Scots, too. Eire had joined of its own free will, or at least become an ally—Matt wasn't too clear on the history; the books in Alisande's library only gave him a vague general outline, and he hadn't had the time to go to Angland and check on the primary sources. He did gather, though, that the Vikings had been pretty thoroughly repulsed, though he wasn't sure how. There was a lot of the history of this universe he didn't know—including what had happened in Latruria. He did know that the capital city of the ancient empire had been named Reme, not Rome, which presumably meant that Remus had won the fistfight, not Romulus—not that it made much difference. Beyond that, he had only the most sketchy outline of Classical history, and what he had was suspect—it sounded entirely too wholesome to be Roman, not that such considerations would matter now. "It is, your Lordship. There are medicinal baths there. Personally, I don't think they heal you so much as just make you feel better—lying around in hot water always has that effect on me, at least."

"*Hot* water, you say? An interesting notion! I must journey there sometime and try it!"

Matt almost pointed out that the count could heat water over the fire right here in his own castle, but bit his tongue in time—the man was likely to try a dip in boiling water. No, let him stay with the natural way.

"So you are a knight of the Bath!" Count d'Arrete chuckled at his own witticism, and his courtiers dutifully echoed him. Matt managed to force a smile himself. He actually *was* a knight of the bath, of course, and the cold tub had been administered in Emperor Hardishane's secret tomb—but there was no need to mention that.

"Ah, you have heard that jest many times, I see," the count said ruefully. "Well, stay and join us at meat this evening, stranger! We are always glad to have visitors, to bring us news of the world outside our domain—but most especially tonight, when my cousins from Latruria are at last able to join us! Their young king has opened the border these last few years, and has now even given permission for his noblemen to journey to visit kinsmen!"

Matt pricked up his ears. Talk about good luck! Unless, of course, virtually all the marcher barons were entertaining relatives—which was probable, if permission had just now been granted. "It has been many years since kin could visit kin, my lord."

"Generations! Not since my grandfather's time have we welcomed our southern cousins! Old King Maledicto kept his border closed by sorcery as well as force of arms! Ah, it is good indeed to see our kin!"

"I shall look forward to meeting them myself," Matt said, with more sincerity than the count knew.

This great hall was considerably less great than Boncorro's. Of course, Matt had never seen the royal castle of Latruria, but he had seen Alisande's court, and the castle of a mere country count suffered by comparison.

Fortunately, Matt wasn't interested in comparing them.

It was a cornerstone of his aesthetic that he take each work on its own merits, and within the context of its own function as well as its designer's intentions. The architect who built this castle had obviously been trying to achieve the optimum balance between comfort and defense, and had succeeded about as well as he could. The hall was large enough to shelter a small army during a siege—or the peasants of the home farms, as well as the gentry of the county, during a feast day. The peasants weren't here at the moment, but the gentry were. Count d'Arrete had meant it when he said he was glad of one more to help him celebrate.

The countess had done at least as well as the architect, when it came to decoration. Faded old tapestries alternated with bright new ones; garlands of flowers obscured the grim old battle trophies. An oversized shield brightly painted with the family coat of arms hung over the high dais, while about the hall hung smaller shields that showed the arms of the count's knights, obscuring the old, dusty, captured flags of foes vanquished. At the far end hung another oversized shield with the arms of the Latrurian branch of the clan.

However, those Latrurians weren't about to let the hidden dinginess go. "These old castles were well enough for defense, cousin, and as trophy cases," Conte Puvecci said with a wave of his hand. "Surely, though, it would be desirable to have a separate, and more pleasant, building, for your daily living."

Count d'Arrete smiled, but Matt could almost hear him grind his teeth. Since he knew who d'Arrete was, it didn't take much deduction to figure out that the other mature male at the high table must be his Latrurian cousin—and therefore that curled hair and pointed beards were all the rage in Latruria. Matt took a quick glance around the hall, noting curly locks and pointy goatees, so he'd know where the Latrurians were—it made for more efficient eavesdropping.

He turned back to the high table just as Count d'Arrete was saying, "There is a feeling of continuity, cousin, of connection with one's ancestors, that can only be gained from living where they lived."

"Quite so, quite so!" Puvecci nodded earnestly. "And when I feel the need for that, I go back to spend a night or two there."

"Alone?" the Countess d'Arrete gasped.

Puvecci gave her a condescending grin. "I know, I know, one is never alone among the ghosts of one's ancestors—or among one's soldiers, for I must needs keep guards posted there; it is, after all, my stronghold, and gives command of the valley. But our new white marble palazzo is far more appealing."

"You must come visit us!" the Contessa Puvecci gushed. "I have found the cleverest painter you can imagine, to adorn our walls with murals and frescoes of the heroes of ancient Reme, and of their goddesses and gods!"

"The marble was expensive," the conte said expansively, "but when one is building for the ages, one must not stint."

Count d'Arrete managed to keep his smile, but it was hard. "Your lands must produce most amazingly."

"They do, they do! Our young King Boncorro was right, insisting that we leave the peasants a larger share of the crop—for it gave them reason to labor with greater zeal! And, of course, leaving his lords so much more of our land's produce gives us far more to work with." Conte Puvecci kept nodding. "He is a good king, a good king! And I think he will grow to be even better."

Matt didn't have to be a mind reader to know that d'Arrete was suddenly finding flaws in Alisande's reign that he had never thought of before.

"I could not truly say life was one continual celebration at King Boncorro's court," Puvecci's son Giancarlo was telling Sir John, Captain of the Guard. "He does demand that we rise before noon to practice at swordplay and tilting, and has each of us oversee the work of some reeve in a distant province, watching the clerks verify the reeve's reports and accounts. He also insists that each of our corps take its turn in patrolling the city at night—so there is very little theft or murder or rape, and it is almost true that even the most lowly born woman may cross the town at night without danger."

"Almost," the count's son, Camano, grated.

Giancarlo shrugged. "There are always accidents."

"Are you never tempted to *be* those accidents, cousin?"

Giancarlo answered with a slow grin. "Why should we? Where did you think those lowborn women were coming from so late at night, cousin?"

"The duchesses hold gatherings every evening," said Lady Sophia, the Puveccis' daughter, "and there is always fizzy wine, and dancing, and song. And the gentlemen, cousin! The gentlemen are so gallant and so handsome as they vie for glory!"

Lady Jeanette d'Arrete was almost green with envy. "Do *all* the young folk stay at his Majesty's court?"

"All who can persuade their parents," Sophia said with a condescending laugh, "and that is *nearly* all. The king has built a whole range of apartments just for us; and I assure you there is much coming and going within that building!"

"How far away are the men's apartments?"

"Why, they adjoin ours, cousin, and there is even a passageway between the two buildings, for use in cold weather! The lady who cannot find a husband there is slow indeed!"

Jeanette was already beginning to turn pale and sigh—while at the far end of the table, Camano glowered and smoldered.

Of course, that could have just been the effect of the flickering light of the torches and candles—but Matt rather doubted that. He had been lucky in his seat assignment—he had to strain to hear what was going on at the high table, but hear he could, and he doubted that the expressions he was seeing on the faces of the younger d'Arretes had anything to do with the lighting.

However, if the little flames helped to obscure the old trophies that the countess couldn't remove without violating tradition, they also helped obscure the signs of age among the mature ladies, who laughed and drank beside their husbands, and gave a glow to the cheeks of the younger women, gentry and common alike, and set a sparkle in the eyes of the young men who paid them court. The serving girls seemed almost as vibrant as the ladies, as they laughed and flirted with the young men. The butler and footmen, of course, did not have that privilege, but the candlelight nonetheless picked out the gleams in their eyes. It was a festive occasion indeed, and everyone was making merry.

Which made Matt wonder about the morose young man to his left. He watched the joyous company with no sign of delight and seemed to brace himself every time he glanced across the table to the blushing young lady who was smiling and making eyes at him. When he did notice, he forced a smile, exchanged a few brief words with her, then glanced away and gazed moodily out over the throng. Each time, the shock of hurt showed in the girl's face, but it was quickly hidden as she turned to her neighbor with forced gaiety. Matt's heart went out to her, and finally, when she turned to her neighbor but found him engaged in conversation on his other side, then turned to her other neighbor but found him likewise engaged, Matt came to her rescue. "Take pity on a stranger, demoiselle, and tell me who these grand folk each may be."

She looked up at him in surprise that quickly turned to gratitude. "Why, those known to me are the knights and neighbors of Count d'Arrete, sir, save for their daughter Jeanette and that young gallant who sits at the end of the high table and is Camano, their son."

"You mean the one who's been giving me nasty looks all evening? What's the matter—doesn't he like strangers?"

That brought a smile of amusement. "Nay, sir, unless they be female. But I think he is more affronted by Squire Pascal, who sits by you, than by yourself."

The young man looked up with a guilty start. "Do you speak to me, damsel?"

"No, sir, I speak *of* you." Finally, a flash of irritation showed in the girl's face, but was again quickly masked. "I was identifying you for your neighbor there; you do not seem to have introduced yourself to he who sits by you."

"True enough—but then, neither has he introduced himself to *me*." The young man turned to Matt. "I am Pascal de la Tour, sir—not yet a squire, but only a squire's son—and this young lady is my neighbor, the Demoiselle Charlotte Espere. Our fathers would have us be betrothed, but have not asked our opinions in the matter."

"Pascal!" Charlotte hissed, blushing furiously as she glanced to either side at her neighbors, who were, fortunately, still earnestly engaged in discussions that kept them turned away from her.

"Be honest, Charlotte," Pascal sighed. "You have no great liking for me, though you do seek to be a dutiful daughter and discover love where it is not."

Tears filled poor Charlotte's eyes. "It is cruel of you to speak so!"

"Is it not strange?" Pascal gave Matt a hard smile. "I speak truth, as the Bible says we should—and folk censure me for it!"

"The truth can be hurtful," Matt countered, "and that the Bible does *not* enjoin—at least, not in the New Testament."

Pascal's eye kindled with interest—or was it delight in a challenge? "Must we choose between two sins, then? Lying, or cruelty?"

"Not unless you're asked for your opinion," Matt answered.

Pascal abruptly lost interest. "You have no more concern for truth than anyone else, I see." He turned away, letting his gaze roam over the room.

Matt contained his indignation at the slight and turned to lean across the table, speaking as low as he could and still be heard by the teenager across from him. "*I* think you should be grateful for his churlishness, demoiselle. At least, this way, you're not apt to wind up in a loveless marriage—and your father can't really blame you."

"He will find a way." But Charlotte looked surprised, as if she hadn't really thought of the consequences. "I thought that if two married, love would grow."

"Not that I've ever seen—and I can think of a lot better reasons for marriage than joining two estates that happen to border each other." Matt glanced up at the high table, looking for a change of subject. "Is that the count's cousin, then?"

Charlotte seemed as glad for the diversion as he. "Yes, that is the Conte Puvecci, with his wife, and his son and daughter."

Matt smiled without mirth. "I'll wager there sits another young lady whose parents are going to try to marry her off to strengthen the family."

"To Camano, you mean?" Charlotte looked startled. "I had not thought . . . but now that you speak of it, perhaps . . ."

"I feel sorry for her."

"You say that, and you do not even know Camano?" The demoiselle turned back to him with a smile. "Of course, I do not, either—but what I have heard of him is enough for me to pity her, too." Her eyes went wide and round. "But I speak of myself, do I not?"

Matt gusted breath in relief. "Yes, except that you don't have to worry about your current trap. Churlish or not, Pascal seems to be getting you out of that."

"So he does!" Charlotte turned with a smile. "*Thank* you, Pascal!"

Pascal's head snapped around, staring in surprise. "For what, Charlotte?"

"For being yourself." Charlotte dropped her napkin and stood. "Come, the fiddlers have struck up a reel, and other folk have gone out to dance! Let us join them!"

Pascal hesitated, looking wary.

"It's a peace offering." Matt gave him an elbow in the ribs. "Get out there and dance with her, you clod!"

Pascal turned on him, fire in his eye.

"She's been your friend all through childhood, hasn't she?" Matt snapped.

That took the heat out of Pascal's anger. "Aye . . . if a girl can be a friend to a boy."

"You know she was, as much as she could be." Matt didn't know anything of the kind, but he liked Charlotte already and didn't see how Pascal could not have liked the girl—until he'd felt threatened. "Get out there and make your peace with her—and don't be surprised if you find a way to make a definite end to the whole problem."

Pascal turned wary again. "How can I? Our fathers—"

"They aren't apt to force you if you're both really dead set against it—and the way you've been behaving, a saint would be dead set against you."

Pascal's head reared back, affronted.

"I thought you coveted truth," Matt jibed. "Go make your peace. In this world, we need all the friends we can get—and in the next one, too."

"There's some truth to that." Pascal put down his napkin and rose. "One dance, then."

"That should be all it takes."

Matt watched them go, heaving a sigh. If only the problem of mass discontent could be solved so easily!

Nearby, he heard some of the young gentry muttering to one another. "They talk as if their lives are constant festival! Oh, so they serve a few hours' duty each day—what matter?"

"Not even that, for the ladies," a young woman said.

"And they are among their own kind!" another youth exclaimed. "They are among folk of their own age and class, with no parents to order them about, living all together with no troubling from the king!"

"Wherefor is he so generous?" another girl wondered, but her voice was buried in the marveling. "A constant round of dressmakers and gatherings!"

"A constant round of flirting with ladies and wenching with wantons!"

"A constant round of drink and song!"

Matt reflected gloomily that he had been right—Alisande needed to start a university. He wondered how quickly he could get it up and running.

"My parents *must* let me go to the queen's capital!" one pretty young maid proclaimed.

"They will not." Another like her sat sulking. "They will say the expense is too great, and I can do well enough wedding Squire Knocknee our neighbor!"

"Squire Knocknee! Why, he is forty if he is a day, and fat and balding, and half his teeth are gone!"

"Aye, and his breath is putrid," the girl said bitterly. "Only think! These young ladies of Latruria can circulate among handsome young bucks with sweet breath, and find themselves husbands for love, not their parents' convenience!"

"So might we, if Queen Alisande would allow it," her brother grumbled.

"Where is she to get the money?" his friend said with sad practicality.

"Where does King Boncorro get his?"

"Aye, and why is he willing to spend it on the young?"

"Why, because he is himself young, and does not wish to be surrounded by antiques!"

"The queen is young, too."

"Aye, but she is married already," a young girl said bitterly. "Married, and with a kingdom in hand—and therefore does she think like an agéd parent, not a young lass seeking love!"

Matt bridled—she had sought love and found it, thank you! Maybe not the most romantic suitor in the world, but—

He sawed back on his own reins. He *wasn't* the world's most romantic husband, was he? Maybe he needed to work on that . . .

Pascal came back, chatting agreeably enough with Charlotte, but somewhat absentmindedly. She didn't seem to mind it this time, though. They took their seats again, and Matt asked, "Was I right?"

"Hm?" Pascal looked up.

"You can still be friends if you agree you're not going to get married."

"Oh! Aye. My father will raise the roof, I doubt not—but Charlotte should be free of blame, since 'tis I who will not have the marriage."

"Not completely free," Charlotte said darkly. "I doubt not Mother and Father will both rail at me for not being able to win your favor, good Pascal—but even as you say, it will be you who bears the brunt of it. I would I could aid you."

Pascal shrugged. "If 'tis too strenuous, I shall simply leave home."

Charlotte's eyes went wide. "Will your father allow that?"

Pascal gave her a bleak smile. "If the quarrel goes as I suspect it shall, he will end by banishing me from his house."

"I do not wish *that!*" Charlotte cried.

"Nor do I, really," Pascal said slowly. "I would prefer to leave with his blessing—but leave I must."

Matt didn't like the sound of this at all. "Why?"

Pascal turned back to him, then glanced away uneasily. Charlotte looked up at him, giving his arm a reassuring squeeze, then said to Matt, "He loves another."

Matt sat still for a minute.

Then he said, "Oh."

After that, he said, "That explains a few things."

"Aye." Charlotte went misty-eyed. "If I had known that, I would never have been . . ." She hesitated.

"Never have been hurt by his frostiness," Matt finished for her. "But how does that tie in with your wanting to leave home, Pascal?"

The young man glanced quickly to either side, then sat down again. "The lady I love is my cousin—but she dwells in Latruria."

"His fourth cousin." Charlotte, too, had taken her seat again, leaning forward in conspiratorial secrecy. "Once removed."

"Perfectly legal and perfectly moral, then. But how did you meet her, if the border has been closed all these years?"

"It has been open for the last few," Charlotte reminded him, "at least, to common folk and gentry."

Pascal nodded. "Last summer both families met at long last and were again one family reunited—and I met Panegyra." He gazed off into space, a foolish smile coming over his face. "Oh, she is the picture of beauty itself, the loveliest and most gentle creature imaginable!"

Charlotte looked down, clasping her hands, and her knuckles went white. Matt interrupted quickly. "Are you of the same station?"

Pascal turned back to him, startled. "Aye—both children of squires, who were themselves children of squires."

Matt frowned. "Nobody wanted to become a knight?"

Pascal's smile thinned into bitterness. "My grandfather Aiello became a squire not by serving a knight, sir, but by virtue of having had a wizard for a father, before the evil king Maledicto usurped the throne."

"Squire?" Matt frowned. "But wouldn't he have become a wizard in his own turn, not . . . Oh! Of course!"

"Aye." Pascal nodded. "Under King Maledicto, white wizardry was banned, even those small magics that drew only slightly on the font of Goodness. It was only by the grace of his lord that Grandfather Aiello became a squire, rather than a peasant or serf."

"His lord's grace, and the money and land his father had accumulated?" Matt guessed.

Charlotte smiled, amused. "If a man has land, you must either give him rank in proportion, or take it away from him."

"And his lord was a good man who refused to confiscate." Matt nodded.

"Perhaps," Pascal allowed, "though family legends speak of a debt owed . . . Well, no matter. The long and the short of it is that my father is a squire, and so is Panegyra's, but I can never become a knight, though she may become a lady." His tone was liquid—pure vermouth.

"By marrying a knight, you mean."

Pascal closed his eyes, shuddering. "Please! My nightmares are enough!"

"I see your point," Matt agreed. "So you want to leave home to woo your cousin, and—"

A blow rocked him. Matt looked up, glaring; that punch had *hurt*! But he was a knight, and chivalry restrained him until he knew whether it had been an accident or not.

It was Camano, the Count d'Arrete's son, grinning down at him. "Your pardon, Sir Knight! I had not seen you there."

"Seen him! Why, you stared directly at him from ten feet away!" Charlotte said indignantly.

"As he might have, if he had any vestige of courtesy." Camano's grin hardened. "He might have given his hosts a glance, now and again."

Matt knew very well that he had—and that Camano had been looking at him at least two of those times. But he was aware of the three young bloods at Camano's back with their hands on the hilts of their rapiers, and he chose his words carefully. "Your pardon, Sir Camano. I became so engrossed in your guests and the beauties of your great hall that I—"

"Engrossed!" Camano cried, and two of the young bloods hooted. "Gross you must be indeed, to be so laggard in courtesy! And as to admiring the beauties, aye, I have seen your gaze roam to every beauteous young damsel in this place. Are you not ashamed, an old goat like yourself?"

Matt was still in his early thirties.

"There is no shame where there is no cause," he said slowly, "but he who has given cause should indeed be shamed."

"An insult!" Camano crowed in delight. "You have heard it, my friends—have I not been given insult?"

"Oh, aye!" "Verily!" "A most grievous insult indeed!" said his backup group.

"Not a bit!" Pascal cried indignantly. "He has given no cause for offense, but—"

Camano's glove caught him across the cheek. "Be still, peasant!"

Matt rose slowly, his hand on his own sword. "Now, that was definitely unchivalrous, Sir Camano!"

"Then prove it upon my body, Sir Matthew of Bath!" Camano cried, suddenly angry. His sword whipped out. "*If* you are truly a knight, or truly Matthew of Bath!"

"I am Sir Matthew indeed." Matt drew his sword, and with a massive shriek, the ladies leapt from their places and crowded back. The men shouted with delight and rose, too, to clear the tables back, and a space fifty feet across suddenly opened around the two men.

"Your people are used to this, I see." Matt glanced at the count and his lady, but they were sitting back complacently, as were conte and contessa. The young folk were leaning forward eagerly. "I gather we're the prime entertainment for the evening."

"Say, rather, that *you* are!" And with no word of warning, Camano lunged.

Chapter
Four

Matt leaped back and aside, parrying, then riposted in time to catch another hasty and ill-timed lunge on his blade. He caught it in a bind, stepping right up to Camano *corps à corps* to say, "No wonder your father was so glad to give me hospitality. Do you d'Arretes always attack your guests?"

"Mind your manners, commoner!" Camano snarled, and shoved Matt away, leaping back. Matt was tempted to hold rock-steady and make the boy look ridiculous, but decided to be a little charitable and fell back a step. Camano slashed and lunged again; Matt parried both times, then dodged the thrust that followed and stepped in *corps à corps* once more, catching the youth's sword hand in a vise grip long enough to say, "Didn't your fencing master teach you how to riposte?"

Camano's answer was drowned in an outraged shout from his buddies, and Matt sprang away—he had just delivered a humiliation, by catching Camano's sword hand. Red-faced and enraged, Camano circled his sword overhead in a figure eight, and Matt felt a twinge of real alarm—if the kid's grip slipped, someone could get hurt! He was tempted to lunge in under the whirling blade, but resisted—Camano might be faster than he looked.

He wasn't. When Camano slashed out with the blade, Matt saw it coming a mile away and had plenty of time to leap back *and* swing his own blade to parry. Metal exploded against metal, and Matt felt the impact all the way up to his shoulder. He leaped back in alarm, realizing for the first time that the kid was actually trying to kill him!

The bystanders shouted and applauded, apparently figuring that Camano had done something skillful. So did Camano—flushed with pleasure, he went into the figure eight again.

Matt was suddenly done with courtesy. With full seriousness he lunged under the whirling blade, slashing Camano's doublet just the tiniest bit with his sword tip, then leaping out just as the youth cut down with a cry of anger. His blade clashed on the floor, and Matt leaped in to hold down the point, then pivoted to swing his dagger straight at Camano's throat. He slowed his stab, though, and Camano just barely managed to parry with his own dagger.

The bystanders shouted in anger and alarm.

For a moment Camano was caught with his arms crossed and his balance precarious. One sidewise kick and Matt could have stretched him on the floor—but it would have embarrassed the young man too much, and his folks were already on their feet, shouting in anger. Matt, ever the good guest, leaped back and let Camano recover.

The boy's sword swung straight up toward Matt's gizzard.

It didn't have much force, coming straight up off the floor and without much room for the swing. Matt sidestepped, brought his own sword up under it, and swung the boy's blade high as he stepped in to mutter, "I *told* you to riposte!" before he leaped clear and waited.

Face flaming, Camano did indeed riposte and moved around Matt warily, sword tip circling—but his friends were shouting objections, and Count d'Arrete signaled to a guard. Two knights stepped in, swords upraised, crying, "Hold!"

Matt was all too glad to step back and lower his blade.

Camano leaped forward, stabbing.

The knights shouted, caught at him, and conveniently missed.

Matt caught the kid's lunge on his blade and circled tight, ending with a sharp downward thrust. Camano's blade struck sparks from the floor again, and Matt set his dagger to the boy's throat. "They said *hold!*"

Camano froze, glaring hatred at Matt, his chest heaving.

"Unhand that boy, sir!" the Count d'Arrete cried.

"Gladly, milord." Matt sprang away—but he brought Camano's sword with him. The boy cried out as the hilt wrenched out of his hand, then he stood there cradling his fingers. Matt quelled a surge of contempt and presented the weapon to one of the intervening knights, then quickly sheathed his own blade before anyone could make an issue of it.

That didn't stop them, of course. Everyone at the high table was roaring in anger, and Count d'Arrete called out, "How poorly you repay our hospitality, sir! Did you not know the lad meant only sport?"

Sport? Yeah, sure, it had only been all in good fun—as long as their boy was winning! But Matt couldn't say that aloud; instead, he bowed and said, "I assure you, my lord, I only answered in sport myself—in sport, and to give a younger knight some edification in his use of the blade."

The court stared at the subtle insult, and the count reddened.

"I'm sorry to see I have offended." Matt bowed again. "Since I have transgressed against your hospitality, I shall take my leave of you. Thanks for this good dinner, sir."

The count blanched; courteous though the words might have been, everyone present knew it for the set-down it was, especially since they all knew that Matt had really been the injured party, and that if there had been any offense against the hospitality of chivalry, it had been Count d'Arrete's, not Matt's.

"Nay, sir, stay!" the count cried.

Matt paused, then slowly turned.

"Right or wrong, I cannot turn a guest out in the middle of the night! Surely there has only been a mistake of intention here, Sir Matthew, not a true wish to offend!"

"Of course, my lord." Matt bowed yet again. "I trust you do not think that I truly intended insult!" Humiliation, maybe, but outright insult? Well, not quite—on his side, at least. "As for young Sir Camano, young men and wine have always made a volatile combination."

Count d'Arrete stared in surprise. Then he laughed, clapping his hands. The whole court took the cue and laughed with him, and the tension was broken.

"Yes, quite apt, Sir Matthew!" Count d'Arrete nodded and chuckled. "I was as hot-blooded as he, in my youth."

"I do not doubt it for a second," Matt murmured.

"Come, sit down!" The count waved at the seat on the bench Matt had been occupying before. "You must still be my guest at board, and yet stay the night in my castle! You shall find our other sports more congenial than this, I trust!"

Matt sat, but he didn't trust anything, not for a second.

A footman showed him to his room with a flambeau and lit a candle on the table before he left. Matt suppressed the urge to tip, and locked the door securely behind the man, then looked out the arrow slit to make sure there was no convenient way for anyone to climb in before he sat down to think over the day's events. There wasn't a question in his mind that Camano d'Arrete had meant to kill him, making it look like an accident—not hard, considering what a klutz the boy was when it came to using a sword. He had taken Matt by surprise, and Matt hadn't really been all that far from using magic.

Everything considered, it made for a very full report to his queen. Matt took parchment, quill, and ink out of his saddlebags and sat down to write.

"My dearest darling," the letter began, and what came after that is absolutely none of our business, at least for the first paragraph or two. Suffice it to say that the letter reassured Alisande on a number of points, then went on to report on the mission she had given him:

> There doesn't seem to be anything resembling a definite plan to make the people discontent. It's just that the families down here have relatives on the other side of the border, and they visit back and forth—and, of course, they talk about the really important things in life, such as taxes and houses and how well the children are eating. For a long time, the Merovencian branches of the families have been able to brag about how well-off they are—but now, the Latrurian relatives are catching up, and even getting ahead in some ways. This is happening with serfs, yeomen, gentry, and nobility alike—the Smiths suddenly feel as if they're falling behind the other Smiths, and the Joneses in Merovence feel that they're not keeping up with the Joneses in Latruria.
>
> It's happening in the marketplaces, too. Peasants come in from Latruria to sell produce for themselves and for their lords, and while they're standing around waiting for customers, of course they get to gossiping with the peasant in the next booth, who's from Merovence. A few potential customers happen by— Merovencian, of course—and overhear the conversation, then ask a few more questions. First thing you know, rumor is spreading through the market that the peasants in Latruria are living in outright luxury.
>
> With the gentry and the lords, the greed is different. After all, they don't have much choice about their houses—they inherited the castles, and there's always the chance of war, so they can't just move out and build mansions. Nonetheless, some of the Latrurians are bragging about building palaces and just keeping the castles as forts.
>
> They all have the luxuries, too, so there's no point in wanting

more. But the young folk can crave excitement—and they do. The rumors of King Boncorro's court are that it is a positive paradise for sybaritic devotees of vice. Of course, rumor doesn't say "vice," it says "fun," but the upshot is the same—there's always something to do, always something exciting going on, always the chance of a duel or an affair, and just time enough to recover from one ball before you start getting ready for the next. The tales of old King Maledicto's court are still hanging around, but where *they* talked about cruelty and depravity and vicious old men ruining the young folk, the stories about Boncorro's court are of the good-natured, generous king letting his people play and have fun while he watches, getting his kicks out of seeing people be happy.

The bind is that there might be some truth in that. If there is, it's going to be awfully hard to fight, because rumors that have facts to back them up have a certain gloss of sincerity to them. I suppose we could close the border and keep the Latrurians out, but somehow it just doesn't seem right to keep relatives from visiting each other, especially since, to these people in the marches, borders are a nuisance during peacetime. It would be wrong to set up and enforce a rigid border watch unless it was really necessary.

Besides, it probably wouldn't work. My world has seen some pretty strong evidence that no border guards can keep out ideas and news. I've picked up some strong hints that the peasants on both sides of the border are accomplished smugglers, and there's no way they're not going to swap stories as they barter goods. So the only thing to do is to boost the standard of living in Merovence and make your court the kind of shining, ideal place that Emperor Hardishane's court was—at least, in the legends.

That's if the stories are true. If they're false, all it takes is a few eyewitnesses to start spreading the truth. I know that truth has a hard time competing against sensational lies, but believe me, I can wrap such a fascinating story around the truth that people really will listen.

First, though, I have to find out what the truth *is*—and there's only one way to do that. So I'll start out for Latruria in the morning, to see for myself. I should cross the border about mid-afternoon, and have some idea of what's *really* going on by noon the next day. Of course, if the rumors turn out to be true, I'll have to go on and visit King Boncorro's court, but that shouldn't take long—I expect to be home in a week, maybe two. Till then, take care of yourself—and try to look forward to our reunion as much as I'm going to.

Thereafter followed a few more paragraphs that were, to say the least, very private, and certainly no business of anybody but Matt and Alisande. They would have reduced Alisande to an emotional puddle, if she had read that far.

Unfortunately, she never got past the bit about King Boncorro's court. By the time her ladies-in-waiting had revived her, they had begun to suspect that something was wrong.

Actually, the ladies-in-waiting had been suspecting for a couple of weeks that something was very, very *right*—but the queen fainting when she read a letter from her husband made the very right turn very wrong, especially when revival brought a flood of tears. Such emotional behavior was very much unlike Alisande—but very like the woman who had been contending with early-morning bouts of nausea for the past fortnight.

They had been looking forward to widespread rejoicing as soon as the news became official—the kingdom was due for an heiring—but their high hopes might be brought low if the poor queen had so bad a shock as to make her miscarry. Almost as bad was the possibility that the child might be born with his father fled or defected to the side of Evil, and a shriek such as Alisande had uttered just before she fainted was cause enough to make them worry almost as much about that. So two of them fluttered about trying to revive her while a third ran for the doctor, and the fourth picked up the letter to scan it quickly. She blushed at the first two paragraphs, turned pale at the next few, and dropped it before reading the last. "No wonder her Majesty fainted! The Lord Wizard sends to tell her he will go into Latruria!"

"Into that land of iniquity?" Lady Julia gasped. "Surely he would not be so foolish!"

"Would he not?" Lady Constance said grimly. "He went into Ibile for no stronger reason than that he had misused the name of God. In truth, his championing of her Majesty's cause when she was in prison scarcely speaks much for his prudence!"

"Ah me, the woes of wedding a gallant but reckless man!" Lady Julia sighed.

"Still," said Lady Beatrice, "he should be reckless only on her behalf, not in spite of . . . See! Her eyelids begin to flutter!"

"Oh, where is that doctor?" Lady Constance cried.

"No . . . doctor!" Alisande protested, forcing herself to sit up.

"No, Majesty!" Lady Constance cried in alarm. "Do not rise so suddenly!"

"Do not speak as if I am ill!" Alisande snapped. "It was a moment's shock, nothing more!" But she stumbled as she pushed herself to her feet.

Lady Constance was there to catch her arm. "What could there have been in that letter to so afright your Majesty?" She glared Lady Beatrice to silence.

Alisande hesitated, torn between her very human need for a confidante and her monarch's duty to take the full weight on her own shoulders. Then she remembered that word of Matt's expedition was bound to become public knowledge, very public and very quickly, and allowed herself to speak. "My dunce of a husband has gone into Latruria!"

The women gasped in shock. It wasn't difficult—they had never heard the queen refer to the Lord Wizard so rudely before.

"But Majesty!" Lady Constance regained her poise first. "Latruria is a kingdom of sorcery and dark Evil!"

"Perhaps no longer," Lady Julia said quickly. "The young King Boncorro may not be so bad as his grandfather!"

"Or may be worse," Lady Constance said darkly. "I have heard tales to chill the blood about the doings of old King Maledicto!"

"Aye—the maidens ravished and tortured, the rebels flayed and quartered." Lady Julia shuddered.

But Lady Beatrice turned deadly pale. "More unnerving are the stories of the folk he had tortured so that he and the folk of his court might laugh at their screams!"

"Laugh, and worse," Alisande said darkly. In spite of herself, she shivered, and her hand went automatically to her abdomen—but she forced it away.

"It is whispered that he commanded his sons be slain," Lady Beatrice gasped, "even that he slew the eldest with his own hand!"

"Aye," Lady Julia said severely, "and that only the youngest was saved from his murderous sire, by his devotion to God—surely a miracle, in the midst of a court dedicated to the Devil!"

"Surely," Lady Constance agreed, "and it is said that it was lust overcame him, and that one sin cracked his holiness enough to make him subject to the evil will of King Maledicto!"

"And that the king would then have slain his grandson," Lady Beatrice finished, "had not some virtuous soul spirited him away into hiding—a hiding so complete that even King Maledicto's sorcery could not spy him out."

Lady Elise burst through the door with a dark-robed graybeard right behind her, puffing as he lugged a heavy satchel. Elise cried, "Here is the . . . Oh! Your Majesty is well!"

"No doctor, I said!" Alisande waved the graybeard away angrily, then instantly relented. "Your pardon, Doctor. It was only a faint, a moment's giddiness, nothing more."

The doctor didn't exactly look reassured. "Still, your Majesty should permit—"

"Nothing! I need nothing! There is too much to do, too suddenly, to permit of time for medicine!"

The doctor started to interrupt, but Alisande overrode him. "*Away, kindly doctor! I must turn to planning strategy!*" And she very deliberately turned away from him.

The doctor glared in outrage—he was one of the few members of the court privileged to do so—but when he saw she was not looking, gave it over and went out the door, shaking his head and grumbling.

"I regret your bootless errand, Lady Elise," Alisande said, "but it was truly for naught."

All four ladies exchanged a very significant glance as Lady Elise said slowly, "A hundred bootless errands I will run gladly, your Majesty, so long as the one that is truly needed be among them. But what gave you cause for such distress?"

Alisande opened her mouth to deny, but before she could lie, Lady Julia said, "Her husband goes into Latruria."

"Oh!" Lady Elise gasped, covering her mouth. "Into that cesspool of evil, where the king is a triple-dyed villain?"

"The new king may not be," Alisande said with asperity. "I have had reports of the conduct of this young King Boncorro, and many of his works are good. In truth, I hear no evil spoken of himself, barring what any monarch must sustain . . ."

"Even yourself?" Lady Elise's eyes went round.

"Even I have had to order the occasional beheading, and the more frequent hanging," Alisande said grimly. "In truth, I have ordered soldiers to their deaths in two wars now, and I do not pretend there was no evil in it."

"But it was for a good cause! Indeed, it was to fight Evil itself!"

"Even so, men slew other men at my orders," Alisande said inexorably, "and I cannot pretend I was innocent of all guilt. No, any monarch must strain her conscience in defense of her people—for the welfare of the commonwealth must be guarded, and where a common man can plead self-defense, a monarch cannot."

"No—she can plead the defense of others!"

"I can and do," Alisande agreed, "and so, I doubt not, does King Boncorro."

"Does he?" Lady Constance said darkly. "Or does he only secure his own power and fortune as well as he may, with least risk to his soul?"

"There is that," Alisande admitted. "Still, if reports are true, I need not fear for my husband's safety."

"Then why *do* you fear?" Lady Constance retorted.

"Because reports may *not* be true." Alisande shivered again. "Send for the Lord Marshal, Lady Elise, and summon Master Ortho the Frank, my husband's assistant. I must call up my armies."

Still pale-faced, Lady Elise bobbed a curtsy and fled out the door.

Queen Alisande turned to Lady Beatrice. "Do you send a fearless groom to Stegoman the dragon, milady—and send a courier to seek for Sir Guy de Toutarien."

Lady Beatrice departed, wide-eyed. It must be truly an emergency for the queen to seek the aid of the elusive Black Knight!

But Alisande and the party she assembled had to go out into the courtyard to meet Stegoman. The dragon could fit through the hallways of her castle in a pinch, but a pinch it was, and quite unpleasant for him, especially since his wings had been mended.

Stegoman lowered his head and raised it in salute—he was one of the Free Folk, not a subject of her Majesty; never mind that he lived in her castle compound now and scarcely ever saw another dragon, except on vacations. "Majesty! Thou dost wish me to fly and bring back my errant companion, the Lord Wizard, dost thou not?"

"You are as perceptive as ever, Stegoman," Alisande answered. "Yes, I do ask that of you—for he has sent to tell me that he will cross the border into Latruria!"

"I knew he would fall into trouble if he did not travel in company with me," the dragon huffed. "But would he listen? Nay, never!"

"He *was* supposed to move in secret," Alisande hinted.

"And is a dragon so rare a sight as all that? Oh, aye, I know—we are, most especially in company with a mortal! Yet I could have laired nearby where'er he sought danger! Then, at least, I would have known where to find him!"

"That much, I can tell," Alisande answered, "or where he was three nights ago, when he wrote his most recent letter: at the castle of the Count d'Arrete."

"That is something, at least," the dragon rumbled, "though as thy Majesty hath said, it was three nights agone!"

"Two days ago he was at the border station near the Savoyard Pass," Alisande offered helpfully.

"That is something more," Stegoman mused. "There should be a road running south from the pass. At least I know where I shall begin to search."

Anxiety stabbed Alisande, and she put out a hand to the warm, dry scales. "Go as cautiously as you may, Great One. I would be loath to lose a friend."

The dragon's mouth lolled open in a sort of laugh. "It is even as you have said, Majesty—the Free Folk cannot travel in secret. Still, I shall fly warily. Fare you well!"

Alisande barely had time to leap back before the dragon sprang into the air, pounding his way aloft with wing beats that boomed and blasted them all with grit and sand. She shielded her eyes, then looked up to watch him circle the keep and fly off toward the south. "God be with you, great friend," she murmured, "and bring you back safely, with my Matthew on your back." Then she turned to the Lord Marshal. "Have you sent to seek out Sir Guy de Toutarien?"

"Aye, Majesty." The grizzled old knight smiled. "His path is like the wind, I know—but he cannot be so footloose as once he was, now that he is wed."

Alisande wasn't altogether sure she liked the tone in which the old knight said that. "*If* he wed the Lady Yverne," she reminded him. "The Princess Yverne, rather, though none knew that of her till she was about to leave. We know only that she rode off into the mountains in his company, and that they *meant* to find a priest along the way."

"I never knew the Black Knight not to do as he had said he would," the marshal told her. "Still, as you have said, he shall be difficult to find. I have sent not one man, but ten, to quarter the mountains and seek him out. Nonetheless, it is a trail two years old, and discovering it will take time."

"Unless he *wishes* to be found," Alisande amended. "Send also to Matthew's friend Saul."

"The Witch Doctor?" The marshal stared in surprise. "I doubt he will come, Majesty. He seems to have little liking for people generally, now that he has found one to dote on."

"His wife Angelique does seem to be world enough for him," Alisande admitted, "at least to judge by report, for we have not seen the man since the two of them went off into the wilderness together.

Still, danger to his friend Matthew may bring him out, just as it brought him to our world—and at least we know where to seek him."

"Aye, in the Forest Champagne," the marshal grunted, "and surely there was never a place so well-suited to a man! A forest named for open land! A wizard who declares he cannot work magic and will not believe in Good and Evil as sources of magical power! Oh, the contradictions are apt, Majesty, most apt indeed!"

"He swears by paradox, I know," Alisande agreed, "and to hear him swear at all makes me shiver with apprehension. Still, we shall need his help if Matthew is truly endangered. Send for him, milord."

"By all Baal's brass!" Rebozo swore. "Could that sniveling young lordling truly be so inept as *this*?"

LoClercchi shrank away from the chancellor's anger. "Surely, milord, you did not truly expect the lad to slay the Lord Wizard himself!"

"No, but I had fondly thought he would at least be a strong enough opponent to force the man into using his magic! Yet what do I find? He was so poor a swordsman that this so-called 'Sir Matthew' scarcely had to work up a sweat, much less resort to wizardry! What do we know now that we did not before? That he poses as a knight and calls himself 'Sir Matthew'—which is a name not uncommon in these lands, even among knights! And that he fares southward, through the pass—which he was almost certain to do, if he came south at all!" He crumpled the tiny note and threw it at the wall. "Nay, this boy Camano has achieved nothing, nothing! Send him a stomachache! Send him a flux! I should give him worse, but pain is fitting for a pain!"

"He has done no harm, at least."

"Would he had! Well, at least we know this 'Sir Matthew' will try to cross the border."

"Shall I send soldiers to set a trap for him, Lord Chancellor?"

"Nay! Instead send a monster to slay him, if he should set one foot across the borderline! A manticore to gobble him up or a chimera to befuddle him! For whether he does or does not intend treachery, it is most definitely *not* in the king's interest for the Lord Wizard of Merovence to come into Latruria!"

"But what harm can he do?" the secretary asked, confounded.

"What *harm*?" Rebozo roared. "You ask what *harm*? The man who stole back Queen Alisande's crown from the sorcerer Malingo? The man who raised the giant Colmain? You know what upheaval followed his entrance into Ibile, his foray into Allustria—and you ask me what *harm* he might do, in a kingdom ruled by a king who will not kneel, nor go into a church? True, Boncorro is not as evil as the kings of those countries were—but I, his chancellor, have no wish to see him dethroned. Do you wish all the old ways to fall in this land, and yourself with them?"

"No, my lord, never!" the secretary said, very frightened. "I shall send to stop him straightaway!"

But the chancellor wasn't listening. He paced the room, muttering, "Good or evil, my King Boncorro is technically *not* the legitimate monarch, since his grandfather usurped the throne and slew the ineffectual former king, himself the son of a usurper of a usurper of a man who was an excellent poet, but a very weak king—and that is how low the line of the Caesars had fallen!"

"Was that poet-king truly descended from the Emperors of Reme, then?" LoClercchi asked, wide-eyed.

"He was, and they spread their seed far and wide, I assure you! Who knows but what this Lord Wizard might unearth one of their descendants to claim the throne from King Boncorro? Nay, best to take no chances—keep him out of Latruria, LoClercchi! Find a way, find ten ways—but keep him out!"

Chapter
Five

Once again Matt wondered how he got himself into these things, and the reflection that it was his loving spouse and liege who had done it this time didn't help much—especially since it had been his own idea to cross the border, and right now that seemed very dumb.

He was still in Merovence, technically, but not by much—only a couple of yards at most, maybe less; it was hard to tell, when there was no fence marking the boundary, or even a dotted line along the ground. But the manticore facing him seemed to have no doubt about the demarcation. "Stay back," it said, grinning—it couldn't do much else, with a mouth like that. "If you cross into Latruria, you are my meat."

Matt eyed the grin and decided he didn't want to take the chance. At least he was talking to a man's head—but it had double teeth, two rows above and two below, and they were all sharp and pointed. Worse, that almost-human head sat on top of a lion's body—if you could count it as a lion's body when it was covered with porcupine quills and had a scorpion's tail arcing up over its back, aiming right at Matt.

He eyed the monster warily, wondering why it was that all the supernatural beasties in this alternate universe could speak fluent Human, when the genuine animals didn't seem to be able to manage a word. Probably because the monsters were magical, and magic seemed to permeate the very air here—they were communicating in their natural medium, so to speak.

"Okay," he said, and turned away.

"What!" The monster stared at him, affronted. "No challenge, no insults, no combat?"

"No sweat," Matt assured him. "I'll just find another way in. This particular pass may seem like the whole world to you, but I'm sure there are other doors."

"What manner of knight are you?" the manticore howled.

"A knight who happens to be a wandering minstrel." Matt pointed to the lute slung across his back. "Do I *look* like a knight?"

"You wear a sword!"

"It's a dagger," Matt corrected. "A big one, sure, but still a dagger."

Actually, it was a very good reproduction of a Roman gladius—with a few modifications. Queen Alisande's smith had forged it very carefully, according to Matt's design, and the two of them together had done their best to sing a lot of magic into it. But Matt was a little uneasy about using it—he knew the quality of his own singing.

"I'll follow you!" the monster averred. "Wheresoever you seek to cross the border, I shall be waiting!" It began to stalk toward him, grinning from ear to ear. "Nay, on second thought, why should I wait? I'll pounce on you now, in Latruria or not."

Matt spun about, alarmed, and swung up his staff, on guard. "Hey, now, wait a minute! Isn't that against the rules?"

"Whose rules?" the manticore demanded, and sprang.

It slammed into an invisible wall, so hard that it seemed to crumple before it fell. It hit the ground heavily—with that much mass, it would have to—and answered itself. "King Boncorro's rules, of course! I should have known!"

"What rules?" Matt frowned. "Why should you have known?"

"Because the king has laid a Wall of Octroi along the border, and enchanted it to keep all monsters out! I never thought he would have been so careless as to craft it in such a way that it would also keep all monsters *in*!"

Matt eyed the beast judiciously and decided King Boncorro hadn't been careless at all. "Makes sense to me. You look as if you could be very useful to a Satanist king. Why should he let his rival monarchs get their hands on you?"

"He is no Satanist, but a vile equivocator!" the manticore spat. "And if I cannot go out, I cannot terrorize the peasants in the borderland at his will!"

Matt was liking Boncorro more and more. "Maybe he's saving you for choice assignments."

"Aye." The multiple grin widened. "Such as devouring a knight named Sir Matthew, who comes in the guise of a minstrel!"

Matt's blood ran cold. Boncorro had an excellent spy system. "The king himself sicced you on me?"

"What king ever did anything himself, that could be a source of blame?" the manticore said impatiently. "Nay, 'tis a subordinate to a subordinate who has laid this geas on me—but think not to overthrow it simply because it comes not from the king himself! I shall be your Nemesis, man!"

For a moment Matt was tempted—it would be interesting to test the strength of his magic against that of Boncorro's minion, and since the Latrurians already knew where he was, he wouldn't change anything if he attracted their attention by using magic. But he remembered that they probably weren't sure he was a wizard, and certainly not the Lord Wizard himself. Better to keep them guessing. "What could *I* do? I'm a mere minstrel!"

"Aye, a minstrel in a world in which magic works by verse and is strengthened by music! Did you think the bards of old Gaul were accounted men of power only for the pleasure their voices gave their tribesmen?"

This was certainly one well-educated monster. "Where did you learn so much history?"

"*Learn* it? I *witnessed* it, mortal! Do you think me a mere kitten of a hundred years' growth?"

Matt felt a chill; he had always tended to react to age with too much respect. "What keeps you going?"

"Only that no sorcerer has commanded my death!"

"Staying alive because you believe you can, huh?"

"Nay—because all of your kind believe I can, and no magician has made it otherwise!"

"Then how come you're antagonizing me, if you think I'm a magician?"

The grin loosened into silent laughing. "Why, do you think I would fear a sapling's magic, when the power of century-old oaks sustains me?"

"No, I guess you wouldn't," Matt sighed, "and that means it's useless for me to try to get around you. Guess I'd better give up." He turned away.

"Do not think to cozen me, mortal!" the manitcore called after him. "I know you plan to lie low, then cross the border when you think I have forgotten! Be sure you cannot find a crossing point that I cannot! Be sure I shall not forget!"

Matt took a deep breath, counted to ten, then turned back slowly. "Look, Manny—I might have some magical power just by virtue of being a minstrel, but do you *really* think I'd be dumb enough to take on a manticore?"

"Frankly," the monster told him, "yes."

Not only educated, Matt decided, but also perceptive. "Okay, then—just tell yourself I'm going back to get some stronger spells." And he paced away, toying with the idea of conjuring up a battery-powered amplifier and an electric lute.

He didn't, of course—he already had enough high-powered verses. However, he did put a ridge between himself and the border and hiked a few miles farther east, until he came to a river. It wasn't much, as rivers went—maybe twenty feet wide, not much more than a stream—but it was going in the right direction: south. So Matt settled down to wait for night, rehearsing a few verses and polishing his magic wand.

When dusk had fallen, Matt started out for the border again, following the little river. It cut through the ridge in shadow, and provided the cover of occasional wind-stunted pine trees. Matt followed it down to the border itself—or at least, what he thought was the border: a row of the wind-stunted pines growing across his path, too close to a straight line to be accidental. He thought some long-ago border guard must have planted them, to make his job easier. There were no border guards in sight now, of course. Not in *sight* . . .

Matt wondered how fast manticores could move.

He started muttering as he came up to the row of evergreens, so that he was actually reciting his spell as he went through them.

> "I leave the trodden paths with mighty heart
> Too near the manticore, within his ken . . ."

He felt a sudden tingling all over his skin—nothing major, certainly nothing painful, but enough to let him know he had passed through some sort of magical barrier. He knew he had just crossed the border, and King Boncorro's Wall of Octroi. Alarm—he felt alarm, and knew he had triggered one; not a bit of doubt that Boncorro knew he was a wizard now, and exactly where he was!

But the king must have known that already, as the manticore had demonstrated. Matt kept on reciting—but he felt unseen forces wrap about him as he did. He always had, but this time they were worse, clamping down on him, fighting him: he found himself struggling to set one foot in front of the other as he called out,

"Safe as when I rode in armor, for my art
Does enclose me as a shield, as it did then!"

A roar seemed to buffet him from all sides, and glowing eyes with multiple glowing teeth beneath came zooming at him out of the gloom. Matt held his ground and started reciting the verse again, waiting for the manticore to collide with his own unseen magical shield . . .

It didn't.

It slowed down a little, very suddenly—but it kept coming. Matt stared foolishly, the verse hanging on his lips, seeing the scimitar claws inch forward, the gaping band-saw teeth glitter as they began to speed up again . . .

That did it. He turned and ran. The tingling alerted him to his re-crossing of the border, but he didn't stop to look—he kept running until a splat and a fortissimo yowl told him the manticore had collided with the Wall of Octroi again. Then Matt turned, chest heaving, and risked a look.

The manticore was just picking itself up off the ground, glaring at him. "Brave knight indeed, to flee rather than fight!"

"I told you, I'm a minstrel," Matt panted.

"Oh, aye! A wizard who chants magical verses!"

"So how many knights do you know who do that?" Matt retorted.

"None." The manticore narrowed its eyes, watching him. "What meat do your thoughts chew, mortal?"

"Tough and stringy," Matt answered. "If you're right, and a min-strel reciting verse is going to make magic happen—and it does, I know *that* from past experience—how come—"

"Your spell only slowed me, but did not stop me?" The manti-core's teeth flashed in the moonlight. "Why, Latruria has been steeped in magic for nearly a century, mortal—but you forget what sort of magic that is!"

"So you're figuring I use Heaven-based magic, and it doesn't work so well in a Hell-focused environment?"

"Why else?" the manticore retorted.

"Good question," Matt admitted—but it was better than the man-ticore knew. His magic had worked well enough in Ibile, and that des-olated country had wallowed in the mire of evil magic far longer than Latruria had—at least, going by what little Matt had heard. No, there had to be some other reason.

"Cease to gnaw at it," the manticore advised. "Your magic will brew no foam here, and that is enough to know."

"For all intents and purposes," Matt admitted—but he knew it wasn't enough. The scholar in him may have been stunted, but it was still there, and wanted to discover the answer just for its own sake—but there was a practical side, too. If he could find out why, he might be able to reverse the effect. Suddenly, he was itching to cross the border and try another spell, just to see what happened.

But not with the manticore there. "You're a very repressive presence, you know?"

"Aye." The steely teeth flashed. "And I shall press you into keeping for supper as well as dinner if you cross again."

"Oh, yeah?" Matt felt a stroke of inspiration. After all, he hadn't really used the wand. He stepped forward again, going carefully, and fired a broadside—meaning he pointed his wand to concentrate the magic, and tried singing the spell.

"Go away from my border, go away from my door,
    Get away from my bankside, and bother me no more!"

It seemed to be working! The manticore's eyes narrowed; it yowled in protest; but it backed away step by step as Matt advanced. He set a foot near the border, set the other foot across it . . .

With a yowl of triumph the manticore sprang.

Matt gave a yowl of his own and leaped back—but steel teeth clanged, and pain seared his finger. In a panic, he looked down—but all five were there, though his index finger was coated with blood. He waggled it, still feeling the sink of horror—but the nail didn't fall off.

"Aagg! Ptooie!"

Matt looked up and saw the manticore spitting and coughing, then sticking a paw between its jaws and wiping. *"Faugh!* What manner of man are *you?"* The monster glowered up at him and accused, "You sought to *poison* me!"

"Oh, no." Matt felt a surge of renewed confidence. "Believe me, I wasn't really planning on having you take a strip of skin off my finger."

"Rejoice that I took no more than skin!"

"I do, I really do." Matt whipped out a handkerchief and wiped off his finger. "But if that's what just a piece of my skin does to your system, imagine what the rest of me would do!"

" 'Twas not your flesh, dunce, but your wand!"

"My wand?" Matt stared down at the stick he had dropped. Sure enough, there was only a stub of it left—and the end was as clean as if it had been polished. "No *wonder* you got a tummyache!"

"Vile poisoner," the monster snarled.

"Hey, you didn't *have* to go biting where you weren't asked." But Matt stared at the stub, severely shaken. That could have been his arm—or his neck!

Worse, he had lost one of his most potent magical aids—and virtually his only chance of piercing the magical inertia of Latruria!

Wait a minute—*what* chance? Obviously, the wand hadn't worked too well, either.

"Do not come," the manticore snarled. "Be advised, be warned! Come not into Latruria!"

Matt summoned shreds of resolve. "If I were a peasant or even an ordinary nobleman, you wouldn't talk that way to me!"

"Aye." All those teeth curved in a grin again. "But you are neither peasant nor ordinary, are you? And the flavor of your wand notwithstanding, I believe I would find *you* to be a man of excellent taste!"

"That's a very old line," Matt objected. However, he had to admit it was effective.

Queen Alisande stepped out onto the battlements to gaze at the rising sun, feeling the loneliness and the sense of abandonment that came with the aftereffects of a bout of morning sickness in her husband's absence. She was going through all this for him, and he was not here to support her through it!

Her lady-in-waiting hurried after her with a fur robe, tucking it about her and clucking. "Your Majesty, no! Not in naught but your shift! And the air so brisk! You shall catch a chill!"

"Oh, I shall thrive, Lady." But the robe was welcome, Alisande had to admit. She clasped the edges and said impatiently, "Thank you, good Elise, but I would be alone to compose my thoughts in the sunrise."

"Majesty, you are not well! You were but now seized with a spasm of vomiting!"

"It has passed," Alisande said in a tone of steel, "and I must needs clear my head with the freshness of the air. Nay, stay near me if you must, but do not speak, for I would have silence."

"As your Majesty wishes," Elise murmured, and fell back a pace, wringing her hands.

Alisande gathered the robe more tightly about her and stared off toward the sunrise, then automatically turned to her right, gazing southward, as her thoughts turned angrily to Matthew, who should have been here to hold her royal head, to hold and soothe, to . . .

Then she saw the spread of vast wings, black against the burgeoning rose of the morning sky, and the long sinuous neck that thrust out ahead of them. She stood a moment, frozen, then turned to hurry back inside. "Quickly, dress me! The dragon Stegoman returns!"

"So quickly?" Lady Elise cried. "In only an afternoon and a night? How could he have found the Lord Wizard so soon?"

"He could not," Alisande snapped. "Pray Heaven he has no worse news than that!"

But he did. Stegoman was still blowing and fuming when Alisande hurried down to the courtyard, and the grooms were hovering anxiously about him.

"Fetch him the side of a steer!" Alisande snapped. "He must be a-hungered after so lengthy a flight!"

"I thank thee, Majesty," the dragon rumbled. "Aye, I am a-hungered—but even more, I thirst!"

"A barrel of ale, quickly!" Alisande snapped to another groom, who paused only to duck his head in a hurried bow before he ran off.

"What news?" Alisande snapped.

"None bad." Stegoman seemed disgusted. "None of any sort! I did not find the Lord Wizard—but I most certainly did find the border!"

Alisande stared. "Has King Boncorro marked it plainly, then? Are not rivers and rows of trees enough for him?"

"It would seem not," the dragon said with disgust. "He has cast some confounded sort of invisible wall all along the border. Not knowing, I flew into it full-force, and 'tis only by good fortune that I did not break my neck! Nay, it sent me spiraling earthward, and I was hard put to pull out of the dive and find an updraft to send me aloft! I tried again, but more cautiously, and slammed into that barrier once more. Then I flew some miles farther west and tried again, but with the same result. I flew back and wended my way east, some miles past my first encounter, and soared once more southward—but the wall struck me on the snout again, and nearly crumpled me anew!"

"Oh, poor beast!" Alisande cried, and stepped up close, her hand rising to the great dark patch at the end of Stegoman's snout. Lady Elise cried out with alarm, but Alisande paid her no heed. "Aye, I can see where the scales are broke away!"

"They shall grow anew." Stegoman pulled his head back a little. "I am grateful for your sympathy, Majesty Alisande, but I beg you to withhold your touch—'tis quite sore."

"Aye, it must be indeed!" Alisande drew her hand back. "But how is this, Great One? My husband told me he had seen folk rowing across the border on the rivers and trudging across it with packs on their backs!"

"Even so; I saw them, too, and not in one place, but a dozen, for I flew along that borderland for twenty miles or more." Stegoman's eyes glowed with anger. "Mortal folk have no difficulty, show no sign even of knowing the exact moment when they cross the border—but I could not cross it!"

A sudden realization of strategy seized Alisande, making her stand straighter. "Dragons are forbidden, then."

"'Tis rank discrimination! Why should we be barred?"

"Why," Alisande said slowly, "because you are the Free Folk, and pride yourself on not serving any but yourselves—most notably, not serving Evil."

"King Boncorro cannot trust us, then, can he?" Stegoman said slowly.

"He cannot. Folk who are evil may, at least, be trusted to do whatever will most advance their own cause—but good folk can be trusted only to do what their consciences dictate, which is not always in the interests of a king! Mere mortal folk can do little damage, but an angry dragon is a fearsome sight indeed!"

"It is." Stegoman preened a bit; whatever influences he might have been immune to, flattery wasn't among them. "Nay, on reflection, I cannot blame the king for wishing to exclude us. I wonder, though, if Matthew shall gain entry through that wretched wall, or if it will keep out any whose will is not in accord with King Boncorro's."

Alisande felt a stab of anxiety. "I hope not, or those of my subjects who have journeyed south to visit would already harbor treason in their hearts. Mayhap if you were to *walk* across the border, rather than fly . . . ?" She frowned. "I own that it worries me greatly, Stegoman, to learn there is so much commerce across that border, that you did see more than a dozen folk crossing in only a score of miles!"

The dragon nodded. "And half of those miles must be impassable, being mountain peaks."

"Indeed! 'Tis bad enough that folk do cross that border in both directions and so readily—but 'tis even more alarming to learn that you cannot join Matthew!"

Stegoman frowned. "Surely, given such a state of affairs, he would follow the course of prudence and . . ." His voice trailed off; then he said, "No. He would not, would he?"

"Nay," Alisande agreed. "We speak of Matthew, after all." She turned away to hide a sudden stab of anxiety—a stab that she felt in her abdomen, and her hand automatically moved toward it. Again she forced it away.

"Your Majesty!" Lady Constance came running up, short of breath. "Your Majesty, a messenger has come from Sir Guy de Toutarien!"

Hope sprang again in Alisande's heart. "Bring him, bring him at once!"

"He comes," the lady said.

The messenger strode quickly up and knelt, bowing his head.

"Enough, man!" Alisande cried impatiently. "There is no time for ceremony now! Tell me your message!"

"Why, your Majesty," said the messenger, standing up again, " 'tis simply that Sir Guy does send to say that he hearkens to your message and hastens to find Lord Matthew and join him."

"Thank Heaven!" Alisande breathed, but amazement followed hard on relief. "How did you find him so quickly?"

The messenger shrugged. "I rode toward the western mountains, and when I came in sight of them, a rider came up beside me. 'Good day, herald,' said he. 'Good day,' said I, turning to look full upon him, and added 'sir,' for though he wore no armor, he was girt around with a knight's belt. 'The mountains are a lonely place to ride,' he said. 'Who could you seek there?' 'Sir Guy de Toutarien, sir,' I replied. 'I have a message from the queen.' 'Why, I am he,' said the knight. 'What is her message?' "

Lady Constance gasped. "He knew you did seek him! But how?"

"How?" Alisande shrugged impatiently. "Who can say? The earth told the grass, and the grass told the trees; then they told Sir Guy. He is so much a part of this land that the very air breathes its secrets to him. 'How' matters naught; it only signifies that he has heard, and goes!"

"He advises that you send me next to seek out the wizard Saul," the herald added, "for surely, says he, two wizards shall be of greater effect than one alone."

"You have named it! Rest, then go!"

"The Black Knight does ask a boon, though, Your Majesty," the herald said.

"He has but to name it!"

"He asks that you shelter his wife and child until he comes again."

"Aye, certes!" Alisande looked up to the nearest knight. "A company of knights, to serve as escort to the Lady Yverne!"

"He said she would come of her own," the herald said quickly.

Alisande stared, horrified. "A gentle lady, traveling with none to guard her? And with a babe! I hope someday to boast that any woman may journey thus in safety in my land—but I would not think it yet!"

A sentry cried out from the western tower.

Alisande turned and followed his pointing arm. There, with the morning sun gilding his wings, came a very strange monster—one with the head of a dragon, the hindquarters of a lion, and the wings of an eagle—if eagles had ever had wingspans of fifty feet.

" 'Tis the dracogriff Narlh!" Alisande cried. "But what does he carry?"

The answer became clear as the monster came closer. A woman rode between his wings, carrying something in her arms.

" 'Tis the Lady Yverne!" Lady Constance cried.

Then they all had to turn away, shielding their faces from blowing dust and grit as the dracogriff settled to the ground—all except Stegoman, who only slitted his eyes and called out, "Well met, cat tail! How came you here?"

"As if you didn't know," Narlh snorted. "I *hate* flying!"

"The more gallant you were, then, to bring me," Lady Yverne said.

"Well, for you, sure," Narlh grumbled, turning his head back to look at his passenger—and she leaned forward to kiss his nose. He yanked his head back, but his scales seemed to redden.

Two knights were already there to help her down. "Descend, Lady! Yet will you not give us your burden first?"

"Only to a woman," Yverne said firmly, and Queen Alisande herself beat Lady Elise and Lady Constance to the draco's side. She reached up, and the lady handed down her precious bundle. Alisande cradled it in her elbow, turning the blanket back to reveal a smooth little face, blinking itself awake. "Oh, how sweet! But come quickly, milady, for he wakes!"

"She." Yverne slid down, the knights catching her at waist and shoulder to ease her fall. She took the baby from Alisande with a smile. "I am blessed that my firstborn is a girl—but I hope also to give Sir Guy a boy."

"I hope so, too," Alisande said fervently. Sir Guy was the secret heir to Emperor Hardishane, and very eager *not* to resume the throne— but it was vital to the safety of Europe, and to the triumph of God and Good, that the male line of Hardishane's descent be unbroken. "Come, you must be wearied!" Alisande led her guest away toward the castle, then turned back to call, "Many thanks, Narlh! Grooms! Fetch this noble dracogriff an ox to eat!"

"Thanks, your Majesty," Narlh called back, then turned to Stegoman. "Your family sent their greetings, just in case I should bump into you, fish face."

"I hope they have honored you as you deserve, feather tip." And the two monsters went away toward the stables, companionably trading insults.

But Alisande didn't notice—she was too busy ogling the new arrival. "Oh, you are so fortunate to have a child so soon!"

"I have not the cares of state to distract my body from its purpose," Yverne said, smiling. "You must load more of your burden onto your husband, Majesty." Then she looked at Alisande more sharply, and stared. "Yes, you must, and right quickly, too!"

Alisande turned away, blushing. "Is it so obvious as that?"

"To any who has borne a child, aye—but do not ask me how. Oh, I rejoice for you, your Majesty! For you, and for all the land!" Then Yverne stared in horror. "But what a time for Lord Matthew to be gone playing the knight errant!"

"Aye," Alisande said grimly, "and the more fool I, for having sent him from me. But he was restless, and I could not see any harm in the mission—nor that it might take any great time, either." She closed the solar door firmly behind them, in the face of an amazed guard. "Come, sit in the chair by the window and nurse, for the babe begins to fret!"

"Aye, the poor thing. I thank your Majesty." Yverne sat down, loosened her bodice, and cuddled the baby against her breast. She sighed with pleasure and satisfaction, gazing down at the little face.

Alisande felt a pang at her own heart, seeing the other woman radiant with happiness. "I regret that I cannot stay to be a proper hostess and give you full company."

"Not stay!" Yverne looked up, appalled. "Your Majesty! You do not mean to go after your husband! Not at such a time!"

"But I must," Alisande said simply, "for what would I do if he did not come back to me?"

Chapter
Six

Matt didn't know which had shaken him more, the close shave or the manticore itself. Either way, it took until nightfall for him to work up the courage to try again—especially since the logical question was, why bother? After all, it wasn't as if Latruria was about to attack Merovence!

Or was it?

What was going on in Latruria that King Boncorro didn't want one of Alisande's wizards to see?

So the manticore itself was answer enough. If the king or one of his officials—say, his Lord Chancellor—had sicced the monster on Matt to keep him out, there must be a really good reason why he should go in! So he pumped up his courage, hunted around in the moonlight, and finally found a fold in the earth that he might have overlooked even in daylight. You couldn't really call it a gully—it was only seven feet or so deep, and scarcely wide enough for Matt to walk through without turning sideways. It looked like the kind of thing a glacier might have gouged as an afterthought on its way back up the peak for the long summer.

And if he might have overlooked it, maybe the manticore had, too—assuming that whatever sort of magical homing sense it had couldn't pinpoint him too exactly.

Which was quite a big assumption.

Too big.

Matt came tiptoeing up out of the cleft on its far end muttering a verse that ought to stop any attackers, just in case—and a yowl of triumph filled the air as an extra couple of crescents flashed in the sky.

"Creep in a petty pace from now till day!" Matt shouted as he leaped back into the gully. "In halting syllables of unrecorded time!" He sprinted back toward the Merovencian border, not daring to look back until he shot out the other end of the drawlet. Then he whirled to look back, just as the yowl ended in a curse as the monster hit the ground. It bounded up again instantly, heading straight for him—but it moved so slowly that before its hind legs had fully cleared the earth, it had time to shout, "I shall be revenged! My master shall banish this spell in an instant!"

"Just glad I had it ready to shout," Matt said with a shudder. He turned his back and walked away, leaving the manticore suspended in midair. Twenty feet more and he heard a sudden thud and a yowl of victory, followed by a SPLAT! and a howl of rage. Matt could almost see the manticore suddenly speeding up to normal, landing, and charging straight at him, but slamming into the Wall of Octroi again. He kept going. If King Boncorro was so determined not to have fellow magicians come visiting, maybe Matt ought to let him have his own way and be lonely—at least, intellectually.

But he didn't quite have it in him to quit. It was that same dogged persistence that had brought him to Merovence in the first place—he wouldn't stop trying to translate an untranslatable fragment of manuscript, had just kept repeating its syllables over and over again until they had made sense—and had found himself in an alien city, understanding a language that had never been spoken in his own universe of universities and political offices for out-of-work actors. Now, for the same reason, he kept prowling about the border, feeling weariness drag at him more and more heavily—but every time he looked south around another rock, there stood the manticore, glaring balefully at him with glowing eyes and glinting teeth. The sky lightened with false dawn as Matt's eyelids weighted with fatigue—so he wasn't looking where he was going, or stepping as lightly as he might have, which was no doubt why he tripped over something that jerked bolt upright with a shout of fear and alarm.

"Sorry, sorry!" Matt backed away, holding up both palms in a placating gesture. "I didn't mean to wake you, didn't mean to trip over . . . Pascal!"

"Why, it is the Knight of Bath!" Pascal threw his blanket back, rubbing his eyes. "How came you here?"

"Trying to cross into Latruria for a, uhm, visit, but I've got a stumbling block . . ."

"Aye—my leg!"

"I *said* I was sorry. Now it's your turn."

"What—to say I am sorry?" Pascal stared, trying to decide whether or not to be offended.

"No—to tell me what *you're* doing here!"

"Ah!" Pascal nodded. "I, too, am seeking to cross into Latruria—for a visit."

Matt smiled, amused. "Well, we seem to be going in the same direction. But why did you camp out on this side of the border?" He wondered if the young man had met the manticore, too.

"There was no reason to hurry ahead, and there was a stream nearby," Pascal explained. "But why have you not yet crossed? You set out a day ahead of me!"

"I've encountered a problem. What made you start right from the count's castle, instead of going home first?"

"Ah." Pascal's face clouded. "As to that, there was some disagreement with my father."

"Oh." Matt instantly pictured a howling fight, ending with a box on the ear followed by a slamming exit. "About . . . Charlotte?"

"Aye. He was not happy to learn that I had told her I did not wish to marry. Her father, too, was angry, and had spoken ill of me to my own father."

"He couldn't understand that not being in love is a reason for not marrying?"

"Not when it was not he who would be doing the marrying," Pascal said bitterly. "He told me that folk do not fall in love, they grow to love one another, as he and Mother had. I asked him if that was why there had been so little joy in their marriage. 'Twas then that he struck me and I stalked out."

"Afraid you might hit *him*, huh?"

"Even so." Pascal looked up, surprised. "You have had an argument much like that?"

"Several. *My* father didn't see any sense in studying literature. Your father did have one point, though—Charlotte's a pretty girl, and she certainly seems sweet."

"Yes, she is!" Pascal said quickly. "A surer friend I could never hope for—but she is not the one I love."

"Oh." Matt lifted his head slowly, pursing his lips. "Yes, that would make Charlotte less fascinating, wouldn't it? So your lady love lives in Latruria, and you're traveling south to see her. What did you say her name was?"

"She is a lady of rarest beauty and grace." Pascal gazed off into the distance with a fatuous smile. "Her hair is golden, her eyes the blue of the sea, her face a marvel of daintiness and sweetness."

"Sounds like love, all right." Personally, Matt thought Pascal was doomed to disappointment, if the girl really was that beautiful. The squire's son was downright homely, with a long face, thin lips, and gaunt cheeks. His only claim to attractiveness was his eyes, which were large, dark, and expressive. Frankly, Matt thought he'd been fantastically lucky to attract Charlotte as much as he had. Of course, her father's orders had helped . . . "How did you say you met this gem?"

"At a gathering last summer. Our Latrurian cousins guested us—and I met Panegyra! One look, and I was transported!"

Not far enough, Matt guessed. "Love at first sight, eh?"

"Aye, and 'twas hard to find a moment to speak to her alone, so hemmed in was she with duennas and sisters and aunts! But I contrived—I bided my time and caught her in a quiet moment, with others far enough distant for me to tell her my name and praise her beauty. She laughed, calling it flattery—but I saw an answering spark in her eyes! She feels as strongly toward me as I toward her! I *know* it!"

"Lovers know many things that are not true," Matt said slowly. "I seem to remember something about being cousins . . ."

"Aye, somewhere low on our family trees—third cousins at least, more probably fifth or sixth. Surely it could not matter!"

"Nothing does, to a lover—at least, not until after the wedding. So she hasn't told you she loves you, and you haven't proposed?"

"Nay, but I am sure she does, and I shall!"

"Seems pretty thin grounds for walking out on your family and heading south to see her."

"But I must!" Pascal raised feverish eyes. "For yesterday, one of my southern cousins told me that sweet Panegyra has been betrothed! Nay, worse—she is to be wed within the month! I must stop her! I must tell her of my burning love, that she may turn away from this gouty old vulture her father would force upon her! I must save her from such a fate!"

"Oh. He's older than she is, then?"

"Aye—twenty years at least! A dotard with rotting teeth, a swag belly, and a breath like a charnel house, I doubt not! How could they entomb so sweet a breath of spring as Panegyra in so foul a marriage, and she but eighteen?"

"Do you really think she'll just cut all her family ties and elope with you?" Matt asked gently.

Pascal's shoulders sagged. "Nay, I fear not. What have I to offer, after all, save a gift for crafting verse, and a heart that would ever be true to her?"

"And love," Matt said softly.

"Love that should set the world afire! Love that should bind her to me forever! Love that should bear her aloft in bliss for all her life!"

Matt felt the vein of poetry in the words, and that was no metaphor—he could feel magical forces around him twitch in response to even so mild a flight of structure in wording. It gave him a chill—he had met a poet who couldn't control himself, kept spouting verses at odd moments, and accidentally made some very strange things happen. "Say—you do know how to write, don't you?"

"Aye." Pascal turned to him in surprise. "Why do you ask?"

"Just make sure that if you get hit with a sudden attack of verse, you write it down instead of speaking it aloud, okay? You do seem to realize that poetry isn't much of a basis for marriage, though."

"Aye." Pascal's gaze lowered. "I am a poor choice, I know, for I have no money, no handsomeness of face or figure—and, now that I have rebelled against his tyranny, will no longer inherit my father's house and lands! Still, I hope to make my way in the world, to win fame and fortune—and if I can only persuade Panegyra to wait for me a year or two, I may prove worthy of her love!"

Five years or ten, more likely—assuming the kid worked hard and had good luck. "But you have to reach her before the wedding."

"Aye!" Pascal sprang up and rolled up his blanket. "There is not a moment to spare! I thank you for waking me, Sir Matthew—I must be off!"

Well, Matt hadn't wanted to say it. "Hold on a minute, friend." He held up a cautioning hand. "You won't get very far, running on empty. How about a bit of breakfast first? Besides, you may find it's not all that easy to get into Latruria."

"It shall be, for me! There is a clandestine route, one known only to a few families. I would not call it truly secret, but if the king's soldiers know of it, they certainly pay it no heed."

"Oh, really?" Matt pricked up his ears. "Say, I've got some journey rations here. How about we pool breakfasts and I tag along when you go?"

"Why, since you offer," Pascal said, surprised. "I own I came away in such haste that I brought only a loaf. Nay, let us become road companions, then!"

"Great!" But Matt's conscience bothered him. "I do have a little problem, though. There's this monster that seems to have fixated on me, decided he's going to have me for lunch, no matter where I cross the border—and he has an uncanny knack of knowing exactly where I am."

"A monster?" Pascal looked up, suddenly alert. "Is it a manticore?"

Matt stared. "How'd you know?"

"Because it has been long known to my family. Never fear, friend—I have an old family charm that will tame the beast."

"A family charm!" Then Matt remembered. "That's right—you said your grandfather was a wizard. You mean you inherited his talent?"

"What, a knack for crafting verses and the sensing of unseen forces?" Pascal said it almost contemptuously. "Aye, I do. All of my family have it, in one degree or another."

"Magic as a dominant trait," Matt muttered, watching the young man as he knelt to feed the coals and blow them into flame. "How much do you have?"

Pascal shrugged. "Enough to recite the old family spells and make them work—to summon brownies to the bowl of milk, that they may aid us; to kindle fire, banish warts, and suchlike."

"Such—like getting rid of manticores?"

"Only the one." Pascal held up his index finger. "It is almost kin, my family has known it so long—and if there were more than one manticore in that county, 'twould be surprising indeed."

"Yes, I can see that." Matt frowned. "If there were two, one of them would gobble the other up. Uh, may I ask why you didn't include wizardry in your catalog of desirable traits for a suitor?"

"Wizardry has been no advantage, in Latruria," Pascal said with a cynical smile, "not for many decades. Only sorcery is prized there—and I will be amazed if that state of affairs has changed greatly under King Boncorro's reign."

Matt frowned. "So you're not interested in learning how to be a professional."

"Nay." Pascal shrugged impatiently. "What use is magic? Who respects the wizard? My grandfather was such a one—and all it brought him was advancement to the rank of squire!"

"You want to be something more, then." Of course the kid did—he'd been born a squire, hadn't he? No progress if he never became anything more.

Pascal confirmed Matt's guess with a nod. "There is little respect in being a squire, Sir Matthew. As you yourself know, one must be a knight, at least, to have any true standing in this world."

"Well, there's some truth in that," Matt admitted. In fact, there was a lot of truth—being dubbed a knight magically gave a man better judgment and the power to prevail against his competitors. People listened to knights, but not to wizards. Matt had found that out the hard way, when he first came to Merovence. "I take it your father couldn't become one, being the wrong kind of squire."

"Oh, nay! A squire is a squire, after all, and he might have won his spurs—if he had wished to. But he was quite content to sit on his home acre, tending his peasants and watching them raise his crops."

"You mean he never even tried?"

"Never," Pascal confirmed. "But so little is not enough, for me! I shall have more, or die trying to attain it! Besides," he confided, "the fair Panegyra might look more favorably upon me if I were *Sir Pascal!*"

Not much chance, Matt thought privately, unless some land and money went with the title—but he didn't say so.

They broke Pascal's loaf between them, shared out some of Matt's beef jerky, and Matt introduced the young man to tea, which was brand new in Bordestang, Queen Alisande's capital. Matt guessed that some enterprising sea captains had found their way to China, and he wondered if those men came from Latruria, as they had in his own universe—where the peninsula was called "Italy."

He expected he would find out very soon.

They doused the fire and set off, Pascal actually whistling, now that he was on his way to the fair Panegyra, and Matt with a growing knot in his belly, now that he was on his way back to the manticore.

Alisande's army stood gathered in the courtyard of her castle in the chill light of false dawn, shivering and grumbling to one another. "We have been waiting most of an hour already!" one soldier complained to his sergeant. "Did not the queen waken when we did?"

" 'Tis no affair of yours when she rises or when she sleeps!" the sergeant barked. "It is your affair only to be on your feet and ready when she calls!" Privately, though, he wondered. The queen had never kept her troops standing about for more than a few minutes before. Had she really slept while they mustered?

"The queen grows lazy," one trooper griped to another. "She would have us up and marching while she sits abed nibbling sweet biscuits."

Food, however, was the farthest thing from Alisande's mind as her ladies supported her away from the basin toward an hourglass chair. "You must sit, your Majesty," Lady Constance crooned. "And whatever you do, you should not be riding when you are in so delicate a condition."

"Condition?" Alisande forced herself to stand straight and tall, though the chair appealed to her mightily. "What condition? A moldy bit of cheese for supper last night, that is all!"

"And the night before, and the night before?" said Lady Julia with a skeptical glance. "Tell that to the men, Majesty, but do not seek to cozen we who have borne children ourselves."

Alisande deflated. Her ladies took the chance to ease her into a chair. "I have not deceived you for a moment, have I?" the queen muttered thickly.

"Well, for a week or two," the elder lady allowed. "But a woman gains a certain glow when she knows there is new life within her, Majesty. The men notice it, but fools that they are, they think it is due to their own presence!"

"Well, it is, in a way," Alisande muttered.

"To more than their mere presence, I should think! But you know your husband will be overjoyed when he learns this glad news, Majesty—and sorely saddened if you should lose the babe while riding after him!"

"I must," Alisande declared, though every fiber of her being cried out to stay home within the thick, safe walls of her castle and let all the silly affairs of the world go by, except for the single truly important business of cherishing the grain of life within her.

But the babe must not be born fatherless!

"I must ride." She lifted her head, rising above the residue of nausea by sheer willpower. "I let him go from me once—I shall not make that error again!"

The ladies fell back before the sheer power of her personality, but the eldest objected, "The welfare of the kingdom requires an heir!"

"The welfare of the realm requires the Lord Wizard!" Alisande retorted. "Do not ask me how I know this—it is the magic of this land, that monarchs know what is best for their countries and their people!"

"Good monarchs, at least," one of the younger ladies murmured—to herself, she thought, but Alisande turned to her, nodding.

"We all remember the days of the usurper who slew my father and had no feeling for the welfare of the land or the people! We must not see such days come again!"

"Therefore you must not risk yourself," Lady Constance scolded, "or the heir!"

"I must." Alisande pushed herself to her feet. "If I do not, if I let myself be shorn of my wizard, the realm shall be imperiled. I must ride!"

But how, Alisande wondered, would she ever fight a battle, if she was to start each morning with her head over a basin!

The "clandestine route"—presumably known only to every smuggler in the territory—was really pretty good; it consisted of a series of caves, joined by sizeable tunnels. They had to be sizeable, after all, since the goal of developing the route had been to smuggle not people, but goods. Matt could see, by the light of his torch, the marks of pickaxes where some of the passages had needed a bit of widening—maybe more than a bit. But from a functional point of view, it was marvelous—Pascal led him behind a small waterfall on the Merovencian side of the border and into a cave that widened as they went farther in. They had to stop to light torches, of course, but there was a whole stack of them, with jars of oil to soak their tow-wrapped ends, sitting about ten feet in from the mouth of the cave—far enough to stay dry, close enough to still be in the light. There was even flint and steel. All they had to do was open one of the jars, dunk the torch ends in, and strike a spark with the flint and steel—re-covering the jar first, of course. Then Pascal set off into the lower depths with Matt following, wondering how many of the royal customs agents on both sides of the border knew about this route. After all, a secret known to two people is compromised, and a secret known to three is no secret at all, so with this route being common knowledge to the border families, it was scarcely possible that the excise men wouldn't know about it—which led to the interesting question of why they ignored its use. At a guess, Matt hazarded, a trickle of trade was to the mutual advantage of both countries—after all, the Latrurian lords no doubt wanted Merovencian wines, and the aristocracy of Merovence probably prized the spices and silks brought in by Latrurian merchants. On the other hand, open and widespread commerce would have robbed the royal exchequers of tariff income.

Matt saw the light at the end of the tunnel and reached out to touch Pascal's elbow. "Remember the manticore."

"Never fear," Pascal assured him—but he went ahead a little more cautiously, reciting:

> "When the Merovencian smuggler
> meets the manticore in pride,
> He will shout to scare the monster,
> who will quail and turn aside.

Then the monster will remember
where his true allegiance lies,
And will hearken to the orders of
the man who bids him rise!"

As a verse, it was good, but it didn't sound like much of a spell, and Matt was amazed that the young man still went on without trembling. He began to mutter his slow-down spell under his breath again, getting it ready just in case . . .

Then Pascal stepped out of the cave, and a yowl split the world.

At the last second Matt found he didn't have it in him to let the kid die alone. He jumped out of the cave, yanking his sword out, seeing the speed-blurred brindled mass hurtling toward them, all teeth—

Then Pascal shouted, "Down, monster! Down, to a son of the wizard who tamed you!"

Matt had never before seen a beast put on the brakes in mid-leap. It was really quite a sight—the manticore twisted in midair as if it were trying to change directions. It did, actually, swerving aside from Pascal and plunging right toward Matt, teeth first.

Matt yanked a sugarplum out of his pocket and threw it, bull's-eye, right between the serrated teeth. *Then* he jumped, as far as he could to the side—right, in fact, on the other side of Pascal.

The manticore's jaws clashed shut automatically, and its throat throbbed with a single swallow even as it twisted in midair again, to land on all four feet. The monster looked very surprised, actually closing its lips for the first time since Matt had met it. Then it began to look very, very pleased. "Delicious! What part of your anatomy was that, O Wizard?"

"Not part of me at all," Matt said, "just some leftover dessert from the banquet two nights ago. I was saving it for a treat."

"I must give you thanks! Perhaps not enough to spare your life, but thanks nonetheless! Quite the most delicious tidbit I have ever munched." Then the manticore began to stalk toward Matt again.

"Hold!" Pascal held up a palm, and Matt had to give him maximum points for bravery, but absolutely none for intelligence.

Then he deducted from his own score, because the monster stopped on the instant, then crouched down and rubbed its head against Pascal's leg, making an appalling grating noise that Matt vaguely recognized as a gigantic purr. The youth trembled, but stood his ground resolutely. However, he didn't take his eyes from the monster for a second as he asked Matt, "When did you pick up that sugarplum?"

"Right after dinner, while you and Charlotte were settling your futures," Matt answered. "How did you get that cat to obey?"

Pascal glanced down and shrugged. "I know not; 'twas truly my grandfather's verse. He it was who first tamed this manticore and forbade him to eat human flesh or steal food of any sort, in return for which Grandfather gave him a bullock a day, or two sheep when the cattle were all eaten."

"Delicious!" The manticore looked up eagerly. "I had never eaten so regularly before! I mourned when the old man died, but grew hungry within a day. Still, in honor to his memory, I would not eat cattle, sheep, or people within his parish—so I fared south to Latruria, and have been here ever since! But it has been a dog's existence, young man—nay, not even fit for a dog! Taking what meat I may, then fleeing with it before the knights or sorcerers come . . . Fighting with armies of peasants for my meals, which is painful, though tasty . . . Enslaved to one sorcerer after another, to feed on grain and their enemies only! Have you come to free me, then?"

Pascal hesitated, and Matt leaned close to mutter, "If you don't, he has to serve whatever sorcerer sicced him on me—by eating me! Not your problem, I know, but . . ."

"But if I free him completely, he may turn on *me!*" Pascal muttered back.

Not softly enough; the manticore said, "Never! I would never munch the flesh and bone of my Master Fleuryse! Nor drink his blood, no matter through whose veins it flows!"

"You really must have liked the old geezer," Matt observed.

"Vastly! He could have slain me, aye, slain me as easily as tamed me! Yet he chose to spare my life, and moreover to feed me!"

Matt could have pointed out that the spell probably would have stopped working if the old wizard had stopped feeding the manticore—hunger has a way of breaking down inhibitions—but it didn't seem like the most politic comment at the moment.

"Then I free you from any other spells or geasa that have been laid upon you," Pascal said, but he cast a worried glance at Matt. "Still, I had only planned to walk safely past you, not to have you accompany me."

"Where you go, I shall bound!" The monster leaped to its feet. "Your paths shall be my paths, your enemies my dinners!"

"But you have to provide alternative menus when there aren't any enemies handy," Matt reminded.

"How shall I do that?" Pascal wailed. "I have no money to buy cattle, no magic to conjure them up!"

"Oh, you'll think of something." Matt clapped him on the shoulder. "And if you don't, I will. Don't look so worried, Pascal—I have a few ducats in my purse. Besides, you never know when a voracious monster might come in handy. Think anybody's gonna try and charge us tolls?"

He turned the young man away, sheathed his sword—and together they set off for the south, the manticore following a few yards behind.

"You do not understand!" Pascal hissed to Matt. "For this beast, fondness for people is tied to fondness for food! If we do not feed it, it will feed on whatever comes first to fang! *I* shall be safe, for I am of the blood of the Wizard Fleuryse, but *you* shall not!"

Matt noticed that the day had suddenly grown chilly. "So I'd better really deliver on that promise to find him food, huh?"

"Aye, or discover a way to part with him!"

There was a growl behind them.

"Careful," Matt breathed, "I think he's got very acute hearing. Haven't you, Manny?"

"Aye," the beast answered, full-voiced, "though 'Manny' is a strange name for me."

"Do you have any other?"

"Nay. None have spoken to me as you do for decades. Even the Wizard Fleuryse called me only 'manticore.' "

"Okay, so 'Manny' is short for 'manticore'—or would you rather I called you 'Ticky'?"

"Manny will do," the monster said quickly.

"Thought so." Matt looked up and saw a peasant shambling down the road, driving a gaunt and spavined cow with lackadaisical flicks of a switch. "Well, look what came to order! Say, fellow, that cow for sale?"

"Sale?" The peasant looked up hungrily, then saw the manticore and froze.

The monster licked its chops.

"That's for the cow, not you," Matt said quickly. "Here, I'll buy it for a silver penny."

The peasant stared at the silver coin, then snatched it. "Take the cow, and gladly!" Then he turned on his heels and ran, as Manny leaped on the cow with a howl of joy. It didn't even have time to moo.

Matt firmly turned Pascal away. "I could tell it was dying of hunger; why not put it out of its misery?"

"It is tough," the manticore complained.

"Don't talk with your mouth full," Matt called back, then to Pascal, "Don't look so sad. Cows turn into food every day."

"It is not that—it is the price! Three coppers would have been enough, and generous!"

"Think so? Well, maybe you're right. I'll haggle a little next time—but there wasn't time just now. Manny looked *really* hungry."

"I was," the manticore mumbled around a bone.

"It was the cow, fast, or the peasant," Matt explained. "Fortunately, I've got enough silver to turn into *lots* of coppers."

"We shall need them," Pascal said with an apprehensive glance at the feeding manticore. "I hope your purse is never empty!"

"Good wish," Matt approved, and decided to see if he could work up the appropriate spell. For his part, *he* hoped that the stories he had heard about the prosperity of Latruria were true—especially the ones about food being plentiful.

Chapter
Seven

Unfortunately, Matt was really very skeptical about the claims of good living in Latruria. The sight of that apathetic peasant and his spavined cow had been enough to remind him that up until a few years ago, Latruria had been the private property of a sorcerer with a reputation for delighting in human suffering. Matt had done a little homework before he started south, spending an hour or so reading up on what little history of Latruria Alisande's library held, and had talked to oldsters he met on his journey about what the southern country had been like during their youth. He couldn't talk to recent travelers, because there weren't any—King Maledicto had closed the border as soon as he seized the throne. The only Merovencians who had been to Latruria between that time and King Boncorro's coronation were smugglers, and so far Matt hadn't had much luck finding any of those—until he met Pascal, of course. Privately, he wondered if this was really the young man's first trip down this way.

But what he had heard from the oldsters was hair-raising. He had decided right away that if he ever got back to his own universe, he could make a living just writing them up and calling them fiction. The only problem was that he couldn't decide whether he should market them as horror or pornography. He ended by deciding that he'd be mortally ashamed if he wrote them at all.

Of course, it could be that his informants had been making up those awful tales. Atrocity stories always grew up around the enemy—like the early stories about Phoenicians throwing babies into the fiery furnaces built into their idols. Only trouble was, archaeologists had found some pretty convincing evidence that the Carthaginians had done exactly that, and they had been a Phoenician colony . . .

So, applying his scholar's caution and training, Matt had made a stab at sifting fact from fancy in the reports of Maledicto's reign, coming to the sad conclusion that most of what he'd heard could have been stone-cold fact. Even after allowing for exaggeration and propaganda, he still thought there was probably some truth in them. Maledicto had delighted in cruelty and encouraged it in his noblemen. But if that had been true, could King Boncorro really have reversed the state of affairs so thoroughly in just six years?

He decided to check his findings under the guise of idle gossip. Besides, he needed to get Pascal's mind off their faithful following monster. "Is it true that King Maledicto indulged in human sacrifice?"

Pascal shuddered. "Aye, from all I hear! He conducted obscene rituals to pagan gods of evil. Their names are only whispered, never spoken aloud."

"Such as Kali and Hecate?"

Pascal shied as if he had just seen a rattlesnake pop up under his feet. "Forfend, Sir Matthew! I *told* you they are never spoken aloud!"

"Doesn't do any harm, in a Christian universe." But Matt wished he could be sure of that; the names he had mentioned could be powerful symbols in their own right. "Probably includes Satan in there under another guise. I also hear tell that he held a party every night, just himself and a few close friends."

Again Pascal shuddered. "Aye, and vile carouses they were, too!"

"Mixing sex and torture?"

Pascal nodded. "And imbibing vile brews that drove them mad with lust."

"Real sweethearts." Matt glowered at the roadway in front of them. "I've also heard that King Maledicto came down with the pox now and then, but got rid of it by transferring it magically to some poor innocent peasant."

"Not always innocent, I will say that for him," Pascal answered, hard-faced. "Innocent folk of any rank became harder and harder to find, the longer he reigned. Must we talk of this, Sir Matthew? I find it distasteful in the extreme."

"I'm not exactly happy about it myself, but I really do want to find out if there's any truth in it."

"Oh, be sure there is truth there! Through all those dark decades, our family did manage converse with relatives, or at least letters, borne by brave smugglers."

"Weren't they afraid King Maledicto would punish them for telling on him, if his agents captured the letters?"

"Tell on him? He boasted of his cruelties! Nay, he wanted them noised abroad, that all might shudder and obey him!"

That unnerved Matt for a minute—but only a minute. Then he plucked back his composure and maintained, "They couldn't know whether or not the rumors were true, then. The king might have been spreading them himself, just to intimidate everybody!"

"Do not doubt their truth! My father's cousin was taken for the king's army, then wrenched from their ranks to be mutilated for his Majesty's sport! There is no question that they would have slain him, had they not already had a maiden for the sacrifice. Nay, they let him go, with stern injunctions to tell all that he had seen!"

That unnerved Matt, for longer than a minute or two. A blood relation was as strong a piece of evidence as he was likely to get, and pretty thoroughly validated all the rumors. It was having to confront the fact that they were true that shook him.

"I had wondered why you carried a lute on your back," Pascal said. "Is it to trade songs of virtue for news of King Boncorro?"

"Something like that," Matt admitted, "and because of that, I'd appreciate it if you'd lay off the 'Sir Matthew' sobriquet. Just plain 'Matthew' will do very nicely, for the nonce." He looked back over his shoulder. "You, too, Manny!"

"My lips are sealed," the manticore promised.

"Somehow I doubt that. I'll settle for you watching what comes out of your mouth a bit more closely than what goes in." He turned back to Pascal. "Mostly I had in mind picking up gossip about the last few years in Latruria—and the current state of affairs. I find it difficult to believe that the new king could have reformed the land so completely, after almost a century of corruption."

"I doubt it, too, and I intend to be extremely cautious as to whom I trust, and into whose power I let myself fall. The king may have forsworn needless cruelty himself, but his noblemen have been trained to it, all their lives, and may not so cheerfully forsake the old depraved ways."

"My thought exactly," Matt said grimly, "and though a knight might be treated with a certain amount of courtesy, a minstrel would not."

Pascal stared at him, appalled. "You have deliberately made yourself their target?"

"Call it bait for the trap." Matt just hoped he would be able to spring that trap if he needed to; he was getting very nervous about how weak his magic seemed to be in Latruria. "As long as there are only one or two knights against me, I can give them a very unpleasant surprise. I just hope I won't have to sing."

The chancellor laid another sheet of parchment in front of the king. "As you commanded, your Majesty—a summary of what we may expect to receive in the various taxes and levies, set against the monies we anticipate having to pay out in the next twelve-month."

"Neatly done." King Boncorro scanned the columns of figures. "Give the clerk an extra ducat's pay—this was new to all of us, and he has invented a very good way to draw it up." He laid the paper down with satisfaction. "It is well, Rebozo! For the third straight year our surplus shall increase—if we hold to this plan. The royal granaries shall be full, even the new score we are building. Famine shall not catch this country again."

"No, your Majesty." The chancellor didn't sound all that happy about it. "Still, the surplus is due more to your own economies than to any increase in revenues. Surely you might now increase the taxes again!"

King Boncorro shook his head. "With taxes low, people spend more, thus giving work to others—who thereby gain money to pay *their* taxes. Merchants are using the money saved to set up new ventures, bringing me more tax money than they did five years ago, even though Grandfather demanded two parts in three, where I only demand one." He nodded, pleased. "Yes, my conjecture is proved true— lower taxes yield higher revenues, though it did take some few years of tight living before the increase began to show. In fact, I see it is time for another experiment."

Rebozo's blood ran cold. "Majesty! Let us recover from your last! Whenever you say 'experiment,' I have premonitions of disaster!"

"This one is easily undone, if it fails," Boncorro said, amused. "Have letters drafted to the noblemen who hold patents of monopoly on commerce in grain, timber, and wool. Tell them that henceforth, any man who wishes may traffic in those commodities."

"Majesty, no! They shall rebel, they shall bring armies!"

"I think not." King Boncorro lounged back in his chair. "They may still be active in the trade themselves, of course—and having held the monopoly and the means of transporting the goods, they shall have a huge advantage over any who wish to enter the trade.

But if they have been charging extortionate prices, they shall find they have no buyers."

"Exactly, Majesty! Their fortunes shall evaporate!"

"They have fortunes enough to maintain them in luxury for the rest of their lives, Rebozo—aye, and their children's lives, too. We speak of counts and dukes, after all, who have vast estates to maintain them. No, they shall not starve—but they shall have to strive if they wish to continue to dominate the commerce of the realm."

"Majesty, how is this?" Rebozo cried, distressed. "A king should not concern himself with commerce, like a grubby tradesman!"

"Every subject must be my concern," King Boncorro contradicted, "from those who grub in the dirt to those who command armies. The lifeblood of the land is trade, Rebozo. The peasants may raise the food for their noble masters, but it cannot feed the folk in the towns if it is not transported to them. The stomach may provide the nourishment, but it does no good if it is not carried to the limbs. If the kingdom is the body politic, the king may be its head, but the army and the artisans are its muscles, the peasants are its hands, and the merchants its blood. That blood has flowed but sluggishly under my father's rule. I have freed it to flow more freely, and do so again now—and the result will be more nourishment for me."

"An excellent analogy," Rebozo said with irony, "but perhaps not accurate. Abolishing monopolies only means that the merchants shall have more nourishment, not you."

"They shall pay their taxes if they wish to be let alone to trade. More well-to-do merchants will arise, even though they charge lower prices to the people who buy—for thereby, more people *shall* buy. More rich merchants means that there shall be more spending *by* merchants, which shall yield richer tradesmen and shall even allow some artists a living, and higher wages for peasants as more and more of them leave the land to become merchants or artisans. Thus shall there be more and more who pay taxes, and my revenues shall increase."

"Well, you are a worker of magics." Rebozo carefully did not say what kind—primarily because he wasn't sure. "If you can make more money flow into your coffers by levying less, it is truly a wonder, and I must not argue with what I do not know. But how if the noblemen gather their armies and march against you, Sire?"

"Then," Boncorro said, tense as a stretched cable, "I shall work some of those magics of which you have spoken."

"You cannot slay a whole army by sorcery!"

"Be not so sure, Lord Chancellor," the king said quietly. "However, slaying armies will not be needed—only slaying their masters."

"You cannot slay dukes and counts out of hand!"

"Why not? My grandfather did. Then, like him, I can replace them with men of my own choosing."

"Their sons shall bring those same armies back on the instant!"

"Then I shall slay the sons, too, and the grandsons, and the nephews, if I must—and all the noblemen know it. They have not yet even tested my resolve, nor, I think, will they. They know I am no saint, like my father, and fear that I may be as cruel and as powerful as my grandfather. No, Rebozo," he finished quietly, "I do not think they will rebel."

Rebozo shivered again, for the tone of the young king's voice had been as remorseless and bereft of emotion as his eyes had been chill and flat. It was almost as if a man of stone had been talking, and Rebozo found that he—even he whom the king loved as much as he loved any—could not be sure whether or not King Boncorro could really rain down destruction on a rebellious army.

He didn't doubt for a second, though, that Boncorro could and would slay every single one of his aristocrats if they sought to unseat him. He might not even have to turn to the power of evil magic, for every single one of the counts and dukes had been so deeply steeped in sin that Heaven surely must aid the young king in defeating them! In fact, it was a perfect summary of Boncorro's strategy—he would commit the sin of killing without the slightest tremor of conscience, and would thereby free his people to be good if they wished it. He would lighten their burdens of despair and fear and even give them grounds for hope—and would thus balance Good and Evil so neatly that surely the sources of magic must be confused as to which he was! In fact, Rebozo suspected that the king wasn't sure himself—or was determined not to be either.

It was impossible, of course. No man could remain exactly half good and half evil for more than half a minute. As soon as he did one more act of good than he did of evil, he would begin the progress toward Goodness—and it would take an act of outright sin to counter it. True, Boncorro was determined not to fall into his father's fate any more than into his grandfather's—but his yardstick seemed to be the good of the people, and surely that must indeed lead him to Goodness eventually.

Rebozo had to do something to prevent that. "If you are going to remove so many monopolies, your Majesty, you should balance them by instituting a new one."

Boncorro stiffened, but he was caught by the word "balance."
"What monopoly can I set up that will *increase* trade?"

"A monopoly on prostitution. No, hear me out! Only think, Majesty—if brothels were legal, but maintained under a monopoly that held the condition that all prostitutes be free of disease in order to do business, more men would patronize them!"

"Aye, to debase and abuse them!"

Rebozo shrugged. "There will be prostitutes whether the law allows it or not, your Majesty—you know it well! Still, you could make it another condition of the monopoly that the women not be beaten by their pimps or procuresses, nor injured by their patrons! You could insist that any who treated them less than gently be hauled before a court—and you could station royal guardsmen within the houses to enforce that law! But you cannot impose any conditions as long as the trade is illegal!"

"But more trade means that there will be more prostitutes," Boncorro said, frowning, "and that girls will be forced into it whether they wish to be or not!"

"Come, Majesty," Rebozo wheedled. "If there shall be more money being spent, as you have said, there will also be more men wanting to buy an hour with a prostitute—and if there shall be more peasants leaving the land and coming to the cities, as you have indicated, there will be more girls drawn into the trade anyway! Why not have them all legally under your own eye, where you may at least insist they not be too heavily abused?"

The king frowned, stuck for a comeback—it was an issue he had never really considered.

"Besides, you know there are some women who really prefer that way of life," Rebozo said.

"Or who choose it, at least." It was as good as a capitulation, even though Boncorro followed it with, ". . . though their number never has been adequate to fulfill the demands of my more depraved subjects. Still, you do make some sort of sense—the women would be better protected under the eye of a duke who is under *my* eye. I shall consider it, Rebozo."

"I rejoice that my feeble counsel has been of use to your Majesty," the chancellor said, beaming. He bowed, thinking, *A blow well-struck for corruption!* He knew full well that the more twisted uses of prostitutes would continue to flourish illegally, as they did now—and that the king, by condoning prostitution of any sort, would be drawn toward the side of Evil. Indeed, convinced by Rebozo's arguments and

bored with his own stable of beauties, he would sooner or later patronize some of those establishments of vice himself, the ones he was
even now discussing. Done once, done a dozen times—then twenty,
then a hundred. Then, as his sexual prowess began to decline with
age, he would be drawn to the more depraved amusements in a desperate attempt to flag his failing powers. The long slide to damnation
was well begun indeed, and Latruria would one day be as securely on
the side of Evil as it was in the old days.

Everybody likes being the center of attention, but Matt was just paranoid enough for it to make him a little nervous. He dismissed it as
stage fright and called out, "Come, good people! Tales and lays, po-
ems and sagas! Listen and lose yourselves in far and fabled lands!"

They came flocking. "Tales from Merovence?" one shopper asked.

"That's neither far nor fabled, but I have the newest stories and
tales." Matt was sure they'd be very new—in this universe, anyway.

"No songs?" one teenager asked, disappointed.

Matt grinned. "I shall play the tunes and chant the words—but believe me, you do not wish to hear me sing."

"True, true," Pascal murmured.

Matt flashed him a mock glare. "You don't *have* to agree with me,
you know."

The crowd laughed, and Matt began to realize that Pascal could be
a very good straight man. In fact, the two of them could really clean
up at every wayside fair between here and—

He wrenched his thought back to the present with a major effort.
He was supposed to be a spy, not a real minstrel! The ham in him was
carrying him away, like Peer Gynt with the Green-Clad One.

"A tale of the far north!" he cried. "A story of the wanderer Peer
Gynt, and his fall from virtue! Who would hear it?"

The crowd clamored agreement, and some of them waved pennies.
Pascal, quicker on the uptake than Matt would have thought, tossed
his hat down at Matt's feet and pitched in a penny of his own. It was
like seeding the clouds, and produced a positive hailstorm of coppers.

"I am persuaded." Matt bowed with a flourish. He began to play
"Morning Mood" from Grieg's *Peer Gynt Suite,* and intoned, "Peer
Gynt was a lad of Norway, where the Vikings came from . . ."

"The sea robbers?" a boy cried eagerly. This far south, the Vikings
were only storybook villains. Matt wondered how the story would go
over even farther south—say, near Sicily. Had the Normans conquered the island in this world, too? "He was of their blood, but was

himself only a poor farm boy whose father had died when he was young. His mother had reared him as well as she might, but he was always willful, and somewhat wild. He liked to ramble the mountain-side with a sling and stones, claiming he was hunting, but really day-dreaming."

The boy's eyes shone, and Matt realized the kid was hearing about a kindred spirit. Well, for him it would be a cautionary tale. "One day, when Peer Gynt was out hunting, he heard a wild pig's squeal— and looking up, he saw a woman. But what a woman! Her form was everything a man could dream of, and her gossamer green gown clung to her in such a way as to show every curve!"

The women muttered, not liking the sound of this—was the min-strel going to say they should show themselves off? That was ex-ploitation for those who did have figures worth looking at, but outright humiliation for those who did not! And the boy in front was beginning to look disappointed. Well, no matter, Matt decided—he would catch them all again when they got to the Hall of the Moun-tain King.

He caught them sooner than that. "From the neck down she was the most lovely of women—but from the neck up, she was a sow! Aye, bris-tles, snout, pointed ears and all, the woman had a pig's head!"

He went on, telling them of the Green-Clad One's seductive invita-tion, of their ride on the back of a boar to the Hall of the Mountain King with its elves and monsters, of their attempt to hold Peer there, and of his escape.

When he finished, the audience let out a collective sigh.

"What then?" the boy cried, his eyes huge.

"Oh, that is a tale for another time," Matt said carelessly.

The audience complained, disappointed—but one man called out, "Have you news of Merovence?"

"News for news," Matt answered. "Tell me what moves in La-truria, and I'll tell you what transpires in Merovence! How fares your king?"

"Boncorro is well, praise Hea—" The man caught himself and glanced around, desperate to be sure no royal spy had heard him. "—praise him! Rumor has it that he sent his men to chastise a knight who still demands that his serfs give him three parts in four of their crop!"

"He has hanged a squire for raping a peasant's daughter!" a young woman said, eyes alight with triumph.

"He has wounded our business," one man complained, "by cutting the taxes on brandy and wool and brocades that come from Merovence and Allustria, aye, even those that come through the country of the Switzers!"

Matt frowned. "How does that hurt your business?"

"Why, I now must charge less for the goods *I* bring in!" the man said indignantly, and the audience laughed. Matt finally got the joke—the man was a smuggler, and the legitimate merchants could now undersell him.

"News for news!" the first man cried again. "How fares your queen?"

"She is well, she is wed!" Matt cried.

"That is old news," a woman scoffed. "Has she birthed a babe yet?"

"No, sad to say," Matt said, with genuine regret, "though we keep hoping."

"More than a year wed, and still no sign of a child?" the woman said indignantly. "What ails her husband?"

Matt stared, caught speechless.

"He cannot be much of a man," another woman opined, "if he cannot get her with child."

"Scarcely a man at all!" the first woman sniffed. "He is a wizard—not even a sorcerer!"

"A wizard, but not a miracle worker!" Matt protested. "Husbands are only the delivery boys—babies come from Heaven!"

The whole crowd fell silent, aghast. "Do not say that word!" a granny cried. "Are you a fool?"

"No, I'm from Merovence."

They stared at him in shock for a moment, then burst out laughing. "Very good, very good!" a portly man chuckled, wiping his eyes. "But what of the crops? We have heard rumors of drought!"

"All false, thank—" Matt caught himself in time, deciding not to offend their sensibilities. "—praises be. The rain falls like a blessing, and the sun beams down."

The crowd began to mutter again, apprehensive, glancing over their shoulders. Matt wondered if, seven years ago, mention of "Heaven" or "blessing" really had been enough to bring a vengeful sorcerer.

If not, King Maledicto had brainwashed them into dreading even the words of goodness. Matt grasped for a change of topic. "The queen has made a treaty with the Free Folk, with the dragons! They shall no longer steal sheep and cattle, and the queen shall arrest the hatchling hunters who seek to steal dragons' blood to sell to sorcerers!" Stegoman had pushed for that one.

Again the crowd muttered, but wide-eyed this time—amazed that

Matt could speak against sorcerers and not get burned up about it. Still, they edged away from him.

"News for news!" But Matt was beginning to wonder if there were a single topic that wouldn't edge into a taboo area, such as sorcery or Heaven. Maybe not, in this world. "But first, let me tell you of Peer Gynt and Solveg!"

The crowd murmured appreciation and came crowding back in, eager for more stories of licentious women. Well, they were in for a disappointment this time. "Solveg was a church-bred woman, a lass who carried a prayer book about her wherever she went."

The crowd edged away again, murmuring with apprehension.

"But she was beautiful!" Matt cried. "Demure, sweet, modest—and beautiful!"

"Not with a figure like that of the Green-Clad one?" asked a teen-aged boy, disappointed.

"Who could know? Her clothing was so loose that none could see! But it was beautifully embroidered, and her skirts swung with the lilt of a May tune as she walked. The aroma of roses seemed to follow her, and so did Peer Gynt's heart."

The boys began to look bored, but the women pressed close, held by the promise of a good love story. Matt told them of Peer Gynt's boastful courtship and of Solveg's interest, though she saw through him in an instant. Still, she found something to love in him anyway—but Peer went off in a huff, offended by her truthfulness.

Then he encountered the darkness cast by the Great Boyg, becoming trapped and unable to fight his way free, as the monster called up harpies to feed on him—but Solveg came, singing hymns, and banished them all by her simple goodness.

The men and boys were riveted by the tale, and the women sighed with happiness—then instantly looked apprehensive again. Apparently this was something really new for them—a story in which virtue triumphed, and they rather liked the novelty. They just weren't sure it was safe, that was all.

Matt and Pascal camped by the roadside that night, Pascal counting the day's take by the light of the fire. "A silver penny!" he cried, holding up the trophy. "They must truly have liked your tale of Peer Gynt, my friend."

"And want to give me good reason to come back and tell them Act Two," Matt agreed.

Pascal looked up, frowning. " 'Act Two'?"

"The second half of the story," Matt said quickly.

"If it is half so amusing as the first, you will make your fortune with it! We have a month's living in this hat!"

"Latruria *is* having a boom," Matt said.

"They have become prosperous, if that is what you mean—but we knew that in Merovence. I fear that you have not learned much new here, Sir Matthew."

"Oh, I wouldn't say that." Matt gazed at the pot that was stewing vegetables and beef jerky. "We've found out that King Boncorro really is trying to make life better for the common folk, but apparently isn't doing it because he wants to do good."

Pascal frowned. "Who told you that?"

"All of them—from their fright, every time I mentioned Heaven or a blessing, or Solveg's church, prayer book, and hymns. They're still scared of evil sorcerers punishing people for even *talking* about Goodness—which means King Boncorro certainly hasn't taken a stand against the forces of Evil, and may not even have a quarrel with them."

"Why, then, would he be doing what is good for the commoners?" Pascal asked, suddenly intent—after all, these were his kind of people.

"Pure selfishness—or, if not pure, then at least basic." Matt reached out to stir the stew. "He has some personal motive, some hope of gain. It might even be that he's enlightened enough to realize that if the people prosper, the king gets richer."

"Why, what an odd notion!"

"It is, around here," Matt agreed, "so I don't really expect that's King Boncorro's reason. I wonder what *is*, though."

"Perhaps you shall find out at the next village."

"Maybe," Matt agreed. "One way or another, at least we should make another haul of coppers. Stew smells about ready, Pascal. Did you say you had a bowl in your pack?"

"The aroma is tempting," a deeper voice answered, "but I prefer my food raw. In fact, I prefer it moving."

"I already paid the farmer a quarter mile back." Matt didn't even look up. "Go have a cow, Manny."

Chapter
Eight

It was nice to know how it felt to be a star. Everywhere Matt went, everyplace he stopped long enough for Pascal to toss down his hat, people came running to jostle each other as they tried to get closer, to see and hear the minstrel. Somehow, it never occurred to Pascal that they might be attracting more attention than he wanted—but it occurred to Matt, sure enough. For himself, Matt didn't mind—he was the bait in his own trap, so to speak. But for Pascal, it was another matter.

"I *am* likely to draw some unpleasant attention from an evil sorcerer or two," he reminded Pascal as the young man poured him another stoup of ale from the inn's pitcher. "I'd really rather you not get thrown into prison for my sake."

Pascal shrugged. "It is worth the risk. Your glory reflects on me, and any ounce of fame is more likely to sway the fair Panegyra to my suit."

Matt just hoped that suit wasn't spades.

That first village turned out to be typical; Matt had learned a lot there, but he didn't find out too much more about conditions in Latruria, no matter how many towns and roadside inns heard his "songs." The people were well fed and well cared for. The country looked very prosperous, and though the serfs and yeomen were deferential when a lord passed by, they didn't cringe, nor did the lords treat them cruelly. The girls in the villages didn't have to turn their faces to the wall as the gentlemen passed by. People gathered around,

winced at any mention of Heaven or blessing, but looked similarly
nervous at mention of the Devil. If ever there was a country that believed in the golden mean, this was it. They had been punished too
often for having spoken of holy matters, and punished too often by
those who were dedicated to Evil.

Matt began to realize all over again that witches and sorcerers
who had sold their souls to the Devil had done it in more ways than
one. They were now completely devoted to evil and wickedness, to
selfishness, hatred, and doing harm to others wherever they could.
The only difference between the mighty sorcerers and the low
seemed to be their capacity for hatred, and the magnitude of their
sins—as Kipling said of the little devils, "They weep that they'd been
too small to sin to the height of their desire." The sorcerers devoted
themselves to their work of misery-making with the single-minded-
ness of the fanatic, whether it was out of despair, a wish for revenge
on their fellow humans, or the feeling that once having turned away
from Heaven, they were doomed irrevocably. If "sold my soul to
rock 'n' roll" meant that the person in question was so totally dedicated to his favorite form of music that there was little room for
anything else in his life, so selling one's soul to the Devil implied
that the seller was totally dedicated to evil and the harming of his
fellow beings. Small wonder that the mere mention of them still
made the Latrurians start looking over their shoulders—or that, six
years after King Boncorro's coronation, there was still a feeling of ju-
bilance, of release, like that of children let out to play on the first
day of spring.

But when grown-ups are turned loose to play, they do it with a
bit more dedication than children, and some of their games are not
nice at all—especially when they have been raised with no mention
of morality.

Matt leaned across the table in the common room of the inn and
murmured, "Every girl I've seen seems to make flirting a major hobby."

Pascal looked up at him in surprise. "Do not all girls?"

So it had spread to Pascal's home in southern Merovence, too. Matt
wondered what had happened to the demure young miss who sat
modestly by and waited for the boys to come to her. Gone and scarcely
remembered, apparently—along with the mammoth and the saber-
tooth. Didn't any of them have enough confidence in their own beauty
and attractiveness to be sure they were male bait?

Not in this inn, at least.

He looked around him, figuring percentages. The common room was long and wide, but low-ceilinged, filled with trestle tables, benches, and smoke rejected by a chimney that was almost drawing properly—not enough to make anybody choke or wheeze, but enough to drift up along the ceiling beams, where a century or so of such vapors had turned the wood black. Laughter and chatter filled the air, along with the clink of mug against pitcher and the sound of pouring. The air was pungent with the aroma of ale and roasting pork. The serving maids giggled at the pinches they drew, or turned on their tormentors with mock severity—or, if the men were handsome enough or looked prosperous enough, batted their eyelashes and exchanged a few double entendres before they hurried away about their errands.

"Your fingers are too hard, sir! Belike from wielding the hoe!"

"Nay, lass, 'tis from counting coins all the day."

"Coins, is it? Your master's they must be—for I see naught but coppers before you!"

"Oh, but there is more in my purse." The man patted his pouch with a grin. "There now, weigh it and see for yourself!"

The girl leaned over to cup her hand under the merchant's purse and judge its weight. "A man of substance, are you?"

The merchant shrugged. "Discover for yourself, if you wish—when you are done with your day's chores."

"And if I find none more appealing than yourself," the girl retorted, "which should not be hard."

"Should it not?" The man grinned. "When should I come to ask again?"

"When the moon is high, if you are not! Enjoy the savories while you may!" She went off with a swirl of her skirts, and the man turned with a grin to the pastries she had left.

"Harmless enough," Pascal judged. "Why do you frown so?"

"Mostly because the man was wearing a wedding ring. Doesn't he even think about his wife?"

"Why?" Pascal shrugged. "He is far from home, and she is not likely to learn of what he does. Besides, do you think she will be any more chaste than he, while he is away on his travels?"

"Well, uh . . ." Matt turned back, feeling very naive. "I kinda had some notion like that, yeah."

Pascal stared. "Is this the fashion in the queen's capital?"

"It will be if she has anything to say about it," Matt said grimly.

"She also might start enforcing some of the rules of chivalry." He nodded toward another amorous tableau. "They could use it."

Here, it was no serving maid, but a lady in her traveling clothes who was sipping her wine and laughing at the remarks a knight was making as he stood beside her, leaning over to look down at her face and her décolletage. Another knight leaned close behind her, looking down over her shoulder, and murmured something in her ear that made her face redden. Then she blushed again at something the first knight said and lowered her eyes, but made no move to cover her décolletage—nor to edge away when the knight in front stepped so close that his thigh pressed against her, leaning close to murmur something, or when the knight behind sat down and slid up tight against her side, leaning around in front to add a comment of his own. She looked up sharply, a glint in her eye, then turned to the first knight and nodded as if accepting a challenge. She rose to take his hand and turn away toward the stairs.

" 'Tis only sport." Pascal frowned. "Why are you so pale?"

"Because those two going up the stairs are *both* wearing wedding rings—and I have the sneaking suspicion that whoever they're married to, it's not each other." Matt turned back to the younger man. "Where I come from, that's counted a deed unworthy of a knight— and as to it being only sport, I have a notion that it's going to become a very strenuous sport indeed."

Pascal shrugged. "Exercise is good for the body—and in any case, 'tis no concern of ours."

"True," Matt said reluctantly. He had to remind himself that though they might be close to Merovence, they were nonetheless not in it.

Nor all that close anymore by medieval standards. They had been moving steadily for at least a week and were almost a hundred miles into Latruria by now. He certainly had no jurisdiction here.

The lady turned back to give the seated knight a saucy, dismissive glance, saying something that apparently wounded him, for he leaped up and drew his sword. The lady fell back with a shriek, and the first knight whirled, his sword whipping out.

"Sir knights, no!" the innkeeper wailed, but his cry was drowned in the clatter of overturned benches and the thunder of feet as the other patrons jumped up and leaped back, pulling their tables with them, leaving a wide clear space around the two rivals—then jostling one another for front-row seats.

"They've done this before." Matt frowned. "Everybody knows what to do."

"Aye, and what to expect. I'll lay a silver penny on the one with the moustache!"

Matt turned to him, appalled. "A couple of men are ready to carve each other to bits, and you're going to *bet* on them?"

"Why not?" Pascal shrugged. "Everyone else does. Besides, they will fight whether we bet or not—so why not wager?"

"We *might* be able to stop them instead!"

"Peasants, interfere with knights? They would both turn on us, and sliver us with their swords!"

Matt turned back to watch, numbed, trying to think of a way to stop them—short of using magic, of course. In passing, he noticed that both knights were wearing wedding rings, but it didn't particularly surprise him.

"Do not be so concerned, Sir—I mean, Minstrel Matthew. Belike their honor will be satisfied with first blood, and none shall be slain."

"You're laying odds again," Matt groaned.

The fight was brief, and made up in verve what it lacked in skill. The knight who had lost out on the lady's favors had a lot of unused testosterone to get rid of, but his rival was riding a high of having already won. Swords clattered and clashed as the two men fenced their way back and forth across the floor—and they did *not* settle for first blood. The spectators cheered when one knight's point scored the other's ribs—but the wounded knight only howled with anger and pressed the fight harder. A loud groan went up from the audience—the people who had bet that first blood would end it, no doubt, and for a moment the clash of steel was drowned out by the clink of coins as the losers paid their bets, then turned right around and set a new stake. Matt noticed two portly peasants working their way through the crowd, collecting coins and putting them into their hats—primitive bookies, no doubt.

Meanwhile, the knight with the bloody chest managed to tear through his rival's doublet, where scarlet stained the cloth, spreading, making its owner spit with anger and redouble his efforts. Finally, one blade stabbed through the opponent's arm, and the sword dropped from suddenly nerveless fingers as its owner howled with pain. The winner yanked his sword free, triumph lighting his eyes, as the man who had been the woman's first choice sank back onto the nearest bench, clutching at his wound. The victor wiped his blade, sheathed it, and turned to offer his arm to the lady. Without the slightest hesitation, she took it—indeed, pressed up close to him with a look that would have melted a beehive—and up the stairs they went, both totally oblivious to the loser.

Blood was welling up out of his forearm, and the innkeeper was shouting for a surgeon, but most of the crowd was making too much noise grumbling about losing or crowing about winning, for any to hear him. Certainly nobody seemed to have the slightest concern for the knight who sat staring at the blood dripping onto the floor. Matt felt a stab of pity for him, then remembered that he had been fighting for the chance to cheat on his wife, and felt only a grim regret that he was himself human. He went over to the man nonetheless and examined his wound. "The blood's flowing evenly," he said. "I don't think he cut a vein or artery, by some miracle."

"Be still!" the knight gasped. "Am I not in enough hazard, that you must speak of forbidden things?"

Matt looked up in surprise. "Forbidden things?" Oh—yes. Miracles. "Okay, you won on a real long shot."

"Nay! I lost the lady's favors!"

"But kept your life." Matt looked up at the innkeeper. "Two measures of brandywine!"

The innkeeper stared, at a loss, but one of the serving wenches had a bit more presence of mind, and brought two small glasses of amber fluid. Matt handed one to the knight. "Drink it. You'll need it."

The man took the glass and drank greedily—and Matt poured the other over the wound. The knight howled and hurled the glass away, but Matt blocked the blow and said, "Just hold on, Sir Knight. That brandywine will do you more good where I've poured it than where you have."

"It burns!" the knight cried. "Oh! The pain!"

"I thought knights never showed their hurts," Matt jibed.

The man went still and gave him a very cold stare.

Matt didn't pay attention—he was busy winding the nearest napkin around the wound. "The brandywine should stop the worst of the flow of blood, and it will make your arm a lot cleaner than you did. I'd tell you to find a doctor fast, but for some reason, I think you might have more luck with a poultice from the innkeeper's wife." He glanced up. "Or from your own."

The knight reddened. "Mind your manners, peasant!"

Interesting, Matt thought—manners mattered, but morals didn't. "As you wish, Sir Knight." He stood up. "I'm afraid that's all I can do for you, though, except for maybe telling you a story to take your mind off the pain."

The man looked up at him with suspicion. "That might be welcome. What is its subject?"

Matt glanced around quickly and noticed the eyes turning toward him at the mention of a story. "Of the Lord Orlando," he told the knight, "nephew of the emperor Charlemagne."

"I have never heard of him."

"Small wonder—he's only a figment in a romance," Matt sighed, "at least, in this world. Still, it's a great story, and it never claimed to be historically accurate. Would you hear it?"

"Aye!" chorused all the customers, and Matt decided to get to work.

One hour and two flagons of ale later, Matt and Pascal were two ducats richer. "Well, we have paid for our night's lodging, and perhaps tomorrow's as well." Pascal didn't seem to notice Matt's part in the earning. "We could hire a chamber for the night!"

Remembering the couple who had gone upstairs, Matt was somehow not as eager for the idea as he might have been. He also remembered the bedbugs at the last inn. "No, let's just wait them out and sleep by the fire." He took his blanket from his pack. "They've started stacking the tables already. Any minute now, the innkeeper should be chasing out the ones who aren't staying the night."

"Well, we shall have to guard our money carefully," Pascal sighed, "but when have we not had to? We should reach my cousin's house tomorrow evening, at least. We can expect proper beds then."

Privately, Matt thought they were much more likely to wind up in the barn—but maybe Pascal was right, maybe the fact that he was planning to run off with his host's daughter wouldn't make any difference. At least, if they didn't tell the squire what Pascal was intending to do, he might not kick Matt out until after the young man had eloped.

Or been immensely disappointed. Personally, Matt thought that was the much more likely option.

When the daytimers had been chased out, and the all-night visitors were all wrapped up and arranged as near the fire as they could manage, Matt noticed that Pascal was still awake, with a brooding frown on his face as he gazed off into space at some unseen horror. Matt told himself it was none of his business, but the assurances didn't work. With a sigh, he sat up and moved closer to his traveling companion. "What's keeping you awake?"

Pascal flushed. "Too much wine, belike."

"Wine doesn't hinder sleep—it helps. That fight bothering you?"

"Only the silver penny I lost on it." But Pascal's answer was too quick, too elaborately casual.

"It *is* bothering you." Matt frowned. "What's the matter? I thought *I* was the one who was preoccupied with morals here."

"You are! I am not! 'Twas only ... well, 'twas seeing that knight go off with that lady, ten years younger than he at least, and realizing what randy goats they must have been, both of those who fought over her ..."

"Oh." Matt straightened. "It isn't blood that bothers you—it's the affluent older man soliciting the favors of the younger woman."

Pascal just glowered at the fire.

"I hope your cousin doesn't find men's brawling attractive," Matt said.

"I doubt it—or at least, I doubt that she is worse than any, in that regard. I have heard that all women thrill to see men fighting over them."

"That's a popular fancy, yes. But you think she might find older men attractive?"

"How could she?" Pascal demanded, his eyes glittering with anger. "He is twice her age at least, and belike is paunchy and foul of breath into the bargain!"

Matt frowned, studying him, then hazarded a guess. "You don't think she'd be able to ignore all that if he were rich enough?"

Pascal shot up from his blanket, face an inch from Matt's as he growled, "How can you defame a pure innocent maid so!"

"I didn't," Matt said hastily, "just made a guess. So you don't *know* that he's ugly and feeble?"

"How could he be aught else?" Pascal bleated.

Matt forced a smile. "Some of us manage to keep in shape, even if we do have desk jobs. But not too many teenagers find forty-five-year-old men attractive. You're probably safe on that score."

"But I have only youth," Pascal mourned, "no beauty of face or form, no wealth, no rank! I shudder to think on it, but I cannot help it, not when I saw that knight ascend the stairs with that lady to their temporary ecstasy! What manner of man is he, who will soon be debauching my fair cousin?"

"Nice question." Matt wondered how the prospective bridegroom had made his fortune.

He also wondered what the knight's wife would say if she ever found out what was going on tonight. He didn't think her own infidelities would insulate her feelings, as Pascal seemed to believe. In his experience, most people thought that their own little sins were perfectly all right—it was just everybody else's that were wrong.

The windows were gray with coming dawn as Matt shook Pascal awake. "Come on, lazybones! I want to get an early start."

Pascal rolled one eye open, took in the light—or lack thereof—and closed his eyes with a groan. " 'Tis not yet dawn!"

"Yeah, but we have a lot of miles to cover, and we don't want to get there staggering and worn out. We want to be at your cousin's castle by mid-afternoon, remember?" Actually, Matt didn't want to be there in the common room when the knight and lady came back downstairs—now that he was a husband himself, he found that he had a tougher time watching other people's adulteries. He resolutely refused to think why.

But before Pascal could even get up, the knight came down the stairs. It wasn't the victorious knight, though, it was the loser—and it wasn't the lady who was with him, but one of the serving wenches, hanging on his arm and laughing gaily at some jest he was making.

Matt realized he was staring and wrenched his gaze away just before the knight happened to glance around the room, smiling, one arm around the girl's shoulders, the other in an improvised sling.

"You look like a fish being served up for dinner," Matt muttered to Pascal. "Better get up and start moving."

The young man had been staring as if his face wore a matched pair of fried eggs. Now he gave his head a quick shake and turned to climb out of his blanket, then fold it up. Matt followed suit, relieved to find that he wasn't the only one taken by surprise.

The knight sat down at a table, still grinning. "I could eat my horse, or at least as much food as he!"

" 'Tis early still, but I shall bring you whatever is hot." The wench favored him with a slumberous look.

The knight laughed softly, with one last tug at her fingers, and she turned away, tossing her head at the chorus of catcalls with which her fellow serving maids greeted her. "Jealous witches! Simply because he did not choose one of *you*!"

"Who else among us was so quick with comfort and nursing?" a buxom wench countered. "Was the loser worth your time?"

The girl smiled and flaunted a brooch.

"Gold!" The buxom one lost her smile, eyes round.

"And more in coin," the wench told her.

The other girls hissed envy.

She tossed her head again and flounced over to pick up her tray. "It is good to be charitable to poor wounded knights."

"Aye, if they be rich and spendthrift!" another girl sneered.

"And lacking in taste," a third contributed.

The chorus of jibes went on until she had taken her tray away, still with a self-satisfied smile; she obviously felt that she had pulled off a coup right beneath their noses. So, obviously, did they.

"I find I have small appetite for breakfast," Pascal told Matt. "Let us take a loaf and eat as we march."

"Good idea." Matt went to the innkeeper to pay their score and pick up some bread. He was glad to see that Pascal's part of Merovence hadn't been completely corrupted by Latruria—yet.

They passed out of the village, managing not to be shocked by the number of people who were up and about—at least to judge by the smoke rising from chimneys and, in the case of peasant huts, smoke holes. Pascal seemed not even to notice, and Matt had become inured to a culture in which people went to bed with the dark and woke with the light. It wasn't quite that bad at Queen Alisande's court, where the candles, fueled by the royal exchequer, burned until well after ten P.M.—but it still made Matt do a mental double-take when he realized that most of the common folk were up and about when he would have been just getting to bed in his protracted college days.

They hadn't gone more than two rods past the village limits when a soft padding behind them made Matt turn around. Sure enough, it was Manny. "Did you eat well?"

"Aye, though the cowherd seemed inclined to dispute ownership with me."

"You didn't eat him, too, did you?" Matt said anxiously.

"Nay. After all, 'twas in your interests he objected."

"Ours?" Pascal frowned.

"Aye. 'Avaunt!' cried he. 'I've sold that beef to a minstrel!' 'He is my master,' quoth I—it galls me, but I find these simple peasant folk cannot comprehend how a monster might be loyal to a family, even as one of its servants might be."

"I have a little difficulty understanding it myself," Matt confessed. "Not objecting, mind you—I guess Great-Grandpa did a better job enchanting you than he knew. So what happened to the cowherd?"

"He did not agree with me."

"I *told* you not to eat him."

"Nay, 'twas with my words he failed to agree, not my stomach. At the last, I became angered and told him that 'twas for me you had bought the steer, and he seemed doubtful enough that he left me to my repast."

Matt sighed. "I can't imagine why."

"Certainly the wisest choice," Pascal agreed. "Then you slept well?"

"Aye; green grass is soft enough for me. Why you plaguey people seem to think you have need of feather beds and such, I cannot fathom—nor why you will not allow me to accompany you into the towns."

"Bad for business," Matt explained. "We're trying to attract crowds, not chase them away."

"So you have said—though I should think that no matter how well they pay you, they would pay better to be sure I would go away."

"Well, yes," Matt said judiciously, "but that way, they might be a little more careful what they said around us, and I'm out to pick up gossip. Matter of fact, with you along, I don't think we'd get close enough to overhear anything they said."

Manny sighed. "Mortals are such flighty creatures. Delicious, mind you, but excitable nonetheless."

"Yes, I've noticed that myself. But for the time being, Manny, we'll keep the present system, if you don't mind."

"Not greatly," the manticore sighed, "so long as you buy me a cow before you go parading into the town. Still, as I've said before, you need only whistle the phoenix's call, and I shall bound to your rescue."

"I remember the notes," Pascal assured him. "But how can you be sure 'tis the cry of a phoenix?"

"Why, because I heard the bird cry out thus just before he burst into flame."

Pascal looked suddenly worried.

"Don't worry, you've done it once already, and nothing happened," Matt said by way of reassurance. He turned back to Manny. "No chance that another phoenix will come to answer it, is there?"

The manticore shrugged. "I cannot say with certainty—but I have heard the phoenix is a most singular bird."

"Meaning there's only one of him, I hope," Matt mused, "though I'm not sure I'd really be all that unhappy to see one."

"Would it not depend on whether it came to help you, or hurt you?" Pascal offered.

"Yes, that might affect the way I felt," Matt admitted. "Now, Manny—when we get to the castle we're heading for, village rules apply, okay?"

"So long as there is a fat bullock staked out for me every night," the manticore said, "I will be as invisible as the very wind. But you will make me feel unloved, mortal."

"How about if I try to find a lady manticore for you?"

Manny's grins widened. "That would be even better than a bullock."

"No promises," Matt temporized, "but I'll keep my ears open for information about one." And they went on down the road, with Matt pondering the complexities of manticore reproduction.

Chapter
Nine

Panegyra's house was a moated grange—a large country house with low walls, a wide moat, and a drawbridge. So big a moat appeared rather extravagant to Matt, until he looked closely and saw that it had been made from an oxbow bend in the river, and that all the squire had needed to do was to dig another arc connecting the two prongs of the U. The house itself was fieldstone, and it was surrounded by a low wall, only four feet high—not enough to keep anyone out by itself, but enough to offer cover to archers trying to keep an enemy away.

"Doesn't look like they're all that sure the peace will last," Matt commented.

"Her great-grandfather was not," Pascal answered. "The land was still in strife then, between the forces of the kings and the counts."

Matt pricked up his ears; that sounded like the medieval Italy he knew. "Did each noble family have a town it more or less owned?"

"Aye, or shared with another noble family." Pascal looked at him quizzically. "I thought you knew nothing of Latruria, Sir Matthew."

"Oh, I've heard bits and pieces—and hold off on the 'Sir,' okay? Around here, I'm just a minstrel."

"As you wish," Pascal said, "though I confess that without it, I begin to lose track of your station. Pardon me if I offend."

"No need." Matt was used to undergraduates trying to be too familiar with the professor. "If I can't win your respect by my actions, the title isn't going to do me much good."

Pascal frowned. "I would have said that it was those who do *not* win respect, who most need the title and station."

"A point, but one I'd rather not admit. For myself, I'd just as soon not be left standing at the station." He turned to the manticore. "Time to head for the tall timber, Manny."

"Where?" The monster looked about at the wide plain, with nothing more than occasional outcrops of trees.

"A point," Matt admitted, "but I'm sure you can find someplace to hide. We paid that shepherd well to leave you two skinned sheep by the big rock in his meadow every night—so don't ramble too far away, okay?"

"I shall not—but do not be gone overlong, I prithee. His flock is not overly large."

"At the price I paid, he can buy sheep and still make a fat profit. In fact, he promised to do just that. Probably thinks I'm a bandit chief with a small army in hiding—so I don't think he'll try to cheat us."

"He had best not," Manny answered, and Matt wondered if it was his voice rumbling or his stomach.

"All this talk of sheep makes me yearn for meat," Pascal grumbled. "Come, friend Matthew! Let us knock on their gate!" But there was a hidden urgency about him; he was as taut as a hound on a leash. Matt gave him a glance, but only said, "Yeah, it has been a long hike. Off we go, eh?"

They crossed the drawbridge, and Matt counted it a healthy sign that there was no sentry stationed to watch. Come to that, the chains running up to the bridge tower were a bit rusty, as if they hadn't been used in a year. Things must have been safe lately.

They came through the tower—really just a stone arch, Matt discovered. He glanced back to see if Manny was watching them, but the manticore had already disappeared.

"Good day! What do *you* here?"

Matt snapped around to see a man with a bucket and brush staring at them as if trying to decide whether or not to scowl—judging their class, most likely. He must have decided favorably, for he forced a smile and turned to Pascal. "I know you, do I not?"

"You do indeed," Pascal told him. "We met at the family gathering last summer, though I fear I do not recall your name. Mine is Pascal de la Tour."

"Ah! Young Master Pascal! You are welcome, sir, I am sure—though your coming is quite a surprise. I am only Anselmo, a footman—I doubt you would have heard my name, let alone remembered it. Come, let me conduct you to Squire dell Tour."

He spoke with a heavy accent, but it was the same language—and Matt had grown accustomed to the dialect as they came south, after all. Anselmo set down his bucket and brush on the doorstep, then led the way into the house.

He brought them to a small, spartan reception room where they waited for a few minutes before the door slammed open to admit a stocky, graying, bearded man in an open robe with open arms. "Cousin Pascal! What a happy chance!"

Pascal rose, just in time for the squire's forward rush to carry the young man into his arms for a bear hug. Matt thought he heard Pascal's ribs creak; then the older man held him back at arm's length, looking him up and down with a grin. "Well, a bit of dust on you, but that's to be expected in so long a journey. What happy chance brings you to my house?"

"Why, a wish to see something of the world, Cousin Giuseppe." The answer was glib; Pascal had rehearsed it at least five times a day, all the way from Merovence. "I had thought it best to begin where I was not a complete stranger—and at the gathering last summer, you and my father did extend open invitations to each other's families."

"We did, we did indeed, and right glad am I of your company!" Squire Giuseppe turned to Matt. "And who is your companion?"

"Matthew, a wandering minstrel who has been good enough to let me accompany him. Even today, I have heard it is not wise to travel alone."

"Indeed it is not—in fact, you are fortunate to have chosen a companion who did not try to cut your purse the first night." The squire pumped Matt's hand. "You are welcome, sir, welcome! I thank you for escorting my nephew! But come, gentlemen, come! You must see my house—then you must refresh yourselves, so that you may come to dinner!" And he swept them out the door and off on a whirlwind tour of his house, complete with names and dates of each ancestor who had built each wing or installed each convenience or had which picture painted or statue sculpted.

He was indefatigable and never seemed to remember that his guests might not be—so when they had finally been deposited in a guest room, Matt sank down on a chair with a sigh. "Now I know what they mean by aggressive hospitality!" He eyed the great copper tub hungrily, but said, "You wash first, Pascal—I think you'll take longer dressing. When do we get to meet this feminine paragon of a cousin of yours?"

"At dinner." Pascal was already half out of his clothes, movements quick and nervous. "I can hardly wait, Matthew! A year and more, but at last I shall see her again!"

"Yes, at last." Matt just hoped the boy decided it had all been worth the trip.

"Your Majesty must not go!" The gray-bearded doctor trembled with agitation. "I have cast the runes, I have gazed within a pool tinted with a drop of your blood—and there can be no doubt! I have seen the babe that grows inside you! You are with child and must not risk the baby's life by going on campaign!"

"I shall take no risks that I can avoid," Alisande said with total determination, "but ride I must, or the child may have no father!"

The doctor's face sank into a tragic mask. "At least ride in a litter," he pleaded.

"What! A warrior going forth to battle in a litter? Who would respect it?"

"I have heard of wounded kings who directed their battles from horse litters," the doctor insisted.

"I am not wounded!"

"No, but you will be if you do not take care. At the very least, Majesty, ride sidesaddle!"

Alisande tried to glare at the doctor, but she couldn't keep it up with someone who was honestly concerned for her welfare. She dropped her gaze. "Very well, learned doctor—I shall ride sidesaddle. Until battle."

"Do not ride in battle," the old man pleaded. "What are generals for?"

Alisande looked up, eyes sparking. "Should not queens be generals, too?"

"Aye, Majesty—if they are not mothers."

"I will not be a mother yet," Alisande muttered, eyes downcast—but she put on her armor with a heavy heart.

Then she took it off again. It no longer fit around the middle.

When she was finally attired, her ladies sighed and ushered her out the door, shaking their heads but knowing it was useless to protest.

As they came out into the courtyard, a shout went up and all the men stood straighter, all eyes locked on their queen, in her hood and coat of light mail, covered by the tabard with her arms emblazoned on it, and her battle coronet on her head. She stood a moment, looking out at them, feeling the old pride stir within her. Then she turned to the groom, who was holding the stirrup of her charger. She nodded and mounted, and her troops broke into another shout. She waved to them, acknowledging their tribute, and called out, "Men, the Lord Wizard may be in peril, for he rides south to learn what mischief brews in the kingdom of Latruria! We ride to be near if he learns tales of woe! It may be war, or it may be peace—but we dare not wait for the Latrurians to decide!"

Another mighty shout went up—then a grizzled sergeant began the surging chant of a war song. The queen smiled and joined in.

But as the last chord sounded, the Lady Constance came riding up on a palfrey, herself clad in light mail, with a surcoat emblazoned with the arms of her family. Queen Alisande stared, astounded. "Milady! What means this?"

"If you are determined to ride when you should not, Majesty, then I must ride with you," Lady Constance informed her. "Do not try to dissuade me! I shall ride with you, whether you will or no—for you must have at least one lady with you, to care for you at such a time!"

Alisande nearly ordered her back into the castle, but she froze with the words of command on her tongue, remembering that receiving loyalty had its prices, and accepting service when it is offered was one of those. She intended to be a leader, not a tyrant, and if she inspired her people to work for her, she had to accept their devotion. So she swallowed the words and let the smile that was straining inside her grow out. "You should not endanger yourself, milady, nor expose yourself to such rigors."

"If you will, Majesty, I will!"

"And right glad I shall be of your company," Alisande said, her eyes shining. "Come, let us ride!"

So she rode out to battle with Lady Constance beside her; she rode out wearing a gown, which she had never done before, with only a light coat of mail over it, and only her battle coronet atop her golden hair. There was a habergeon of heavy ring mail tied behind her saddle, though, with her helmet atop it. She rode sidesaddle, which she had never done before—but she did ride, head lifted high and proud, blond hair blowing like a banner, and her knights and footmen shouted with joy at the sight, then broke into an old marching song as they followed her.

Out beneath the portcullis they rode, over the drawbridge and down the winding road to the plain, the troops marching behind them. Off they went, with the soldiers chanting a marching song, out across the valley floor—but an hour later, as they came up to the crest of the hills that surrounded the plain, she saw a lone rider in full plate armor silhouetted against the sky, sitting his charger and waiting for them. Her heart quickened with hope, and as they came up level with him, the face became clear, but the armor stayed black, and she saw that it was indeed he! "Sir Guy de Toutarien! You are well met indeed!"

"As are you, Majesty." Sir Guy inclined his head as a courtesy between equals, not any token of subjection.

"But why have you not come to visit your spouse?"

"We have said our good-byes already." Sir Guy fell in beside her, and the army shouted with joy. Sir Guy turned to grin and wave, acknowledging their acclaim, then turned back and went on. "I would not trouble her heart again when I must be gone in an hour's time. What of *your* spouse, your Majesty?"

"Why else would I ride south?" Alisande said with irony. Then her face creased with anxiety. "But tell me, Sir Guy—the messenger brought some talk of the Witch Doctor, Saul . . ."

Sir Guy contrived a look of sympathy. "I found him, Majesty, and spoke with him. The Lady Angelique is well, and they have indeed married, but there is as yet no sign of children."

Well, Alisande thought, at least she wasn't coming in last. "That is good news, Sir Guy—but will he come to aid us in search of Lord Matthew?"

Sir Guy sighed. "Alas, I fear he will not. He persists in his claim that he is not overly fond of other folk—"

"Which the Lady Angelique stands to deny, if not to ameliorate," Alisande said crisply. "What does he, that he will not come?"

"What he terms 'research,' though why he should search again where he has presumably already searched, I cannot tell."

"Indeed! And what is it he searches for?"

"Ah! That, at least, I can say," Sir Guy replied. "He still pursues his old goal."

"What! Still seeking a magic that may work without drawing on either Good or Evil, God or Satan?"

"As earnestly as ever," Sir Guy said, rather embarrassed for his friend. "He is absorbed in his studies and says that he does not wish to interrupt them unless 'tis a matter of dire emergency."

"Why, this case is just such an emergency!"

"Matthew is not yet in peril of his life, Majesty." Sir Guy drew something out of his armor, dangling at the end of a chain. It was a ball about an inch across, perforated with tiny holes. "However, the wizard Saul gave me this talisman."

Alisande frowned, peering closely at the bauble. "It is singularly unremarkable, though its silver polish is pretty enough. What use is it?"

"It is a talisman he has made, that we may call upon him if Matthew is truly imperiled."

Alisande eyed the little ball warily. "How will it do that? Surely it cannot ring—it is a dumb bell!"

"Aye, but if we say the right words, it shall become most truly outspoken," Sir Guy told her. "If we speak the phrase, it will make its mate, which Saul wears on his belt, to ring—or, at least, to give off a beeping sound. *Then*, promises Saul, he will talk with us, and if Matthew is sufficiently imperiled, he will come with all the speed a wizard may summon."

"Fair enough," said Alisande. "What is this magical phrase?"

"It is a set of numbers." Sir Guy frowned; obviously it made no sense to him, either. "Nine one one."

"Nine, one, and one?" Alisande stared. "What mystical significance has *that*?"

The hall was bright with the sunset, but there were four-branched candelabra waiting to be lit, all down the center of the long table. The dozen members of the family swirled about the room, chatting with one another, as Squire Giuseppe led Matthew and Pascal in. "Sons and daughters! Cousins! Hearken!"

Everyone stilled, turning to them expectantly, all gazes probing Matt and Pascal. Matt suspected they had been the hottest item of conversation in the house all afternoon. One young lady managed to step in front of the two men who had threatened to obscure her view—a blond vision in silk and taffeta, with a long braid curling down over one creamy shoulder, huge blue eyes seeking out Pascal. He saw her and went stiff as a hound on point.

Matt took a closer look—this must be Panegyra. In beauty, at least, she certainly seemed worth all the fuss. He reserved judgment on her personality.

When the introductions were done and they were sitting at the table, Pascal muttered, "I must be alone with her!"

"Easy, boy, easy," Matt muttered out of the corner of his mouth, managing to smile about at his table companions. "Push it too fast, and you may get us kicked out of here. Take your time, fit in, and wait for your chance."

"There *is* no time!" Pascal whispered. "For all we know, she may be married within the week. Can you not *contrive* a chance?"

"That doesn't strike me as very likely," Matt said to his neighbor on the other side.

"Not likely to have an alliance between Merovence and Latruria?" The lady stared at him. "But why not?"

"It's a question of trust," Matt explained. "When you've been enemies for so long, a few years isn't exactly time enough to start believing your neighbor has nothing but good intentions."

"Will you not *answer*?" Pascal hissed.

"Hm?" Matt looked up as if the young man had said something surprising, then whispered, "Calm down and be polite, or you'll be out of here before dessert!"

"Surely you can at least hold the company's interest while I step aside with her!"

"Oh, all right," Matt grumbled, "but if you try to elope, don't expect me to hold the ladder."

"Ladder?" His neighbor on the other side stared.

"A ladder of diplomacy." Matt turned back to her. "Each rung is another advancement in trust, then in treaties—cultural exchanges, trade agreements, and so forth. When you get to the top, you can develop a full-scale alliance."

"Perhaps even a dynastic marriage?" His middle-aged neighbor dimpled prettily.

Matt forced a laugh. "Yes, but that might have to wait until King Boncorro has married, and both royal couples have children."

"Surely Queen Alisande can rid herself of this lowborn trickster she has wed."

Matt just stared for a second.

"At least last till dessert," Pascal muttered out of the corner of his mouth.

Matt forced another laugh. "No, I don't think there's much chance of that. She seems thoroughly enamored of him."

"Besotted," the woman sniffed.

Matt decided he was going to have to watch his step—*very* carefully.

When the last course had been devoured, the squire leaned back in his chair and said, "Minstrel Matthew! Will you not give us a song?"

"Why, I'd be glad to," Matt said slowly, "but perhaps a little dancing first might settle the stomach."

Whatever the squire thought of this bit of lunacy was drowned out by the joyful shriek from the younger generation. They were on their feet and clearing the tables back on the instant.

"Not so fast, not so fast!" the woman next to Matt protested. "At least let me stand up and step back first."

"Oh, all right, but hurry!" the young man near her growled.

"The dishes!" the squire's wife cried. "Have a care for the . . . oh!" The last accompanied by the sound of crockery breaking.

"If you must clear the tables, take the dishes out first!" the squire bellowed.

"Well, if we must, we must," one of the girls snapped, "though there are servants for that sort of thing."

"Then give them time to do their tasks!"

"No, we would rather do it ourselves," another girl said.

Matt stepped back, dazed. "Sorry," he said to the squire. "Didn't know I was going to stir up such a hornet's nest."

"You did not, I suppose," the man grumped. "They are always like this nowadays."

The tables cleared away, the young folk assembled in the center of the floor, one calling, "Give us a reel!"

"Nay, a jig!" cried another.

"A hornpipe!" cried a third.

"A hornpipe is only for sailors, lout!" snapped a girl.

"And jigs are only for peasants," he retorted, "though what difference it could make to one so clumsy as yourself, I could never—"

"Speak not so to her!" Another young man stepped in front of the girl.

"People, *people!*" Matt held up his hands placatingly. "How about I just play it, and you figure out what it is?"

The suggestion met with unanimous protest, but it was too late— Matt had already started playing. "Hail to the Chief" sounded a little odd when played on a lute, but nobody knew the lyrics, so they couldn't very well protest about the sentiments. They did gripe about the rhythm, loudly and vociferously, but when Matt kept on playing in spite of the griping, they simmered down and started dancing to it. At a guess, Matt decided, it was a reel—some kind of line dance, anyway.

He plucked the final chord, and instantly a boy was calling, "Too sedate! More spirit, minstrel!"

"Why?" Matt returned. "Is the castle haunted?"

Wrong line—everybody immediately glanced over their shoulders.

"Of course it is," the squire said, scowling, "and our ghosts are not the sort of which we wish to be reminded. Play something jolly, minstrel, or I'll see you given the haunted chamber this night!"

Matt wondered if the spectral company could be any more disagreeable than the live, but he said, "As you will, your Honor," and began to play a tune that had recently been popular in Bordestang— ever since Matt paid a minstrel to start singing it around the streets.

The young people looked up, startled, then began to nod in time, smiles growing, and turned to one another to begin a dance that Matt decided was well on its way to developing into a minuet.

As they finished, one girl cried out, "How pretty! Are there words to it?"

"Yes, and they're even out of copyright," Matt answered, then rode over the confused looks as he began one of Shakespeare's hits:

> "Tell me, where is fancy bred?
> Or in the heart, or in the head?
> How begot, how nourishéd?
> Reply, reply!
> It is engendered in the eye,
> With gazing bought, and sighing fed.
> Let us all sing Fancy's knell!
> I'll begin it—'Ding, dong, bell!' "

"Sing it with me!" he cried, then repeated the line. A slight murmur answered him, and he called out, "I can't hear you!" then played it again, with a little more verve from his impromptu chorus, but not enough, so he called out, "What did you say?"

"Ding, dong, bell!" everybody called back, looking angry.

Sheesh, Matt thought, *what a bunch of sourpusses!*

One fat and surly squire in a rich but gravy-spotted brocade surcoat under a velvet robe, scowled and said, "Have you nothing more fitting?"

"Squire Naughtworthy is to marry my daughter," Matt's host explained. "Surely he would not wish to hear of the death of true love."

Marry his daughter? Matt took a closer look at Squire Naughtworthy. He was graying—fifty, at least, with little piggy eyes, a blotch of nose, and a ruff of beard. The mere thought of an old satyr like that with pretty young Panegyra made Matt's blood run cold—but he noticed that Pascal was drawing the young lady aside for some private conversation, so he went on to the next verse. The audience sang the chorus line with a bit more verve this time, and Matt, emboldened, switched over to the version from *The Tempest*:

> "Full fathom five thy father lies.
> Of coral all his bones are made.
> Those are pearls that were his eyes.
> Nothing of him that doth fade,
> But all doth suffer a sea-change

Into something rich and strange.
Sea-nymphs hourly ring his knell.
Hark! I hear it . . ."

And everybody joined in, with relish:

"Ding, dong, bell!"

Everybody, that is, except Squire Naughtworthy, who turned purple and bellowed, "Would you rush us to our graves?"

The whole room fell silent, the whole family staring at him, taken aback.

"My pardon, your Honor," Matt said slowly. "I did not know you had a son."

"I have not! But you clearly spoke of a man my age!"

Matt smiled with feigned relief. "No, good squire. I did not tell you how old the son was." And before Naughtworthy could blast another objection, Matt struck the strings again, calling out, "Ding, dong, bell!"

"Ding, dong, bell!" The young folks grinned and sang it all the harder for Naughtworthy's grousing. He turned magenta and swelled up for another blast—but his host very obviously disagreed with his complaint. He looked pleasantly surprised, and Matt guessed that it was the first time he had ever heard all the young folk agree on something—rather quarrelsome household, this. But Pascal and Panegyra were edging away toward the screens passage, so he decided to give his hosts a lesson.

"Oh, the Hatfields and McCoys,
　They were jolly mountain boys,
　Till they both came down to town to do some dancing,
　And a McCoy there, stamping low,
　Trod on a Hatfield's toe,
　And old Anse, he hollered loud to stop their prancing.

"Now, a swollen toe's not bad,
　But this sullen Hatfield lad,
　Bore grudges long way out of all abettin',
　So he hid behind a rock
　Where McCoys were known to walk,
　And as one passed by, the Hatfield shot his head in.

"Anse Hatfield took exception,
　Complained of vile deception,
　and led a troop of clansmen to the border.

But the oldest male McCoy,
Known as Randall, pride and joy,
Saw them coming and laid ambush for a slaughter."

Matt had them spellbound, but the greedy looks on their faces weren't quite what he had hoped to evoke. Still, he was started now and couldn't very well change songs in mid-verse—and Pascal had disappeared with Panegyra in tow, so Matt figured he had better hold the company's attention awhile longer.

Accordingly, he finished up the whole feud, managed to wipe out both families more thoroughly than the original feud had, then treated them to a brief scene in Hell where "old Devil Anse" met the real thing.

The last part had them shuddering and looking over their shoulders again as he finished, and the squire frowned. "Has Pascal told you the history of our house, then?"

"Nay, cousin." Panegyra had led Pascal back in during the last verse, looking flushed and very pleased with herself—but Pascal had a hangdog look that made Matt's heart sink. He obviously needed a jolt, so Matt said, "You didn't tell me you had resident haunts here."

Pascal looked up, but didn't quite focus. "Haunts? . . . Aye. What house of any age has them not?"

Matt was possessed of a sudden overwhelming curiosity at just what the girl had told his young friend, but he couldn't very well come right out and ask. Instead, he said, "That's true, but most of the ghosts I've heard of haven't been malicious—just misunderstood."

Pascal came out of his mood with a shudder. "Not this ghost, I assure you! Or the worst of them, I should say."

"True," the squire said judiciously, "and you have not even seen him, only heard tell of him." He turned to Matt. "We think him to be the ghost of my ancestor Spiro, who built this house—and seems to think himself still entitled to hold it."

"He's not willing to share?" Matt said carefully.

"He would not if he could prevent it," the squire said, "but he cannot—he is bound to the chamber in which he died."

Matt grinned. "And that's the room you were going to put me in if I was a bad boy, eh?"

"Oh, I would not truly have done so," the squire protested—but Matt didn't believe him.

Still and all, when finally he retired, he had no complaint with the room they did give him—obviously a guest room, since it seemed to have been dusted in a hurry, though not too successfully, and the soot on the hearth looked to be ready for carbon 14 dating. The wall hangings were old enough to be brittle, but they were heavily embroidered and very attractive, and there was a very nice painting on the wall, though Matt really preferred his nudes to be somewhat less Neolithic in build. He did wonder why he had been moved out of Pascal's room, then realized it might have been by Panegyra's request. Well, getting away from the young man's snoring wouldn't be all that tough. He was just starting to unbutton his doublet when there was a knock at the door. He froze with a button halfway through the hole and called, "Who is it?"

"Pascal," came the muffled voice. "Let me in, I pray!"

Well, so much for getting away from him. Matt stepped over to the door, drew the bolt and let the young man in. "Thought you were planning to sleep someplace else tonight."

"Matthew!" Pascal stared at him, genuinely shocked. "Surely you do not think the fair Panegyra would—"

"No, but I figured *you* might." Matt raised a hand to forestall the youth's hot rejoinder. "I see I was wrong, though. No, you wouldn't do a thing like that, would you? Not to her, anyway. So what *did* the two of you talk about?"

"Alas!" Pascal sank down on the bed, head in his hands. "She owns that she does not find me detestable, even finds me comely—but she will not bend from her father's rule!"

"She won't run away with you, eh?"

"Aye, and she owns that it is because she shudders at the life of poverty and hardship such a course of action would mean, even for the few years it would take before I built a good living for us."

Matt thought it would take a bit longer than a few years, at least for the kind of living Panegyra had in mind. "She likes the soft life, huh?"

Pascal nodded heavily. "Not so much that she has a love of luxury, as that she fears poverty—and she fears what my fate would be if her father should catch us."

Well, at least the girl was honest, though she added a bit of embroidery. Still, if it spared Pascal's feelings, what harm was there? "And she doesn't shudder at the sight of Squire Naughtworthy?"

Pascal shivered. "She claims to think him handsome, though I cannot see why!"

"Some women are attracted to older men," Matt said slowly, "even to men old enough to be their fathers—and they find strength and, um, prosperity, attractive. Signs that the man would be a good provider. It's possible, Pascal." But in Panegyra's case, he didn't think it was likely.

The youth moaned and dropped his head back into his hands. "She is sure he shall be a veritable kitten in her hands, that she will even persuade him to take her to King Boncorro's court!"

"Men will do a lot for a pretty bride," Matt sighed, "but I don't think this one can get her into court—he's just a squire, after all. She *might* change her mind, Pascal."

"What could change it?" the young man said bitterly.

"A knighthood," Matt said slowly. He had to give the boy something to work for, something to hope for. "Or even becoming a squire with a definite chance of graduating to knight."

"Aye!" Pascal's head snapped up, his eye catching fire. "Women ever do dote upon men of arms—and a knight's rank is surely better than that of an elderly squire with no prospect of rising higher!"

Matt wouldn't have called Naughtworthy "elderly," but he wasn't about to slacken the head of steam he'd been trying to build. "That's the spirit. A uniform always gets 'em, even if it's made of iron." Privately, though, he doubted that Pascal had much of a chance of climbing the social ladder, or that Panegyra would really care much if he did. From the sound of her, she would definitely choose the older, wealthy squire over the younger but penniless knight. No, all in all, Matt didn't think Panegyra was worth all the devotion Pascal was heaping on her. Love never did have much to do with the head, though.

A cold gust suddenly struck, and the candle went out. In the sudden darkness, Matt froze, then asked carefully, "Pascal?"

"Aye." The younger man's voice trembled.

"Did I leave the window open?"

"This chamber *has* no window!"

Matt was just beginning to realize that his host might have a peculiarly nasty sense of humor, when a faint moan began, swelling in a second to surround them, battering at their eardrums, and a pale, misty, glowing figure seemed to rise out of the bed to tower over them, grinning and drooling into its beard. It was a man, wearing a robe over a belted, knee-length tunic, with a medallion hanging from a chain about his neck. His eyes were holes, and his mouth split into a grin of malice and gloating pleasure, then split farther to reveal pointed teeth as he raised his hands, showing fingernails that stretched into claws, poised to stab and pierce.

Pascal shrieked and dove under the bed. An eldritch howling filled the night, and he came bolting back out, shrieking even louder, pursued by a ghostly hound the size of a German shepherd.

"Get behind me," Matt snapped, and stepped between the dog and Pascal just in case the young man was already too far gone to be able to understand.

"Fool!" the ghost chortled, winding up to pounce, and the hound howled and sank its teeth into Matt's leg. Fear clamored through him, but he reminded himself that ectoplasm can't interact with protoplasm, and felt only piercing cold in his leg. He ignored it and recited,

> "From ghosties and ghoulies and long-legged beasties,
>   And things that go bump in the night,
>   Dear Lord, preserve us!"

It didn't rhyme, but boy, did that old formula work! The dog gave a howl that sounded as if its tail had been twisted in five places, then sank out of sight even as the ghost of the man screamed in frustration and fear, and winked out.

The darkness was awfully quiet for a minute.

Then Pascal asked, in a quavering voice, "Friend Matthew?"

"Here." Matt tried to sound reassuring. "Just stay put, Pascal, while I kindle the candle."

"Do not!" the ghost's voice snapped out of the darkness. "Begone from my chamber! Or even your L—your appeal will not save you from my wrath!"

"Oh, come off it!" Matt snapped. "If you could have resisted the Lord—"

The ghost gasped in pain.

"—you wouldn't have run at the mention of the word," Matt finished. "And it's a pretty general word, at that! I didn't even specify Whom it referred to! Can you imagine what it would have done to you if I'd used a Name?"

"And what I would have done to you!" But the ghost's protest sounded feeble.

So feeble that Matt ignored it. "What are you getting so huffy about, anyway? You've got to know that we're just guests . . ."

"That man who is with you is of my blood!"

"Nonsense—you don't have any left." But Matt wondered how the ghost could tell. Ectoplasmic genetic imprints? Could ghosts read DNA code? "Even so, you know he's not a regular part of the household, and that we had no choice about which room we were given. What makes you so territorial, anyway?"

"I built this house!"

"And left it to your son," Matt finished. "What's the matter? Was he too eager to inherit?"

The room was ghastly quiet for a moment. Then the ghost's tone was bloodcurdling. *"How did you* know?"

Chapter
Ten

"Just basic reasoning," Matt said quickly. "That would give you something of a score to settle, and even if you had no way to do that—"

"No way?" the ghost said bitterly. "He laughed at my anger; he mocked at my pain!"

"Yes, the younger generation has no respect for its elders. Couldn't you get back at him after he died, though?"

"Nay. He was not tied to his chamber by the violence of his death, he—his soul plunged like a stone into the depths, screaming as it went." Sparks glowed in the ghost's hollow eyes. "*That* was my revenge!"

"Then why do you keep trying to take it out on whoever sleeps in your room?"

"If you had suffered as I have suffered, you, too, would pounce upon any who happened within your reach!"

Matt shuddered. "I hope I wouldn't! Is *that* all it is—just a colossal bad temper?"

The ghost fixed the glowing sparks on him. "What else should it be?"

"An attempt to communicate," Matt said. "If it is, I'm not getting the message."

The ghost just stood glaring at him, and Matt felt a thrill of accomplishment. Pascal stared at him as if he were a superman from another world.

"There was a broken promise," the ghost finally said.

"And you think the current generation might be able to mend it, if they cared enough to do the research? You're not exactly behaving in a manner calculated to inspire concern."

"Nay, but any should wish to be rid of me!"

"Enough to look through the family records and try to find a reason for your haunting." Matt nodded. "Well, I'm only here for the night, so I don't have time for extended research. How about you just tell me?"

The ghost glowered at him, but said, "I am Spiro, the first squire of this manor. I built it—but I did not mean to lie near it for eternity."

"Then it sounds as if your goals coincide with the current squire's," Matt said. "I'm sure he'd like to get this room back—though I must admit he seems to find it useful to hold over people's heads as a threat, if they're naughty."

The ghost's head snapped upright. "You mean he uses me as his whip and his goad? Why, the poltroon, the vile villain, the—"

"—inheritor of tradition," Matt said, cutting him off. "I gather he's just keeping up what his forefathers have done. So where—" Then the significance of the name hit. "Spiro? That's Greek!"

"Your perception amazes me," the specter said dryly. "Aye, I am Greek—and longed to return to my native Athens, to the Parthenon and the groves of Academe. I had intended to depart in two years' time, and my son would have been rid of me—but he could not even wait that long!"

"Sure—you were going to take all the money with you. Probably sell the land, too, and he knew he didn't have money enough to buy it."

"I doubt it not," the ghost said with disgust. "Yet I had always intended that if I did not return to Greece to finish my days, then my bones would!"

Matt lifted his head slowly. "So. If they were to ship your coffin back to Greece, your ghost would go with it."

"Aye—and once there, I could shuffle off that mortal coil and pass to my reward."

"You . . . *sure* you want to do that?"

"*I* have naught to fear of the Afterlife, foolish youngling!"

"Maybe some time in Purgatory, but all in all, you think you did as much good as bad in your lifetime? Well, then, be glad you died before King Maledicto came to power."

Squire Spiro shuddered. "I am. That blackguard would have made short shrift of any man who sought to abide by the rules of chivalry, let alone the Commandments!"

"You don't fear the Lord?" Matt frowned. "Why did you back off when I recited the old charm, then?"

"You asked Him to preserve you from ghosts, fool! If I honor Him, of *course* I will honor those whom He protects." Spiro drew down his brows, turning his eyes into caverns as he frowned. "But you are no mere minstrel, are you?"

"About that return to Greece," Matt said hurriedly. "I'll mention it to the current squire, but I can't promise anything. If he wants a haunted chamber more than a usable one, he may opt to keep your mortal remains here."

"If he does, then I shall howl night and day, I shall groan to break all hearts, I shall give him never a moment's rest, I shall—"

"Haunt the whole house?" Matt said brightly. "Make it *all* unusable? Can you do that?"

The ghost looked daggers at him. "Nay. I am ever drawn back to this chamber. But I can make unceasing racket herein!"

"You might do better just not to bother anybody," Matt pointed out. "Then he wouldn't have any reason to keep you."

"But no reason to spend the money it would take to ship my bones back to Greece and bury them and be rid of me, either!"

"True," Matt admitted. "Sure you can't offer him some sort of inducement?"

"There is a treasure I buried," the ghost said slowly, "since I had begun to mistrust my son. Two hundred years ago, it was only enough to take my bones back to Greece, but now—"

"—what with inflation, the price of gold has gone up, and it's worth a small fortune?"

"Aye. When my body is buried near Athens, I shall come back to this house once, and once only, on my way to Purgatory, to tell him where to dig!"

"Giving him a nice, tidy profit." Matt nodded, satisfied. "Good business all around, and everybody's happy. Okay, Squire Spiro, I'll broach the issue to your descendant in the morning. Of course, I'd be a bit more persuasive if I'd had a good night's sleep . . ."

"My descendant is not the only one who needs a bribe, I see," the ghost grumbled. "Very well, minstrel, I will leave you in peace for this night. But if you betray me, I shall find a way to smite you, soon or late! Remember that where my blood and bone may go, my spirit can go, though it takes a ruinous effort and causes me great pain!"

"Meaning that you can follow Pascal, if he sticks with me?" Matt cocked his head to the side. "Interesting! An ectoplasmic DNA link goes even further than I thought. Still, not to worry, Squire Spiro—what I said I'd do, I will do. I can't speak for your descendant, though."

"You need not; gold speaks loudly enough," the ghost growled. "Well, then I'll leave you for this night—but remember your promise!" And with that he winked out and was gone.

The room was totally silent, and totally dark, for perhaps a minute more. Then the candle glowed to life again of its own accord, revealing a shaken and sweating Pascal, who mopped his forehead and said, in a tremulous voice, "That was amazing, Matthew! But I think my ancestor was right—you are no mere minstrel, and are even more than a knight, are you not?"

"Me?" Matt protested, all innocence. "Pascal! If you don't know my secrets, who in Latruria does? Off to sleep, now. If I were you, I'd take a blanket and head for the barn. I don't particularly fancy sleeping in this bed alone, but I think I'll get all sorts of kudos if I can emerge bright and fresh in the morning. *You* don't have to, though."

The primary kudo was the look of shocked amazement on the faces of the squire and his family when Matt came in to breakfast the next morning. He allowed himself a feeling of satisfaction as he sat down behind a huge slice of bread that was serving as a plate, and accepted a portion of something fried from a serving girl. He nodded a pleasant thank-you, then looked about at the family with a bright smile. "Good morning!"

"Ah . . . good morning," the squire said. "Did you . . . sleep well?"

"Oh, very well, thanks! Took a little while to calm down and doze off, that's all."

Pascal nearly strangled on his porridge.

"Remarkable," the squire's wife murmured, and Panegyra was staring at him with awe—no, not awe, Matt realized: fear.

"You had no . . . dreams?" the squire pressed.

"No, but I did have an interesting conversation with the resident ghost." Matt looked up. "Really very reasonable man, once you can get him talking."

The squire turned white as a sheet. His wife nearly fainted, and Panegyra almost fell off her chair. Fortunately, she fell toward Pascal, and he caught her neatly and helped stabilize her. She murmured her thanks as she resettled herself, and Matt wondered if the move had been entirely accidental.

"You . . . managed conversation with the ghost?" the squire stammered. "You . . . you were not . . . afraid of him?"

"Well, sure, anybody would be, the way he appeared out of nowhere!" Matt said. "But I know an old charm or two—minstrels collect those sorts of things—so he backed off and tried to order me out."

"And . . . how did you refuse him?" The squire's wife was recovering nicely.

"I asked, 'Why?' " Matt said simply.

"And he *told* you?"

"Well, there was a little more to it than that." Matt was beginning to enjoy himself. "But the long and the short of it is that he wants to go back to Greece."

"Wants to go?" the squire said blankly, and his wife seized his arm. "Instantly, husband! Whatever he wishes, give it! If we can be rid of that specter, it will be well worth it!"

"Let us first see the bill before we pay it," the squire said cautiously. "It is old Spiro's ghost, then?"

"The founder himself," Matt confirmed. "That's why he feels he has a right to have the room to himself—he not only built it, he also died in it."

"The grandest room in the house!" the squire's wife wailed.

"But how can he go back to his homeland?" the squire asked, staring. "He is dead!"

"Yes, but he seems to think that if you can dig up his coffin and ship it back to Greece, he'll go with it."

"It might be worth the attempt," the squire said, gazing off into space.

"Worth?" His wife dug her fingers into his arm. "Worth it a hundred times over! Then we can have the chamber exorcised, reopen the bricked-up windows—and *we* can reside there!"

"There will be some expense in it," the squire warned. "There is the summerhouse you wished to build—that would have to wait a few years."

His wife turned away, sulking. "All the best families have one!"

"All the best families have at least one ghost, too," her husband reminded her.

"We have two to spare—I shall not miss this one! He is so disagreeable, so malicious, so . . . frightening!"

"But is he worth your summerhouse?"

"Oh, aye, I would say he is!" The wife capitulated. "But there shall still be enough money to redecorate the room, shall there not?"

"Plenty," Matt said. "He left a few gold pieces buried someplace on the estate, to dig up and pay for his passage when he was ready to sail—but he was killed first."

The squire turned avid. "Where is this treasure?"

"It's not *that* much," Matt warned. "He said that once his carcass is back in Athens where it belongs, he'll make one last visit on his way to Purgatory, to tell you where it's buried."

"I may have my summerhouse still!" The wife clapped her hands.

"I wouldn't go *that* far," Matt cautioned.

"He said it is no treasure—belike enough to cover no more than the shipping and reburial of the coffin—and it may be a lie, to induce us to do what old Spiro wishes. Still, it is worth the gamble," the squire said.

"But there *should* be enough for redecoration," Matt said.

"There should," the squire agreed, then turned back to Matt. " 'Tis a noisome task, digging up a coffin that is two centuries old."

"Lots of wormholes," Matt agreed, "and probably falling-apart rotten. If I were you, I'd have a new casket waiting that was large enough to hold the old one—and I'd dig double-wide, so that you can set the new coffin right next to the old one before you try to lift it."

"A coffin inside a coffin? The notion will bear thought," the squire mused.

"I'll leave you to think about it, then." Matt finished his last bite and stood up. "You'll pardon me if I have to eat and run—but I'm bound for the king's court; I hear he's generous to musicians."

"He is?" the squire said blankly, and Panegyra's eyes lit. "Surely, Father! His court is always filled with music! You do not think his courtiers dance to their own singing, do you?"

"Please!" Matt shuddered. "Amateurs are bad enough in their own homes!" And he managed to make it out the door while the squire's wife was still trying to decide whether or not to be offended.

They swung down the road with a long, easy stride. Matt was pushing the pace a little, hoping that sheer exertion might pull Pascal out of the doldrums. "Buck up, squire's son! At least she didn't tell you that she *doesn't* love you!"

"No," Pascal admitted, "but she did not say that she does, either."

"The fortunes of romance," Matt commiserated. "I had that problem with a girl, too."

"You did?" Pascal looked up, eyes wide with hope. "What did you do?"

"Everything I could," Matt told him. "Made it clear that I was doing my best for her and wasn't planning to stop."

"What happened?"

"Oh, she finally admitted that she loved me."

"What did you do then?"

"I married her—after a very long wait. So do your best to prove your worth, and you never know what could happen." From what Matt had seen of Panegyra, though, he thought *he* knew—but at least the effort might give Pascal a new interest in living.

The young man was frowning, though. "If you have married a wife whom you love, what are you doing wandering the roads so far from your home?"

"Who do you think sent me?" Matt retorted. "Look, just because she loves me, doesn't mean she wants me hanging around the house and getting underfoot all the time. Say, who are those kids on the road up ahead?"

Pascal turned to look, and stared at the large, boisterous group coming into sight around the next bend. "None that I know—but why are there so many of them?"

"I was hoping you could tell me," Matt replied. "Well, let's go ask."

They caught up with the happy songsters, who were passing a bottle of wine from hand to hand—and if one of the boys occasionally paused to sip the wine from a girl's lips, who minded? Not even the half-dozen middle-aged couples who swung along a little way in front of the pack of juveniles, with occasional glances back at their traveling companions. Matt left the young folk to Pascal and went ahead to the nearest mature pair—who, he noticed, were holding hands, but not wearing wedding rings, not even the little brass circlets most peasants wore. "G—" He was about to say "Godspeed," but caught himself in time. "Good day, good folk! Where are you bound?"

"Why, to the capital, of course!" said the man. "To the king's town of Venarra!"

"Why should we languish in the hamlets of our births?" the woman asked. "There is nothing but boredom and grinding labor there! We shall go to Venarra, where all are paid in gold for their work, and there is continual revelry!"

Matt had a notion they were due for a severe disappointment, but it wasn't his place to say so. He did notice the use of the plural, though. So they had come from different towns—which meant that, in a society like this one, they had probably never even met before. Was he looking at the saturated end of a long-delayed love story? Or a tale of double adultery? He decided not to stay too close, in case there was an angry husband following with a knife—not to mention an angry wife. "I take it this gaggle of overgrown children are bound toward Venarra, too."

"Oh, let them enjoy life while they may!" the woman said, and the man agreed. "Before they must settle into the traces, let them kick up their heels awhile."

Matt knew from his own generation just how long that while could be—but surely not in a medieval society! "You sound as if you speak from experience."

A shadow crossed the man's face, and the woman said, "Which of us does not?" She held up her hand for display. "See the wrinkles, the shriveling, the calluses? I do not rejoice in them, believe me! But any woman who has reared a family shall show you the same. Unless, of course," she said bitterly, "she is wealthy enough to have servants, who may then ruin *their* hands for her!"

Matt guessed that he was speaking to a former chambermaid and mother. "Ah, yes, sweet lady, but what would any of us do without mothers to care for us?"

"Then there should be fewer of us," she retorted, "so that a woman might have fewer years of drudgery. Nay, let the husbands bear the children, if they want them so badly! Let the husbands rear the ones they claim to treasure, but would as soon kick as feed when they come home o' nights! And let the women go free!"

Not all women enjoyed mothering, Matt knew—and the more often he heard diatribes like hers, the greater he thought their number must be.

But that was in his own world. In this world, it was a very new idea indeed. "Have you done that, then?" He forced a grin. "Left a husband to take care of his children?"

"I have," she said with a defiant toss of her head. "If he wants them so badly as to beget one after another upon me, then let him care for them! For myself, I shall seek excitement and adventure— and, aye, revelry and pleasure!"

"You, too?" Matt asked the man. After all, it was kind of a logical conclusion.

The peasant shrugged. "My wife was at me night and day to cease trying to order her about and order the children about. At last she cried that she would be better off alone, for all the good I did."

The woman frowned, moving a little away from him. "She did not say that she wished you to go!"

"Not in words, no," he said, "but in her looks, in the tone of her voice, in the hatred flashing from her eyes, she did."

"So you think that you should lord it over your wife?" The woman's tone was dangerous.

"A wife, yes." The man grinned and caught her close around the waist. "But a woman who comes with me for revelry and delight, and the pleasures we may give one another—nay. I have no claim upon her, nor she on me, but only company, while we are agreeable to one another!"

He pulled her close for a kiss, and she yielded, but without quite as much zest as she had before. At a guess, Matt decided, this was the first time the two of them had discussed that particular issue.

Pascal showed up beside him with a grin, eyes shining. "They have all left their parents and the labor of the plow and the kitchen, to seek wealth and gaiety in the king's capital of Venarra, friend Matthew!"

Matt eyed him narrowly. "You sound like you think they're doing the smart thing."

"Well, they may not have found wealth," Pascal said, "but they have surely found gaiety! If you will excuse me, friend Matthew, I find their company quite enjoyable!"

He dove back into the happy, singing throng. Matt gazed after and saw him flirting with a pretty girl. Well, it certainly did pull him out of the doldrums over Cousin Panegyra—but it didn't say much for his fidelity to her. Admittedly, the treatment she'd given him was only one step from a brush-off, but more vicious, in its way, since it was designed to keep him bound to her—no doubt she was one of those girls who rated her worth by the number of boys she kept on strings, which boded ill for her future as wife to an older man. Pascal was ripe to lose himself on the rebound, for better or for worse. Matt hoped it wasn't worse.

On the other hand, the merry band did afford excellent cover for Pascal, and Matt wasn't exactly going to be glaringly obvious with the middle-aged adventurers. Okay, he was a little young, being only in his thirties, whereas everybody else looked to be in their late forties or early fifties—though in a medieval society, that meant they were probably late thirties, or younger; sometimes peasants looked positively ancient by thirty-five. Okay, so being right between the two groups, he stood out a bit—but he was a minstrel, and nobody would be surprised to see him attaching himself to such a festive crowd.

Matt, however, was a little concerned about this southward migration. These village kids just didn't know enough to be able to cope with the big city—and none of the elders were wearing wedding rings; he suspected they had all kicked over the traces, just like these first two.

"All" because he could see more of them ahead, as the roadway straightened out—two groups of youths, laughing and passing a skin of wine from hand to hand, and several smaller groups of older people, talking and jesting and flirting just as baldly as their juniors.

Was half the countryside migrating to Venarra? And what was the other half doing at home, abandoned? Besides taking care of the kids, of course—if they were even bothering to do that.

He found out when their band stopped at a wayside inn for lunch— along with half a dozen similar groups.

"We are full inside!" the harassed landlord said, standing in the doorway, waving them off. "We will gladly sell you meat, bread, cheese, and ale—but there are no more places to sit!"

In a few minutes he and his serving-girl staff had a thriving business going in take-out orders—but as the older folk stepped up for service, a middle-aged woman came out of the inn door and berated them. "You clods, you lumps of earth! You have no more heart than a stone! Would you leave your wives and children to the wolves, then? Would you sacrifice them to your own greed and lust? For shame!"

The older travelers looked up in surprise. Then one buxom matron threw back her head and laughed. "I have not left a wife, I assure you!" The whole crowd joined in her laugh, with a note of relief.

The woman flushed. "But you have left children! The pretty little ones who sucked at your breast—you have left them to the blows and rages of their father! You have left your husband to fend for them all, trying to plow the fields and somehow manage to care for the little ones! Can there be anything but disaster for any of them?"

"It would have been disaster for him if I had stayed," the errant wife retorted. "I doubt not he will find a woman to fill his bed—let *her* care for the children!"

"Care for your own!" another woman called, and the whole crowd broke into angry hooting and insults. Red-faced and trembling, the woman went back inside the inn.

Matt put a coin in Pascal's hand. "Two of those little meat pies and a flagon of ale, okay? I think I want to go inside and hear the rest of this."

"Nay, then, I'll come with you," Pascal said.

"Suit yourself."

"I cannot—I am no tailor."

Matt gave him a doubtful look. "Maybe I could work you into the act, after all. Well, let's venture." He stepped up to the doorway.

The landlord spun to block his way. "All full, I said. No entry!"

"Not even for a minstrel?" Matt brought the lute around and struck a chord.

The landlord's eye lit, but he said, "There is no seat."

"I usually stand while I'm working, anyway."

"I will not pay!"

"It's okay—my partner will pass the hat." Matt nodded to Pascal, who yanked off his cap.

The landlord gave him a quick look that weighed him and found him harmless, then stepped inside and nodded. "Enter, then."

Matt stepped in with Pascal right behind him. A few of the other travelers saw and surged toward the door with a yell of delight, but the landlord stoutly blocked their way. "Only the minstrel, so that he may entertain!"

The crowd grumbled and groused, but didn't try to push their luck.

Matt stepped into the comparative gloom of the common room, to hear the woman who had been standing in the doorway still running her stream of invective. "Poltroons and adulterers! Abandoners and jilters! They deserve no better than hanging, any of them!"

"They shall learn the error of their ways." The man sitting across from her clasped her hand, gazing at her with concern. "They shall come straggling back in grief, I fear, Clothilde. They shall come straggling back, begging for alms to take them to their homes, where they shall pick up the traces they have kicked aside, sadder but wiser—all of them. As my Maud shall, and your Corin."

"I shall not take him back, not if he comes crawling! Not after he has left us without so much as a word of parting!"

"We must forgive," the man murmured. "We who remain must be steadfast."

"Not too steadfast, I trust." Clothilde raised her eyes to his, her bitterness transforming into a hot-eyed stare.

The man goggled, then squirmed, taken aback. "We are both married, Clothilde!"

"Does your Maud care about her bond? Does my Corin care about his ring? Nay, call him mine no more!" Clothilde angrily pulled her ring off her finger. "If they will not keep faith, why should we?"

The argument hit the peasant hard, you could see it in his face, and for a moment his longing was written naked on his features. Matt glanced at Clothilde more closely, and could understand the man's desire—she was still a fine figure of a woman, and he could imagine what she must have looked like twenty years before. At a guess, the man had burned for her when he was a teenager—but when she married someone else, he had fallen hard on the rebound, then settled for second best.

Could that have had anything to do with why Maud had left?

"If they do not feel bound to us, we should not feel bound to them!" Clothilde gripped his hand with both of hers, eyes burning into his. "Nay, this could be our revenge upon them! What harm could there be in it, Doblo?"

"What harm indeed!" he said deep down in his throat, and his hand trembled as he clasped hers and he rose. Together they turned away to mount the stairs.

That brought Matt's attention to the sounds he was hearing overhead. Now he knew what the stay-at-homes did in Latruria.

Pascal was looking around and frowning. "Are there none here of my own age?"

"No," Matt said. "All the young folks are out there, joining the crowd that's heading south. Take off your hat and get ready to pass it, Pascal. I'm going to have them rolling with mirth in a few minutes. They won't start thinking about the lyrics until after I'm gone."

But then, they *would* start thinking. He knew that.

An hour later, as they came out to join the other travelers, who were finishing up on lunch and preliminary encounters, Pascal shook the cloth bag they had bought from the innkeeper and shook his head, marveling. "Make them roll with mirth you did, and made them generous into the bargain! But where did you learn that song about man's slavery to sex, or his lying when he sought to resist temptation, or the moon over the street by the docks?"

"From two men named Brecht and Weill. Never met them myself, but I just love their songs."

"Do you truly believe the folk there will think about the meanings of those ditties when you're gone?"

"Oh, yes," Matt assured him. "You bet they will—maybe even soon enough to prevent disaster. Brecht designed them that way." He wasn't sure that was the issue the playwright had wanted his audience to think about, though. "Have Latrurians always been so loose, Pascal?"

"Not from what I heard at the gathering last summer," the young man answered. "The old folk were remembering how life had ground them down, with toil in the fields from sunrise till sunset, then laboring to keep the hut from falling down until well after dark."

"Not enough leftover energy to philander." Matt nodded. "Now that the taxes are down and the draft oxen aren't being taken by the landlord, though, they can fill their bellies with only eight or ten hours of work a day."

"There is time to think of games and songs," Pascal agreed. "Ah, the miserable folk! To have had their lives so poor for so long!"

"Poor indeed," Matt agreed, and assured himself that all he was really seeing was people adjusting to having some leisure time again. Now that they all had decent housing and clothing, they had become discontent, wanting something more, but not knowing what—so they fought boredom with affairs. "I'm surprised none of them seem to worry about their spouses finding out what they're doing."

"How," Pascal asked, "when their spouses are a hundred miles away?"

Something about his tone bothered Matt. He gave the youth a sharp look and saw that Pascal had a faraway look in his eye. "You aren't thinking about having an affair with Panegyra, are you?"

"If I cannot dissuade her from marrying that old fool—why not? She cannot truly wish to lie with him. I might have to make it seem like a kidnapping, but I do not think she would be loath."

"Pascal," Matt said carefully, "that could be very dangerous."

"What could be wrong with it?" the boy challenged. "If everybody else is having sex without marriage, why not we, too?"

Well, it was natural to think that the peer group was always right. Matt had to try to counter the idea, though. "But the errant husbands will be back when they find that they're not going to make their fortunes in the capital—and when they come home, some neighbor who has a grudge against the wife will tell on her."

"If they truly thought that," Pascal argued, "why would they take the risk?"

"Because the danger of discovery adds some excitement to a very boring life, especially if you think you're tied down to it because you were the one who got left with the kids. You heard Clothilde—part of her argument is revenge on her husband. How's she going to have that revenge unless he comes home and finds out what she's been doing while he's gone? And what do you think is going to happen when he does?"

They found out at the next inn.

Chapter
Eleven

Matt and Pascal were playing another inn—like the first, travelers stayed outside with take-away orders while the locals got together to commiserate inside, and Matt and Pascal had played their way in. Matt was just finishing "There Is a Tavern in the Town" with a sing-along chorus, when the Irate Husband came slamming in. "Where is he?" he bellowed. "Where is that cur Simnel? Where is the thief who has stolen my wife?"

A couple jumped up at the back of the room, the man turning to scrabble frantically at the window latch while the woman jumped in front of the I.H. " 'Stolen,' forsooth! Taken up what you cast away, more likely! So now you have come back from your philandering, and think I shall be yours again, Perkin?"

"You *are* mine!" Perkin was in no mood for sweet reason. "And I shall beat you soundly to show it to you, Forla! What, do you think this puling coward will protect you?" He swept her aside with the back of his hand and lunged past her, grasping at the pair of heels that were just disappearing out the window. He bellowed in frustration and turned to charge back out the door. His wife was in no condition to interfere—a knot of sympathetic women were gathered around her, counseling her to lie still.

Pascal stared at Perkin as he disappeared through the doorway. "He is bent on murder!"

"Some men take sexual jealousy to extremes," Matt agreed. "After all, it's the only honor they have." For himself, he was rather shocked that none of the other adulterous husbands seemed at all inclined to stop Perkin. "Come on, let's go outside. I want to see how this ends."

Pascal stared at him as if he were mad, but when Matt headed for the door, Pascal came along in his wake.

As they rounded the corner of the inn, Matt handed his lute to Pascal and checked his dagger to make sure it was loose in its sheath. There Perkin was, charging after his rival! They were just in time to see him bring down the fleeing man with a tackle that would have done credit to an NFL halfback. Simnel kicked at his pursuer's face in a panic—and connected. The attacker let go with a howl of rage, then leaped to his feet and swung a haymaker that grazed the fugitive just as he was regaining his feet, and sent him staggering. The Irate Husband followed up hard and fast, fists pumping like the pistons of an engine. The fugitive did his best to block, but most of the punches got through. He howled in anger and slugged back—and one of his blows clipped Perkin on the chin. Perkin rolled away and sank to his knees. Simnel shouted with satisfaction and followed up, punching and swinging a haymaker. Perkin's head rolled aside with one punch, but he surged up inside the haymaker, a knife glinting in his hand.

"That's just a little bit too much," Matt said, and stepped in to catch Perkin's arm, twisting the knife out of his hand. "No steel!"

"What business is it of yours?" bellowed a voice behind him, and a rough hand yanked his shoulder, spinning him around just in time to see the fist that cracked into his jaw. Matt sank to his knees as the world went dark for several seconds, shot with sparks. He shook his head and staggered up, vision returning just in time to see his attacker pull a knife from his boot.

The blade came in low. Matt dodged, and the thrust went short. Then Matt jumped in to try to catch the knife arm, but the attacker was too fast for him—he pulled the blade back, then slashed. Matt leaped back just enough to let it swing past him as he drew his own dagger. Crowd voices shouted with excitement, but he blocked them out and concentrated only on his antagonist. Matt saw the man's eyes flick downward, to his own knife, and he slammed a kick at the elbow. The man shouted as he leaped back, then lunged with a speed that caught Matt off balance. Matt managed to twist enough so that the knife only grazed his side; he heard the cloth tear, and the searing pain made him suddenly realize that the thug was very, very serious. He wasn't just out to even the odds in an entertaining fight over a woman—he was out to kill Matt!

What had he ever done to him? They were total strangers!

He brushed the thought aside—all that mattered now was staying alive. Could a peasant knife artist really bring down a belted knight?

He could, Matt saw in the next two passes. The man's skill was just too great; he had to be a pro. What was he doing here, at a roadside inn near a rural village?

File the fact for later. For now, leap back from that blade, draw him into lunging, then lunging again, then again and again . . .

Finally the attacker lunged just that much too far, off balance for just half a second, and Matt whirled in, catching the knife arm in an elbow lock and pushing down. The man howled with the sudden pain, and his knife dropped from suddenly nerveless fingers. The crowd shouted with delight, but Matt just spun back in, set his blade against the man's throat and growled, "Who paid you to kill me?"

"None!" the man blustered. "None needed to, when you butted into a fight that was none of your—" The sentence choked off in a rattle of pain as Matt hit a nerve center. "Nay, no more! I'll tell! The man who paid me was—" Then, suddenly, his eyes rolled up and he crumpled to the ground.

The crowd cheered, and half a dozen men surged in to lift Matt up on their shoulders. Matt held on, their clamor ringing in his ears while he let the sudden numbness within him fade. When they set him down inside the tavern and thrust a mug into his hand, he faked laughter and sipped a little, nodding thanks for their shouted compliments, then started a drinking song. In a few minutes the men were all swinging their tankards in time to the music and bawling the chorus, leaving Matt free to welter in morose remorse.

Why? Well, the peasant who burst in the door said it best. "He is dead!"

The whole room went instantly silent. Matt froze.

Then Forla asked, in a trembling voice, "Who?"

"Simnel," the man cried, and Forla burst into tears, wailing, "Oh, my love! To have found you so late, and lost you so soon!"

"Be still, woman!" her husband snarled as he staggered in the door. His face was a mass of bruises, and blood trickled from a cut on one cheek, but he lurched toward her, lips drawing back in a snarl.

She saw him coming and screamed.

Then a man in a fur-collared velvet robe strode in the door. A gold chain held a medallion over his breast, and his gray hair and lined face made him look all the more stern as he pointed at Perkin and shouted, "Seize him!"

A dozen men leaped to obey with shouts of glee.

"Who is this guy?" Matt muttered to Pascal.

"The local reeve, by the look of him," the youth answered. "Someone with more sense than blood lust must have gone to fetch him."

The reeve stepped over to the biggest table in the room and sat himself down majestically. "The court is now convened! Who will serve as jury?"

There was an instant clamor of eager willingness, and hands waved to volunteer.

"You, you, you . . ." The reeve picked his jury by pointing at them one by one, until he had twelve good men and true.

Well, twelve men, anyway. Out of the corner of his eye Matt noticed Forla edging toward the door, then slipping out. The reeve may not have known how the case was going to come out, but she sure did.

On the other hand, the reeve probably had made up his mind before the trial, to judge by the way he ran it. "Perkin, husband of Forla!" he snapped, pointing at the cuckolded husband. "You are charged with the killing of Simnel, of your own village!"

"He had cuckolded me!" Perkin cried. "He had bedded my wife!"

"Then you admit to killing him?"

"I had every right!"

"Did you kill him? Yes or no!"

"Yes!" Perkin shouted. "As I would kill any man who laid a hand upon her! Do you tell me I am wrong?"

"Do you tell him he is wrong?" the reeve demanded of the jury. The twelve men put their heads together for a quick, muttered conference, then turned back to the judge. The tallest said, "He was right to kill Simnel. It was adultery."

"The killing was justified!" The reeve slapped his hand on the table. "Set him free!"

The men holding Perkin stepped back, letting go, and the cuckolded husband stood looking about him, rubbing his arms where they had gripped him, looking dazed. Then fire lit his eye and he demanded, "Where is she? Where is my faithless wife? Where is Forla?"

The whole room went silent. Then the men began to mutter to one another, concerned but excited, and the women exchanged uneasy glances.

"Where is she?" Perkin shouted.

"They can't think it's right to let him kill her, too!" Matt protested.

"I think not," said Pascal, "but they shall not mind if he beats her sorely." He was very pale.

"Where is she?" Perkin bellowed at the women. "You know, do you not? Tell me where!"

They rocked in the blast of his rage, but the stoutest woman said, with determination, "We know not where she is fled—but fled she has, and the more fool she if she has not!"

Perkin snarled and raised a hand, but the reeve thundered, "Nay! This one is not yours to abuse!"

Perkin cast an uneasy glance at him, then turned and bolted out into the night, bellowing, "Forla! Where are you, Forla? You may as well come forth, for I shall find you soon or late!"

"Come on," Matt said urgently, and led Pascal toward the door.

But a matron stopped him with a hand on his arm to say, "Do not fear for Forla, minstrel. You are a good man, and no doubt seek to save her, as you sought to save Simnel—but you need not. Where she has gone, no man can follow."

Matt wasn't sure what she was referring to, but it did reassure him. "Thanks. I need to be going anyway, though. Good night, goodwife."

She flushed. "Good woman, rather! Though I was a good wife indeed, till my husband fled." Then anxiety creased her face. "Do not follow Perkin—for he is maddened now and might strike you down without knowing what he did!"

"I'll stay out of his way," Matt promised. He patted her hand. "By the way, what do you think the jury would have decided if it had been the other way around—if Simnel had killed Perkin? If the adulterer had killed the husband?"

"Simnel would have been outlawed," she said grimly, "with his life forfeit to anyone who wished to kill him, for revenge or for pleasure, or for any reason at all."

Pascal blanched dead white.

The woman noticed and scowled at him. "Are you an adulterer, too?"

"Not yet," Pascal answered, "and I think not ever—now."

As they slipped out the door, Matt said, "Wise decision, if running away with Panegyra, or even officially kidnapping her, would give her fiancé grounds to kill you out of hand, and the local reeve and jury would virtually ignore it."

"It does seem the wisest course," Pascal agreed. "Do you think they would do that to me even if we eloped before she married him?"

"I don't doubt it for a second," Matt assured him. "In fact, even without having done anything, I think we'd better go, and go fast!"

Pascal glanced at him in surprise, saw the grimness there, and hurried down the path toward the main road with him.

As they came out onto the highway, Pascal asked, "Shall we not wait for our fellow travelers?"

"Yes," Matt said, "five miles down the road. Then we'll let them catch up."

"Why the haste to go so quickly now?"

"Because that man I fought is dead," Matt said, "and I don't want to be around when the locals discover it."

Pascal's eyes went wide and frightened. Then he turned away, paying serious attention to making speed. "They will be after you with the reeve and all his men!"

"I don't think so," Matt said. "I don't think any of them will even recognize him—I'm pretty sure he's from out of town."

"Why?" Pascal was getting very used to staring.

"Because he was a professional assassin—I could tell by his style."

"Oh! Then you killed him because if you did not, he would have killed you!"

"No."

"Then *why*?"

"I didn't kill him at all," Matt explained. "I forced him to tell me who had hired him to kill *me*—but before he could talk, he died."

"Sorcery!" Pascal gasped.

"That was my guess, too. You might want to find a different traveling companion, Pascal. Almost anybody would be safer."

The young man didn't answer for several minutes; he only hurried along, watching the road and keeping pace with Matt. When he did speak, it was only to say, "I must think over my future again."

"Yes," Matt agreed. "That might be wise."

"Hell and damnation!" Rebozo swore. "Can you not find a single assassin who is competent?"

The secretary cowered away from his master's anger—Rebozo was, after all, a sorcerer, and a powerful one. Now was not the time to remind him that, so far, he had chosen all the assassins himself.

"First that fool of a knightling in Merovence, then that debacle of a manticore, followed by a ghost who proved to be as easy to bribe as any clerk—and now this! Two tavern brawls in a row, and neither slays him? Are your assassins all fools and oxen, or is this wizard of Merovence proof against any assault?"

The secretary grasped at the last phrase. "Perhaps, Lord Chancellor. He is, after all, Queen Alisande's Lord Wizard—and her husband. Perhaps he *is* invulnerable to all but the mightiest spells."

"Yes, perhaps he is." Rebozo calmed with amazing speed, gazing off into space. "Her wizard—and her husband! Ah, if we could capture and hold him, we could bring that proud queen to her knees, and all of Merovence with her, at our mercy!"

The secretary shivered at the audacity of it—and the danger. "How could we hold so mighty a wizard?"

"With sorcery," Rebozo told him, "sorcery of the foulest sort. The king might have to join with me in such an effort, if the wizard proves too much for me alone—but we shall attempt it! Send word to that chowder-headed reeve that he has tried the wrong man! Bid him arrest this wizard for the murder of your agent!"

"It shall be done, Lord Chancellor." LoClercchi scribbled out a quick note, then passed it to Rebozo, who sealed it—carefully not signing it—then worked his magic over it until it disappeared in a flash. He leaned back and nodded, satisfied. "The note shall appear by him, no matter where he may be. He shall lead forth his men to capture and hold that wizard forthwith! If all goes well, he will be in our power by dawn!"

But the secretary knew better than to think all would go well—at least, if the minstrel really was Matthew Mantrell, Lord Wizard of Merovence. And if he was, it might be better if they did *not* capture him—for rather than ransom him by money or deed, Queen Alisande might very well march south against Latruria, with all her armies behind her. The secretary found himself wondering if King Boncorro was really ready for a war.

Alisande was ready for a war, and growing more ready with each passing minute. The only problem was that so far, she had no one to fight. Of course, they were still in her own country . . .

As they rode, peasants working in the fields looked up to see the marching army and the silver figure at its head with the glitter of sunlight on her crown. They shouted to one another and came running, to cheer their queen and bow as she passed. No one rode out to command them, none forced them—they came to catch a glimpse of her of their own free will. Alisande's heart expanded within her at the sincerity of their devotion. Perhaps she was doing right by them, after all. She turned to watch them straggling back to their work as the vanguard passed . . .

. . . and saw a flutter of wings beating upward, a bird launching itself into the sky.

Launching itself? Surely not! It sprang up too smartly for that, lofted too high as it was still unfurling its wings. Was some loyal peasant releasing his tame pigeon to honor her?

A crossbow quarrel sprang up to meet the bird—sprang up from her own army, behind her, and a soldier broke ranks to run and catch the tumbling, bloody ball of feathers as it fell from the sky!

Alisande stared, outraged, frozen by the sudden, callous stroke. Then anger broke loose. "Bring me that man!"

The soldiers looked up, startled, then amazed by their queen's wrath. Red with anger they might have understood—but pale with rage? Over so little a thing as a pigeon?

A squadron hustled the luckless crossbowman out of the field and up to the queen, where he stood like the Ancient Mariner with a very small albatross, while his queen sat fuming above him. "For shame, sirrah!" she cried. "Are you so starved that you must seize upon every tiniest scrap of meat? For surely, one pigeon cannot make a pie! Do I feed you so poorly that you must devour every feather that floats by? Is there not enough food in my wagons to feed an army, that you must seek your own provisions from the countryside?"

It was her tone that did it, more than the words—the sheer icy rage that daunted the crossbowman and made his hands tremble. Again and again he tried to protest, but he was so terrified that no words came. "Royal rage" was no empty phrase, not now!

"Surely there was but little meat on its poor tiny carcass—but there was as much life in it as in you or me! By what *right* do you deprive a fellow creature of breath? What need was there for killing?"

In answer, the soldier held out the tiny carcass with shaking hands—but two fingers held up a foot, so that Alisande could clearly see the capsule tied to its leg.

She stared, taken aback. Then she glanced at the sergeant and nodded. He plucked the capsule from the bird's leg and passed it up to her. Alisande opened it, shook out the scrap of parchment inside and read. Her face settled into hard, grim lines.

Nonetheless, she looked down at the crossbowman. "You could not have known this was there."

"Nay, Majesty." The man swallowed thickly. "I am countrybred, and saw only the escape of meat that might help feed a peasant's family."

"Give it to the next peasant we pass, then!" Alisande commanded. "For now, get you back to your sergeant! Good fortune has saved you—but see to it that you shoot no more birds without reason!"

"Yes, Majesty! I thank you, your Majesty!" The crossbowman ducked his head, then ran off, relieved.

Alisande sat staring after him, amazed at her own reaction. Why had she taken the death of a mere pigeon so hard? She had killed hares, even deer, for her own supper, and never thought twice about it! She had flown hawks to seize just such birds as this, and never given it a thought! Where had this sudden concern for even the tiniest life come from? And what did it bode for her prowess as a general?

"What was it, Majesty?" asked Lady Constance.

The woman was right—she should have been far more concerned about the message, than about the messenger. "A spy's report, to the Chancellor of Latruria," Alisande replied. "Some one of my peasants has learned to read and write, and taken the pay of another sovereign!"

"Or is not truly one of yours at all?" Lady Constance said quietly.

"If that is the case, he is a most brave man," Alisande said grimly. "Sergeant! Alert the home guard to seek out a peasant who keeps pigeons and can read!"

The man ducked his head and ran back along the ranks.

"What did it say?" Lady Constance asked, eyes wide and round.

"Only that the Queen of Merovence rides south with her army."

"Why, that is not so damaging!" Lady Constance said in surprise. "There is no secret in this—every peasant in the parish knows it, and rumor will spread the word almost as fast as that pigeon could fly!"

"True," Alisande agreed. "It is not the news itself that angers me, but the simple fact of a spy living so close to my castle."

"Small wonder in that," Lady Constance said with irony.

"Again, true—we must expect that every monarch about will set spies upon us, even those who are our friends. But to know that we will be shadowed every mile of the way, that the Chancellor of Latruria will not only know of our coming, but will surely know our exact strength, down to the man! And what the chancellor knows, King Boncorro shall know!"

"We could not hope to take him by surprise, I suppose." Lady Constance sighed.

"No, we could not," Alisande said with regret. "I suppose it means no more than that King Boncorro is competent, or has competent men about him—but it serves notice on me to brace for a true battle." She turned to her adjutant. "Give orders to shoot down any pigeons that we see flying near."

The man nodded and turned away, but that odd pulse of pity welled up in Alisande again, the lament that any living thing should die without need, and she called out, "No, stop! It is ridiculous to even attempt it, when for every bird we see, there will be five that we do not! Let them go, mine adjutant—it is better that we know how much King Boncorro knows, than that we believe he knows nothing."

And she set her face firmly to the south, ignoring the adjutant's stare of confusion, no matter how quickly it was masked.

Chapter
Twelve

Five miles was all it took for the twilight to thicken to the point at which Matt had to call a halt. "If we go any farther tonight, we might as well go wandering among the trees—we won't be able to see any more out in the open."

Pascal shuddered. "Not the forest, I pray you, friend Matthew! There are still so many outlaws that one does not ask whether one will be robbed, but when."

"Doesn't sound too good," Matt said. "This road passes through the forest, doesn't it?"

"Aye, but my relatives have told me that the road itself is safe. The king's foresters and reeves have seen to it that the trees are cut back for seven yards to either side, and the reeves' men patrol it frequently."

"So travelers are never robbed anymore?"

"Almost never."

Matt didn't like the sound of "almost," but reminded himself that they had a backup. "Okay, Manny! You can come out now!"

There was a moment's pause, during which Pascal sidled around to put Matt between himself and the only nearby outcrop of trees—so of course the manticore stepped out from the boulder behind him. "I thought to accompany you openly on the road, mortals, but there were too many other folk abroad."

"Yiiii!" Pascal's head seemed to jump a foot, though his shoes stayed on the ground, stretching him out, then snapping him back.

"He does move quietly," Matt agreed. "Yes, Manny, thanks for staying undercover. Half of northern Latruria seems to be hiking south on the highway."

"The other half are staying at home seducing one another," Pascal grumbled.

Matt could see he was beginning to have doubts about Panegyra's fidelity—and this before she had even married! But the man was far too old for her, and Matt thought Pascal was right—the little snip would probably be planning her first affair even as she was marching down the aisle! Assuming she wasn't working on her second. Or third, or fourth.

But maybe he was doing her an injustice. He turned to the manticore. "I've got a question, Manny."

"I am hungry." Both sets of teeth grinned.

"I paid a farmer to tie out a brace of goats for you—he seemed to be overstocked, judging by the state of his clothes."

"Where!"

"Ah, ah!" Matt wagged a forefinger, then pulled it back quickly, just in case. "Answers first, before you get my goat!"

"I thought they were the farmer's."

"Mine now—I bought 'em. When Pascal introduced us, you mentioned that somebody had sicced you on me."

"I had been commanded to eat you if you crossed the border, aye." The manticore's tongue slurped around its lips. "It took little urging to induce my accord."

"Good thing you didn't follow through—I'm not a man of good taste." Pascal winced. "That was old."

"That's why it didn't taste good anymore. Besides, I believe in recycling. So tell me, Manny—who was it who told you to put the bite on me? Of course, if you can't say . . ."

" 'Tis simplicity itself!" the manticore assured him. "The man who bade me gobble you was Rrrmmmmmmmmm . . ." His lips sealed themselves shut and his eyes widened in astonishment. "Mmmm! MM, mm!"

"I was afraid of that," Matt said unhappily. "What's your name, manticore? Not your true one—I can see you wouldn't want to go spreading that around. Just the nickname I've given you."

"Mmmmmanny!" Then the manticore clacked its jaws shut, looking even more surprised.

"Easy for *you* to say. But how about this guy who compelled you to hunt me? What was his name?"

"Mmmmmmmmmmmmmm . . ." The manticore stared in outrage. "Mmmmm! Mmm, mmm, mm!"

"Can't even get his mouth open this time." Matt sighed. "Okay, what's the name of my partner, here?"

"Why, he is Pascal!" Then Manny frowned, puzzled, and opened and closed his jaws a couple of times.

"Don't worry, they work just fine—as long as I don't ask you to tell me who told you to get me. What was his name, by the way?"

This time the manticore hesitated.

"I know, I know, your lips are sealed—or will be, if you try." Matt held up a hand to forestall the answer. "Don't blame you for not even wanting to try—the condition might become permanent, and then what would those poor lonely goats do? Not to mention all the spare cattle that are for sale between here and Venarra. Okay, Manny, go find 'em. They should be staked out in a meadow about a mile back."

"I go!" the manticore cried with a toothy grin.

"Just try to snap 'em up before they even know what hit them, okay?"

The manticore pouted. "I am a cat, Matthew! A large one, and mixed with a scorpion and a hedgehog, perhaps, but a cat in bulk, and a cat in nature!"

"Yeah, but just feed, okay? No recreation. Okay, go."

The manticore disappeared in a blur.

"Remind me not to get *his* goat." Matt turned away. "Well, let's pitch camp, Pascal."

"Are you not concerned that the reeve may send his men after you?"

"Not terribly. Nobody seemed to notice my would-be murderer dying, in all the excitement over Perkin and Simnel." Matt remembered the scene with a shudder. "Besides, out of sight, out of mind." He only wished they were.

"Well, mere living is a hazard, in Latruria," Pascal sighed as he dropped his pack. "I was mad to come here!"

"Lovers generally are—and you really were mad for a sight of Panegyra. Don't worry, you weren't exactly the only mad soul in that house."

A low moan began all around them.

Matt froze. "Speak of the—" He clamped his jaw shut; in Latruria, it probably wasn't a good idea even to speak about speaking of the Devil. "—of the ghost, and you hear him moaning!" He turned around. "That you, Spiro?"

"How did you know?" A wavering tendril of mist curled up from the ground, thickening and spreading to a little above Matt's head. The top of it sculpted itself into the rough semblance of a human face.

"Deduction," Matt answered.

"A form of reason? Foolish mortal!" The face firmed into Spiro's countenance, and the body began to define itself into clothing. "When you deal with the supernatural, what good is deduction?"

"If it's good enough for the tax man, it should be good enough for you," Matt answered, nettled. "What's the occasion? Decided it was going to be too long before they gave your room to some other poor sucker, so you might as well track me down and have another try?"

"Nay." The hollow eyes scowled down at him. "I have come to thank you, if you must know!"

Matt stood frozen in astonishment for a minute, then said slowly, "Well, I guess I must, if you're going to say it. Uh, you're welcome, Spiro."

"I have not even thanked you yet!"

"Okay, so I'm premature. My mother always said I was. Let's try again. Uh . . . glad to see you, Spiro."

"A pleasure, minstrel." The ghost bowed.

"Say, how's it been going?"

"Most marvelously well! The current squire has already unearthed my coffin and built another around it. Even as we speak, it trundles through the night toward Genova, where it will take ship for Greece!"

"Hey, congratulations!" Matt grinned and reached out to pat Spiro on the back, then thought better of it.

"I never thought he would agree so quickly!" Pascal said, eyes wide.

"Who should better know the nature of my descendants?" the ghost said dryly. "Nonetheless, he succumbed to his wife's pleading—and his own dislike of my claim on the manse, no doubt! I must thank you indeed, minstrel, for I shall soon be all at sea!"

"Must run in the family," Matt said with a glance at Pascal. "Well, I'm really glad for you, Spiro—and glad I could be of service." He almost volunteered to help out if the ghost developed any further little problems, but caught himself in time.

Besides, Spiro beat him to it. "I am in your debt, mortal, and I dislike that state. If you need my aid, call upon me."

Matt stared. Then he recovered and said, "Oh, that's not necessary! I was just trying to help out a little, that's all." As a matter of fact, all Matt had really been doing was trying to get a very intimidating specter out of his room. He felt guilty about taking any kind of payback for it, even gratitude.

But Spiro was determined. "I must repay my debts, mortal! That is the nature of Purgatory!"

"Well, uh, thanks—but you're going to be in Greece!"

"I shall be farther than that, if I have any choice," Spiro assured him, "and I have, or I would not be here. Nay, even from Purgatory, I can hear and come to aid you—in whatever manner a soul may, who has Passed Over."

"I'm sure there's some medium of communication there," Matt assured him. "Okay, nice offer! Thanks, Spiro! If I need a friend Over There, I'll call! Assuming I can find a way to send a message, that is."

"You have it." Spiro nodded at Pascal, who instantly did the best he could to become invisible. Unfortunately, there was no cover besides the tent, and he hadn't even started to pitch it yet.

"Pascal?" Matt turned to frown at his friend. "He's no medium!"

"Nay, but he is of my blood," Spiro assured him, "and blood speaks to blood; like will to like. Have him call upon me, and I shall hear."

"C-C-C-Call?" Pascal stammered.

"Have you no wits?" Spiro demanded. "My blood has grown weak if it reposes in such as he!"

Pascal stared. Then his face darkened and he stood up straighter, clenching his fists.

"Ah, that is better!" Spiro allowed himself a smile. "Never forget that you are the son of a squire, lad—especially if you truly seek knighthood! Stand tall and remember your honor! Even as your friend does." He turned to Matt with a frown. "I would think you were a knight, if you were not so plainly a minstrel."

"Appearances can be deceiving." Matt just hoped they were. He needed a quick change of topic. "Say, if you founded the whole line, then you must have been the wizard!"

"Nay, he was my son."

"Then you must have something of his talent for magic."

"Not 'must'—but I think I may have a trace." The hollow eyes creased in a smile. "I shall hear young Pascal call, never fear—and I think I may find a way to answer. Farewell!"

"G'bye." Matt waved as Spiro's form blurred into the tendril of mist again and sank into the ground. Matt watched it recede, then gazed at the bare grass. "Well, I always said I needed every friend I could get."

"Then you must have some very odd friends indeed!" Pascal wilted, knees gone rubbery. "I am amazed that you are so undaunted! You truly are a knight!"

"Yeah, well, just don't noise it around." Matt turned back to the pile of canvas. "You want to cut the sticks for the tent, or shall I?"

• • •

The low whistle brought Matt out of a light sleep. He looked around, but the campsite lay still in the pale light of a quarter moon. There were no trees, just the boulder and a copse across the road. Maybe a night bird?

Then the whistle came again, and Matt was sure no bird really sounded like that. He was on his feet with his dagger in his hand in an instant, fumbling for his sword. "Pascal! Visitors!"

His answer was a snore.

"Pascal!" Matt hissed. "Wake up!"

"Oh, do not trouble him," said a deep voice, and harness creaked as mounted figures loomed up out of the night. "It is yourself whom we have come for."

Well, that let out bandits. Matt brought his sword out slowly, turning it to make sure the moonlight gleamed off its twenty polished inches. "And who might you be?"

"I am Vanni, bailiff to the reeve of this shire—and these are my watchmen."

"Oh." Matt lowered his sword. "Well, that's a relief. What can I do for you?"

Pascal, awake now, stared at him as if he were crazy, but rose to stand at his side.

"You can come with us." Vanni sounded a bit surprised himself. "We have come to arrest you in the king's name."

Matt stood still for a few seconds, letting the news soak in—and, oddly, found that he had almost been expecting it. "On what charge?"

"For the murder of a man."

"I murdered no man." Matt frowned. "Who is my alleged victim?"

"We do not know his name," Vanni answered, irritated. "He was a stranger—the man with whom you fought."

"Oh." Matt shrugged, making sure the movement made the light gleam on his blade again. "No problem there—I wound up fighting in self-defense. *He* tried to kill *me*."

"I did see the stranger wielding a knife," one of the watchmen said.

"And I saw the minstrel strike it out of his hand," Vanni snapped. "Innocent or guilty, it is not for us to say." His gaze stayed on Matt. "It is only for us to bring you to the reeve."

Why did he have the feeling that the reeve was not going to give him an unbiased hearing? Matt wondered. Maybe the mention of the king? "The stranger just died all of a sudden. His heart stopped. I had nothing to do with it."

Vanni barked a laugh. "Died while fighting you, and you had nothing to do with it? Nay, surely!"

"We're in a land of sorcery," Matt countered, "and you doubt it?"

Vanni frowned. "The young king is no sorcerer!"

"What kind of magic does he work, then? Even in Merovence we've heard that he's powerful enough to protect himself—and in a kingdom with a lot of unemployed and vengeful sorcerers running around, that's no mean skill!"

"The king's magic is not your affair," Vanni snapped. "Obeying his law is!"

"I did." Matt decided it was time to call in reinforcements and raised his voice. "Didn't I, Manny?"

"Indubitably," the rich voice said out of the night.

Vanni frowned, peering into the darkness beyond the circle of fire-light. "Who said that?"

"I did." The manticore stepped into the light, grinning and lashing his tail.

The horses screamed and tried to bolt. A few of them managed it, with riders shouting halfhearted protests. Most of the men fought their mounts to a standstill, though—and looked as if they wished they hadn't.

"The minstrel obeyed the king's law in every particular," the manticore said, giving Vanni the full double grin.

Vanni goggled at the monster, then managed to wrench his gaze back to Matt. "What manner of man are you, who keeps company with a manticore?"

"Just a traveling companion, really," Matt answered. "Manny isn't so much with me as he is with my friend, here." He slapped Pascal on the shoulder. The young man gulped and managed a rather queasy grin. His nervous glance was ticking back and forth between the bailiff and the manticore so regularly that Matt found himself wondering if his eyes were run by clockwork.

"The *youth*?" Vanni stared down at Pascal.

The young man's lips twitched in an attempt at a grin. "He is an old family, ah, friend."

"A DNA-linked spell," Matt explained.

Vanni's stare snapped up to him. "Are *you* a sorcerer, too?"

"No," Matt said truthfully. After all, Vanni hadn't asked if he was a wizard. "But I've heard talk about it."

Vanni forced himself to look the manticore straight in the eye again—a brave man indeed, Matt decided. "Is your name truly 'Manny'?"

"Of course not," the manticore spat. "What fool would let his true name be known far and wide, so that any passing sorcerer might enslave him? 'Twas one such incautious lip-slip that gave this youth's ancestor power over me, to bind me to himself and his family for all my days! Forbear, foolish man—I will not step into your trap." His toothy grin lolled wider. "Though you might step into mine."

"I asked only from curiosity, I assure you!" It was amazing how fast Vanni could backpedal, even on a horse.

"Say, Manny," Matt asked, "do you remember my telling you not to eat human flesh?"

"Aye," Manny said, his grin now so wide it was amazing his own head didn't disappear into it. "And bitter am I about it, for mortal folk have a most excellent flavor."

"I was thinking about taking it back."

"Were you indeed!" Manny looked at the reeve's men hungrily, and a slab of tongue drooled out of his lower pair of teeth to circle around his lips, slurping.

"I am convinced of your innocence!" Vanni said quickly. "I thank you for your testimony, minstrel—and friend! I shall return to my master the reeve and tell him of your arguments, so monstrously persuasive!"

Or of my persuasive monster, Matt thought. "Why, thank you, bailiff. It would really be quite an inconvenience to have to go back to your village."

"But *we* shall." Vanni reined his horse around. "Ho, men of the Watch! Back to our quarters!"

"I am sorry to see you go," Manny pouted.

"Perhaps another time," Vanni said uneasily. "It has been fascinating to make your acquaintance! I shall tell my grandchildren about you."

"You're too young," Matt protested, and Manny concurred. "You cannot have grandchildren yet."

"No, but I intend to. Farewell!" And away they rode, barely managing to hold their horses in from blind flight. Matt caught a few mutters about, "Manticore for a friend! Can he be more fell than it, then?" "He seemed pleasant enough." "Aye, one you could pummel with impunity." " 'Tis quite unfair—one never knows who will have powerful friends."

As they disappeared into the night, Matt turned to the manticore. "Thanks, Manny. You take a hint beautifully."

"Hint?" The monster stared. "I spoke in all earnestness, Wizard! Did not you?"

• • •

The next day passed without incident. Matt and Pascal joined up with another group of roistering travelers, much larger than the first; a few discreet inquiries revealed that this crowd comprised three or four smaller groups that had all set out from different villages with the same purpose: living the good life in Venarra. There was constant laughter, constant singing, and the wineskins passed freely from hand to hand. Matt wondered where they found the money to buy them.

He found out at the next wayside inn, where the landlord sold them provisions at what had to be cost or below. In fact, when a few of the peasants took the wine and forgot to pay, he made no mention of it—just looked tense and nervous until they had finished lunch and started on. Looking back, Matt saw him wipe his forehead and collapse onto a bench with relief. Matt could sympathize—there were at least fifty men in the group, thirty of them young, and all of them strong and able enough so that together they could have torn that inn apart. No wonder the landlord had wanted to keep them in a good humor.

Matt had also noticed that the servers were all male, and all wound tight as springs, as if nerved up to expect trouble. There wasn't a one of them who wasn't carrying a small club hanging from his belt. At a guess, Matt decided, the landlord had told the serving girls to hide and called in his hostlers, plus men from the nearby village, to hurry this crowd along. They were probably having to go through this at least once a day. Matt was impressed—it would have been more in keeping with Latruria for the landlord to use his female personnel to try to keep the vagabonds satisfied enough not to cause trouble. Of course, there were more women than men in the group, but still . . .

Still, he proved to be wise, as Matt found when the crowd came upon a peasant girl working in the fields but sneaking covert glances at the wanderers. Matt could almost see her wondering whether or not she should join them—but she must have decided not, when the boys gave a shout of glee and started chasing her. They coursed as hounds chase a pretty doe, and brought her to bay the same way, then took her down, and what they tried to do to her was not pretty at all.

Tried, because Matt muscled in, holding off the boys with wine, jokes, and occasional punches that everybody could pretend were all in good fellowship. He did all this while he was giving the girl a recruiting spiel about the joys of the capital, emphasizing all the fun she could have with boy after boy, then sent her home to pack without asking whether or not she wanted to. He turned back to face a glaring semicircle of youths, but grinned easily and rested his hand on his sword hilt as he said, "Well, back to the road, eh, lads? I doubt not she'll catch up with us when she wishes."

The looks they gave him made him determined not to turn his back on a single one of them—but they glanced at his sword, noticed that he didn't have his lute on his back, and let themselves be moved by his jolly slaps on the back off toward the roadway again. Matt sang them Kipling's "Smuggler Song," with its refrain, "Turn your faces to the wall, my dear, as the gentlemen pass by," and they took the excuse to start grinning and feigning good spirits, though every glance said its owner would delight in seeing Matt spitted upon his own rapier, if he'd had one.

Of course, Matt was so intent on trying to calm them down that he temporarily forgot the power of verse in this world—and that melody strengthened the impact of the words. When they caught up with the crowd again, they found everyone reveling in the goodies that had magically appeared among them. The girls oohed and aahed as they fingered the laces, the men got drunk on the brandy, and Matt was quite content to let them give King Boncorro credit for long-distance generosity. Somehow, he wasn't eager for fame at the moment.

As twilight drew in, they came to a large open meadow where another couple of groups their size were already encamped, more or less. Local peasants were bringing in pigs, and the travelers were gleefully spitting them over slow fires. More wineskins appeared, again courtesy of the locals—anything to keep the strangers from foraging. The vagabonds proceeded to eat, drink, and make merry, and the locals faded away into the dusk—but several of them cast envious looks back over their shoulders as they went. Matt gave them two days before they hit the road themselves.

It was the wildest party he had ever been to, even including his one visit to Mardi Gras in New Orleans. There was a carnival atmosphere over the whole throng, a hundred fifty strong; inhibitions were thrown to the winds, along with random articles of clothing. No, not random—the more cloth that went sailing on the breeze, the more purposeful the selection became. Matt was shocked to see couples tumbling to the ground right out in the open, without the slightest attempt at concealment or seeking of privacy, eagerly stripping one another with laughter and lewd comments.

Of course, he was a little more shocked to discover that he was shocked. Was there still a Puritan lurking deep within him? Or just a romantic who held the quaint old notion that sex should somehow be linked to love? Of course, he supposed love didn't *have* to be private—but if love there was, then lovemaking grew out of intimacy, which cannot by its nature be public, for if it is, it is no longer intimate.

He didn't seem to be completely wrong, judging from the young lass sobbing on the shoulder of another girl, who was leading her toward the outer edges of the crowd, her face a study in compassion and anger.

"He told me last night that he loved me!" the teenager sobbed. "And here he is, stroking that hussy who just joined us today!"

"There, there, Lucia. Perhaps it is only the wine." But the look of hatred the older girl threw at a callow fellow who was unbuttoning a giggling young woman's garments said that she didn't believe her own lie for a second.

"He was the first man I ever let bed me! He told me he loved me!"

They passed beyond Matt's hearing, to his relief; he felt a pang of sympathetic hurt for poor little Lucia. Her dreams had already crumbled, after only a day or two. Maybe now she would go home, though . . .

But no, she couldn't, could she? Not in this culture, not without the man who had taken her to bed—if you could call a patch of grass a bed. He looked around for Pascal, to remind him to be a gentleman, but he was gone. A moment's panic ended with concern as he saw his traveling companion drinking and laughing with a group of five other young people. One of the girls was making eyes at him; another was stroking his arm.

Pascal? Homely Pascal?

Matt began to suspect there was something going on here besides mere lust. Of course, maybe he was being unfair—Pascal might be attractive in ways Matt couldn't see; after all, he couldn't look through a woman's eyes.

The older folk were looking on with indulgent smiles, then glancing at each other with knowing looks that turned lustful as, slowly, they kissed, decided they liked the flavor, and kissed again, deeper and longer. Work-worn hands began to loosen ties and buttons—but the middle-aged did seek some kind of cover—even if it was only a bush—before they took anything off. A bit more decorum? Or only an unwillingness to display flesh that was no longer in its prime?

Matt noticed one of these more mature women leading a young girl away—only this time, both of them were sobbing. Matt couldn't detect any family resemblance. He decided the young weren't the only ones having their hearts broken.

Nor girls, either. One young man was huddling in the shadow of a cask, glaring down into his mug and muttering, "I told her I loved her! Why would she lead me on like that, then turn away to that great lout?"

"At least she let you bed her last night," said his buddy.

"Yes, and I thought it meant she loved me! All day I was burning for her, aching for her! Then she laughed at me and turned away with *him*!"

"Courage!" His friend clapped him on the back. "Give as good as you've gotten! There is no shortage of willing wenches here! Bed another and let her see how little she meant to you!"

The brokenheart looked up with a glint in his eye. "That would be the fitting revenge, would it not?"

They got up and sallied forth into the crowd, while Matt watched with his blood running cold. Okay, so the kid would bury his pain in some other girl—but what would that do to *her*?

You worry too much about other people, he told himself sternly, but himself wasn't listening.

Now that he looked around with those last few conversations in mind, he detected the signs of the aftermath—the hard, brittle tone to the laughter, the determination, the desperation with which the young folk were pushing themselves to have fun. The girls were throwing themselves away, the boys were scalp-hunting—all of them trying to convince themselves that sex didn't really matter. *Pleasure shouldn't be so much work,* Matt thought. He remembered when he'd been in the same state, after the breakup of his first big romance. The rebound had been hard, and he'd ricocheted for a long time, slamming into a lot of walls. He winced at the memory of the people he'd collided with, and wondered how badly he'd hurt them. Any pain Alisande had caused him, he'd more than deserved . . .

He wouldn't do that to her. Never.

He wondered about Pascal. What kind of shape would the boy be in, come the morning? What would happen to him tomorrow night?

"A tankard, friend!" A buxom woman at least ten years Matt's senior sailed up to him with a foaming mug in each hand. "Will you not join in the revelry?" The look she gave him left no doubt as to what she thought his place in the festivities should be.

"Why, thank you!" Matt took the tankard with forced cheerfulness. "But before I take part, I must give part, for I am a minstrel, and song is my donation!" He took a drink that wasn't as deep as it looked, handed back the flagon, and struck the strings of his lute.

After all, she couldn't quibble if his hands were busy making music, could she?

"Will there not be time for music later?" she asked, pouting.

She was still a very attractive woman, and Matt wondered how much of her own escape from mundanity had to do with a desperate determination to enjoy using her charms before they finally faded. He rippled out a sequence of chords, grinning at her, and tried to remember that the verses would work magic, and which song would have the least ruinous effect.

What else?

> "Alas, my love, you do me wrong
> To cast me off discourteously,
> When I have loved you oh, so long,
> Delighting in your company!
>
> "Greensleeves was my delight,
> Greensleeves was all my joy,
> Greensleeves was my heart of gold,
> And who but my lady Greensleeves?"

The crowd quieted and turned to look at him, listening. There were still pockets of giggling and sighing and moaning, but the simple fact that he could hear them meant people were paying attention. Matt sang on, remembering how many verses Childs had chronicled, and choosing among them carefully. He thought he was having a good effect—but remembering what one professor had told his class, about which feminine profession wore green sleeves in the high Middle Ages, he could only hope. He struck the last chord and bowed, doffing his cap as the crowd broke into applause with cries of "More! More!" But before he could begin again, several women of all ages crowded in, eyes shining, with such choice comments as, "Can you finger me as well as you do your lute, minstrel?" "Shall we make music together?" "Is it true you only sing about things you cannot do?"

"Never run away with a musician," Matt counseled. At least they had crowded out the matron with the first invitation . . .

A shout of anger, the sound of a blow, and a chorus of cries of alarm and excitement. The women swung around, avid for the sight, and Matt's heart sank. Was that what came of singing about broken hearts in this universe?

Apparently not—the wench who was the cause of it all stood to the side, eyes glowing as she watched two stalwart youths face off, each with a knife, one with his shirt open and the love bite already swelling on his chest, the other with a day-old mark on his neck and all his clothes buttoned more tightly than he no doubt wished. "Villain! She is mine!" He shouted, and leaped forward, slashing at his rival.

Chapter
Thirteen

The rival jumped back, but not far enough—a streak of crimson appeared across his belly. The girl screamed, though whether with horror, delight, or both, Matt couldn't tell. The rival blanched and leaped farther back—into a wall of hands that shoved him forward to meet the blade of his foe. He howled with anger and slammed a fist into the other man's jaw—a fist with a knife sticking up from the top. The jealous lover reeled back, blood welling from a gash on his cheek, then charged back with a roar. The rival lunged, but the jealous lover blocked the blade with a cloth-wrapped fist and struck for the chest. The rival blocked, but he had no wrapping, and the blade nicked his knuckles. He shoved hard with a shout of rage, though, then sprang back to yank a shawl from a woman in the crowd, who shrieked protest—but he paid no attention, only began whipping his fist in circles to wrap the cloth around his forearm as a shield.

The jealous lover struck before he could finish.

The rival blocked and stabbed, but the jealous lover blocked, too, and they sprang apart.

The crowd booed.

They actually booed, incensed that nobody had been slashed.

That did it. Matt decided he had to put a stop to this, somehow—especially since he was hearing angry shouts from two other places in the crowd, and quick glances showed a fistfight breaking out off to the left, and a couple of older men going after each other with cudgels, off on the right. Matt swung his lute into firing position, took aim, and struck a chord—not that anybody could hear it. They couldn't hear his voice, either, amidst all the yelling, but he sang anyway:

"Gonna lay down my sword and shield,
Down by the riverside!
Down by the riverside, down by the riverside!
Gonna lay down my sword and shield,
Down by the riverside,
Ain't gonna study war no more!"

Nobody could hear him, of course, but he went on singing doggedly away. It did cross his mind that a religious song might attract some very unwelcome attention in a country like this, but though the particular song on his lips might have been a spiritual, it didn't actually mention the Deity or the Savior, or any other specifically religious words. Maybe it was those very associations that gave it the power to cut through the magical inertia of Latruria, for it did seem to be working—the duelists in front of him slowed, the anger fading, uncertainty replacing it until, finally, the jealous lover hurled down his knife with a snarl—right between the rival's toes—then turned on his heel and stalked off. The onlookers crowded back out of his way, wary of his thunderous face. The rival watched him go, frowning, then sheathed his knife and turned away. The girl who had been the cause of it all ran to touch him on the arm, but he shook her off with a snarl and strode away into the crowd. Neither felt proud of himself, that was obvious. The girl glared after the rival in indignation, then pivoted to glare after the jealous lover in fury, then finally tossed her head, a dangerous light in her eyes, and stepped up to a good-looking youth who had been watching. "Would you forsake a damsel so easily as that, handsome lad?"

The boy answered with a slow grin. "Nay, surely not! Not one so fair as yourself! Come, shall we dance?"

"Pay the piper first," the girl said—and sure enough, now that the excitement was over, an older man was unlimbering a small set of bagpipes. Matt felt a bit indignant about the competition, but he couldn't really claim that the man was horning in on a songster's territory. The young fellow paid him, and the piper coaxed his instrument into a wheeze. Matt winced. No, he certainly didn't have to worry about competition.

The bag inflated, the pipes droned, and the chanter began a merry melody. The boy and girl began to dance. Others joined them, and soon a score of couples were prancing merrily over the turf while the sounds of the other two fights ceased. Matt glanced at the two areas uneasily, but all four men were still on their feet, though glaring blackly at one another, so Matt decided to take a little credit for it. Not aloud, of course—especially with that piper going. He was into full swing now, and if he wasn't very good, he was certainly loud. Well, as long as the young folk were dancing, they couldn't very well be fornicating—although, looking at some of their movements, Matt wasn't all that sure. The postures and undulations became steadily more suggestive, and Matt turned away, suddenly realizing how very much he was missing Alisande. As long as he'd been staying busy, he hadn't thought of her more than once every couple of hours, and that in a rather platonic way—but work had suddenly begun to remind him that he was male, and therefore to remind him of his chosen.

What was it doing to Pascal?

There he went, flying by in a stamping, hip-thrusting dance, movements that Matt was quite sure he had never known until now—but he was a fast learner, and the girl who was teaching him was very dedicated. Not very pretty, but dedicated—and with a figure well calculated to cheer a disappointed lover.

Then they were gone, faces flushed with the dancing, but also with drinking. Matt looked about him and saw that they weren't the only ones. Only an hour after sunset, and most of the young folk were staggering—and at least half of their elders, too, the ones who were still standing. Of the forms on the ground, some were madly coupling; the ones who weren't, were passed out cold, reeking of ale. Most of the bushes were shaking their leaves and rustling, but the ones that weren't emitted the sounds of abused stomachs rebelling.

Come to think of it, the innkeepers may have been giving the ale away for free, but they weren't exactly shabbily dressed. Matt tried to picture each of the three he'd seen, noticed that they were all wearing unpatched clothes of good cloth and that their wives wore jewelry. That might have come from selling food and renting rooms, but he had a notion a lot of it came from selling beer, too. By local standards, they were wealthy—but if they could afford to give the stuff away to buy off potential troublemakers, it wasn't because they charged high prices. In fact, the first innkeeper's prices weren't bad at all. If he'd been doing well, it was only because his countrymen drank a great deal of beer. Everything considered, Matt decided, it was lucky that medieval Europe hadn't had access to much in the way of narcotics.

Pascal went whirling by in the round of dancing again, laughing too hard and eyeing his partner with desperate purpose. He had definitely thrown himself into it with a certain wildness, with the air of a man who is anxious to forget.

"Dance with me, handsome minstrel!"

Matt turned in surprise. The woman was about thirty, still attractive, and her figure was generous.

"Why thank you." Matt forced a smile. "But if the minstrel dances, who will play the music?"

"Why, the piper." She swayed closer, fluttering her eyelashes.

Matt thought he must be a fool or a testosterone deprivation case, to feel only the slightest stirring of response. "The piper will tire."

"But will the pipe?" she asked, and stretched up to plant her lips on his in a firm, demanding kiss. Her tongue teased his lips, and he was shocked to feel them part—by reflex? But her body was pressing against his, he could feel each curve all too warmly, and he realized it had been far too long since he had spent an evening alone with Alisande . . .

The thought of his wife cooled his heating ardor, and he broke the kiss, gasping. "I . . . thank you, damsel, but—"

She broke into a peal of laughter. "Damsel? Why, thank you, gallant sir, but 'tis ten years and more since I was wed!"

Matt knew better than to ask if she was a widow. He was dimly aware that the crowd had mostly swirled away, that they were standing at the fringes now. "It has only been a year for me, plus a few months. No, my wife and I are still very new to the business, and still very excited about it."

"Give it a few years," the veteran advised. "You will find it boring enough—and find that a kiss and caress on the side will rouse you to greater heights with your wife." She demonstrated with another kiss.

This time Matt was warned, and he kept his lips firmly closed—until he felt a hand smoothing over his buttock and sliding around toward the front. He gasped out of sheer surprise, and that maddening tongue deepened the kiss. She felt his response and moved back with a low, throaty chuckle. "So then, you are not so faithful as all that, are you? Come, sweet chuck!" And she kissed him again.

This was definitely too much. Never mind that a healthy body will respond to any touch—Matt didn't *want* to respond, damn it! He took the lady by the waist and pushed her firmly away—but she clung, her mouth a veritable suction cup . . .

Pain rocketed through his head, a rocket that must have been heading for the stars, because they were there suddenly, and the world was tilting, more and more, until it jarred up behind him. Dimly, he could hear the woman chuckle again, feel her hands, though they weren't searching in any way armorous this time, they were searching for his purse, and there was another pair of hands busy, too, trying to wrench at his belt, his sword . . .

Then his vision cleared just enough for him to see a huge blade sweeping down at him out of the darkness. Panic shot through him and he tried to roll, but his body wouldn't respond . . .

A roar filled his ears. Something slapped up under his shoulder and sent him spinning.

Under the circumstances, he didn't mind.

The roar broke again, and there was a lot of screaming, some of it masculine. There was a pounding that faded. Finally, Matt managed to push himself up off the ground. The world tilted around him, then reversed direction. He caught his breath and swallowed his stomach back down to where it belonged, squeezed his eyes shut, waited for his inner tilting to stop, then tried looking again, and saw . . .

A great tawny wall of fur.

It looked vaguely familiar, so he tilted his glance upward, up and up and straight into a grin—two of them, and Manny's eyes twinkling with amusement up on top.

"You said I could not eat them, man," the manticore said, "but you did not tell *them* that."

"Th—Thanks, Manny." Matt pulled himself up to a sitting position, amazed that he ever could have thought this beast was his enemy. "They . . . they got a lot closer that time . . . didn't they?"

"It is easier to overcome a man," Manny reflected, "if you do not give him a chance to fight."

"There is that," Matt agreed. "Get him busy with a willing wench, then sap him from behind."

"It somewhat galled the wench," Manny observed, "that *you* were not willing."

Matt smiled ruefully. "Or at least, that she had to keep me rolling for a while before my engine would catch."

The manticore frowned. " 'Engine'? What device did you use?"

"Only a lute," Matt sighed, "but apparently that qualifies as a lethal weapon in this universe." He looked around and saw his instrument, miraculously uncrushed. He took it into his lap, checking, but finding no more than a scratch. "Remind me to be *very* careful who's around when I sing songs."

"With all due respect, minstrel-knight," Manny said, "I doubt that it was either your words or your songs that brought on this . . . encounter."

"No." Matt stared down at the lute, brooding. "It's the same sorcerer who's been trying to kill me all along, isn't it? But why?"

"Why not?" Manny replied. "A manticore needs no more reason for killing than hunger. Perhaps your foe needs not even that."

"Am I *that* big a threat? Just me alone?"

"It would seem so—and in the midst of this carnival, who would know you had been slain for any reason more than jealousy over a woman?"

"If anybody even bothered to look that far," Matt muttered. "Yes. Perfect cover for a murder, wasn't it?"

"Perhaps not perfect," the manticore said judiciously. "If it had been I who did it, now—"

"Uh, yes, I'm sure you would have managed it much more efficiently." For some odd reason, Matt wasn't in the mood for hearing the gory details of the manticore's no doubt fabulous plan. He climbed to his feet, trying to ignore the piercing pain in his head. "Let's say it may not have been perfect, but it was certainly good enough."

"Nay. Almost."

"Right. *Almost* good enough." Matt took an experimental step. "I'm still alive, aren't I? Thanks to you, Manny."

"It was nothing," the manticore assured him. "Anything for a friend."

"I'll try to return the favor some day." Matt looked around him at the merrymakers, most of whom were no longer standing. "It just makes you wonder why putative Christians are so busy breaking the Commandments."

The manticore winced. "Please! If you must use strong language—"

"Uh, yes, sorry again," Matt assured him. He'd forgotten that the creature had been so long a pawn of evil that words associated with virtue might be offensive to it. "And I suppose nobody can be openly a Chr—religious, even under the new regime. In fact, most of them probably aren't at all."

"Not so. King Boncorro has let it be known that he will not move against any who worship as they please."

"And nobody believes him. They think it might be a ruse to bring all the believers out into the open, where he can cut them down. Having been persecuted for a hundred years might tend to make a person paranoid. Besides, there's no assurance Boncorro won't be bumped off, and his throne usurped by a sorcerer—and *then* where would they be, the people who had started going to church again? Still, you should be able to tell them by the way they live—by moral conduct."

"Not under the old king," Manny said. "Even if people lived morally in private, they did not necessarily want it known."

"Morality became a matter of taste, eh? And Boncorro hasn't seen any reason to change that."

"Other than to let people who want to be moral, be so, no."

Matt nodded. "Besides, the moral folk wouldn't have left spouse and children to go trooping south to Venarra—and the kids might be in rebellion against moral parents as easily as they might be running away because they *had* no morals."

"You might say it is unpopular," Manny said thoughtfully. "Moral living is not considered to be in the best of taste. Your northern prudery never did have all that strong a hold here. The folk of ancient Reme lived lives quite scandalous by your standards. Their descendants have been somewhat tempered by the preachers, but not overly much."

"Yes, I've heard about the Roman orgies," Matt said, "but I thought they were only for the people who could afford them."

"Smaller purses yielded smaller vices," the manticore agreed. "But the city was Reme, mortal, not Rome."

"Oh, yes, I forgot—the other brother won the fight here."

" 'Other' brother?" Manny frowned down at him. "Why should Remus have been the 'other' brother? Surely that would have been Romulus!"

Matt was about to protest that the whole story of Romulus and Remus had just been a myth, but was hit by a sudden stab of uncertainty. Sure, it had been a myth in *his* universe, but here it might have been documented fact. "They were orphans who were suckled by a she-wolf, right?"

"Nay. Their nurse was a wildcat."

Matt let that sink in. If the whole story of the she-wolf were just a symbol to express the inner nature of the Romans, what did that make their analogs here? A lynx was just as much of a hunter as a wolf, but went after smaller prey, and wasn't anywhere nearly as rapacious—except in self-defense, or defense of its young. What kind of people could have established an empire just because they were good at self-defense?

Paranoids, probably. If they defended themselves all the way into North Africa, Spain, Asia Minor, and England just to make sure nobody would attack them . . .

Or diplomats?

That had a better sound to it. After all, in the myth of the founding of Rome, Romulus was the one who had started building the wall for a future city, and Remus was the one who had made fun of him and jumped over the wall to show how useless it would be. Then Romulus had killed him . . .

But here, Romulus had lost—and his city had been founded by the descendants of the man who didn't believe in walls. "So Reme has no wall to guard it."

"Wall? Around Reme?" Manny stared at him as if he were insane. "Why would the citizens have done that? 'Twas not Babylon or Ninevah, after all!"

"I thought we were discussing its morals. But if they didn't have a wall, what happened when the Etruscans attacked?"

" 'Attacked'? Surely that is too strong a word for two bands of young bloods who steal a few maidens from one another!"

Matt stared. "But . . . but Lars Porsena . . . Horatio at the bridge . . ."

"Ah! I have heard of Horatio. He it was who persuaded Lars Porsena and the other Etruscan noblemen to come confer with the elders of the Latini, under a tent on the broad plain beyond the Tiber! He it was who quieted their acrimony, who showed the Latini how the raids and even the deaths wrought by the young men's skirmishes appeared through Etruscan eyes—and Lars Porsena, not to be outdone, explained for his folk how the raids must have looked to Latini eyes. They built a bridge indeed, a bridge of understanding between people! Worse luck," he said, in a sudden change of mood. "There are better pickings for manticores when war bellows loud about the land." He licked his lips, remembering the taste of human blood.

Matt had to get his mind off that subject. "So what did they do about the raiding?"

"Why, each nation agreed to restrain and rebuke their young men, but to allow them to come courting properly, if they wished—and, to drain off their youthful urge for swordplay and glory, they established the Circus, where the young men could fight with blunted swords for fame—and even fortune, for both peoples paid into a fund to confer prizes upon the winners."

"The gladiators were free men?" Matt stared.

"Of course." Manny scowled down at him. "What would you have had them be—slaves? How valiantly would they fight, who were forced to?"

It did make a lot more sense than the way Matt's Romans had done things. "So the Remans didn't defeat the Etruscans, they married them?"

"Aye, and out of their union grew the great empire of Latruria, whose soldiers marched out to protect all the civilized world from the howling hordes of barbarians."

Well, Matt had heard that line before. "Sure—and they protected all the other nations so well that they wound up owning them."

Manny shook his head. " 'Owned' is too strong a term. They led, they showed the Greeks and the Egyptians the Latrurian way of fighting, and learned theirs; they learned from every nation they protected, and taught them the use of the legion. But 'conquered'? No. Each nation in turn asked to join the Federation of Latinis and Etruscans, and Latruria was glad to embrace them, for the barbarians were growing in numbers and skill. It was too much to ask that each nation be accorded a syllable in the name of the empire, though, so Latruria it remained—not Latrurigreegyptolibiberi—"

"I get the point," Matt said quickly. "So it was a friendly federation of states that just happened to be ruled from Reme, huh?"

Manny shrugged. "It was Horatio who built the bridge of understanding; it was his countrymen who excelled as diplomats and teachers—aye, and in commerce, too. Of course the Senate met in Reme, and just as surely, every provincial nobleman longed to see Reme before he died."

"And all voluntary and from enlightened self-interest," Matt said, feeling numb. "How about Judea?"

"Those stiff-necked fanatics?" Manny said with a snort of disapproval. "They who would not ask Reme's help, Reme wisely let be, but when the Medes—"

"Medes?" Matt frowned. "I thought the Eastern empire was Persian."

"Nay. Alexander had sounded the death knell of the Persian empire long before. 'Twas the Medes."

Matt shrugged. "One man's Mede is another man's Persian. So what did they do to the Jews?"

"Why, conquered them, of course. They pounced upon the Jews and conquered them with the Latrurian way of waging war. I ween Judeans wished then that, rather than be conquered by a member of the Federation, they had accepted the help Reme offered."

"Sure—members of the Federation would have been barred from fighting one another." Matt felt numbed. "I assume the Medes used Reme's laws and penalties?"

"All did." Manny pursed his lips, puzzled. "Why do you ask?"

"Just making a guess as to what might have happened to a man

convicted of blasphemy. Crucifixion was still the penalty, I guess—
even though it wasn't Romans who did it."

"Remans!"

"Right," Matt sighed. "Remans. What did they do about Carthage?"

Manny grinned. "Outbid them, of course, time and time again—
and Carthage would not hear of a merger. After the defeat, it was the
visionary statesman Hannibal who convinced his countrymen that if
they could not beat the Remans, they should join them. Therefore did
he send an embassy to Reme with rich gifts—"

"Including elephants?"

"Then you *have* heard the tale!"

"No, but something like it. So Carthage stayed Carthage, but
joined the Federation?"

"It did indeed, and became a mighty power for welding the empire
together with strands of gold and silver."

"Commercial colonialism got an early start here," Matt reflected
wryly. "Hard to see how an empire like that could ever fall."

Manny shrugged. "Did it fall? Or was it merely too successful? It
civilized the barbarians all about it, after all—even the Huns, when
they hacked and slew their way in; but the legions engulfed them,
punished their leaders, and sent them home with rich gifts for their
kings."

Matt stared. "The *Huns* joined the empire?"

"No, but they learned from it, and ceased to roam the steppes with
their herds. They became herders still, but within their own farms—if
you can call it a farm, when it encompasses miles and has only grazing land and fields of oats . . ."

"I'd call it a 'ranch,' " Matt said sourly. "If they managed that with
the Huns, what happened to the Gauls and the Germans?"

"Oh, they became more Reman than the Remans! Even those silly
folk on that northern island who painted themselves blue and stiffened their hair with chalk, even they began to build Reman houses
and baths, and wear Reman clothes! But they began to think that they
could fare better by themselves, and broke away from the Federation.
Then older states followed their lead and one by one declared themselves independent. Reme looked up one day and discovered that it
was alone, though it had many friends. But when those friends began
to make war upon one another, it had no justification for seeking to
stop them. Oh, they sent diplomats to plead and explain, but the
Gauls and Germans and Goths, in their pride, would not listen. Then
at last, the Vandals, in their arrogance, sacked Reme, and the day of

empire was most definitely done. Hurt and angered and bitter, the men of the Tiber turned inward, rebuilding their city and swearing to care no more about the other nations, only to take care of their own."

"So." Matt glowered down at his lute. "They finally built Romulus' wall for him, eh?"

Manny turned to him, startled. "An odd thought—but when I think of it that way, you are right. It is not a wall of bricks and stones, but of pride and bitterness—yet it is nonetheless a wall."

Matt looked up. "Where did you learn all this? You don't strike me as the bookish sort."

"I have not struck you at all," the manticore returned, "though I was tempted at first."

"Evading the question, huh?"

"Not at all." Manny drew himself up. "How do I know all this? I and my forebears have long memories, man!"

Matt stared. "You *saw*?"

"Not I myself, but my great-grandsire. Well, he did not see Romulus and Remus," the manticore admitted. "If you wish my opinion, I think they were naught but myths. But my great-grandsire came to life when the Latini were still rough tribesmen and the Etruscans already cultured gentlemen. He saw Horatio, but could not come near the tent to hear the great conference between Horatio, Lars Porsena, and their respective elders. He saw them come out of the tent in amity, though, and was severely disappointed."

Yes, because peace meant leaner pickings. Matt hurried to change the topic. "How much of it did you personally see?"

"Only the breaking apart itself." The manticore sighed. "I came to life about seven centuries ago. I thought then that it boded well for me and my kind, for state would war upon state—and I was right. Then the sorcerers came—"

"And they muzzled you?"

"Muzzled, aye, and harnessed," Manny said with disgust. "I had begun to wonder why I bothered living, till you came to amuse me."

"Nice to know I have a purpose in life." So the empire had only been dead a couple of centuries before Hardishane came marching out of Gaul to reunite the whole of Europe and squash the sorcerers, or at least drive them back far enough so that they didn't do much damage. Obviously, therefore, the sorcerers had proliferated during the breakup; Matt thought he saw their hand in the warring between Gaul and Germany and between Gaul and Iberia. He wondered about the full story of the behind-the-scenes power plays between Good and Evil.

Well, maybe he'd have time to do the research someday. Of course, he didn't have his Ph.D. yet, but it would make a great dissertation topic.

Well, he'd worry about it in the morning—say a morning a few years away. For now, the talk had calmed him; he was even beginning to feel a bit sleepy. He wasn't the only one—all about him sodden snores drenched the night and lovers lay sleeping in one another's arms. A few roisterers still teetered by the light of the moon, but from the way they swayed, they'd be down soon enough, too.

"It's looking almost safe," Matt said. "I don't suppose I could talk you into standing guard while I catch a little sleep?"

Manny shrugged. "'Tis the least I can do, considering the vast number of sheep and cattle you have bought me these last days. Not quite so tasty as—"

"Yes, well, if you're hungry, I can always find a few more," Matt said quickly.

"Do not bother; I shall behave." But Manny looked about him hungrily. "Sleep, and have no worries." He turned his back, but not quite quickly enough; Matt heard him muttering about the atrocious waste.

Well, if he couldn't trust the manticore, he could at least trust Pascal's grandfather's spell. Matt turned over, cradled his head on his arm, and didn't quite have time to be surprised at how quickly he fell asleep.

He woke up. Under the circumstances, that rated as an accomplishment.

He woke up and looked around carefully. The manticore was curled up cat style right next to him, the stinger on its scorpion tail sticking out of the ball of fur. Asleep or not, Manny was a guardian to give would-be assassins second thoughts.

Matt started to sit up . . .

The stinger whipped around and poised above him. Matt froze as Manny uncoiled enough to reveal wide-open eyes filmed with sleep. "Who stirs?"

Matt had moved barely eighteen inches, and that pretty slowly. "Light sleeper, are you?"

"Deep, but I waken quickly nonetheless. It is only you, then?"

"Just me." Matt swallowed. "I was, uh, thinking about getting up."

"Go, then. You can defend yourself when you are awake—if you do not let females of your kind hold your attention."

"That wasn't what you think."

"No, it was—for I think she pursued, and you sought to retreat. I confess I cannot understand your species."

"It's called 'morality.' "

"As I said," the manticore growled, "I understand it not."

And that, Matt mused as he plodded down toward the little stream, was the manticore in a nutshell. Not that he was all that different from any other member of the feline family—it was just that, having a human face, Matt had sort of expected some other human attributes, such as a conscience. He should have known better—the double set of teeth should have tipped him off.

It seemed that the manticore wasn't the only one lacking an understanding. Everywhere Matt went, he heard isolated sobbing. Some of the girls were curled up weeping quietly next to their snoring mates; others were sitting up alone. Not all of them, no—not even a quarter—but too many. His heart twisted with the urge to comfort, but he knew better than to intrude.

He found a copse of trees for his morning ablutions, knelt by the stream to wash his hands and face and shave with his dagger, then turned back toward the camp just as the girl in the homemade noose jumped off the stump.

Chapter
Fourteen

Matt took in the rope snaking up from the noose to pass over the limb overhead and down again to where it was tied around a lower branch, but by that time he was already running, yanking his sword out, and he managed to slash through the rope just before the girl hit the top of her arc.

She crashed to the ground with a cry of anger and despair, then rolled up to her knees, huddled and sobbing.

Matt sheathed the sword and went to her slowly, wondering what to do, what to say. "Do" was obvious enough—comfort her—but what to say while he did it?

The girl solved the problem for him. As he knelt down beside her, she moaned, "Go away! Is not my shame enough, but that you must see it, too? Gooooo!"

"I don't see any shame," Matt said firmly. "I only see a pretty girl, who could have a wonderful life, giving up when she doesn't have to."

"Does not have to!" The girl whipped about, glaring up at him. "What do *you* know about it? Losing your virginity is cause for a man to boast! For a woman, it is always cause for shame, even if she has gained a lover who will be true to her forever . . . And if he will not stay true . . ." Her face puckered, and she turned away as the tears flowed with renewed vigor. Matt held out his arms, but she ignored him, curled into a ball of misery.

"Bess!" cried another girl's voice, accompanied by a lot of thrash-

193

ing and rustling of underbrush. "Bess! Where have you gone?" There was anxiety in the voice, even fear.

"Here," Matt called, then asked, "Is your name Bess?"

His only answer was a wail of grief.

The thrashing stopped, and the other girl pushed the branches aside to stare in shock. "What have you done to her!"

"Only cut her down before she could stay up." Matt climbed to his feet and went toward the new arrival. "She won't take any comfort from me. See what you can do."

The older girl stared at him as he went by. "You are too old for her!"

"I know," Matt said over his shoulder, "but somebody else didn't." And he went on his way, resisting the temptation to look back, but hearing the soothing murmuring and the awful tearing cry as Bess threw herself into her friend's arms.

Matt hoped he would never learn the rest of the story. Had she only wakened to find her seducer gone? Or had he gone off after some other girl while Bess was still awake? Or something worse? No, all in all, Matt hoped he never found out—and if he met the man, he hoped he wouldn't know it.

As he went back toward Manny, he saw most of the people beginning to stir, sitting up with hands pressed to their heads and moaning, or crying as Bess had been crying. Here and there a couple sat up beaming into one another's faces, but there were definitely very few of them.

"I have *brought* the magistrate! You will stand up and take your oath like a man, or you will go to the Devil!"

Matt turned, staring. Half a dozen hard-faced men were standing around a disheveled teenage couple with pitchforks poised to stab.

"But I do not wish to marry!" the boy cried, and the girl's head snapped up with a look of dismay that transformed into aching hurt.

"You should have thought of that before you took her to bed," a grizzled man said grimly. "But take her to bed you did, and you will marry her or die!"

"In front of a *magistrate*?" the boy wailed.

A squire in a robe stepped up. "Aye, in front of me! I shall testify that it was justified! Up and swear, or die with my blessing!"

"You will marry, come back to the village, and settle down like the good husbandman you will become," the grim old man snapped.

"But I do not *want* to go home!" the girl wailed. "I want to go to Venarra!"

"The only way you will go there is if he goes ahead of you and finds work enough to support you both in decency! What, my lass, did you think there would be better than this for you in Venarra? You shall swear, too, or we'll spit him like a pig!"

Alarm in her face, the girl scrambled to her feet. "Come, Williken! I would not see you dead!"

The boy climbed to his feet, face thunderous.

Matt decided not to linger. As he went away, he heard the magistrate beginning to intone the ritual. He did notice that there was no mention of God—but at least there was no mention of the Devil, either.

He looked about the field, noticing a few other groups of men carrying scythes and pitchforks. Some of them had found their quarry and were holding them while they waited for the magistrate; some of them were still hunting. Matt wondered what kind of a life two kids could have if it began like this. Well, at least it would be legal . . .

But there were no priests on hand, and he saw at least two parties digging graves. Some of the fights over women had gotten out of hand. Matt shuddered as he realized he could very easily have been one of the bodies being lowered into the ground, in hasty, improvised graves with nothing to mark them. He turned away from the sight, to look down at the sound of sobbing coming from nearby . . .

And almost tripped over Pascal.

Pascal looked like the eked-out remains of a secondhand illness. His face was battered and bruised—either several small fights or one humdinger. His eyes were bloodshot, his hands trembled, and his face was the color of melted beeswax. He winced at the sound of Matt's footsteps, and Matt could imagine the headache that produced such oversensitivity. Pascal was hung over so far that he was about to fall in. His face was a container for misery, but even so, he sat with his arms about a young woman whose body was racked with sobs. His face was a study in consternation; he obviously didn't have the faintest idea what to do, but felt the need to do *something*. "I know, Flaminia, I know," he was murmuring. "It is the greatest of pains, to be scorned by one you love . . . Only two days ago—"

"Did she promise you marriage and bed you, then steal away when she thought you slept?" the young woman flared. "But no, if she had you would have rejoiced! It is different for men!"

"I would not," Pascal said with full conviction. "But we did not share a bed, only a few minutes in a garden."

"Ah, but if she had taken you to her bed, you would have found your ardor remarkably cooled in the morning!" At least the heat of the girl's anger was drying her tears.

"I did not think so then," Pascal said slowly, looking directly into her eyes. "No, I still think bedding her would not have changed me—but meeting you, hearing your voice, your mirth, your wit . . . It is strange, but Panegyra seems less than she did . . ."

Flaminia froze, staring at him. Then she recovered herself enough to snap, "So you would desert her!"

"I cannot," Pascal said simply, "for she would not exchange promises with me, no matter how many I offered. No, she is to marry a man old enough to be her father, and has no interest in breaking off with him. She enjoyed flirting with me, aye . . ." His gaze strayed. "Yes, I see it now! She was toying with me, enjoying the game, tantalizing me! Why did I not see that before?"

"Why indeed?" the girl said, but her tone had lost its steel. "Do not be too hard on her—every woman enjoys that sort of play. But did she give you reason to think she might return your ardor some day?"

"Now that I think of it, Flaminia, no," Pascal said slowly. "She told me that if I were a knight, and wealthy . . . Ah, friend Matthew," he said, blushing.

Flaminia looked up, horror-stricken. "Another who knows my shame," the girl said bitterly, and scowled back down at the ground. "I could never go back to my village now, not in such disgrace."

"None need know save yourself!" Pascal assured her.

"Two boys in three days? Be sure that one of them will tell, if the other does not! Gossip will travel back to my village, Pascal, and if you know it not, you have never lived in so small a place. Of course you have not, squire's son," she said with even more bitterness, "and you cannot know the petty cruelties of peasant women! But believe me, I do, and I shall not open myself to them! No, I cannot go home. I must go on to Venarra—but Heaven knows what the men there will make of me!" The tears overflowed again.

Pascal reached out again to gather her in. She resisted for a second, then tumbled into his arms. "There, there, sweet chuck," he soothed. "You may yet marry."

"Marry!" she wailed. "What tailor would buy soiled goods? What groom would be wanting a wanton?"

"You are only a wanton if you choose to be," Pascal said slowly. "There are men who can understand that a woman has made a mistake, has let herself believe gilded lies, but will never do so again."

"I will not, be sure of it! Lies have been my undoing—I shall never heed them again!" She pushed him away, tears still streaming down her face. "So do not tell me any more of them! Where is the man who would wed a lass who is no virgin? Where could I find such a fool?"

"I cannot be sure," Pascal said, looking straight into her eyes, "but I might be such a fool—if I were in love with the woman."

Flaminia froze, staring at him.

" 'Wise fool, brave fool,' " Matt quoted softly.

"*May* be," Flaminia said in a flat tone.

"May." Pascal nodded. "I have only known you one evening, Flaminia, and an hour this morning. But if I were to come to know such a woman as yourself, I might find myself in love, and—"

"To wed a wanton would be foolishness indeed!"

" 'Motley's the only color,' " Matt quoted, "for fools wear motley, and I realized long ago that every man is a fool in some way. The only choice any of us poor males really has is to choose which kind of fool we'll be."

Flaminia looked up at him, as if startled to realize he was still there. "Do not bear word of my folly, I beg you!"

"I wouldn't dream of it," Matt assured her, "and word just might not spread, because there's so much of this sort of thing going on. You're not exactly going to stand out in *this* crowd."

Flaminia lowered her eyes. "I am scarcely one to speak about foolishness, am I?"

"You are," Matt contradicted, "and so am I. Only those of us who have really been guilty of folly can know what we're talking about when we say the word."

Flaminia caught the trace of humor in his words and looked up with the ghost of a smile—sardonic, but a smile. "Then you, too, have been a fool?"

"Many times," Matt assured her, "and worse, I was foolish enough to keep taking one more chance on being a fool again."

He studied her face, wondering what Pascal saw in her. The nose was a little too thin, the cheeks gaunt, the eyes a little too closely set—but they were huge, those eyes, and the lashes swept across them like curtains! She certainly was not a beautiful woman, not even pretty. Handsome, maybe. It must have been her mind, her wit, and the fact that Pascal's wizard grandfather still moved in his veins enough to make him appreciate words and honor the one who could craft them into sharpness.

"Have you ever been a fool for a woman?" she went on.

"Many times," Matt assured her. "That was the chance I kept taking. The last chance was the biggest folly ever, for I fell in love with a woman far too good for me."

Flaminia stiffened. "What did she do to you?"

"Married me," Matt said, "finally—and that was *her* greatest folly. But maybe it will turn out to be as wise for her as mine was for me."

She smiled, thawing a bit. "If you are wed, what are you doing so far from her?"

"Trying to find her something she asked for," Matt told her. "Foolish of me, isn't it?"

"Perhaps," Flaminia said, with a smile that held back amusement. "But there is a point at which foolishness becomes wisdom." She turned to Pascal. "Your friend has wit."

The look Pascal returned was so blank that she laughed and leaned forward to kiss him on the cheek—and Matt noticed once again that her figure was nothing short of spectacular. Certainly enough to cloud a young man's judgment—or attract the wrong sort. "I think you'd better come along and take care of him, damsel. Pascal, you *do* need taking care of, don't you?"

"Oh, without doubt!" For once, Pascal picked up a cue. "If no one watches over me, I am apt to do very foolish things indeed!"

"Why, so am I." Flaminia climbed to her feet, pulling him up with her. "So perhaps you should stay near me and guard me from my own foolishness, too. Do you think I should let you?"

"Without question!"

"No, not without question," she said with a roguish smile. "I am apt to ask you very many questions indeed, for I have an enormous curiosity about the world around me, most especially the things I have never seen—and woe to you if you answer me falsely!"

"I shall be careful to be honest," Pascal assured her, "and if my honesty is not always truthful, it shall be no fault of mine."

Flaminia frowned at him, then glanced at Matt. "Can you tell me what he means? How can honesty not be truthful?"

"Why," Matt said, "because he'll honestly tell you everything he knows and believes, but he might be wrong. After all, if you ask him about the queen's capital of Bordestang, I'm sure he'll tell you every rumor he has heard about it—but he hasn't seen it himself, so some of the rumors may be false."

Flaminia laughed—a sound with the beauty of song—and pressed Pascal's arm close. "I think you may have some ghost of wit yourself, friend Pascal! Come, let us put this tiresome crowd behind us and find the road to the south by ourselves!"

"They shall catch up with us," Pascal warned, falling into step beside her.

"Perhaps," Flaminia said, "but I think they will be better company by that time. We can wait for them in the shade when the sun grows hot."

"Better listen to her," Matt advised. "She's no fool."

But as they started to pick their way through the litter of unconscious bodies, a beefy young man came reeling up with a lopsided grin. "Ah, there you are, my betrothed! Come, kiss me good morning, then!"

He was nicely calculated to inspire ardor in the most finicky of women—muscles like melons, guileless blue eyes in a handsome ruddy face, blond hair, and a devil-may-care jauntiness. Unfortunately, those blue eyes were bloodshot, and he was also unshaven, smelled like a brewery that had been converted into a cockroach-haven hotel, and was weaving and stumbling in what he no doubt thought was a straight line.

Flaminia froze, the color draining from her face. Pascal stared in alarm as the big young man reached out for her, chuckling.

She slapped his hand aside, her color returning and flaming high. "Nay, Volio! Do you think you can seduce me, then leave me to bed one doxie after another and come back to take me again?"

"Aye." The grin turned nasty. "For you are mine, are you not? We are betrothed!"

"No longer! Oh, if only you had given me a ring, so that I might throw it back in your face!" Flaminia blazed. "I shall not be your doxie, neither wed nor unwed!"

"But you must." The nasty grin widened to gloating, and he reached out again. "For if you do not wed me, then you shall be a slut. Come, chick."

"Go!" she cried. "Go, and never come near me again! For I had rather be a fallen woman than a betrayed wife!"

"Why, then, a fallen woman you are," he said, "and shall fall to me again."

Flaminia caught the reaching hand, twisted it sharply, and bit.

Volio howled, eyes staring in shock. Flaminia leaped back with a cry of triumph, letting go of the hand. "You shall not touch me again!"

"Oh, but I shall!" Volio shouted, and the bleeding hand slapped the side of her head, hard. Flaminia fell back with a cry of pain; Matt just barely caught her. But Pascal howled with outrage and leaped in, slamming a fist into Volio's face.

Volio fell back, staring in utter stupefaction, pressing his hand to the fresh new pain. Then he brought his hand away, saw the blood on it that streamed from his nose, and came for Pascal with a snarl, swinging a haymaker.

Pascal blocked with his left as if he were parrying a rapier cut and slammed a hard right into Volio's belly. The big young man staggered back with a grunt of surprise, and Pascal followed it up, whirling his right fist like a rapier, then slamming it into the side of Volio's head.

But Volio blocked, as if he was catching a sword blow on a buckler, then riposted with his right and caught Pascal a blow that sent him reeling back a few paces. Volio followed hard, but Pascal ducked just in time, his shoulder slamming into Volio's belly. Pascal straightened up, staggered, but held Volio on his shoulder just long enough to dump him in a heap from five feet up. Then he stepped back, shaking his head to clear it as Volio caught his breath then scrambled up, snarling, "None of your peasant's wrestling tricks!"

"Peasant!" Pascal cried, affronted, and feinted twice to draw Volio's left, then stepped in to crack a blow across his cheek.

"No!" Flaminia cried, surging up out of Matt's arms toward the fighters—but Matt held her back. "No, damsel! You'll just get them hurt more! Don't worry, if it gets too bad, I'll break it up."

"Then why not break it up now!" she demanded.

"They need it," Matt said simply, though he meant it differently for each man.

They had obviously both been trained—but as swordsmen, not as boxers. Right fists whirled high in figure eights as if they were wrapped around hilts, lefts blocked and counterpunched, and most of the blows were aimed at the chest. Every now and then one of the boys slipped and caught the other on the cheek or chin, but it was definitely by accident. Matt began to think he was going to have to break it up, after all—they were causing each other a lot of pain, but no damage, nothing even remotely decisive. Flaminia wept, crying Pascal's name, and kept trying to struggle free to help him, but Matt held on tightly. "Don't worry—pretty soon they'll both drop from sheer exhaustion. Neither of them is in the greatest shape this morning."

Just then Pascal leaped in past Volio's guard, threw his arms around his chest, lifted and whirled, throwing Volio to the ground. The young man surged back up to his feet with a bellow. "Villain! Would you use a peasant's wrestling tricks with me again? Have at you!" And he charged with a roundhouse swing.

Pascal ducked under it, seized Volio's knee and straightened up, heaving. Volio squalled and went flying backward, arms windmilling.

He landed with a heavy, meaty sound, and lay struggling, gasping for breath again.

Pascal stood over him, eyes alight with victory, fists clenched, waiting.

"Oh!" Flaminia gasped, hand coming to her mouth.

Matt kept his hold tight.

Volio floundered to his feet, growling, "Would you fight for her honor when she has lost it?"

"Foul blot!" Pascal shouted, and swung an uppercut at Volio's jaw.

Unfortunately, Volio straightened up just then, and a little too fast; Pascal's fist caught him right in the solar plexus. His eyes bulged and he stiffened, gasping for air like a fish.

Pascal stared, frightened by what he had done.

"He can't breathe!" Matt shouted. "Put him out of his misery until his lungs start working again!"

Pascal came unfrozen, slamming the uppercut at Volio's jaw again. This time he connected, and the beefy young man's eyes glazed. He slumped and landed with a very solid thud.

Flaminia tore loose from Matt's hold with a cry of distress and ran to Pascal. "Oh! Are you hurt? Surely you must have suffered sorely!"

"Nay, not I." Pascal grinned, enjoying the touch of her hands on his bruises. "Look to your fiancé, if you must aid one who suffers."

"Him?" Flaminia turned and kicked the inert fighter, hard. "He is no fiancé of mine, and I have told him that! How I hope he does suffer, for he has deserved every blow you gave him, and ten more for each!"

"Oh, I think he'll be aching aplenty when he comes to." Matt knelt beside Volio and checked his pulse, just to make sure. "No permanent harm done." Of course not—neither of them knew the first thing about unarmed combat. There might have been accidents, sure, but barring that, there had been no danger. "Count yourself revenged, damsel—as much as a woman can be." Matt looked up. "But he might have friends. I suggest that when he does come to, the two of you might be smart to be a mile or so away?"

"Yes!" Flaminia whirled to Pascal, eyes wide with fright. "You did not know! He is the son of a knight, one who lives not ten miles from here! When that one discovers how his son has been hurt, he is sure to send his men after you!"

Pascal registered alarm, but said gallantly, "I shall not go unless I guard you as I do."

Matt was nodding. "The son of a knight and the son of a squire?

No wonder you were both fighting the same way—you were both trained in swordplay!"

"Of course," Pascal said, surprised.

"But this time, the squire's son won out, because he hadn't been worried about lowering himself to learn wrestling from the peasants. I guess you had a good education after all, Pascal."

"You must flee!" Flaminia cried. "If they catch you, they will flog you within an inch of your life—or beyond!"

Pascal seemed shaken by that, but he still spoke gallantly. "If die I must, then die I will, so long as it saves you from that lecher's paws!"

Flaminia almost melted—right into Pascal's arms. For a moment their bodies were twined tightly together as she reached up to give him a long, steadily deepening kiss. Pascal's hands stuck out behind her back, taken by surprise, as if they didn't know what to do—but they learned quickly, cradling Flaminia's waist and shoulders, then tightening and beginning to caress.

Matt looked away, whistling cheerfully.

Finally, Flaminia broke the kiss, breathing, "Oh, you are the bravest and most noble of squires! But you must not risk yourself for me!" Pascal started to object, but she laid a finger across his lips. "Fear not—I shall not turn back to that oaf Volio. I shall run away to the greenwood instead, and join a band of outlaws!"

"That doesn't exactly sound like all that safe an alternative," Matt warned.

"Not unless I run away with her," Pascal said stoutly. "Come, Flaminia! Shall we turn outlaw together?"

Flaminia hesitated, torn between a gush of gratitude and a draught of fear for him.

"Take him up on it," Matt advised. "You can change your minds about your destination once you're on the road—but for now, you would definitely both find it healthier someplace else."

"I shall not go if you do not," Pascal warned. "No woman is safe without an escort in this land."

Flaminia gave him a slow and sultry smile as she swayed back into his arms again. "Why, then, I shall go with you, or you with me—but I enjoin you to tell me if you tire of my company, and tell me straightaway, not by little hints and slights! Promise me that!"

"Why, then, I promise," Pascal said slowly, "but how if I do *not* tire of you?"

"Why, then, do not tell me," she said merrily, and gave him a quick but very sound kiss, then pirouetted out of his arms, though still holding onto one hand. She looked back over her shoulder at Matt. "Will you wander with us, minstrel?"

"Yes, I think I will," Matt said slowly. "After all, I'm traveling your way."

But they hadn't even heard the end of his sentence—they were both gazing into each other's eyes, laughing, a little breathlessly, as they set out toward the road.

On the road, they passed small groups of young folk, with one or two of their elders, heading back north, looking wan and washed-out, or grim and morose. For them, at least, the party had come to an end before they reached Venarra. Matt wondered if they might not turn out to be the lucky ones—especially when they passed by an acre or so of chewed-up ground that had obviously been the camping place of a group that had gone before them. Off at the side, near the trees, were five rectangular mounds of earth with small pieces of board at one end of each. No crosses, not in a country that was only just beginning to think about bringing religion out into the open again—just pieces of board. Matt took a quick detour from Pascal and Flaminia to see if there were any words carved on the improvised headstones. There were—all variations on, "Here lies the body of a youth who left home to seek fame and fortune in the king's town." Just that—no injunction to pray for the soul, of course, and, thank Heaven, no stern moral lesson about their fates. But no names, either. These kids—and maybe some midlife-crisis cases, too—had been buried by the local villagers, the few who had stayed at home. Their road companions hadn't even cared enough to stay around to give them a funeral.

Matt was very glad to catch up with Pascal and Flaminia again.

With the resiliency of youth, the two were laughing at one another's jokes as they argued with mock earnestness over the comparative merits of line dances and circle dances. Within minutes the topic had changed to the color of the stream they were passing over—whether it was grayish-blue or bluish-gray. They debated the case with great seriousness, each one coming up with a reason that was more ludicrous than the other's for about three rounds, before Flaminia began to break up into giggles and Pascal burst into laughter. Matt followed along behind, letting the smile grow, and letting their humor and camaraderie warm the chilly spot within him.

Chapter
Fifteen

The sun peeked over the horizon, the huge gates opened, and the crowd of runaways poured through into Venarra with a delighted shriek.

It was echoed by a collective hum from the crowd waiting inside the gates; it sounded suspiciously like "Yum!"

Each of the mature men was instantly visited by a prosperous-looking, if flashy, city man or woman; each mature woman was accosted, too. If couples tried to stay together, the city folk wheedled and cajoled and showered them with flattery that gradually pulled them apart. That happened with the young folk, too, though much more quickly. Girls with shining eyes were listening, entranced, to the blandishments of older, motherly looking women—and if the paint on their faces was a little too thick or too flashy, well, wasn't that the way all city women looked? Matt picked up a few odd sentences as he hustled his two charges through the ring of human sharks, firmly keeping them in hand.

"Yes, dear, a place to stay till you've learned your way around Venarra," one grandmotherly sort was saying. "Clean sheets, and a way to earn some money—sisters to show you how things are done—and ever such handsome gentlemen to come calling!"

"But why are you willing to help us so?" a starry-eyed girl was asking another woman decked in costume jewelry.

"Why, bless you, child, welcoming newcomers is my pastime," the woman gushed. "It is my charity!"

The clamor of promises of glamorous living even caught Flaminia's ear. She twisted about to try to watch the beldame who was professing altruism. "Why, how good of them! Why do I not go to her house, friend Matthew?"

"Because once you're in, she'll never let you out until you're well and truly corrupted," Matt said grimly. "The charity she has in mind is for you to give her every penny the handsome men give to you in return for your sexual favors—and most of them won't be terribly handsome, or very young, either. It's a business doing pleasure with her."

Flaminia paled, but wasn't willing to admit her mistake so readily. "What are they telling the boys, then?"

"The same thing, for some of them—and their customers won't all be rich old women. For others—"

"It's an easy job, mate!" A flashy juvenile crowded up to Pascal. "All you have to do is take this bundle across town to a house on Fleet Street!"

Pascal looked tempted, lifting a hand, but Matt said, "And you'll be just fine, as long as nobody catches you—but if the Watch should happen to look in that bag, you'll spend the next couple of years in prison, and you won't even be able to tell them who hired you."

"What business is it of yours, mate?" the youth asked, turning savagely on Matt.

"My friends are always my business," Matt said, "sometimes even my enemies are." He let his anger out in a wolfish grin. "Want to be my enemy, bucko?"

The youth stepped back, trepidation in his eyes.

"Yuh. I do," growled a basso behind Matt's shoulder.

Matt turned and found himself facing an expanse of bulging, hairy chest with a row of buttons on one side and buttonholes on the other. He followed the breastbone up to an unshaven chin, a cauliflower nose, and two gleaming piggy eyes over a gap-toothed grin. Matt felt his stomach hit bottom and bounce back up, but he scowled his fiercest and said, "You know what you're getting into?"

"Yuh," the big beefy man said, and a huge fist came out of nowhere and struck sparks inside Matt's head just before a wall came up and slammed into his back. He straightened his legs, pushing back against the wall to hold him up while the ringing in his ears faded to the point where he could hear the big man's guttural laughter while he held a furious, flailing Pascal six inches off the ground. Flaminia's mouth was wide open, but Matt couldn't hear anything over the big guy's hooting.

Except, maybe, the ringing of his lute strings when the instrument bumped into his side as he stepped away from the wall. He caught it and held it up—miraculously, it was undamaged. It must have swung wide about him as he shot backward, and thus slapped into his stomach instead of the wall. Matt staggered up to the giant, slipping the strap off his shoulder and reminding himself that he was a belted knight. That meant, among other things, that in this universe he could hit a lot harder than anyone his size ought to be able to.

He staggered up to the thug, holding out the lute. "Here—hold this."

The man blinked with surprise, dropped Pascal—Flaminia cried out and ran to pick him up—and took the lute. Matt nodded and slammed a right into his jaw.

The big man dropped the lute—fortunately, it landed on Pascal—and staggered back. His buddies shouted in anger and charged in. Matt ducked the first punch, kicked the legs out from under the other punk, then straightened up just in time for the first guy's left to smack into his chest.

Of course, the hoodlum had been aiming for his face, but the blow still knocked Matt back, staggering—and the big guy bellowed and waded in, slab fist winding up for a very final punch.

Matt knew when he was outnumbered. Knight or not, up against three seasoned street fighters he didn't stand a chance, unless he pulled his sword and started slicing—and he was reluctant to kill these guys without knowing why they deserved it. Also, there was the little problem of the local constabulary, who might take a very dim view of a tourist killing off three of the locals, even if they weren't paying taxes. That meant that there was no way out but magic. If it worked here.

But if he was going to run a spell, he had to do it fast—he ducked, and the big guy's first haymaker whizzed by overhead, but the next one would probably hit. Matt stepped inside and cracked another uppercut into his opponent's jaw. That would slow him down, but not for long—and Matt caught a jab in the short ribs on the way out. Wheezing, he nonetheless managed to chant,

> " 'Neath my clenched-up fist, like diorite, he fell,
>   And I left my views on Art hammered hard upon the heart
>   Of this mammoth thug, whose friends all ran pell-mell."

The big guy snarled and came at him again. Matt gulped, hoping the spell would work right, feinted with his left and, as the big guy lifted his right to block, bopped him soundly. The big guy stared at him for a second before he toppled.

The other two punks stared in surprise, too, at their buddy's inert body.

"So much for the main course." Matt pushed up his sleeves and started for the pair. "Now, about dessert . . ."

They didn't even stay to curse him—they just ran.

Matt watched them go, almost trembling with relief. Either his magic had worked ever so slightly, or he really had managed to fake out the big guy, and seeing him beat the unbeatable had scared his sidekicks—all thanks to Matt being a knight. Presumably having been knighted by a legendary emperor overcame even the antimagic field of Latruria.

But then, that was the way his magic had been working here—if it had been. There was every possibility that reciting verses was merely giving him an extra edge of self-confidence, by his believing he was working magic. If so, he intended to do nothing to puncture that illusion.

He turned back to his two young charges. Pascal was holding Flaminia, Flaminia was holding the lute, and they were both staring at him with wide, frightened eyes. "You are a more powerful fighter than I took you for, friend Matthew," Pascal said, but Flaminia blurted, "How did you manage *that*?"

"Not as well as I could have," Matt said grimly, "or I wouldn't have had to start fighting. Come on, let's get away from here. The Watch will be swooping down any second now."

"But why?" Pascal protested. "The fight is over!"

"Safest time for them," Matt assured him. Besides, he knew that if any sorcerer had been paying attention, they would have picked up the traces from the spell he had just worked and know there was a rival magic worker in town. He was very sure that King Boncorro maintained a twenty-four-hour magic sentry—he must, since he was still alive and on his throne.

Not that it really mattered, of course. Boncorro, or one of his advisers, seemed to have known where Matt was every step of the way. In fact, it was a good possibility that the trio Matt had just chased off was one more group sent out to kill him.

He didn't really think so, though. They hadn't come close enough to success. No, this was just the same kind of reception that greeted any new arrival in Venarra.

As they entered one of the streets that led away from the plaza around the gate, they passed one of the more mature couples who had been with them. The woman, with her hands on her hips, was accusing, "You said you had gold in your purse!"

"I did." The man held up the ragged stumps of two thongs tied to his belt. "The louse cut them through, and I never even knew!"

"A fine guardian you are," the woman said with withering sarcasm.

Flaminia plucked Matt's sleeve and pointed. "Yonder goes one of the beldames who greeted us, with three of the girls in our party in tow! Let us follow them—mayhap she will give us lodging for the night!"

So she didn't share Matt's skepticism. He waged a brief struggle within himself, then decided that she couldn't come to *too* much harm with himself and Pascal near. "Okay. Let's go look."

They followed the quartet down a broad concourse, keeping their distance. The madame was pointing out the sights. "Yonder coach, with the team and the footmen, is that of the Contessa of Mopona— see you her crest on the door? And yonder is the Theater of the Comedia."

But the girls were still watching the coach with great, huge eyes, waiting for a peek at the grand lady within.

They went on down the boulevard until the girls were dizzy with the sights—then the older lady led them into a side street that very quickly turned into a maze of lanes.

"This city is grown much less grand of a sudden," Flaminia said, staring about them.

Laundry was pegged to ropes that ran across the street. Peddlers hawked their wares, and grimy children played on the cobbles. The procuress wound her way adroitly between them. Matt slowed the pace, keeping the party just barely in sight.

"We will lose them!" Flaminia said impatiently.

"No," Matt said, "but we don't want them to know we're following."

They passed another mature couple they knew from the road, being guided by an enthusiastic young city man. "Only a little farther, and you shall see the bridge for yourself!"

"Then we can truly buy it, and charge toll to everyone who would pass?" The man fairly licked his chops at the prospect of riches.

"Indeed you can! I shall give you a lawyer's deed to it!"

"But it must cost a fortune," the woman said anxiously.

"Not a bit! It will cost you only . . . How much did you say you had in your purse?"

Matt hurried his charges ahead.

"Can they truly buy a bridge?" Pascal asked, eyes round.

"No," Matt said, "but they can lose every penny they have, trying."

"We must stop them!" Flaminia protested.

"If we do, we'll lose the madame and her flock of gullible little geese," Matt told her, "and I think they're about to lose something more than cash."

Flaminia blanched and hurried on.

They turned three more corners, then came out into a narrow street of tottering houses. It was dusk, and lean, wasted-looking men were coming out to hang red lanterns over every other doorway.

"Here is my house!" The beldame waved at a doorway—and waved harder.

The ferret-faced man in the doorway whisked his lantern behind his back, then pasted on a smile and bowed. "Welcome, mistress! And have you brought us guests, then?"

"Aye, Smirkin—three lonely girls, fresh from the country!"

"Fresh meat for the grinder, you mean." Matt came up right behind her.

"Away, rogue!" The woman turned on him sharply. "Get you hence, or I'll call the Watch!"

"Why, 'tis the minstrel!" one of the girls said in surprise.

"Ask her what she sells in there," Matt told them.

"I sell nothing!" The woman drew herself up indignantly.

"Don't you really?" Matt climbed the steps. "That's funny. Half the houses on this street have red lanterns, and . . ." Suddenly, he yanked Smirkin through the doorway. The man squalled, bringing up his hands to ward off a blow—and one of them held a red lantern. Unlit, but his other hand held a tinderbox.

"She's in the same business everyone else is here," Matt told the girls. "The red lantern is the sign of a brothel. She's right about one thing—she doesn't sell anything, only rents them by the hour."

"What is that?" one girl said, eyes wide.

"Women," Matt said, "for men to do whatever they want with, short of killing." He turned to the proprietress. "Or do you allow that, too?"

"You lie, sir!" she said indignantly.

"No, but all the girls you bring home do lie—lie down, that is, or suffer until they're willing to." He turned back to the country girls. "Let's go. There's someplace better for you than this."

"Do not believe him!" the madame cried. "He seeks to use you for his own purposes!"

The girls hesitated, uncertain.

The door of the house across the way burst open and a half-undressed man shot out, with a huge burly brute behind him. "Be off with you! If you've no cash to pay, you can't have her!"

"But I had money!" the man bleated. "Gold! She took it while I was undressing!"

"The more fool you, for letting her know where it was," the bouncer said contemptuously. "Go on, get your clothes on and get out of here!"

The girls turned pale.

"Yes, that is my business, too!" Suddenly, the nice old granny had turned into a sneering harridan. "But you'll come to it sooner or later, my chicks, so why not sooner?"

"Never!" the tallest girl cried indignantly.

"No? Is there a one of you that's still virgin, after that carnival trek you've taken? Where do you think you'll find husbands? What work do you think you can find in a town overflowing with girls new from the country?" She shook her head. "Oh, no, sweetings—this is the only bed you'll find, and the only bread you'll eat. You can starve until you're willing to take it, until you throw yourselves into the trade with no training or bracing—or you can come in now, and learn the business properly and at a decent pace."

The girls shrank back, looking very frightened.

"There are other choices," Matt told them. "Let's go." He strode down the steps and away. They followed him with relief.

"Go then, fools!" the harridan screeched at them. "But remember where this house is, for you'll need it within the week!" And to Matt, "A pox on you, minstrel! A pox that you will give to them! Did you think him a rescuer, girls? No! He's just a pimp, come to steal you from a procuress!"

"No, I'm not," Matt told the girls. "I'm not going to keep you, just find you a safe haven for a couple of days."

The girls still looked uncertain, but followed him, shuddering at the harridan's screeches behind them.

As they came back into the high street, a sergeant came strutting along. "Hup! Hup! That's right, lads, at the barracks they'll give you fine clothes like mine, and each of you a bright new florin! Then dinner, and bed with a score of brothers!"

Eager young men trooped after him.

"Why, there is Berto!" one girl cried. "And Samolo, and Gian! Are they going to be soldiers, then?"

"Looks like it," Matt said, "and the sergeant will become a lot less friendly as soon as they're safely in his barracks. Even so, they've got a better choice than you girls have—at least they'll have room, board, and safety."

"And all for nothing but the risk of their lives," Flaminia said darkly.

"I think I would prefer that," said the thinnest girl, with a trembling voice.

"Where will you take us, minstrel?" one girl asked.

"To the . . ." Matt's voice trailed off. He had been about to say "the church," that always being a safe place for girls needing sanctuary and advice—but in Latruria the churches were boarded up, and the few priests still ministering to the faithful weren't about to go public just yet.

"We'll find you jobs," Matt told them. "You can clean house, make beds, cook meals, that sort of thing."

"But that is what we fled our village to escape!" one girl protested.

"Where is the wealth of Venarra, the continual parties and fine clothes and dancing?" asked another.

"In the palace," Matt said, "and the mansions of the wealthy. Rumor lied to you, damsels."

The youngest girl began to weep. "To come so far . . . to have lost . . . have lost . . ."

"Your home is still there," Matt told her, ignoring what else she might have been saying. "If worse comes to worst, you can join one of the bands of people going north."

"Not the wasted, haunted ones!" the tallest girl cried, looking up in horror.

"Better to join them before you're washed out, too," Matt said, "but in the meantime, if you want to be able to earn the money to enjoy the life of Venarra, we'd better find you some honest work."

They trooped along behind him in silence for a few minutes. Then the oldest girl said bitterly, "We shall have to get it ourselves, shall we not? No one will get it for us!"

"No." Matt shook his head sadly. "No one will. You have to pay for what you get, one way or another—and if anybody tells you he can get it for you without any cost to you, he lies. He may not know it, but he lies."

Matt may have known the ways of cities better than the girls did, but that didn't mean he knew the ways of *this* city. He took them into a tavern, to ask a few discreet questions and learn the lay of the land—but the questions must not have been discreet enough, for the jolly-looking man he was asking only laughed and said, "New come to Venarra, are you?"

"Does it show so badly as that?" Matt asked, deflated.

"I'd know you in a minute, and I've only been here a year and some months myself!"

"Then there *are* jobs!"

"Yes, if the Burglars Guild lets you learn the trade."

Matt stared. "Burglars Guild?"

"Yes. We keep needing new members—so many of them go to the king's gaol, and half of those to the noose. No, there's always room for a newcomer who's willing to learn to steal. You and I, now, minstrel, might do great business together—you holding the attention of a crowd while I slip into their homes . . ."

"Well, maybe some other time," Matt said, abashed. "How about girls' jobs? Is there a Housemaids Guild?"

The burglar gave him a tolerant smile. "There is, if you're looking for that line of work—though I'd scarcely call it a guild, more of a gossip club."

"Better than nothing," Matt sighed. "Where do I find them?"

"In the Street of Rough Hands. Can't miss them—there are always young women standing about the door, waiting to be sent out."

"And older women, trying to recruit them into a different sort of housework?"

The burglar grinned broadly. "No, the Housemaids Guild keeps a couple of bruisers about to scare off the jackals. Your young charges will be as safe there as anywhere. The young man, now, might do well to join my guild."

Pascal glanced about nervously.

"Thanks," Matt said, "but he's not limber enough for second-story work."

Pascal looked up indignantly.

"Anyone can learn to cut a purse," the man offered.

"Yes, but I'm afraid that if he starts cutting leather, he'll get carried away and start cutting skin."

"Ah." The burglar nodded. "No, that kind of thing is out of our purview. He might try the Murderers Guild."

"Yes, of course." Matt was feeling increasingly nervous. "Say, do you folks take care of armed robbery, too?"

"No, that's the Thieves Guild."

Matt could imagine what the jurisdictional disputes must have been like. "You can only take things when people aren't around, huh?"

"Not around, or sleeping. We can steal, but cannot rob."

"I don't suppose you set fires, either—or steal people?"

"The Arsonists Guild and the Kidnappers Guild?" The burglar scowled. "You are not really looking for that sort of work, are you?"

"No, but I'd like to know what to steer clear of. Any kind of crime that isn't organized in this city?"

"None that I know of, no," the burglar admitted. "Still, there is always someone about who will dream up something new."

Matt shuddered at the notion and decided to get out of town before someone invented racketeering. "Well, thanks for all the info." He turned away, then stopped and turned back. "I don't suppose the heads of all these guilds have the same last name, do they?"

"Only the Thieves Guild, the Burglars Guild, and the Murderers Guild," the burglar said. "They're Squelfs. The Gamblers Guild, now, with the Pimps Guild and the Peddlers guild, they're Skibbelines. All the rest are DiGorbias."

The girls shivered, wide-eyed, and Pascal swallowed heavily. Matt didn't blame them—he was feeling the same sort of chill inside that they must have felt—but his curiosity was piqued one more time. "The Peddlers Guild? Peddlers are criminals here?"

"Only the ones who sell you what you can't get in the shops."

"Oh." Matt couldn't help himself. "Uh, what *do* they sell?"

The burglar's grin widened even more. "Anything you want."

"Right." Matt turned away, "Thanks, friend! Come on, folks, let's go."

They found the Street of Rough Hands just as the sun was setting. The bouncer snarled at them, but when Matt explained that he had brought some young women who were looking for honest work, the bruiser sent one of the loitering girls in to call the boss. She came bustling out, a matronly sort in a blue dress and white apron, saw the new arrivals, said "Ah!" with a nod, and came down to look them over from head to toe. "Well, you'll need a bath and a chance to wash your clothes, at the least. Go to the house next door, where the house warden will give you supper and a bed until you can find your own quarters. We'll take it from your first week's wages, of course, and we take one part in ten from all your wages after that—one part in five for as long as you live with us. Anyone hires you, they pay us, not you, and we pay you your share. If we catch you setting up work on your own, you're still in the guild, but out of our services. Any questions? No? Off with you, then!"

Bemused, the girls turned away. The boss woman turned to Flaminia with a scowl. "You don't wish to go with them?"

"Not yet," Flaminia hedged. "The minstrel needs our help with other business first, I think."

"Well, you look honorable enough." The matron gave Matt a quick inspection. "You brought these poor deluded lambs to our doorstep, anyway. We can't take them all, mind you, but we do what we can."

That explained why *they* hadn't had a recruiter just inside the gate. "I understand. Not all that much call for housemaids, is there?"

"Oh, there is work aplenty!" the woman said. "The town has swollen enormously since good King Boncorro came to the throne! The nobility have come flocking in—bored to death in the country, and eager for the delights of the city, now that there's no chance the king will demand their wives in his bed, or themselves for his arena. So they have left their lands in the care of stewards and come to Venarra for excitement—and they all need food, and furniture, and new houses, and clothing, and all manner of silliness."

"So there's a sudden increase in the number of tradesmen and merchants?"

"Yes, and they are all growing rich off the trade—so their wives are wanting to spend more time in the shops and less at the housekeeping. No, there are jobs aplenty for girls who can clean and mend—but there are far more girls coming in. The peasant folk wish the exciting life, too, and far too many of them find it, but on the wrong end."

"Yes," Matt said grimly. "The noblemen want to be entertained, don't they? And there aren't enough clean and open amusements."

"There are diversions aplenty, young man!" the matron said indignantly. "You'll find you have far too much competition here—there is a minstrel on every street corner! Aye, and a theater in every boulevard, though their plays are very bad, and more what you would expect to see in a brothel than on a stage."

"Yes," Matt said grimly, "the pimps always learn early on that the theater is a great place to advertise, on stage or off. Isn't anybody trying to keep them out?"

"Trying, aye." The matron gave him a hard smile. "Has anyone ever succeeded?"

"Well, they have in my country—but it took a hundred years or so. How about music—concerts of a dozen musicians together? That's harder to corrupt."

"Oh, there are whole bands of musicians playing in great halls every night, and livery stables, fencing masters, taverns for the lowborn and parties in palaces for the highborn."

"But you don't recommend the new arrivals try to find jobs in them?"

The matron made a face. "Certainly not for the girls! You have heard what I think of the theaters, and the troupes of dancers are every bit as much apt to abuse as to foster! Music's another thing, I suppose, but it means learning to play or sing really well, and that's no quick undertaking, as I am sure you know."

"Yes, it did take me a few years to learn to play the lute." Matt had needed something to fill the spare time while he waited for Alisande to set the date.

"The dancers and players are poorly paid," the woman said, "but a living is a living, I suppose."

"Yes, if that's all they're after." Matt frowned. "But if the plays and dances are really bad, they must be pretty unhappy about doing them."

"Bitter, I would say—quite bitter." The matron shook her head, looking angry, almost frightened. "At least, the few who have come to me for employment have complained of it. They tell me there are a few of the players who will never leave the theater, they are so ardent about it—but my ex-player women think those ardent ones to be mad, or nearly so. Certainly they will rage and rant, at a moment's notice, about the paucity of mind in the folk who come to see them, and the poverty they must endure—and what they call the hollowness of the soul."

"Yes, I've run into artists like that," Matt said, "though most of ones I've talked to have been painters and poets." He didn't mention that he had once thought of himself as being one of them. "They start feeling that there is no substance in their culture for them to draw on."

The matron frowned up at him. "Oddly put—but it has the sound of sense, even though I think I do not understand all of what you mean. I only wish that I could provide a living for all these poor souls who feel themselves stretched so on the rack of fashion."

"But you can't," Matt said sympathetically. "Too many girls and not enough work, and you'd stop making profit."

"Profit? What is that?" the woman said impatiently. "We make a living, and so do they."

Matt's opinion of her went up. "Are you open to donations?"

"Donations?" The woman stared. "You mean gifts of money? Whatever for?"

"To help protect more of them." Matt fished a gold piece out of his purse and pressed it into her hand.

She stared at it, then looked up at him, her composure shaken. "Thank you, young man—but I'll hold this a week before I spend any of it, so you can come back for it if you find you have need."

Matt nodded. "Very prudent. But I'm sure I won't need it back."

"I'll wait all the same," she said doggedly. "Keep it or not, I thank you—your heart's in the right place."

"Thanks." Matt gave her a sardonic smile. "Like you, I just wish I could do more." He turned back to Pascal and Flaminia. "Time to start pub-crawling, folks."

"What is a 'pub'?" Flaminia asked.

"Anyplace where they serve beer and wine to people with more money than sense." He turned back to the matron. "Thanks ma'am—and good night."

She watched them go, brow puckered with worry, shaking her head.

Pascal and Flaminia seemed rattled. "There is far more wickedness in this city than I had thought," the young man said.

Matt shrugged. "What would you expect, when it was the capital of evil for so long? Interesting to hear her call Boncorro 'good'—but even if he were, he couldn't reform his town completely in just a few years."

"And from what I have heard," Flaminia said, "he is *not* dedicated to Goodness—it is simply that he is not dedicated to Wickedness, either."

"But his reign has produced more!" Pascal burst out. "Or as much, but of a different sort! It has brought the noblemen flocking into town to prey upon the innocent, and the country folk in to be their meat!"

"That's one side of it, yes," Matt said, frowning, "and as far as that goes, Boncorro's try at a worldly culture without any teaching of values *has* produced a great deal of emotional suffering and exploitation of the weak—but on the other hand, nobody's starving or homeless, or at least very few."

"I have seen many beggars," Pascal objected.

"But they have been far from starvation," Flaminia pointed out.

Matt nodded. "Plus, I haven't seen any dead bodies in the streets, though maybe that only means that it's the wrong time of day. No, I think I'll have to meet this king and talk with him a bit before I make up my mind about him."

"Meet the king?" Flaminia looked up, frightened. "Surely you are jesting!"

"He must be," Pascal agreed. "Why, to meet the king might be as dangerous as it would be exciting!"

"No, I really do want to," Matt said.

"*I* do not," Flaminia said certainly.

"But you shall," said a voice behind Matt's ear, and he was just beginning to turn when the pain burst on top of his head and spread through it. He fought to stay conscious even as he felt himself falling, but all the good it did was to give him a quick glimpse of Pascal struggling in the hands of one bruiser while another swung a truncheon, and to let him hear Flaminia's screams as two more men closed in on her. He was just realizing that they wore livery when the darkness closed in.

Chapter
Sixteen

Matt's first blurred impression was of a lot of cobblestones. After a minute he realized from the discomfort that he was lying on more than cobbles. Then he realized that there wasn't anyone anywhere near, though there did seem to be a goodly number off in the distance, there—lined up, pointing, gesticulating.

Then the headache hit.

Actually, it had been there all the time—it just required a certain level of consciousness to feel it. His vision stayed blurred, and he gasped with the agony of it. He begged his pulse not to beat, because every throb made his head split all over again.

Fortunately, he didn't beg in rhyme.

Through the blinding pain one thought bored: he couldn't possibly function with his head splitting, and there was only one way to make it stop. What the hell? Whoever the chief sorcerer was around here, he knew where he was, anyway.

> "When headache's pounding till you're done,
>   Get ibuprofen on the run!
>   Instant-acting, long and wide,
>   Analgesic, be inside!"

The improvement startled him. Suddenly, the headache was only a dull, persistent pain at the back of his head—not as successful a spell as it would have been if he had tried the same verse outside Latruria, but good enough. He raised a hand to touch the spot the pain radiated from, then thought better of it—he didn't need to start another explosion. In what was left of his mind, he made a note to check himself for concussion when he had time to find a mirror—or conjure one up, more likely.

With the pain reduced to a bearable level, he could take stock of his circumstances. Now that he thought of it, he remembered being hit on the head, remembered . . .

Flaminia's abduction!

In a panic, he looked around for Pascal, and saw . . .

A wall of tawny fur.

He stared at it for a second, realizing why the onlookers were staying so far back. Then he looked up slowly to the double grin above. "Hi, Manny."

"It is good to see you alive again, mortal."

Matt pushed himself up to a sitting position, very carefully. "Somebody tried to kill me again, huh?"

"Yes—one of the soldiers in wine-red tunics. He changed his mind when I dropped down beside you."

"Dropped down? How'd you get into the city, anyway?"

"Why, I leaped atop the wall, then sprang to the nearest housetop and prowled across the roofs."

"Like any cat." Matt nodded.

"I kept you in sight all the afternoon, disappointed that there was no need of me."

"Bet you were real happy to see them jump us, huh?"

"Yes. I could not prevent them from striking, but when the wench was secured and the leader turned back to you with a lifted knife, I knew my moment had come and dropped beside you with a hiss of joy. He was somewhat startled to see me."

"I'll bet. How was he?"

"Too quick to catch, alas."

"Too quick for *you*?" Matt stared.

"Yes. He shouted a few words I recognized from long ago, and disappeared, along with his soldiers and that scrumptious tidbit of a young woman."

Matt thought that Pascal would probably agree with him on that last, and that reminded him. "Seen Pascal?"

"Yes. He is on my other side—" Manny glanced away, then back. "—only just now waking."

"Safe, then—sort of. You say you recognized the soldier's words?"

"Aye. They were in a language from the East."

"How far east?"

"From Persia, I believe he called it—the magus who had come to Reme to teach the priests new ways to read the auspices and haruspices."

"Auspicious indeed." So the language had been Persian, or maybe older. Chaldean? Sumerian? "What did the leader say?"

"Only, 'Return whence we came!'" The manticore frowned. "Few words indeed, to accomplish so much!"

"Not really, if he had left a spell hanging in the air and only needed a few final words to put it into action. What did he look like?"

"Difficult to say. He was masked, you see—but he had gray hair and beard, was tall and lean, and wore a robe of flaming orange."

"Just your standard sorcerer, except for the color of the robe." Matt frowned. "Could have been any senior magus. Any distinguishing features?"

"Only his knowledge of an old and arcane tongue, and the fact that he did attempt to enslave me with a spell of obedience in that tongue."

Matt looked up, startled. "And it didn't work?"

"Of course not," the manticore said with disdain. "I already walk under the old geas laid upon me by the ancestor of your friend Pascal, and renewed by that young man himself. They enjoined me by the power of Goodness, which is greater than the evil source of that sorcerer's power. He would have had to remove Pascal's spell before he could lay a new compulsion upon me."

"So you were protected by loyalty."

"Protected in more ways than one." The manticore shuddered. "It is highly unpleasant to labor in a sorcerer's command! Some tasty meals, aye, but they do not compensate for being restrained and constrained when I wish to ramble. Would that I could take revenge!"

"But they're too powerful for you, huh?"

"Or too quick. I almost caught this graybeard on the tips of my claws, but he disappeared a half second too soon."

"Too bad about that." Matt suspected he had just personally encountered the sorcerer who had been trying to have him assassinated all along. Apparently he had become fed up with his klutzy hirelings and decided that if he wanted the job done right, he'd have to do it himself. But why kidnap Flaminia?

Just in case the sorcerer failed to kill Matt, of course. This way, Matt would have to come after the sorcerer. Or was Flaminia herself important in some way Matt didn't know about? Or maybe Pascal? It seemed unlikely, but you never knew. "How's your liberator doing?"

The manticore glanced down on his other side. "He rises."

Pascal's head appeared above the manticore's back. He looked like yesterday's hashed browns unsuccessfully warmed over, but all he could say was, "Flaminia!"

"Stolen away," Matt relayed. "We have to go get her back." It didn't even occur to him that there might be another option. "Of course, we have to figure out where she is." He pushed himself to his feet and went over to the spectators. They gave way before him, and some turned to run. "I'm not going to hurt you!" The way Matt felt, he couldn't have damaged a plate of spaghetti. "I just want to know whose soldiers those were."

They didn't even try to deny having been there when the soldiers jumped Matt and his party; they just looked at one another with wide, frightened, but incredulous eyes. "He is a foreigner, after all," one of them said.

"Aye," said his friend. "You can tell that by his accent."

Matt frowned. "What difference does that make?"

"It is why you did not recognize their livery," the man explained.

"Meaning their boss is so big and important that anybody here would know him just by his colors?" Matt didn't like the way this was going. "Okay—who is he?" But the creeping dread in his belly told him that he already knew—he was just hoping he was wrong.

"They are the royal colors," the citizen said. "Those were King Boncorro's men."

Matt just stared at him for a moment. Then he gave a short nod. "Thanks. Any idea why they would want to kidnap our young woman?"

Again, the passersby exchanged glances, and a woman said, "Why would any young man abduct a young woman?"

Matt stood frozen.

"King Boncorro is a young man, after all," one of the men said defiantly. "He is a good king, but he has a healthy young man's appetites—and he will not touch the daughters of the noblemen, as his grandfather did."

"That is why the noblemen have come flocking back to Venarra," another man said stoutly, "with all their money—because he treats them with respect, they and theirs."

"So he makes it up by snagging any of the peasant girls who catch his eye, huh?"

"His eye, or his soldiers' eyes," the woman said darkly.

"Still, the king may not find her to be of interest," the first man said, in an effort at consolation. "Be of good cheer, friend—if the king does not fancy her, she will be brought back here unharmed. None dare touch her, unless the king gives his leave."

"And he never has," another woman pointed out.

"How about if one of the lords takes a fancy to her?"

The woman shrugged eloquently. "A nobleman, desire a girl that the king finds unattractive? He would not dare be so far off the fashion!" She said it with a certain smugness—as well she might, since it was probably one of her own defenses.

Matt wondered how the king's taste ran. "Well, thanks, folks. I'll take my manticore and go now."

They looked relieved, and certainly no one moved to stop him. As he came back up to Pascal, Matt said, "Bad news. Those were the king's men who snatched her."

Pascal blanched—not that he had much color left to begin with. "But why?"

"Because she's a reasonably attractive young woman," Matt sighed, "and apparently, he has his share of vices."

Pascal began to tremble—whether with fear or anger or both, Matt didn't want to know. "We must free her! But how?"

"I was just saying I wanted to meet the king, wasn't I?" Matt sighed. "I won't say this gives us a good opportunity—but it certainly gives us a good reason."

Privately, though, he knew this had to be one of the dumbest things he had ever done. If that sorcerer really was the one who had been trying to bump him off all along, he would sure as Hell know Matt was coming—straight into his jaws. If the sorcerer worked for the king, the chances were this kidnapping, and the attempt to assassinate Matt, had all been ordered by Boncorro himself. Matt knew he would just have to go in with all enchantments up and ready. He thought of trying a disguise spell, but suspected it would be useless, since the sorcerer had already penetrated his cover once.

There was one shred of hope: maybe Boncorro had *not* ordered this abduction. The townspeople seemed to be familiar with peasant girls being kidnapped on spec—on the chance that the king might desire them. Maybe the sorcerer had just been out shopping for his master— and if it had been his own idea to kidnap Flaminia, maybe it had been his own idea to assassinate Matt.

Maybe. But Matt wasn't putting any money on it.

"But how are we to find a way into the king's castle?" Pascal wailed. "One does not simply walk up to him and demand to speak!"

"No," Matt said. "One walks up to the nearest nobleman. Come on, let's go find one."

He turned away. Pascal glanced at the manticore, startled, but the monster only shrugged and jerked his head toward Matt. Pascal swallowed and followed the wizard.

When they looked back, the manticore had disappeared.

In this town it was always a short walk to the nearest boulevard. The districts changed from grungy to grand in two blocks. Matt took up station on a street corner and began to play. Pascal, with conditioned reflexes, threw down his hat. A passerby stopped to listen, then threw in a copper when the song ended. Another passerby joined him. Soon the hat was half full, and Matt had a crowd.

Then he saw the nobleman's retinue coming.

Matt timed it so the nobleman would just be passing as he sang:

> "Oh, a private buffoon is a lighthearted loon,
> And you'll listen to all of his rumor.
> From the morn to the night he's so joyous and bright,
> And he bubbles with wit and good humor.
> He's so quaint and so terse,
> Both in prose and in verse,
> So all people forgive him transgression.
> My lord, bend the rule, and take up this fool
> To the king, for he loves his profession."

The carriage stopped and the aristocrat peered out through the door, no doubt wondering what there was about this minstrel that was so compelling—he didn't *sound* all that funny.

Matt went on:

> "I've jibe and joke, and quip and prank,
> For lowly folk, and men of rank!
> I cry my craft, and know no fear,
> But aim my shaft at prince or peer.
>
> "I've wisdom from the East and from the West
> That is subject to no academic rule.
> You may find it in the jeering of a jest,
> Or distill it from the folly of a fool!
> If it's offered to the king in any guise,
> The sponsor, he will favor with a will.
> Oh! He who'd rise in courtier's circles high
> Should take the king a jester, and his shill!"

The nobleman laughed, and his lady joined in. He wiped his eyes and said, "Well-spoken, minstrel! In fact, hilariously spoken! Climb up behind, for you must come with me to the king!"

Some show of reluctance was in order. "But your Lordship—"

"Get up behind, I said!" The nobleman frowned. "Are you under the illusion that you have a choice?"

"No, my lord! Right away, my lord!" Matt slung his lute across his back and leaped up to the perch on the back of the coach, calling, "Come on, Pascal!" Then, to the footman who had already moved over to make room for him, "He's part of the act."

"Part or not, there is no more room!" the man protested. "There is scarcely enough for three, let alone four!"

"Number four," Matt said, standing up and grabbing a footman's handle, "you'll have to sit between my feet and hold onto my ankles."

"Stand fast," Pascal begged as he hiked himself up onto the moving seat, and off they went, with the disappointed commoners protesting loudly, and Pascal trying to count his hat with one hand, the other elbow hooked around Matt's shin.

Off they went, with Matt reflecting that either the mangled version of Gilbert's verse had been funnier than he knew or his magic was getting stronger. Maybe it was just a matter of getting adjusted to the Latrurian environment.

Matt just hoped he wasn't adjusting too far.

The sentries didn't even bat an eye as their party drove over the drawbridge and into the courtyard. The coach drew to a halt and the footmen hopped down to open the doors. Matt and Pascal hopped down, too, and started to follow the nobleman and his wife, but a footman caught Matt by the elbow. "Through the kitchens, you! You're no better than the rest of us!" And he led Matt off firmly, while his mate took Pascal in tow.

Definitely, he had not worked this spell just to meet the royal cook. "But your master wants us to sing for the king!"

"He will send for you when it is time." The footman clearly didn't think much of this way of hiring new staff. "You'll stay in the servants' hall, or whatever sleeping chamber they afford you, until then."

The "sleeping chamber" turned out to be a ten-by-six-foot space with a four-foot-high ceiling that sloped rapidly down to six inches—they were under the eaves. Matt warily eyed a dark spot in the overhead boards and decided not to rest his lute underneath.

The loft was hot and stifling. He could hardly wait for dusk. "Everything considered, Pascal, let's hang out in the servants' hall."

" 'Hang out'?" Pascal gave him a blank look.

"Loiter. Idle. While away time when we don't have anything to do. Pester the servants and find out about the king."

Pascal's eyes lit.

"Come on." Matt headed for the curtained hole that served as a door.

He tried out the strength of his new spell by singing it to the off-duty servants, then following it up with some popular songs from his own world and time that he had found singularly disagreeable. The servants gathered around with wide eyes and tapping toes, hanging on his every phrase. Grins broke out and people began dancing. Matt decided that the spell worked like a charm. Come to think of it, in this universe, it *was* a charm.

Either that or rock music had a more universal appeal than he was willing to admit, even when it was played on a lute by a third-rate amateur . . .

"Ho, minstrel!" It was the lord's footman at the door again, the one with his face in a permanent sneer. "Your master summons you!"

"Why, then, I shall obey with alacrity!" Matt struck a final chord and nodded to Pascal. "Let's go."

The servants grumbled in disappointment as Pascal followed Matt toward the door. "Don't worry, we'll be back," Matt assured them, then wished he hadn't. Sometimes he had trouble keeping his promises.

They wound a tortuous way through halls that had been accumulating sudden turns for centuries, then came up to a stout oaken door banded with brass and flanked by two guards. The footman announced, "The minstrel Matthew and his assistant Alacrity, responding to the summons of Conte Paleschino."

Matt turned to him, puzzled. "My assistant . . . ? Oh, right."

The left-hand guard scowled. "We have permission for a minstrel to enter with you, but none other."

The footman frowned, but Matt said quickly, "Don't worry about it. Pascal can hobnob with the off-duty servants while he waits for me. In fact, I thought you had struck up an acquaintance with a young lady there, hadn't you, Pascal?"

"Aye," the young man said, giving Matt a very direct look in the eye. "There is a young lady there who is quite fascinating. She dwells with the women who wait upon the king, and seems to partake of their beauty."

The footman frowned, incensed, but the guard gave Pascal a sly grin. "Aye, lad, back to the servants' hall with you, to deepen your acquaintance. Can you find your way?"

"Oh, I shall ask if I have need." Pascal turned away. "I shall see you when you have finished, friend Matthew. I trust you shall be well-received and shall play long for them."

"Thanks." Matt could take a hint. Pascal was trusting him to keep the king and his men occupied for a long time. Well, he would do his best to play along—a very long.

He turned back to the guard. "Okay. Do I get to see the king now?"

"No. You see his Lordship." The guard nodded to his mate, who swung the little door open. The footmen pushed in front of Matt, snapping, "This way!" Matt let him go first, and followed him in.

The huge room they entered was lit only by candles around the walls, and a row of small, narrow windows high above. Matt glanced up, just to check, and sure enough, there were guards stationed next to the windows, on a catwalk that went completely around the huge room. Those weren't windows, they were arrow slits. Each embrasure was filled with tinted glass—tinted not by intention, Matt supposed, but by imperfect glass-making. Still, the muted background light that it gave the throne room was really very pleasing, especially when it was highlighted by the two ten-branch candelabra at either side of the steps that led up to the throne.

The dais wasn't really very high—only three feet or so—but it was enough to make the king decidedly the center of the room. Matt took a quick glance—all he could manage, as he followed the footman who was weaving through the crowd. But he retained the image of the king and studied it until he could look again.

He didn't have time, though. The footman was standing by the nobleman from the coach, who didn't seem to be anywhere nearly as tall now that he was standing on the floor. In fact, he was shorter than Matt, if you didn't count all the hair piled up on top of his head.

"Milord." The footman bowed. "The minstrel is here."

"Very good, very good." The count shot Matt a keen glance. "You had best be as amusing for the king as you were for me, fellow."

"I shall do my best, my lord." Matt bowed, managing to keep a straight face—if the count knew that Matt technically ranked him, he would have had to push his jaw shut. Of course, if the count knew that this minstrel had been born at a station lower than his own, he would have had apoplexy. Matt entertained a brief vision of the count having apoplexy with an open jaw, then put it resolutely behind him as his new "master" brought him up to stand before the dais. The count bowed, and Matt followed suit. "Your Majesty!" the count cried. "May I present the minstrel of whom I spoke!"

A ripple of interest passed through the ranks of the crowd of courtiers—anything to break the boredom, Matt decided. If he was amusing, all well and good. If he wasn't, they'd have fun watching him be flogged.

But when he looked up at King Boncorro, he had difficulty believing this handsome young man would flog a minstrel just for poor singing. The bilious, scrawny old man standing behind him—well, he looked ready to flog Matt right now—but the king himself was in his mid-twenties, about ten years younger than Matt himself. His face was open and seemed guileless, his blue eyes frank and honest, his nose straight and his chin firm without being too large. He looked like a real nice guy, all-American and addicted to Mom's apple pie. Of course, Matt reminded himself, these people didn't know about America—for all he knew, it might not be there; he hadn't gotten around to looking yet—and probably didn't know about apple pie, either. If Boncorro was really skilled at deception, one of the first things he would have learned was to look honest and guileless. Matt decided to withold judgment, but couldn't help liking the kid anyway—which, no doubt, was just what Boncorro intended.

"A minstrel, are you?" the young king asked. "Can you sing?"

"No, Majesty," Matt said honestly, "but my lute can, and my mouth says the words."

The crowd emitted a noise that sounded as if they weren't sure whether or not to laugh. Boncorro decided the issue for them by giving a chuckle. "Not only a minstrel, but a jester, too! What songs can you sing, then?"

"I can sing you of my trade, Majesty."

"To sing of singing?" Boncorro's smile firmed with amusement. "Well, then, let us hear it!"

Matt sang "I've Jibe and Joke" again. The crowd went silent at the first line and stayed that way so thoroughly that Matt knew they were charmed—literally. Boncorro listened closely, too, with an agreeable smile, but with a guarded look that told Matt that the king knew well and truly that he was being subjected to a spell, but that it didn't bother him. He was that sure of his own power to dispel the charm, if he thought it necessary. Matt's blood ran cold at the thought of that kind of power in one so young. Of course, Boncorro could have been wrong— he might not have been as powerful as he thought . . .

Then again, he might.

When he finished, the crowd applauded, and Boncorro nodded approval. "Not bad, not bad at all—and your voice is far better than you led me to believe."

"Well, yes," Matt conceded. "I'm just not too good at hitting the right pitch, your Majesty, that's all."

The king smiled. "Well, your words were so fascinating that we did not concern ourselves with it. What is this 'wisdom of the East' of which you speak?"

Matt was curious. "Is your Majesty not more concerned with what thoughts a minstrel would consider to be the wisdom of the West?"

"No," the king said, with absolute conviction. "I know what we of the Western world consider to be wisdom—it is religion, and I'll have none of it, or the magic of Evil, and I'll have none of that, either."

The old man standing behind the throne looked very upset at that. Somehow, Matt didn't think he was the religious type.

"Why, just as your Majesty says." Matt was taken aback by the young man's intensity—but then, he had known other people who had rejected religion with an almost religious fervor. "Maybe you *would* prefer the wisdom of the East."

"What is it, then?"

The old geezer behind the throne was watching Matt very narrowly. Matt mustered his wits, trying to oversimplify drastically—not too hard, considering how little he knew. "Broadly speaking, there are three kinds—but the one of them is so like that of the West that I think you would find it of little interest; it has to deal with who should take orders from whom, and how to keep things orderly in a kingdom."

"You are right," the king said impatiently, "I know enough of that already. And the other two?"

"The one teaches that all life is more suffering than joy, and that the main goal in living is to be able to escape life."

Boncorro frowned. "Why, a naked blade can accomplish that soon enough!"

"Only if death lets you stop existing," Matt pointed out, "without going to Hell."

Boncorro became totally still. "I think I do wish to learn this wisdom. How can one cease to exist when one is dead?"

"Only with great difficulty," Matt said, "for this wisdom teaches that unless you have lived the life of a saint, you will be reborn in another life, and have to live it over again, and the next, and the next, until you *do* manage to live a life of perfect purity."

Boncorro relaxed, disappointed. "There is no profit for me in that. I am a king, and cannot live a life of purity, for we who rule must ever make the hard choice between the lesser of two evils. Besides, I wish to make my life one of pleasure and joy, not one of suffering."

"And your people's lives, too?" Matt watched him keenly.

Boncorro shrugged. "If their happiness will make my life more pleasurable, yes—and I think it will. The more they prosper, the more tax they can pay, and the more wealthy I will become. The more content they are, the less likely they are to rebel, and the less difficulty I will have keeping this crown on my head."

So. A materialist, and one devoted to the good of his people, even if his reasons were less than noble. On the other hand, Matt wasn't all that sure he believed the king was really so self-centered.

"What of this third form of Eastern wisdom?" Boncorro demanded.

"Alas, Sire! I fear it will interest you even less, for it teaches that everything that exists is only a small part of a greater, single whole— that all the universe is one unified entity, and that human happiness can be gained by working to live in harmony with all the rest of the world about you."

Boncorro smiled sourly. "If that is so, then even the wolves and lions do not know of that harmony, for they slay and feed on other animals."

"That *is* a problem," Matt admitted, "though I'm sure the Taoists have an answer for it. Unfortunately, their idea of living in harmony with the rest of the universe involves learning how to eat as little as possible and do without anything but the absolutely essential belongings—even clothes."

Boncorro gave him a cynical smile. "No, I do not think that wisdom will make my people happy, and will certainly not make me so—unless it teaches how a king may cease to exist when he dies."

The old guy behind him looked very worried.

"No, your Majesty," Matt admitted, "Just the other way around— they try to find eternal life, by living lives of virtue."

"Which doubtless entails poverty." Boncorro gave him a sour smile. "What use eternal life, if there is so little of pleasure in it?"

"There is spiritual rapture," Matt clarified.

"But only for the virtuous? Nay, I think competent kings could not gain that inner pleasure."

"So do they, your Majesty. In fact, one sage actually came right out and said that governing a kingdom would make it impossible for him to live a virtuous life."

"Perhaps he did have some wisdom, after all." Boncorro gave an approving nod. "Tell me of him."

"A king sent his men to invite the sage to come advise him on the best way to govern his kingdom. They found the wise man in the wilderness, wearing worn, rough clothing. He refused the king's invitation. They asked him why, and the sage said, 'What would you expect a turtle to say, if you invited him to dinner—when the dinner was going to be turtle soup, made out of himself? Would you expect him to be delighted to come to the palace, or to prefer to continue to draggle his tail in the mud?'

" 'Why,' said the messenger, 'he would refuse.'

" 'And so do I,' said the sage. 'Be off with you, then, and leave me to draggle my tail in the mud.' "

The king stared in surprise, then threw back his head and laughed. "A point most apt, and a sage indeed! But it is an insight that is of no use to me. So much for the wisdom of the East."

"But there is another Western wisdom that you might find more useful," Matt said, desperate to keep him interested. "There is also the learning of the ancient Greeks, who had begun to search for knowledge that came from neither Faith nor Wickedness."

"Yes, I have heard of that." Boncorro sat forward, his attention suddenly focused. Matt was surprised at the force of the young man's gaze. "They say that scholars have unearthed scrolls that were moldering in libraries, or even dug them from the earth sealed in jars, and that, slowly and with great pain, they have begun to translate them. I have even read a few of their ancient tales of their gods and heroes. But how is it that you, a mere minstrel, know of this?"

"Ah, your Majesty! A minstrel's stock-in-trade is news, and the discovery of things long past is just such news as I thought to have in store, for a king's court."

"Why, what foresight you had." Boncorro grinned. "Have you read these scrolls, then?"

"Alas! I am fortunate to be able read the language of Latruria itself, let alone that of the ancient empire or its elder neighbor! But I have heard that scholars have uncovered the thoughts of a man named Socrates."

The old geezer behind the throne gave a start of alarm. Matt gave him a closer glance—he had a long white beard and a perpetually worried expression. His eyes narrowed as he met Matt's gaze, and Matt suddenly felt a very definite dislike for the man. Heaven only knew why—he looked nice enough, if rather dyspeptic.

Then he remembered that Heaven might very well know why, indeed.

"Majesty." The old geezer took a step closer to the throne. "Surely such talk of long-dead Greeks is a waste of your most precious time!"

"It beguiles me, my Lord Chancellor," the king said.

"But it is surely of no—"

"I said it beguiles me, Rebozo." There was sudden iron in the king's tone, and the old man took a quick step backward. "Now, minstrel, tell me of this Greek of whom you have heard. What manner of man was this Socrates?"

"Why, what men term a 'philosopher,' your Majesty."

" 'Philosopher'?" Boncorro frowned. "Let us work that out from the roots . . . It means, 'lover of wisdom,' does it not?"

"It does, your Majesty, though I personally think the term may have been misused," Matt said, with a hard smile. "Socrates claimed to love truth and to be preoccupied with searching for it, but from what I've heard of the man, his searching discussions with his students really seemed to be more a very subtle way of persuading them to agree with his ideas."

Boncorro smiled with slow amusement, and Matt tried to ignore the restless shuffling and coughing from the spectators who, having the traditional courtier's attention span—i.e., that of a gnat—were beginning to become bored. But the king seemed almost excited. "And how does a man go about searching for truth?"

The old geezer's alarm turned into five fire trucks and a hook-and-ladder.

"Alas!" Matt said. "I know so little of this Socrates! But it seemed he thought all knowledge could be gained by reasoning, through a system called 'logic.' "

The geezer relaxed a little.

"I have heard of this logic." Boncorro frowned. "Wherein do you find it lacking?"

"It is more a question of *how* one finds it lacking, not where," Matt said sourly. "The only way is to test its findings by observation of the real world, then perhaps even to attempt to put those findings into practice on a small scale; they call that 'experiment.' "

The geezer's alarm was back, and had added a paramedic van.

Boncorro smiled slowly. "And how shall one test the conclusions of logic against reality, when they concern the human soul?"

"That, no one can do," Matt affirmed. "That is why such matters should be the only true domain of philosophy."

Boncorro threw back his head and laughed. All the courtiers looked startled, especially the old geezer—but he sent the paramedics home and began to relax.

"I think that I will keep this minstrel about awhile, to play the fool for me," Boncorro said to Conte Paleschino. "I thank your Lordship for bringing him to me, but I shall relieve you of his upkeep for the time being. I must find a way to reward you for this, my lord."

The count fairly beamed. "No reward is necessary, your Majesty. Your good regard is enough."

It sure was, Matt thought sourly—especially since the king's good will would sooner or later be transformed into hard cash, by grants of land or monopolies. Well, Conte Paleschino had won some royal favor, the king had won a new and rather odd jester-minstrel, and Matt had won access to the king—so everybody had gotten what they wanted out of this transaction.

Except, maybe, the old geezer behind the throne.

Chapter
Seventeen

Matt found his way back to his garret, and found it stifling hot. It seemed that all the heat of the whole castle had risen to this one little space under the eaves. The tiny window was open, with Pascal sitting by it stripped to the waist and sweating buckets. He was staring out at the sunset with so dejected a look that it could have set an example for all bloodhounds.

Matt closed the door gently, then sat down across from him and a little way back. After a while Pascal said, "You need not be silent, friend Matthew. This is not a funeral."

Isn't it? Matt wondered. "You were in time, then?"

"In time for what?" Pascal said impatiently. "In time to meet Flaminia? Yes, for the servant girl contrived to bring her down to the hall, with two of the other . . . handmaidens to accompany her. They were most beautiful," he added as an afterthought.

But not beautiful enough to distract him from Flaminia, or ease his current depression? Matt frowned, puzzled. "You spoke with her? She hasn't been . . . harmed?"

"Nor bedded by the king? No, though he may choose to sample her delights this very night." Pascal shuddered.

"So we're in time to save her from a fate worse than death?"

"Yes," Pascal said, "if she wants to be saved."

Matt stared. "You don't mean she *likes* the idea of becoming one of the king's concubines?"

"No, she assured me of that."

Matt waited. When nothing else was forthcoming, he prodded. "You didn't believe her?"

"Well, let us say that she spoke with no great amount of conviction."

Matt frowned. "She doesn't figure it's her duty to her country or anything like that, does she?"

"No, but she was fairly bursting with excitement about all the delights of the women's quarter. She has taken a perfumed bath and is now clothed in silks. She is learning to paint her face, and finds the company of the other women . . . congenial."

"Dazzled," Matt interpreted. "The other girls don't see her as competition?"

"They have at the least been most friendly, and are all beautiful." Pascal caught his breath, then said, "Very beautiful."

"So she's flattered just to be in there with them." Matt found himself wondering why Flaminia *was* there—she wasn't exactly a raving beauty herself. It must have been her figure, and the way she moved, and the air of sensuality she exuded . . . Yes, come to think of it, he could understand why the sorcerer had picked her to take home for Boncorro. He wondered if the king would. "The other women are happy about this, too?"

"Most happy, as I have seen myself. They are peasant girls who would never have known such luxury as this, and might well have been compelled to wed men they did not love, by circumstance or by their fathers. This way, at least, their lover is handsome." He said, with sarcasm, "It would seem that none of them needs to be forced to share a bed with our glorious lord and master the king!"

Matt couldn't blame him for a bit of jealousy. "But aren't they worried about what will happen to them when his Majesty tires of them?"

"Not at all, since it has already happened to a dozen of their number. He sent them away with gold and jewels worth a small fortune. For peasants, they are wealthy. They had no trouble at all finding husbands, for they are beautiful, after all—and now had excellent dowries. In fact, the other girls say they lord it over their husbands, who dare not treat them harshly, for fear of the king."

"You're afraid for her, aren't you?"

Pascal gave a short nod. "For her, and afraid of losing her." He gave Matt a bleak smile. "Is that not amusing? I cannot properly say that I have her—yet I am nonetheless afraid of losing her! We have given one another no promises, we have not shared a bed—I have but dried her tears, and laughed and jested with her! Is it not amusing that I should be so smitten so quickly?"

"Yes, I'm just quaking with laughter," Matt said dryly, "but that's the way it happens sometimes. She isn't definitely lost to you, though."

"No," Pascal agreed, "but I fear that she will be, between the prattling of her newfound friends and the dazzle of finery. I fear that present luxury and future riches may gloss over and make her forget that there is yet something to be said for virtue, and for true love."

Matt sat very still, waiting, not looking directly at Pascal.

"Oh, yes, I told her that I love her, friend Matthew," the young man said bitterly, "and her smile glowed, she clasped my hand more tightly for a moment, and assured me that she loved me in return."

Matt watched him carefully. "That sounds like cause for rejoicing."

"It might have been—indeed, my heart did leap with gladness—had she not begun to seem distracted within a few minutes. I spoke to her of escape, and she said that it was useless to try, for their quarter is heavily guarded and she did not wish to risk my going to prison, or worse."

"You don't believe that she was really concerned for you?"

"Oh, I suppose I do," Pascal sighed, "but if she was truly unhappy where she was, or truly frightened at the thought of the king's attentions, she would have been glad of my help and willing to risk all to escape."

Matt tried to see it from Flaminia's viewpoint for a minute. It wasn't as if she would be losing her virginity, after all, and Boncorro was vastly more attractive than the young man who had seduced her first. In fact, the young king really was very handsome and exciting . . .

But Matt was a man and never had been very good at understanding the feminine point of view. He was sure he did Flaminia an injustice. That she intended to enjoy the advantages of the king's harem for a little while, he didn't doubt—but actually having to go to bed with the king was another matter. Still, he knew just how difficult it could be to resist temptation . . . "I take it she has become an ardent fan of King Boncorro's?"

"Aye," Pascal said grimly. "I told her that risks mattered not when it was a question of her safety, but she told me that she was frightened for me and was sure that the king would not hurt her. I demanded to know what sort of paragon of virtue he was, and she proceeded to tell me."

Matt squeezed his eyes shut in sympathetic pain. Nothing like singing the praises of the Other Man to the one who has just told you he's in love with you. "She told you how handsome he is?"

"Not in detail, no—only that he is, and that all the other girls are besotted with him—there are one or two who even dare dream of becoming his queen—and that she felt quite sorry for them, for she knew they were doomed to heartbreak."

Trying to remind herself, no doubt—but Matt knew a chance to gain information when he heard one. "How about whether or not he's a good king? Or a good human being? Did she mention that?"

Pascal shrugged, exasperated. "How should she know?"

"Just gossip," Matt said, "but gossip can tell you a lot, and she seems to have been hearing plenty of it. He sounds as if he's charming, at least to his wench corps." Of course, just *having* concubines was definitely wicked—but he did seem to treat them humanely, even with care and consideration. Matt knew, from his own brief encounter, that the man was charming and did seem to be trying to do right by his people, whatever his motives. But was he effective? "If he gives orders, are they obeyed?"

"Why, I should think we can say yes to that, simply from the changes we have seen ourselves, as we came through Latruria," Pascal said, surprised. "Whether those changes are good or not is another matter."

"So is their real source. I've heard of many kings who have really been just false fronts; it was their advisers who actually ran the country. But the only adviser I've seen so far is Chancellor Rebozo, although he doesn't seem terribly evil, or terribly powerful. In fact, he doesn't seem to be able to *do* much—he's scared of the king."

"It would seem that everyone is," Pascal said slowly. "Flaminia did indeed say that King Boncorro does not issue edicts very often, but that when he does, no one dares disobey him."

"Oh?" Matt sensed pay dirt. "I take it some of his concubines have tried?"

"No, but one or two have incurred his anger. Flaminia told me, as a jest, of one girl who tried to work magic upon the king, to warp him into being obsessed with her and with her alone—"

"Love philter." Matt nodded. "Even a minstrel hears about that—constantly. I take it she didn't succeed?"

"Nay. The king knew in a moment what she was doing. Sharp pains racked her body; it was her screams that brought the other girls to see. But the torture lasted only a minute, perhaps less; then the king commanded *her* to drink the philter. She did, and dotes upon him still, so devotedly that she will do anything he says—even to escorting other women to his bedchamber."

"You mean he humiliates her like *that*?" Matt said indignantly.

"No, but when another wench taxed her with it in jest, she said in all sincerity that she would do it."

"Okay, so he dominates his harem," Matt said, numb. "How about his kingdom?"

Pascal shrugged. "The wenches have heard his chancellor arguing with him—for it is Rebozo who recruits virgins for him. The king did not argue, but only told the chancellor again and again what to do, and would not yield."

"Odd to discuss affairs of state in the harem—or women's quarters, I think you said they call it."

"Perhaps not; the issue was the future of the first woman King Boncorro discarded. He instructed the chancellor to see to it that she was laden with gold and gems, then escorted in state to her home. Rebozo argued furiously, claiming that having been favored with the king's attentions should be reward enough for any woman—but Boncorro was adamant."

"So she was taken home in triumph?"

"Well, not at first. Rebozo sought to bundle her quietly out of the castle with nothing but the clothes on her back—but a spasm of agony seized him, and he ordered his men to fetch her gold and gems, and a palanquin. Then the pains stopped."

Apparently, Flaminia had been a regular font of information. Matt could picture her, bubbling over to Pascal about this masculine paragon, her eyes alight with excitement—and he felt another stab of sympathetic pain. He tried to move the subject a little further from home. "Well, I gathered from my brief chat with him, that he's been steadily putting economic reforms through, and apparently no one has successfully defied him. He does seem to be effective—especially if he can detect a love potion and induce pains in a seasoned sorcerer."

Pascal stared. "The doxie who sought to entrap him was a sorcerer?"

"No, just a girl who knew a few simple spells," Matt said impatiently, "or who had bought a potion from a village witch. I was talking about the chancellor."

"*He* is a sorcerer?"

"I assume so, until I'm proved wrong. He's old enough to be left over from King Maledicto's administration, which would mean he would have *had* to be a sorcerer. It's probably still a qualification for office."

"Perhaps not. Flaminia says the king himself wields magic like a sword, but is no sorcerer."

"He's *not*?" Matt stared. "How would *she* know?"

"Gossip, again," Pascal sighed. "The ... experienced concubines say that a man will speak more than he intends when his head is on the pillow ... afterward. The women may feel compelled to hold their tongues when speaking to those not of their number, but certainly feel no such reservations among themselves."

"Well, this must be one thing the king doesn't mind slipping out." In fact, Matt found himself wondering if the king might be using his concubines as a way to plant rumors—surely an unworthy thought. But he remembered Boncorro's insistence on not accepting either religion or wickedness, and decided the notion fit. "Where does he get his magical power, then?"

Pascal shrugged. "I suspect that only he knows. All he has told his doxies is that he does not truly comprehend the magic that he uses, but has only memorized words and gestures, then repeats them at need—but surely that is false."

Matt could believe it, though, and the mere thought was enough to make his hair snap to attention. All Boncorro would have had to do was to watch sorcerers at work, then mimic what they had done—and remember which spell went with which effect. Could he have done that with good wizards, too? But where would he have seen any?

Worse, if he didn't really understand what he was doing, he could very easily make a mistake that could spell disaster. Matt shuddered and hoped the king had been lying to his concubine, as well as with her. "One way or another, he certainly seems to make sure people do what he wants—and if Rebozo really is as high-powered a sorcerer as I think he is, Boncorro must be a magical giant!" Either that, or Hell had its own reasons for keeping him on the throne.

Hell, or Rebozo?

"I think we'd better get you out of here," Matt said.

"Not without Flaminia!"

"Yes, that's what I had in mind."

Pascal stared. "How will you manage *that*?"

"By taking a risk," Matt said. "A risk for me, that is—shouldn't be much hazard for the two of you." After all, his hit-song spell had worked inside the castle, even though it was presumably saturated with sorcery. Either Boncorro or his chancellor knew him for what he was, or at least knew him for a wizard, so they wouldn't be surprised if he worked magic within the castle. That might mean they were watching him, ready to pounce, but Pascal and Flaminia couldn't be faulted for that.

Of course, the sorcerer who had been trying to stop him from coming into Latruria, and trying to kill him once he was in, might not have been either king or chancellor, but someone else—say, the constable or lord marshal or such. Matt knew he had to keep an open mind about that, or he wouldn't be suspecting everyone he met, which could be fatal in enemy territory.

"It will make it easier if the two of you are together," Matt said. "I'd rather make one rescue attempt than two. Can you get to Flaminia?"

"Aye; she and her fellows are to go into the town this afternoon, to procure more finery to bedeck them for the king."

"A shopping trip?" Matt stared. "Isn't the king worried that some of them might sneak off to meet lovers?"

Pascal shrugged. "I do not think he cares. Flaminia had heard that several of the wenches have lovers among the guards, and several more have lovers in the town. The king cares not who else enjoys their company, so long as they are there when he wants them."

A most enlightened monarch—or one who was honest enough to admit he was running a brothel. Matt wondered if his spells included prophylactic incantations, to protect him from venereal diseases. "Makes it easier for him to dump them when he gets tired of them, huh?"

"Aye." Pascal's smile was sardonic. "They already have husbands waiting, in a way."

Well, European peasant men had lived with the droit du seigneur for centuries, and had married anyway—not that they'd had much choice. "So we can just stroll out across the drawbridge and meet her in the garment district?"

Pascal nodded. "As simply as that."

"How will you know where to find her?"

"I think that I can send word through my new friends in the servants' hall," Pascal said slowly. "There should be little hazard to them—though I should think they will expect my thanks to take a rather substantial form."

Matt reached into his purse and handed him some substance.

They were loitering, definitely with intent—just standing on the corner, waiting for the girls to go by—when a passing soldier noticed them and glared suspiciously.

"He is glaring suspiciously," Pascal said nervously.

"He's right, too," Matt agreed, "but let's try not to let *him* know that." He slipped his lute around to the front and began to pluck the strings. "Foggy Mountain Breakdown" sounded a little odd without a banjo, but it did draw a crowd. Mollified, the soldier gave them one last glower, then went on his way.

Pascal, never one to waste an opportunity, threw down his cap. Matt struck a final chord, and pennies spattered into the hat. Matt glanced around, didn't see anything resembling a retinue, and started in on "Darling Corey." The audience didn't seem to know what "mash liquor" was, but they certainly seemed to catch the drift of the rest. But as he hit the last chorus, one of the listeners glanced up, then let out a whoop. "The king's doxies!"

"Profit!" cried several voices, and the crowd suddenly diminished by half as shopkeepers ran to trot out their finest finery. Matt looked up and caught his breath.

That definitely had to be the largest concentration of feminine pulchritude he had ever seen in one place at one time, even counting the beauty pageants on TV. There were at least twenty girls, all of them in their twenties, every single one of them stunningly beautiful. These doxies may not have been without smocksies, but they certainly gave the impression that they were. There wasn't all that much naked skin showing, really—only a plunging neckline here and a bare midriff there—but the cut of the clothes, and the way the girls moved in them, certainly gave the impression that you were seeing every iota of the woman's charms, at the same time as it made you frantic to see the rest. Matt decided the garments must have been enchanted.

They swept by in a cloud of perfume that dazzled the senses, and left Matt throbbing with desire. It must have been laden with pheromones—or charmed to charm. Of course, the two possibilities were entirely compatible—sorcerers and wizards only specified end results, not ways and means. A vagrant touch of sanity managed to push through Matt's miasma of hormonal vapors—these girls might have been enchanting, but they also might have been enchanted.

The king's concubines swept by, chattering and laughing—but they left a bit of jetsam behind, a new face in the crowd, but one Matt knew well—Flaminia, eyes shining with the excitement of forbidden adventure. "Play for me, minstrel!"

Matt stared. If he looked at her coldly and objectively, he would still have to say she was no raving beauty—but looking at her coldly and objectively was something he could no longer do. Whatever spell the sorcerers laid on the royal consorts, it was working overtime on Flaminia. Her eyes seemed to beckon, no, to pull; her smile made her lips seem more than enticing—compelling.

Compelling all too well—Pascal was moving toward her with a

fixed gaze and robotic step. Matt managed to catch him and steer him back toward guarding the hat, then struck the strings and began to sing.

> "Soldier, seek not, do not find!
> Soldier, ask not—do not mind
> If she is lost or she is fled.
> Forget her, let her go to wed!"

He managed another verse, enjoining the crowd to forget they had ever seen Flaminia. Since they had to forget her, they drifted away, looking bored—which was just fine with Matt.

Of course, that could have just been the effect of his singing, and the songs definitely lacked both character and action. The guards might just not have noticed she was missing yet. Matt wished he could be sure whether his magic was working or he was just having good luck.

As the last listener turned his back, Matt slung his lute and grabbed Pascal before he could quite manage to catch Flaminia in an embrace that would have shamed a sumo wrestler. "Come on, let's go!"

Flaminia looked definitely disappointed for the half second before Matt caught her wrist and yanked her along. He dragged the reluctant couple down the street and into the arcade he had checked out earlier. Keeping the two of them moving was a major task, since all they seemed to want to do was to stop in the middle of the street and grapple, and never mind who saw. But Matt *did* mind, and kept them in motion, even though he was right between them and they kept trying to reach around him to get at each other. In fact, they were growing frantic, and beginning to get angry, when Matt finally slung them into a shadowed alcove, panting. "Now! Go to it!"

They did, falling into one another's arms with a fervor that made Matt long for Alisande, and the way they were groping each other with their mouths glued together certainly didn't help his concentration. Even so, Matt raised his hands and chanted,

> "In the wood, where, if they wish to, he and she
> Upon faint primrose beds may choose to be,
> Or on the fruited plain away to steal,
> Through magic that doth lovers' flights conceal,
> Thence from Venarra turn away their eyes,
> To seek new friends and truer companies!"

The combined form of the entwined lovers began to fade, then grew more vivid again. It began to fade again, but came back again—again and again, pulsing.

No surprise. Matt could feel the Latrurian environment fighting his magic. In desperation, he sang the first thing that came to mind for young people:

> *"Gaudeamus igitur, juvenestum sumus!*
> *Gaudeamus igitur, juvenestum sumus!*
> *Post jocundum juventutem,*
> *Post molestam senectutem,*
> *Nos habebit sumus, nos habebit sumus!"*

It must have been the Latin that did it, for the resistance let go with a shock. There they were—and there they weren't! Not quite instantaneously—they sort of did a fast fade, so there was no gunshot crack of air rushing in to fill a sudden vacuum. Matt lowered his hands, relaxing—at least they shouldn't have attracted any undue attention.

Which made it all the more puzzling when the finger tapped his shoulder and a voice right behind him said, "Most neatly done. I could not have been more adroit myself."

Matt froze. He knew that voice.

Then, very slowly, he turned around. "Good afternoon, your Majesty."

Chapter
Eighteen

"I trust it is a good afternoon indeed," the king replied. "Let us go out from this arcade into the sunshine, so that you may look your last upon it."

Matt stared at him while he waited for his stomach to hit bottom. He saw Rebozo and the ranks of soldiers behind the king, and the unremitting hostility in the chancellor's gaze, and felt his stomach take another plunge. Nonetheless, he managed to say, "Can't have been all that neat, if I attracted your attention. You were just waiting for me to try this, weren't you?"

"It was a trap most neatly laid," Boncorro confirmed. He turned to the chancellor. "I must congratulate you, Rebozo, on so adroit a piece of maneuvering. You chose exactly the right damsel to abduct."

The chancellor smiled and bowed. "It was nothing, Majesty. This foolish do-gooder is so lacking in suspicion!"

Why was it that paranoids created more paranoids? "I take it your Majesty is sore about losing a very promising concubine."

"What, that?" King Boncorro tossed his head in dismissal. "She matters nothing, nor does her swain. Indeed, I hope they will be happy together."

But Rebozo's eyes flashed with malice, and Matt realized that he was apt to track down Pascal and Flaminia out of pure spite.

"You, on the other hand, matter a great deal," the king said. "It is customary for a man of power to announce himself when he enters another country—surely when he comes to the court of its king."

"Who, me? I'm nothing!"

"I think you mean that, in some strange way." Boncorro regarded him narrowly. "I can only say that your humility is excessive. Any wizard who can overcome the spells of allure laid about my women's quarters is no mean wizard indeed."

"Well, it was nice to know Flaminia hadn't really been all that fickle."

"You are a wizard, of course," Boncorro said.

Well, that put it to the test. Matt wished Christianity let you deny it to save your life once or twice—but he had to declare his loyalty. "I am, your Majesty—but you are, too."

"I suppose I must be, since I am not a sorcerer." Boncorro sighed. "But I will not take power from either Heaven or Hell, as you no doubt know."

The chancellor flashed him a glare of annoyance, very quickly masked. Matt had guessed rightly—he was a sorcerer. "I had gathered that, yes. But how, then, do you work magic?"

"By virtue of a prodigious memory." Revenge could always be postponed in favor of a good chance at shop talk. "You might say I grew up with it—I watched my grandfather work his spells, as I was compelled to do along with half the court, that we might tremble at the mere thought of disobeying him. He never thought that I would remember every word, every gesture, since they were meaningless to me. In like fashion, I saw my father work spells that, he claimed, drew on the power of God or His Saints—in fact, he taught them to me, most earnestly."

Matt had caught the word "claimed." "But you don't believe his power really came from God?" He loved watching Rebozo wince every time he said the word.

"No, no more than I believe that sorcery truly draws on the power of Satan," Boncorro said with a cynical smile. "I do not believe in either one, nor in Heaven or Hell."

"Is that why you're so interested in trying to find a spell that will make your soul cease to exist when you die?" Matt asked slowly.

"Be still!" Boncorro's eyes flashed with anger. With an effort, he controlled himself and forced another smile. "Let us say, at least, that I deny that the sources of magic may be either Good or Evil."

"Then where does the power come from?"

"Is it all around us. To ask where it comes from is useless."

Matt remembered going through that stage. "So you just go through rituals you've seen and memorized, and don't worry about why they work?"

"That is the case. What matters 'why'? All that matters is that they do most surely function!"

"Well, it helps to be able to figure out new ones," Matt said slowly, "or to understand why they sometimes don't work out quite the way you expect."

Boncorro gave him another narrow glance. "You speak as one who knows—and only the mightiest of wizards would think so precisely about the origins of his power."

"I have told you!" Rebozo snapped. "He is the Lord Wizard of Merovence!"

Matt stood very still, giving Rebozo a promissory glare.

"Is this true?" Boncorro demanded. "Are you her Majesty's wizard?"

Again that confounded Christian insistence on honesty! If it just hadn't been a direct question . . . "Yes, your Majesty. I am Matthew Mantrell, wizard to Queen Alisande."

"And her husband!" Rebozo's eyes glittered with satisfaction. "We have caught ourselves a most valuable hostage, your Majesty!"

"Yes, if we can hold him." But Boncorro's sudden enthusiasm seemed to be of another sort entirely. "What would *you* say is the source of my power, Lord Wizard?"

"The power of kingship itself, your Majesty," Matt answered. "A rightful king gains great power from his land and his people, for he is their head and representative. But his power is even greater if he is properly anointed."

"Be still!" Rebozo's hand cracked across his mouth.

Matt's head rocked; then he glared at the old man. "Try that again, and I promise you can keep the wrist."

"Treat our guest with courtesy, Lord Chancellor!" King Boncorro rebuked. He turned back to Matt. "Though you have been somewhat lacking in courtesy yourself, coming into our kingdom as a spy."

"Well, I'm sorry about that," Matt said, chagrined. "One thing just led to another, you know. I was planning on an official visit later on . . ."

"If you thought I was not an evil man." Boncorro smiled, without rancor. "Well, what is your judgment?"

"That you are fundamentally decent," Matt said slowly. "In fact, that you are basically a good man, and a good king. That means you are also drawing on the powers of God and His Goodness."

Rebozo let out a keening of pain, but Boncorro shook his head with dogged insistence. "No! I am a man of vice, and have had to work evil to hold my throne, to keep my kingdom orderly and my people prosperous! I have executed murderers and rapists; I have banished priests who preached against me; I have enslaved thieves and pimps for tens of years' hard labor! I am no saint, Lord Wizard."

"I didn't say you were," Matt answered. "But you have had the good of the country at heart."

"Only so that it may increase my wealth and security!"

"If you say so," Matt sighed. "But I gather you have a very deliberate program of reform, to improve life for everybody. Mind telling me the overall plan?"

Boncorro frowned. "Surely you have seen it for yourself!"

"Yes, I think I've figured out what you're doing and why," Matt said, "but I'd like to find out whether or not I've guessed right. Mind telling it to me clearly and simply?"

Boncorro shrugged. "It is clear and simple indeed, though it took me long enough to reason it out." His smile became quite charming. "I had time enough to devote to it, however, while I waited for my grandfather to die."

The chancellor looked up, startled. Apparently, he hadn't heard this part before.

"I saw the poverty and squalor of the peasants for myself," Boncorro went on, "and heard Baron Garchi, the country lord who fostered me, grumbling often about the grinding burden of the king's taxes and how we should have to manage with less in order to pay them. I could not believe anything but that my grandfather himself must be badly in debt, though his debtors dared not seek payment— and I discovered I was right, when I came to the throne; the treasury was empty, and a host of moneylenders respectfully paid me visits."

"Fortunately, you had figured out what to do about it."

"I had, between lessons and . . . sports. I reasoned that the king's poverty must have come from the peasants' poverty, for if they had no more to give, he would have no more to take."

Matt nodded. "That makes sense. So you figured Item One was to find ways for the peasants to raise more grain."

"No, to keep more of what they already raised—and Item Two was to make certain their lords would not steal it from them. So I lowered taxes and appointed reeves to see that the lords collected no more than was their due."

The chancellor scowled fiercely.

Boncorro noticed and gave him a smile. "You did not approve of my reforms, did you, Rebozo?"

"Nay, Majesty, and still do not! Disaster shall yet come from these newfangled notions!"

"Not so quickly as it would have come from maintaining the old ones," the king returned.

Well. So Boncorro *could* enforce his will, even on his inherited Lord Chancellor. Matt decided he must be stronger than he looked—although he had to admit the young man was looking stronger every minute. "What was Item Three?"

Boncorro turned back to him. "Encouragement of trade—for no matter how much wealth my people produce for me, I shall be richer yet if they bring in gold from other lands. I could go on at length, Lord Wizard, but the long and the short of it is this: the king must plan the flow of money as a farmer must plan the ditches he digs to bring water to his crops—and manure them well, as assurance against starvation. The chance of profit encourages the peasants, tradesmen, and merchants to produce more." He gave Matt the winning smile again. "Thus far, it has seemed to work."

Matt nodded. "A planned economy combined with private enterprise—good recipe. You're way ahead of your time, King Boncorro."

"Aye." Rebozo flashed Matt a venomed glance. "But what shall he do when his time catches up with him, eh?"

Boncorro laughed, richly amused. "I shall never fear rashness, Rebozo, for I shall always have you beside me to croak of doom!"

The last thing Rebozo needed was to have somebody encourage the king—so Matt did. "When your time catches up with you, O King, it shall give you the wealth of Midas."

"Yes, it will." Boncorro gave him a keen glance. "Money makes more money, as seeds make more grain—but I see that you know of this, Lord Wizard."

"I know about capital and investment, yes."

"I shall remember that spell." Boncorro's gaze was suddenly intent, totally concentrated as he sucked up Matt's words to engrave them into his memory. "Is there more to it?"

"Yes, but it takes a long time to tell, and I know only a little of it. You seem to be ahead of me, anyway."

"Perhaps," Boncorro said guardedly. "My ideas have yet to prove themselves in fullness."

"Especially since you have more changes to make," Matt inferred.

Rebozo stared in alarm.

Boncorro's lips pursed in amusement. "You are quite perceptive, Lord Wizard. I can see that you would be a dangerous enemy indeed."

"Yes," Matt said, choosing his words carefully, "but I could also be a doughty friend."

"Aye, if we both served the same Power—but since I serve only my own interests, I doubt that we shall."

Rebozo almost collapsed from sheer relief. Matt realized that the chancellor had been afraid he would try to convert Boncorro. "It wasn't just your father and grandfather you copied spells from, was it? You had other wizards show up to try to persuade you to serve God."

Rebozo winced and glared hatred at him.

"Yes, I did," Boncorro said slowly, "though how you could have guessed that is beyond me. Still, a worthy effort deserves a worthy reward, Lord Wizard, so I shall tell you of it. I could scarcely go for a walk in Baron Garchi's woods without a holy hermit popping out of the underbrush to show me wondrous spells as evidence of the power of God. I took their spells, but left their Faith."

"It made sense, while you were still an impressionable young boy," Matt said judiciously. "There was a chance they might have been able to convert you, and through you, when you came to power, the whole kingdom."

"They were fools!" Boncorro's eyes flashed. "They succeeded with my father, and what happened to him? A dagger in the back, an early death! Satan's minions have too firm a hold on this land; they would never have permitted a saintly prince to become king!"

Rebozo relaxed and gave Matt a vindictive glare.

"So," Matt said slowly, "your grandfather was a Satanist who devoted himself to every sin he could think of, and made as many people miserable as he possibly could. That disgusted your father, so he rebelled by becoming holy and devout, dedicating himself to doing good works—and he tried to protect himself by learning as many Good-based spells as he could."

"The more fool he! What profit did it give him?"

"Probably a lot, but not where you can see it." Matt ignored Rebozo's murderous glare and went on. "Be honest. You admired him, didn't you? Even loved him, maybe—and decided you were going to be just like him."

For a moment he thought he had gone too far, for the murderous rage in Rebozo's eyes was echoed in Boncorro's. Matt hastened to add, "But what does a little kid know, huh?"

Boncorro must have missed the sarcasm, because he relaxed, and the mayhem faded from his face. "Even as you say—it was foolishness. I learned that from the point of the assassin's knife that slew my father."

"So you grew up rebelling against both Good and Evil—but you were smart enough not to let it show until Grandpa was dead. Didn't *his* death make you wonder about the power of Evil?"

"No, but I think that my grandfather began to have second thoughts when Father was slain. Surely he must have realized that his wickedness had not brought him happiness!"

"No, Sire!" Rebozo protested in alarm. "What could make you think that?"

"Why, your own reports, Rebozo." The king turned to his chancellor. "You told me that he was sunk in gloom for the last ten years of his life."

"Nay, Majesty! The revels began again only a few weeks after Prince Casudo's death, and were wilder and more intense than ever!"

"Almost desperate, you might say?" Boncorro smiled thinly. "As if he was striving mightily to gain pleasure, but found he could not, no matter how depraved his sporting?"

"I said no such thing!"

"You did not have to," Boncorro said with a hard smile.

"So the missionaries haven't given up on you yet," Matt said slowly.

The chancellor's head snapped up so sharply that Matt had a wild hope his neck might break. It held, worse luck, but he stared at Boncorro in total and absolute panic.

"You see far more than most men, with very little evidence." Boncorro frowned. "Still, it is even as you have guessed—ever and anon, as I am going through town or forest, an innocent-seeming beggar will pop up to trumpet the virtues of Faith to me. Will they never learn?"

"Probably not, when your reign is such a huge improvement over your grandfather's—though I do wonder if maybe your reforms haven't produced just as many Hell-bound souls as his cruelty did."

Boncorro looked very interested. "Why, how is that?"

"I've seen it on my way south," Matt said slowly. "The extra money and leisure have made people start itching to have Heaven on Earth. They've heard rumors of the high life here, and are flocking in to get their share of excitement. They're holding a continual party on their way south, with drinking binges and free sex all around. Husbands are leaving their wives, wives are leaving their husbands, and young people are leaving their villages."

"Why, herein is pleasure," Boncorro said, "not misery!"

"Yes, but they're sinning hand over foot—and ending up in misery when they get here. It's almost as if they're using up a lifetime's worth of pleasure in a few months. They come into Venarra broke and exhausted, and find out that the king isn't giving everybody a fortune on a silver platter, and that there aren't even enough honest jobs to go around. They stagger back home to their villages drained and pale, or die on the way."

"He lies, Sire!" Rebozo cried. "They parade in by the score, yes, but many of them stay in Venarra!"

"Yes—in the brothels and the jails. The girls get recruited by the pimps and procuresses, the boys get taken on as apprentice thieves. They make life more dangerous for your average citizens and steal wealth instead of making it."

"They are not forced to it," Boncorro countered, "though I see I must set up some sort of scheme to keep them from having to sell themselves or die."

Rebozo gave Matt a glare that could have blistered his skin, if he had only been able to say aloud the spell that went with it. He couldn't, of course—not with his king listening.

"Perhaps work for the men, building more barracks to hold a larger army," Boncorro mused, "or repairing all the bridges and halls and monuments that my grandfather let fall to ruin—"

"Nonsense," Rebozo scoffed. "Where would we get the money?"

"True." Boncorro nodded. "We must find them work that will bring in its own revenue—that, in addition to public works."

Matt interrupted before the man reinvented the whole New Deal. "How about the women?"

"The very thing!" Boncorro snapped his fingers, turning to Matt. "Set them to weaving! Train them to the finest in needlework—most of them excel in it already, if Baron Garchi's peasants are any guide. We would export carpets, tapestries, the finest in craftmanship!"

"But it is men who are weavers!" Rebozo was beginning to sweat.

"Not in their own homes," Boncorro countered, "and not in other countries. No, let us build a new industry with some of these truant country lasses."

"The crown cannot risk so much!"

"The crown is the only one who can." There was steel under Boncorro's tone now. "Naetheless, I would not have the crown own everything—"

Rebozo let out a bleat of agony. "Of course the crown owns everything! Your Majesty, if you must persist in this folly, at least ensure that all the revenues come to yourself!"

"No, I must manure my fields." Boncorro looked off into space, a certain whimsical light coming into his eye. "We shall find some enterprising young merchant who wishes to work twenty hours a day for the next six years or so, and lend him the money to begin such an industry—no, five young merchants! Then, as they pay us back, we shall find other young merchants to begin similar works! What a marvelous idea!"

"Socialistic capitalism." Matt was keenly interested in watching a power play in action—not that there seemed to be much Rebozo could do to stop the king. Either he wasn't really a very powerful sorcerer, or the king was.

Of course, Rebozo might have been playing a more subtle game than either of them realized . . .

"What was it you said?" The king's attention returned to Matt.

"I would say your Majesty is a materialist," Matt said carefully. "Somewhat idealistic perhaps, but a materialist nonetheless."

"Not if materialism is a religion." Boncorro regarded him narrowly again.

"Well, it seems to be, to some people—but rest assured, it isn't to you. You seem to have introduced something entirely new to medieval society."

"Have I indeed! And what is that?"

"Secularism," Matt said. "Worldliness that is neither wicked nor virtuous in itself."

"Why, then, a secular king I shall be! For I have most thoroughly rejected both Good and Evil, Lord Wizard, of that you may be sure!"

"No wonder, having seen your grandfather killed by the one, and your father killed in spite of his devotion to the other. But as I understand this universe we live in, your Majesty, you don't have that kind of option—you *have* to be one or the other. Even if you manage to balance the two during your lifetime, you can't escape the consequences after your death."

"Be still!" The king scowled. "Bid me not think of mine end when I am still young!"

"Memento mori." Matt wondered if Latin here was close enough to the Roman language of his own world for the king to understand it.

Apparently so; Rebozo's stare verged on panic. But Boncorro's education was apparently lacking, for he only frowned and said, "I will *not* think of the afterlife, not until I have found some mystic charm that will make my soul cease to exist completely when my body dies! I may not receive the rewards of virtue, but I will at least cheat Satan of the punishments of wickedness."

And to think most people wanted immortality! "How would you feel if I started a speech to you by saying, 'O King, live forever!'?"

"An intriguing notion! Do you know how it may be achieved?"

"Afraid not," Matt admitted.

"Still, it is a worthy line of inquiry," Boncorro said judiciously. "I shall have to find a sorcerer of an inquisitive turn of mind and set him to the investigation of it."

The chancellor stared in surprise, then developed a very thoughtful look.

That was one train of thought Matt figured he'd better derail. "Your people say you are a good king, your Majesty—even a great one." After all, a little flattery never hurt.

Boncorro grinned, lapping it up. "I would never deny it." But there was a guarded look in his eyes; he knew flattery when he heard it, and suspected the motives. "Your magic, now, Lord Wizard—do you draw on the power of Goodness?"

"Oh, yes," Matt said, "though it's sometimes accidental."

Rebozo looked at him as if he were primed to explode, but Boncorro only frowned. "By accident? How can one be good by accident?"

"You should know," Matt said, amused. "However, in my case, it's because I'm preoccupied. You see, I'm usually more concerned with the power of poetry than with its source."

"Why, what a fascinating notion!" Boncorro cried. "I have always loved verse! In fact, I intend to install a Poet Laureate when my treasuries are restored to their proper level!"

"Even kings have to stop and think about what they can afford," Matt sighed, "in this case, a venture that definitely won't produce a profit."

"Yes, but perhaps you have found a way to do so!"

"Oh, I doubt that," Matt said. "Even here, poetry doesn't exactly make gold."

"By reputation, though, it has made you powerful!"

Matt shrugged uncomfortably. "The pen is mightier than the sword, your Majesty."

"Is it indeed?" A slow smile curved Boncorro's lips. "Let us experiment, Lord Wizard!"

A chill fanned out over Matt's back. "Oh. You've decided to test how strong I am, huh?"

"You could call it that." Rebozo gave him a nasty grin that revealed some gaping holes in medieval dentistry.

"Yes, let us look at it as a test of your powers!" Boncorro urged. "For I would hate to be thought lacking in hospitality, even if the guest is uninvited! We shall accord you accommodations, Lord Wizard!"

Matt frowned. "Let me get this straight. You're going to give me a place to stay, and that's going to test how strong a wizard I am?"

"It is a matter of the sort of accommodations," the chancellor said, his eyes glittering.

"Oh," Matt sighed. He settled his lute more firmly on his back. "You mean I get to spend the night in the dungeon."

"The night," Rebozo agreed, "or much longer."

"So the test of my powers is finding out if I can escape from your dungeon?"

"If you are so mighty a wizard as to warrant my listening to your advice," the king said, "you will no doubt be able to escape my prison with ease."

Matt shook his head sadly. "Really, your Majesty! I had expected better of you!"

"Oh?" Boncorro said in surprise. "Surely you realize that I cannot have you wandering at liberty about my kingdom, Lord Wizard! Are you so certain of your ability to escape, then?"

Matt shrugged. "I've escaped from a few jails before this, and I'll be surprised if yours is much of an improvement." He looked up at the guards, who were shuffling their feet nervously. "Well, let's go to it, boys!"

"You do not object?" Rebozo asked, amazed.

"Object? Of course I object! But I don't *mind*. I always meet the most fascinating people in dungeons." As long as Flaminia and Pascal were safe out in the countryside, a night on moldering straw might even be restful.

The chancellor gave Matt a whetted glance. "His Majesty has a special dungeon for competing magi! If you can escape this prison, Lord Wizard, you must be doughty indeed!"

For the first time Matt began to feel a stab of doubt—doubt that built quickly into apprehension as Boncorro spread his hands and began to chant in a language Matt didn't even remotely begin to recognize. He had always mistrusted foreign languages, ever since he pulled that D in Freshman German. Besides, how could you counter a poem if you didn't know what it meant? Not that that had stopped the postmoderns . . .

Boncorro spun his fists together as if tying a knot—and disappeared.

Disappearing, Matt was used to—he'd come up against half a dozen wizards and sorcerers who could disappear. But he'd never before run into one who could take everybody else with him—as well as all the buildings in the vicinity, and the cobblestones of the street, and, now that you mentioned it, even the sky and the sun.

He hadn't taken the light, though. At least Matt could see everything that was left, even if the light was gray and wan and formless. It was the epitome of indirect lighting—it didn't even cast his shadow. Of course, that could have been because there was no surface for the light to cast his shadow onto—and it might have been pale because it was filtered through all that fog.

All fog—everything was fog. Matt looked about him—it was like being inside a cloud, only this time there was no jet plane around him. Just to check, he looked underneath him, but all he could see was more of the same gray mist. He stared about him wild-eyed, trying to stifle the panic that was climbing up his throat. He told himself that he should take a bold step forward to break out of this prison—but found that he was afraid to. Okay, there seemed to be something solid beneath his feet just now—but was it the only spot of substance in this pocket universe?

He stood, tense and stiffened, afraid to take a single step, to move so much as an inch for fear of a never-ending fall. He had to give it to Boncorro—as a dungeon for sorcerers, this was a beauty!

Well, at least the king had been right about one thing—if he could get out of this one, he would definitely be somebody worth listening to—that is, if he could still talk.

Chapter
Nineteen

Ortho the Frank stopped abruptly, holding up a hand. The horseman behind narrowly managed to avoid a collision, and that only by swerving his cantering steed to the side, which made the rider next to Ortho sheer off, and the man behind him rein in with an oath, while the man to the side of the man to the side had to pull over, but not quite as much. A knot in the traffic flow developed, and the army ground to a halt.

Fortunately, Queen Alisande had been on Ortho's other side—in fact, that was why the rider behind had swerved wide though the huge presence of Stegoman the dragon might have had something to do with that, too. But she was nonetheless peeved at having her cantering army coming to a stop. Still, she knew better than to tax a wizard while he was doing his job. After he was done with his job, maybe . . . She wrenched her mind away from a sudden craving for oatmeal with sauerkraut sauce and asked, "What moves, Ortho?"

"Your husband." Ortho's voice seemed distant, reverberating from a long journey bouncing off cavern walls. "He is in great trouble, very profound."

The thrill of fear banished all thoughts of oatmeal, even if that sauerkraut sauce *would* be delicious right now. "Is he in peril of his life?"

"Nay. There is no danger of death."

Alisande relaxed a little and couldn't help thinking that sauerkraut was vastly underrated. She put the notion aside with resolute insistence and focused her attention on the problem. "What danger can he be in, then?"

"Danger that he may be doomed to dwell in a dungeon cell," the wizard breathed, "that he may never win free again, never return."

Panic gripped Alisande all over again. To be bereft of her husband, and especially at a time like this . . . ! She turned in her saddle, waving a clenched fist aloft. "Onward, men of mine! To Venarra! We must pry open the king's castle as if it were a nutshell!"

A shout of approval answered her, but as it died, a different kind of shout went up from the vanguard. Alisande turned, wondering what it might be.

"A courier comes," said Sir Guy, and beside him the dragon Stegoman lowered his great scaly head to say, "He wears King Boncorro's colors."

Alisande turned to the messenger with a glare that could have melted a glacier. "What does your master wish, sirrah!"

The courier pulled in his horse, amazed and frightened by the total absence of protocol. "Your Majesty!" he stammered, and dismounted to kneel. "I bear greetings from King Boncorro, through the mouth of his chancellor, Lord Rebozo!"

Which meant that the king might not know of this errand—but if he did, the words had better be to Alisande's liking. "What says the Lord Chancellor?"

"He bids you welcome to Latruria, Majesty, and asks if you have come seeking Lord Matthew Mantrell."

Alisande stiffened. "I have indeed!"

"Then he bids you be easy in your heart as regards the Lord Wizard's welcome here, your Majesty, for Lord Matthew is no longer in Latruria!"

Alisande stared, feeling the frisson of danger, very sinister danger, spreading icy needle jabs all over her skin. "Is he not, then?"

"Nay, Majesty, though, says the Lord Chancellor, the Lord Wizard was severely lacking in courtesy not to announce himself openly, but to come in secret, like a spy."

All expression left Alisande's face; the criticism felt like a slap. "You may tell the Lord Chancellor that my husband has ever had a taste for going in disguise among the common folk, that he may have a truer sense of their needs—and that I am sure it was concern for the relatives of Merovence's folk that led him across your borders. But where has my Lord Matthew gone?"

"Why . . . the Lord Chancellor did not say!" the courier stammered. "I would be surprised if he did know, Majesty!"

"He speaks the truth," Ortho muttered, his gaze still halfway in some other world.

The truth as he knew it, Alisande amended. She, however, was quite sure that Chancellor Rebozo did indeed know where Matt had gone, and suspected that what Rebozo knew, his master knew. "You may give the Lord Chancellor my greetings and tell him that I am pleased to learn of the hospitality he has offered my husband. Tell him that I shall find a way to return the favor in equal measure." There, she thought, let him hear that and tremble. "But tell his Majesty that, since I have come this far, I shall press on to Venarra and make a visit of state. I have not, after all, had the opportunity to congratulate him on his coronation."

The courier paled, catching the implied rebuke—which, of course, he was very right to do; Alisande was still smarting at not having been invited, though she knew well that inviting the ruler of a kingdom dedicated to the Rule of Right to the coronation of a king dedicated to the Rule of Might was like inviting a dozen wildcats to a dogs' party.

The courier ducked his head in a bow, leaped up and scrambled back onto his horse. If anything, his face was paler than before. He turned his mount . . .

And found himself hemmed in by a sea of hostile faces.

"Conduct our guest to the edge of our army," Alisande purred, "and see him on his way with every courtesy. We would not, after all, wish our message to go astray."

"It has already been heard," Ortho breathed, like a breeze in leafy branches.

Alisande didn't doubt it for a second; she had dealt with sorcerers before. She had noticed a beetle clinging to the courier's shoulder and had thought that it might indeed be enchanted to send the sound and sight of this meeting to Chancellor Rebozo, or at least to allow him to focus on the scene in his crystal ball, or pool of ink. "Send him forth with all ceremony! For surely, it is ceremony that is our concern now!"

The courier glanced at her with apprehension. She noted with approval that the man must know the ways of the court well, to catch the implication that she knew that King Boncorro knew what she was thinking that he was thinking, so that all that was left to do was to go through the motions. She watched the man ride away, reflecting that he was wise to be apprehensive. Only the motions, yes, but those motions might be the handshake of peace or the blows of war.

Her attention turned inward for the moment; reflexively, she pressed her hand to her abdomen, hoping for the first time in her life that it would not be war, not now. Yes, she hoped indeed that King Boncorro would receive them with outward hospitality, would go through motions that at least said they were not enemies, though also not friends.

She found herself hoping that his kitchen stocked sauerkraut.

Bad enough that everything was misty—now it was getting dark, too! Matt had finally summoned the willpower to risk a very tentative step, and when the yielding surface had held up as he gradually transferred his weight from one foot to the other, he had risked a second step, then a third. There was a floor there, all right, and occasionally he actually saw wisps of dry grass poking through the mist around his ankles, so he assumed it must be ground. Besides, it was very uneven, and he stumbled a lot.

After a while dim shapes seemed to be hulking in the mist, darker gray amidst lighter gray, but when he moved toward them, they faded. Were they really mirages, or was he somehow going astray when he thought he was going right at them?

At least he wasn't going to die of thirst—all he had to do was open his mouth, and in a minute enough moisture condensed to calm his needs. He was definitely getting hungry, though, and very tired.

Then the light began to go.

The only thing worse than twilight in a strange place is darkness when everything has been twilight already. It did occur to him that he might have been in London on a bad day, but it didn't seem very likely—unless the whole city had gone on vacation at the same time. Besides, they would have had streetlights, and here he couldn't see any light at all.

So, everything considered, he was overwhelmingly relieved when one of the shadow shapes lasted long enough for him to come up to it, though it filled his whole field of view—even if it was the darkest, gloomiest, most forbidding castle he had ever set eyes on, made of black granite and dripping with rivulets of moisture. As he came up to it, the fog seemed to lift, becoming a lowering sky instead of an environment in its own right. Off to his left he saw a brackish, turgid lake that extended a pseudopod to feed the castle's moat. Looking down, Matt saw dark water with a greenish tinge—the first color he had seen in this alien environment. Now that he thought of it, he glanced down at his own parti-colored clothing, but instead of brilliant red and blue and yellow, it all seemed to be just different shades of gray, with only a hint of hue. Anxiety touched him—this dampness had to be bad for his lute! He had to get it indoors, preferably near a roaring fire—if this strange pocket universe *had* fire . . .

He looked down at the moat again and thought he saw lumps in it. If he did, they were moving. He looked away with a shudder, thinking that he would have preferred to see teeth and glowing eyes. But the drawbridge was down, the portcullis drawn up, and never mind if its spikes did look like fangs, if the doorway itself reminded him of a hungry mouth, he took a step onto the tongue—no, that was a draw-bridge—and another step, and another, until he was nearly at the doorway.

A scrabbling and a thump, and a troll popped up from beneath the drawbridge, fangs glittering in its watermelon-slice mouth. Fingers with talons of steel reached for Matt. He backed up, but heard a splashing behind him, with a thrashing and thumping as something aquatic was climbing up onto the bridge, while two more trolls climbed up behind the first one, gibbering with insane glee, and two sea serpents reared their heads up from either side of the drawbridge, mouths yawning wide as they came toward him.

All he could think was that whoever owned the castle had really overdone it. The fear was remote, not even pressing—this couldn't be real, it was just too much.

"Fooood," said the smallest troll, the one only seven feet tall.

"Toll!" the foremost troll demanded. "One arm!"

"Toll!" the second echoed. "One leg!"

Matt cried,

> "Be that toll our sign of parting, troll!
> All trolls and monsters without thanks!
> Keep thy teeth from off my arm,
> And get thy forms off of these planks!"

The trolls howled in surprise and anger, and the sea serpents hooted in rage—but they disappeared, fading into the mists, and whatever was behind Matt gave a honk like an eighteen-wheeler in dire distress, but it only managed two more approaching thumps before its voice seemed to dwindle like a spray of mist. Matt turned quickly, but was only in time to get a vague impression of a bloated, elongated shape with lots of teeth in its tail—as well as all the hundred or so in front—before it, too, was gone.

Matt just stood there blinking for a minute. He had expected the spell to do *some* good, but not *this* much! Maybe to knock the monsters back for a minute or two, to give him time to figure out a plan of action—or even to have sent them all running away. But to just *fade*? As if they'd been made out of the mist itself?

Illusions. They had to have been illusions, mere illusions and nothing more. No wonder he'd felt that the lord of the castle had been overdoing it!

He strode into the castle a bit more confidently—if all he had to worry about were illusions, he was perfectly safe. On the other hand, he'd been trying to banish his own illusions for a dozen years now and hadn't had too much success. Of course, these were somebody *else's* illusions . . .

He stepped in under the portcullis, but it didn't crash down on him at the last second, and no giggling microcephalic giant tried to bisect him with an axe. There wasn't even a huge and horrible black hound from Hell pouncing on him with a howl.

It made him very nervous.

He ran through the entrance tunnel, then, very cautiously, he stepped through the archway at the end. Still no terrors attacked him. He looked about him and found he wasn't in a courtyard, as he had expected, but actually inside the castle proper—the great hall, in fact. There weren't any windows, but there were torches in sconces along the walls, sending up trails of greasy smoke—and, at the far end, a dais with a canopy. But it looked old, almost rotted; if it hadn't been for the torches, Matt would have thought he was in an abandoned ruin.

Suddenly, twinkling lights glimmered on the dais and in the center of the room. Matt braced himself as the light turned into a coruscation, clouds of sparks that pulled together and settled and became . . .

Gorgons. Matt didn't turn to stone, but he almost wished he had—they had snakes for hair, and their mouths opened into grins with fangs. Lamias joined them, and harpies, and something rustled and chirruped above his head. It was almost as if he had confronted the male monsters outside and the female monsters inside—except for the half-dozen old men with yellowed beards and obscenely carved staffs, who cackled and discussed him with gloating grins, then pointed at him all together and shouted, "Destroy him!"

With a shout of delight, the lamias and the gorgons charged, and whatever it was that was chirruping swooped.

Matt dodged, just in time for a huge black widow spider to swing through the space where he'd just been and slam into the charging mob of monsters. They screeched, and the giant spider emitted a shrill blast of sound that sent the gorgons' snakes stiff and made them clap their hands to their ears.

It gave Matt time enough to sort them out.

> "Uncommon kinds of monsters! Whose breath I hate
> As reek o' the rotten fens, whose loves I prize
> As the dead carcasses of unburied men
> That do corrupt my air—I banish you!"

The monsters all screamed, the spider loudest of all. Matt clapped his hands over his ears as he repeated the verse again, and louder, just for good measure. The monsters blew apart in showers of sparks, showers that faded, except for all the scrawny old men. They turned to Matt, pointing at him and shouting something in that blasted archaic language that he didn't understand. He suddenly found himself sinking; the floor had become quicksand and was sucking him down—or was that himself melting from the feet up? He looked down, decided he was melting, and sang,

> "Solidity, it's creeping up on me!
> My thighs are like granite,
> My knees, they began it.
> Solidity, it's creeping down o'er me!
> My shins strong and steady,
> My ankles quite ready.
> My feet stout for kicks,
> My toes like small bricks!
> Solidity! I'm all at one for me!"

The pack of wizened men flung up their arms and started chanting, but Matt beat them to the punch line.

> "All your likenesses must go
> And banished be, to leave you so
> Alone, original, unfeigned,
> And only your own substance gained."

He just hoped none of the men were having an identity crisis. Of course, they were probably all just illusions, too . . .

All the ugly men gave a chorused single squawk of outrage that diminished rapidly as they faded, shredded, blew away . . .

Except for one.

Matt frowned at him. "Scat! Scoot! Go on! Get away!" He underscored it with shooing motions.

"Get away yourself," rasped the survivor. "This is *my* castle!"

Matt stared. "Oh! Sorry." He tried to recover his aplomb and not stare—but really, the little old man looked as imaginary as any of the other monsters—scrawny, yellow-eyed, his beard grungy from lack of washing . . .

Matt frowned and looked more closely. He wasn't really that old, actually—more like middle-aged. He just *looked* old, because of the white beard, and the white hair flowing down around his shoulders—only it wasn't yellowed from lack of washing. That was its natural color. And he wasn't really short or little or stooped with age—his shoulders were hunched up defensively, his head pulled down to glare. Sure, he was holding his staff in both hands, but he wasn't really leaning on it—he was ready to wave it like a magic wand, which it probably was.

He *had* to have done all that deliberately, to look like less of a menace than he really was. Didn't he?

But those yellow eyes were huge, with the whites showing all around them, and glittering with malice. His garments were soiled and faded, but they were sumptuous, or had been once—brocade and velvet. Matt couldn't help thinking that they were just the right thing for the climate; the only thing that would have been even better was a raincoat.

The owner jabbed a finger at him and shouted something unintelligible, and Matt suddenly felt an irresistible interior urge, one that would ordinarily have sent him on a frantic search for the garderobe, only he was sure he didn't have time, and besides, it was all just an illusion anyway, so he called out,

> "The cheese stands alone,
> In my blood and bone,
> All throughout my viscera,
> The cheese brings me home!"

The urge went away, but the yellow eyes sparked with anger, and the staff snapped out as its owner spat another indecipherable verse. Sparks glittered all over the floor and turned into cockroaches, scurrying toward Matt; he could almost hear them thinking, *Yum!* He wondered what they thought he was—but while he was wondering, he was chanting.

> "Hey! Where y' going, y' crawling ferlie?
> Not to me—too big and burly!
> Run to him, who seems decayed!
> His scent is yours, so make a raid!"

For a moment he blushed with shame—how could he be so gauche as to mention Raid around a cockroach? But if the insects had noticed, they gave no sign—only turned and ran toward the lord of the castle.

The old man cursed, then spent a few minutes in an anticockroach spell of his own. Matt used the time to think up an all-purpose antidisgustant verse—but when the bugs had coruscated and effervesced into nothingness, the yellow eyes turned back to Matt with undisguised loathing and said, "I shall not be rid of you so easily, shall I?"

"I don't think you'll be rid of me at all," Matt said, "except maybe by asking me nicely to leave."

"Will you not leave?"

Matt sighed. "Well, that's not quite what I meant by 'nicely,' but I guess it will have to do. Okay, I'll walk out—but I would appreciate answers to a few questions first."

"I give nothing to any man!" The grubby one raised his staff as if to strike and began to recite something in that confounded antiquated tongue again.

Matt got his counter in fast and first.

> "His heart is turned to stone;
> He strikes it, and it hurts his hand.
> His hand therefore, is stone,
> And all his body banned
> From flesh and bone.
> All is rock! His head alone
> Is live!"

The owner's voice ran down into a croak and stopped. He stood poised, staff raised to strike, but unable to as his body turned grayish.

"Well, now, that's a bit better attitude!" Matt strolled up to go slowly around the man, inspecting him from every angle. "Actually, that posture isn't really the best attitude in the world, but it could be worse."

"You could not!" The man's voice had an undertone of gravel. "Loose me, Wizard, or it shall be the worse for you!"

"Oh, I don't think so," Matt said casually. "You're a wand slinger, see, so I doubt any verse you come up with will have much effect without that stick to direct it—and what little power your spells might have, I'm sure I can counter."

The yellow eyes gleamed with fury, and the sorcerer began to recite again.

"Everything considered," Matt said quickly, "it would be a lot easier for you just to answer a few questions for me. Then I could unfreeze you and go away."

The sorcerer paused in mid-syllable.

"Of course, if you *do* manage to do something lethal to me," Matt pointed out, "I won't be here to unfreeze you."

"I can deal with that myself!"

"Sure. You could unfreeze somebody *you* had turned to stone," Matt said, "but could you counter a spell of *mine*?"

The sorcerer just gave him a very black look.

"Let's start with: how did you get here?" Matt asked. "The king sent you, for openers."

"Openers indeed! I was the first—but only the first of a dozen! And there shall be more!"

Matt nodded. "Makes sense. However, what the king didn't explain to me, before he blasted me here, was why he didn't just execute anybody who wouldn't come to heel. You know, off with their heads, then burn the body just to make sure. Why not?"

"He did that with the worst of them," the sorcerer grated, "they who sought to overthrow him."

"But you were no threat to him personally? You just didn't want to stop torturing your peasants?"

"Something of the sort," the sorcerer admitted. "I had no designs upon the throne."

"Yes, I noticed it wasn't terribly ornate. I thought Boncorro was tolerant, though. All you had to do was live by his laws."

"And cease to slay priests?" the sorcerer demanded. "Cease to despoil nuns? Cease to seek to bring about the misery of every soul near me, that I might send them to Hell? What use would there be in living, then?"

"So. You were incorrigible and unreformable." That put in a thought. "Did the king even *try* to reform you?"

"Oh, aye. He bade me mend my ways three times. At the last, his fool of a reeve shrank quaking from my sight, so I knew 'twas not he who told the king how I had amused myself with the peasant lass—so I know that King Boncorro must have had other spies within my castle, perhaps even the cat I had bought to attend to his other spies."

Matt decided he did not like this man.

"He appeared in my hall with the sound of thunder and with fires gushing away from him—the showy fool! 'What?' I said. 'Will you send me to a monastery?' 'Nay, nor even presume to tell you to renounce your pact with Satan,' said he, 'for your soul is your own affair, and no reform will affect your Afterlife save that which you work yourself.' "

Matt listened closely. This didn't sound like the atheist the king professed to be. "Sounds like common sense."

"The more fool he, to presume to find laws that govern the consequences of the soul's deeds! He commanded me to forgo my pleasures, though, 'For what you do to my subjects,' he said, '*is* my concern.' The conceited prat! I spat in his face. It was for that he sent me here."

"Three strikes and you're out of his kingdom." Matt nodded. "In fact, out of his whole world. Interesting that he still honors the number three."

"There is nothing mystical in that!"

"That's what they tell me. And you just happened to find this castle sitting here?"

The sorcerer stared. Then he laughed, a nasty, mocking sound. "Why, you understand nothing of the nature of this realm, do you?"

"Oh. So you built it yourself?"

"Aye, with my own two hands," the sorcerer said, sneering. "There is a quarry not far from here, and I am stronger than I seem."

"Yes, that's why I don't want to get too close. Did you make the quarry, too?"

The sorcerer eyed him narrowly, finally beginning to realize who was mocking whom. "What a fool's remark is that! How can one make a quarry?"

"I thought that here you could make anything—like that." Matt pointed at a wall, imagined a pickaxe, and willed it to appear. Sure enough, it did, swinging at the granite.

"No!" the sorcerer cried in alarm, and a huge hand appeared, seizing the pickaxe and throwing it at Matt. Quickly, he willed it to disappear, and it faded into thin air. Then he imagined an even bigger hand holding a ruler, willed it to appear, and made it strike the sorcerer's construct on the knuckles.

"Well enough, then," the sorcerer said with disgust. "I will banish mine if you will banish yours."

Matt nodded. "On the count of three."

"Nay—five!"

"Okay, five," Matt sighed. He considered telling the man that five was a holy number in some religions, then thought better of it—apparently it didn't matter, as long as the religion wasn't Christianity.

After all, this part of this world ran on Christian concepts, or against them. "One . . . two . . . three . . ."

"Four—five!" the other sorcerer counted, and Matt's hand disappeared. The sorcerer laughed as his giant hand rushed at Matt's head. Matt did some quick imagining, and a huge chain appeared fastened to a ring in the wall. The other end was fastened to a chain in the hand. It slammed down onto the floor and scrabbled its fingers furiously, trying to reach him. Matt's hand appeared over it with the ruler again.

"As you will," the sorcerer sighed, and his hand disappeared. Matt nodded and banished his. The sorcerer growled, "If you know that all here is illusion, why did you ask?"

"I come from a school that likes to have its guesses confirmed," Matt explained. "So this whole realm is a pocket universe so thoroughly saturated with magic that I can dream up anything I want?"

"Even so," his enemy grunted. "This whole castle is the product of my imagination."

Matt decided that this boy really needed a psychiatrist.

"In this realm-between-worlds to which King Boncorro has banished us," the sorcerer explained, "anything imagined can appear to be real."

Matt shuddered. "The ideal place for people who want to delude themselves!"

"Oh, they need not come here," the sorcerer said with a curl of the lip. "They who wish to find their Paradise on Earth are doing exactly that. Now that there is money enough, they are looking away from the Afterlife and toward the here and now, forgoing their families to seek only pleasure."

Matt remembered the roisterers he'd met on the road south, and shuddered.

The sorcerer gave him a toothy grin. "That pleasure is fleeting, of course—and only builds up a debt that must be paid. After summer's plenty comes winter's famine, and fools follow the search for pleasure into ways that lead them here—or to death and damnation. What an idiot is King Boncorro! For in seeking to make his folk happier, he has only given them the means of their own destruction!"

"He claims he doesn't care, as long as it means more money for him." But Matt frowned. "Are you trying to tell me that the king's new order has actually produced more Hell-bound souls than King Maledicto's reign?"

"Aye, for in place of the fear of old Maledicto and his devilish masters, Boncorro has given them—nothing. He does not punish the priests, but he has not brought them back, either." The sorcerer grinned, savoring the idea. "The people have no guide in the use of their newfound prosperity, nothing by which to decide what to do and what to avoid."

"You mean that because the people have lost any sense of religion, they can't have faith in anything?"

The sorcerer winced. "Spare the words that burn, Wizard! You have almost the sense of it—it is not that they cannot have faith in anything, but that King Boncorro has given them nothing to have faith in! In place of the fear of Hell, he has given them no hope of anything beyond this world—so they pursue only worldly joys and pleasures. Not knowing what to do with the sudden leisure that has befallen them, they have themselves fallen prey to the temptation that comes their way."

"You mean it's harder for them to hold onto their faith, now that they don't actually need it."

"No, I mean that there is no faith for them to have! It is the king who sets the example, but he embraces no beliefs and preaches none—so his people have none, either!"

"And this pocket universe is the perfect example of what happens: when you have the chance to make your dreams come true, but no yardstick to measure which dreams are good for you and which are destructive, you get bogged down in your own neuroses."

The sorcerer grinned wickedly."Odd terms, but an agony of heart quite clearly stated."

And it was, of course, what he was living day to day—unless he was one of the few who had control over his illusions, not letting his illusions control him. No wonder this was a prison fit only for sorcerers and wizards—for anyone else, it would begin as Paradise, then turn into a torture chamber of the subconscious, and finish by being a killing ground.

The sorcerer's eyes flashed. "Be sure that I can control my imaginings!"

"So the secular monarch needs to find some sort of values to replace religion." All Matt could think of was how the Soviets had made Communism assume many of the aspects of religion. It had indeed been a secular religion, in its own way.

All of a sudden he couldn't take this conversation any more. This sorcerer was too right about what was wrong. "Think I'll go looking and see if there's anybody else here who really knows about mind control," Matt said. "Thanks for the overview." He turned and started for the gate, then remembered and whirled around, his finger stabbing out—just in time for him to think up a lightning bolt that exploded the elephant-headed giant belly dancer with carnivore's fangs that was reaching for him with its trunk. It burst into a shower of sparks and was gone. "Don't try it," Matt told the sorcerer sternly, "because I'm making myself a little familiar, right now, to watch you closely and alert me if you come up with any other monstrosities for stabbing me in the back."

The sorcerer glared at him. "You remove all the fun of this world!"

Matt suddenly realized that, to the sorcerer, he had been put there only for the man to play with—that, like all other people, his sole reason for existence had been to amuse this monster of depravity.

Monster of depravity? Was that why all his creations were depraved monsters? "Just don't try it," he warned. "So far, I haven't tried to hurt you. Don't tempt me—I don't have much resistance."

"Oh, I think this realm will tempt you to your fullest," the sorcerer assured him.

Matt resolved, then and there, not to imagine up a single item for his own amusement or pleasure. Trouble was, he'd never been much good at keeping resolutions. But he did manage to walk out of the dank and fetid castle, his back prickling every inch of the way, expecting attack.

A dragonfly from the moat zoomed past him, hit the wall, and turned into a tarantula. It scuttled up the stonework, and Matt relaxed. Just to test it, he glanced through its eyes, and saw the sorcerer making a wolf with a head on each end. Matt produced a huge saw, cut it down the middle, and made them all disappear. He walked on out, listening to the cursing behind him with great satisfaction—but he didn't relax until he'd made it across the drawbridge and a hundred yards away. Then, with one final shudder, he loosed his binding spell, put the foul sorcerer from his mind, and set off to find out if there was anyone good in this befogged wasteland.

Actually, he was ready to settle for someone just a little bit good. He wasn't in any shape to be picky.

Chapter
Twenty

They watched the herald out of sight. Then Alisande turned to Sir Guy, resolutely banishing thoughts of a strange chill-white concoction in a clear glass standing cup, with some sort of dark brown sauce oozing over the top of it, and said, "How now, Sir Guy? How shall we save Matthew without bringing a war down upon our heads?"

"I would say," the knight said slowly, "that we must first discover how Matthew may be in dire danger, but not in Latruria."

"*Is* he gone from Latruria?" Stegoman rumbled.

"A good thought." Alisande turned to Ortho the Frank. "How say you, Wizard? Is your teacher in Latruria, or not?"

"He is not." Ortho's gaze still probed a distance only he could see. "Yet he is nonetheless in dire peril."

The ice of fear enveloped Alisande's heart. Ice! That was the stuff in the standing cup! But not really ice, either . . . "He . . . he is not in . . . a realm of the Afterlife?"

"No," Ortho said with complete certainty. "He is not in Hell, nor Purgatory, nor any of the realms of the dead. He is in a place that both is and is not . . ." He shrugged, his eyes coming back into focus. "I cannot explain it more clearly than that, your Majesty; we have not the words. It is a wizard's realm; let it rest at that."

Stegoman scowled. "A wizard's realm, and Matthew cannot break free of it?"

"Not by himself, no."

"And can you not aid him?" Sir Guy demanded.

"Alas, no," Ortho sighed. "I am a willing wizard, Sir Knight, but not a terribly powerful one."

"Then we must *bring* a terribly powerful one." Stegoman swung his head toward Sir Guy. "Is this not the emergency of which the Witch Doctor spoke?"

"It is," Sir Guy agreed, and turned back to Alisande. " 'A clear and present danger,' he said. This is a present danger, though its nature may not be clear."

"Yet it is clearly a danger." Alisande turned to Ortho. "Is it not?"

"Most clearly indeed, your Majesty, and if it is not present now, it will most quickly become so!"

"Then there is no more time to wait," Alisande said to the Black Knight. "Summon the Witch Doctor!"

Sir Guy loosened his gorget and drew a most unspectacular bauble out from the protection of his breastplate. "This is the amulet he gave me."

Alisande frowned at the ball on its length of dull iron chain. It was a globe of metal perhaps two inches across, perforated with dozens of tiny holes arranged in diagonal rows—serried ranks. " 'Tis most unprepossessing, Sir Guy."

"It is," the Black Knight agreed. "The Wizard Saul says appearances are of no importance—only function and substance do matter."

Alisande shuddered. "I pity his lady, Angelique!"

"Be assured, she has their cottage well in hand," Sir Guy told her, "and he rejoices in its appearance as he does in hers."

Alisande frowned. "Does he not see that his pleasure in her beauty, and the loveliness she creates about her, give the lie to his claims not to care about the outsides of things?"

"With respect, your Majesty," Ortho said, "Lord Matthew has told me that the wizard Saul has never been troubled by his contradicting of himself. What does the amulet do, Sir Guy?"

"It will take my words to him." Sir Guy pressed a little nubbin on the side of the cylinder that held the amulet. "There is a charm I must recite, to make it carry my voice . . . 'Breaker, breaker! Nine one one! Come in, Wizard Saul! Mayday! Mayday!' "

Alisande frowned. "But 'tis mid-June, Sir Guy, nigh to Midsummer's. 'Tis long past May Day."

Sir Guy shrugged. "Who can comprehend the ways of wizards, Majesty? He told me that it means 'help me' in a language called French—muh aid-ay—but that makes scarcely more sense, for I have never heard of such a tongue."

Alisande glanced quickly at Ortho, but he only shrugged, looking as baffled as she.

"Nine one one! Mayday, Wizard Saul!" Sir Guy said again, then, "Oh! I forgot! He said I must loose the nubbin when I am done speaking!" He lifted his thumb, and the button rose. Saul's voice crackled out of the amulet, surprising Sir Guy so much that he dropped it. Fortunately, it swung by its chain, reverberating with the little tinny voice that somehow they could recognize as Wizard Saul's. "You've gotta let up on the button, Sir Guy! I'm talking, but you can't hear me if you don't let go! Raise your thumb! Lift up your finger!" Then, oddly, the voice broke into song.

> "I lift up my finger and I say,
>   'tweet, tweet, now, now, come, come,'

"Am I sounding as daffy as I think I am? Hey, wait a minute—how can you answer if I'm still talking? Okay, Sir Guy, I'll give you a chance—I'll shut up for ten seconds. You press the little button again and tell me if you can hear me. Remember the incantation? It's, 'I read you loud and clear.' Got that? Okay, let's try it."

"He might give me a chance," Sir Guy said, annoyed, then pressed the button. "As it happens, I do remember that—I read you loud and clear, Wizard Saul! Though I do not read you, truly, only hear you, and why you think this spell will work when it has neither meter nor rhyme, I cannot think!"

He let up on the button just in time to hear Saul say, "Well, I knew that. Don't worry about the verse, I enchanted it when I built it, and it will keep working unless you break the indicted thing. Over."

"He says 'over' to signal that he is done talking," Sir Guy explained, and pressed the button. "Wizard Saul, we have just received word that Matthew is in danger. He seems to be imprisoned, but we cannot say where—it seems to be some sort of wizard's realm."

"We pray you come to his aid, and quickly!" Alisande called into the amulet, then added as an afterthought, "Over."

For a moment there was no sound. Sir Guy frowned, and was just about to press the button again when Saul's voice sounded from the bauble. "Yeah, I'd say that's a good reason for putting my experiment on ice. It will take a few minutes to shut down, then a few more to square things with Angelique, but give me, oh, half an hour, and I'll be with you."

"There is no need to be with us!" Alisande protested, and Sir Guy pressed the button in time for the amulet to catch her words. "Only find a way to be with *him!*"

"Over!" Sir Guy said, and let go of the button.

"Be with him. Gotcha," Saul's voice said. "I'll work on it. Any other instructions? Information, maybe?"

Alisande glanced questioningly at Ortho, who shook his head, and Sir Guy said, "You know all that we know now, Wizard Saul—except that word came from King Boncorro's chancellor, Lord Rebozo, saying that Matthew is no longer in Latruria. The knowledge that he is in danger came from Ortho, who has been Matthew's assistant for some years. Ortho also tells us that Matthew is in a strange sort of wizards' realm that is neither part of this world nor of any domain of the Afterlife—but cannot explain what he means. Over."

"Well, if anybody would be wise to him, it would be his research assistant," Saul's voice said, "at least, when it comes to magic. How did you know, Ortho? A dream? A waking vision? A hunch? Excuse me, I mean 'a feeling.' Over."

"A feeling," Ortho said, "but far more than that. There was, of a sudden, a sensation that I walked through mist, that the whole world had become insubstantial, and that I would never find my way out, for there were no landmarks. Over."

"Yeah, that sounds pretty convincing," said Saul's voice. "I'll start work on it and see if I can find anything—or anybody. Report back to you this evening. Over."

"Over and out," Sir Guy said, and let up on the button. "Well, your Majesty, we have done what we may."

She nodded. "It is in Wizard Saul's hands now."

"Shall we, indeed, press onward?" the dragon rumbled.

"We shall." Even though she was no longer in her own country, Alisande still knew instinctively what was best for Merovence; in this universe, the Divine Right of Kings was no empty theory. "We shall discover what we may, for I know in some manner that it shall be vital to us all that we be in Venarra when Saul finds Matthew. Forward!"

They marched, the army newly resolute, Ortho now with hope to balance his dread, and Alisande wondering whether the cold white substance in the clear dish could be snow, and if possibly they might have some in King Boncorro's kitchens.

Matt didn't really relax until the dark castle had disappeared into the mists behind him. Then he slowed down to a stroll and decided to admire the scenery. The only problem was that it was awfully hard to admire a continuous expanse of gray mist—so he started making his own.

He began small, with a miniature snow-globe scene, right after somebody had shaken the ball—and sure enough, there it was, ahead and off to his right. The little house looked charming, the snowman actually waved at him, and the flakes drifted gently down. Of course, being so small, it seemed to be far away—but what the hey, it was all illusion, anyway.

On an impulse, Matt left it standing for a while, thinking about something else—say, making a succulent fruit plate—until he was fifty feet past it. Then he looked back—and sure enough, it was still there, even though he hadn't been watching it, and had very deliberately *not* been thinking about it. The snowman hadn't turned to watch him go, but you wouldn't expect that a snowman would. So any illusion he conjured up would stay there until he deliberately wiped it out. Matt was tempted—after all, it was a harmless little scene—but the antilitter habits of his own world took over, and he carefully thought of it disappearing as if erased with an art gum. No doubt he just imagined that the snowman looked a little bit panicked just before its head disappeared, but he felt a trifle guilty, anyway.

Then he turned around, pondering the possibility that illusions could gain even more of an independent existence here.

The bowl of fruit sat before him, looking every bit as delicious as he had imagined.

Matt stared—he hadn't even willed it into existence, just imagined making it, with lingering delight. In fact, he had worked up an appetite just thinking about it—so maybe that was why it had appeared.

Gingerly, he reached out, selected a slice of melon, and bit. It was definitely the best melon he had ever tasted—exactly as he had imagined it should be, succulent and flavorful and moist. The moistness helped a lot, since he hadn't found a drinking fountain yet. He finished the melon, ate a few more pieces of the fruit, then imagined the whole plate fading into nothingness. Condensed mist wasn't very satisfying; the fruit was, and the comfortable feeling in his stomach stayed. Why not? It was just as easy to create the illusion that he was well-fed as it was to create the illusion of a fruit plate.

He strolled along, fabricating butterflies and songbirds as he went. They fluttered and flew about him, then went winging off to spread glad sounds everywhere else in this pocket universe. With all that depressing gray stuff, they were needed.

Matt came to a halt with a sudden thought. If he could leave illusions lying around the landscape, couldn't other people? And if his could make noise and taste good and fill the stomach, maybe somebody else's could draw blood with sharp teeth, or inject agony with a very big stinger. He decided to proceed a bit more cautiously.

It also raised the question of what happened to the odd imprisoned magico who died here. Could his soul escape to the Afterlife, or did it have to hang around this vale of mist? Admittedly, sorcerers would probably prefer to hang around—paybacks are hell, literally in this case, and Hell wasn't apt to be cheated, especially by a pocket universe created by a man who wasn't even trying to be saintly. So the odds were that Hell would have no trouble reaching in to yank one of its debtors out. But the ghost of a wizard might be another matter, though why it should want to linger around here when it had Heaven waiting, Matt couldn't think. Of course, if it was expecting a long session in Purgatory, that might be another matter—so Matt decided to be wary of wandering ghosts.

After starting with alarm at three different wraiths that turned out to be just thicker-than-average swirls of mist, he decided that, no matter what, he needed sunshine. The idea of creating the sun itself was so audacious that he had to think twice about it, but he reminded himself that it was only an illusion, not a real sun. In fact, just to keep himself from getting confused and also possibly suffering radiation sickness, he imagined it as a ball of pure light, not flaming at all, and only a hundred feet overhead. Sure enough, it appeared—or its light did, filtered through the mist. As he walked, he imagined the mist melting away under the sun's heat—and there it was, his own portable sun, sitting up there at the zenith . . .

But he had imagined it as having just risen. And, come to think of it, he had imagined its light as being golden, not white, not yet. What was going on here?

Especially what was going on as the lifting mists disclosed a beautiful park, lush lawns bordered with flower beds in a dozen colors and textures, trees whose leafy boughs were so regular that they might have been sculpted, hedges and bushes that definitely had been, and here and there among them all, pools of water with stunning miniature scenes and fountains, and elegant, almost Classical, statues.

Matt went up to one of the statues, wondering, and decided that it really was Classical, at least in style. Someone had studied the Greeks and Romans thoroughly, and done a painstakingly accurate job of mimicking their style. The feminine form was tantalizingly real, its posture inviting and graceful, but its face a study in the calm, cool self-possession that he had seen in so many pictures of Greek statues.

He went a little farther, wondering, looking all about him. There wasn't a single religious statue among the lot—or at least, nothing that was Christian or Hindu or Buddhist; these figures might have come from the Greek and Roman pantheons, but if so, they were only idealized versions of the human.

Human! That was it! Someone had rediscovered the value and potential of the human body and, presumably, of the human mind! These weren't Classical statues, they were Renaissance! But this was the Middle Ages; this universe hadn't rediscovered the Classics and begun the rebirth of knowledge yet.

Wait a minute—when he had mentioned old Greek tales, Boncorro had said that he had heard of such discoveries, had even read a few. The Renaissance had started in Italy when the English knights were still slugging it out with broadswords, and Latruria was Italy by any other name. Had he arrived just in time for the beginning of the Rebirth of Art and Learning? Matt wondered.

Or was it going to be stillborn? Was King Boncorro going to keep it locked up here, instead of letting it loose?

Anger surged, but faded into puzzlement. King Boncorro was far too interested in learning, and in finding alternatives to religion, for him to have deliberately banished a scholar. Was there some Latrurian equivalent of Petrarch or Abelard imprisoned here? And if so—why?

The park opened out to reveal a manor house of alabaster, gleaming in the noon glare—and *now* Matt recognized that sun! It was the magical, clear light of Italy and Greece that he had read about. Whoever lived in that house really knew his subject.

As he came closer, Matt saw that the building wasn't really all that imposing. Oh, it was no cottage—but it wasn't a palace, either. In fact, unless he missed his guess, it was a Roman villa, but scaled down to be comfortable for one man. His respect for the owner went up—he had some humility and wasn't greedy. He could have anything he wanted, but what he wanted wasn't ostentatious or overdone—it was simple, but very elegant in its simplicity. The proportions were perfect, the colonnade behind it harmonizing beautifully with the house itself. The paved court in front was welcoming, as it led up to a portico that was the one element of the house not accurate historically, but blending so well with the Classical style that Matt found himself thinking he must have missed something major in his overview of

Classical architecture. Of course, that had only been two weeks out of a survey course, but still . . .

Wait a minute! This *wasn't* part of the Classical style—it was something new, an innovation, but developed in perfect harmony with the spirit of the sunlit Golden Age of Greece, expressed in Roman style! Whoever this man was, he was eclectic, and not afraid to try something new.

Matt had to meet him. He walked up to the door and was surprised to find a huge brass knocker that could have come off a door in sixteenth century Florence, but somehow blended exquisitely with the Roman style. He lifted it, let it fall, waited a minute, then lifted it and let it fall again. He was mildly surprised that there were no reverberations echoing away into cavernous depths, then surprised at himself for being surprised. No, of course there wouldn't be, would there? Not in a sunny, airy, open house like this.

The door swung wide, and an old man stood there, bald, a little stooped, with a Roman nose, a thin-lipped smile, and a bright, inquisitive eye. "Good day, friend! You are a friend, I trust?"

"Not yet," Matt said, "but I think I'd like to be."

"Are you a philosopher, then?"

"I can't really claim that." After all, he hadn't even written his dissertation yet, let alone received his Ph.D. "I just enjoy learning."

"But not enough to claim you love knowledge, eh?" The man smiled, amused. "Perhaps you love women more? Or one woman?"

"One," Matt confirmed. "I suppose you might say I flirt with knowledge, but I wouldn't want to marry it."

"Ah!" The man laughed. "Whereas I, my friend, most exquisitely enjoy flirting with beautiful women, but have chosen to marry knowledge! Have you read the works of the Greeks?"

"Only some," Matt admitted, "and I studied modern languages, never did learn Latin or Greek."

"But you are a scholar!"

"No, only a professional student."

Finally, the man frowned. "You must explain the distinction to me—but first we must see to some refreshment for you. Come in, come in!"

As Matt stepped inside the door, the old man held out one hand as he closed the door with the other. "I am Arouetto. And you?"

Well, here it came. This was the chance of friendship, or the making of an enemy—but Matt didn't feel like lying to this guy; he instinctively liked him. "I'm Matthew Mantrell."

Arouetto stared. "The Lord Wizard of Merovence?"

Matt braced himself. "The same."

"I have heard of you, have heard of the breadth of your scholarship! Oh, do come in, seat yourself! We must talk, at length and of many matters! Come, come!"

Arouetto hurried away down a hall and through a doorway. Matt followed, bemused. Nice to know he wasn't counted as an enemy— but it was a bit of a surprise to hear this stranger sing his praises, especially for his scholarship. Maybe, by the standards of this world, he knew enough to be *called* a scholar—but Matt knew the truth.

On the other hand, he knew a mathematician who had walked through the commencement line, taken a proud look at his Ph.D. diploma, and said, "Well, now I know how much I don't know." Maybe it went with the territory.

But sitting down did have a nice sound. He followed Arouetto.

They passed through the door into the atrium. That bright Italian sun beat down, but Arouetto was leading him to a marble bench in the shade of a wall, with a little table beside it. "Seat yourself, my friend! I know—the marble is hard. But a cushion will soften it!" He stared at the white surface, and suddenly there was a brocaded cushion covering its top, fitting its shape exactly. "And something cool to drink!" Arouetto stared at the tabletop, and a crystal goblet appeared, beaded with moisture, for the purple liquid inside it was iced. Arouetto looked up, beaming. "It is convenient being in a world of illusion, is it not?"

So he knew. "How long did it take you to figure that out?" Matt asked slowly.

"I did not—I fear I am slow of thought. It took an encounter with a braggart sorcerer, who thought to intimidate me with the range of his fantasies." Arouetto smiled. "But he did not know the Classics, knew nothing of the Hydra or the gorgons. He fled screaming when he met them, and by the time he remembered they were only illusions and could be fought, I had already dreamed up this villa. Its walls were proof against all his monsters, for I fear the man had little learning, and less imagination." He sat down on a bench next to Matt's, the little table between them. "How long did it take you, my friend? Being a wizard, you no doubt knew it for what it was quite quickly." A goblet with chartreuse liquid appeared in his fingers.

"Well, yes, but I was *trying* to figure it out," Matt said, "and when you're deliberately trying to cast a spell, and it works better and faster than you'd expected, you kind of get a hint." He took a sip; it was unfermented grape juice, cold and delicious. "Apparently, King Boncorro decided it would be better for me to be working my magic in here than in his kingdom."

"So you confronted the king himself! A wizards' duel?"

"Don't know if you could say it was a duel," Matt said slowly. "I was too busy talking and not being suspicious enough; he took me more or less by surprise. I can understand why he'd want me out of the way, though—I did come into his kingdom in disguise, after all. To be frank, I was spying."

"And he found you out." Arouetto nodded. "Or was it his chancellor, Rebozo?"

"It was Rebozo, and he would as soon have cut my head off as glowered at me—but Boncorro decided to send me here instead. He said it was a test to find out how powerful I was. If I can figure a way to get out of here, I pass."

"In which case, he will know that he must use every spell at his command to slay you." Arouetto nodded. "I would recommend, Lord Wizard, that if you do manage to fly this congenial prison, you escape to some place far from King Boncorro—and take me with you."

Matt swirled the liquid in his goblet. "I should think you would like it here."

"Oh, it is certainly far more luxury than I could manage in the real world, and I am able to surround myself with beauty that I can only dream of at home! But it is lonely, Lord Wizard. I may not wish to marry, but I do enjoy the company of kindred souls—and corresponding with the few others who have discovered the delights of the old Greek and Reman books."

"I can understand that. I saw some of your statues coming in, though, and they're masterful. Did you just remember works you had actually seen? If you did, I'd like to meet the sculptor."

"I did remember the statues of the Greeks and Remans that I have seen myself, but for the others, I imagined people I knew, then undressed them in my mind and set them on pedestals, in stone."

Matt smiled. "It's a good thing none of them can see their statues."

"Oh, they would not recognize them!" Arouetto assured him. "I begin with faces I know, but change them so that the resemblance is lost, but the beauty preserved."

"And change them toward the Greek ideal while you're at it, I'll bet—and the same for their bodies. I haven't seen too many modern people who have those builds."

Arouetto smiled with delight. "You have caught me! But yes, there is a certain sameness to all the faces, and to the bodies, too. It is the Classical style."

"I take it you enjoy working with nudes."

"If you mean, do I find sexual pleasure in it, the answer is yes," Arouetto said. "I caress the feminine form divine with my mind as I am making it appear on its pedestal—but I take equally great delight in the contemplation of its proportions and its line and grace, when I am done."

He was honest, at least. "I might accuse you of glorifying the human form."

"Might, but would not?" Arouetto smiled wickedly. "So you, too, believe that human beings are perfectible!"

"Well, yes, but they're depravable, too," Matt said slowly. "I do think our race has an amazing number of good qualities and hidden potentials—though I sometimes despair of them ever being developed."

"Still, you have faith in humanity?"

"I'm afraid I do," Matt sighed, "though it does make me feel gullible. I wouldn't say I believe that *all* people are born fundamentally good, but I think *most* of them are. Doesn't always last until they're grown up, of course. I take it you *do* believe humanity is good in and of itself?"

"Oh, I think that people are wonderful! They are a never-ending source of wonder and mystery, even the bad ones! But yes, I find that there is more good than bad in them, and believe that we as a species can be made perfect."

"You are definitely a humanist," Matt said. "What else are you?"

Arouetto spread his hands. "I am a scholar who seeks to become a philosopher. That is all."

"That's enough, Heaven knows." Matt noticed that the man didn't flinch at the word "Heaven." "But how do you make a living?"

"I inherited enough to live in comfort if I lived plainly," Arouetto said, "and found that I had to make a choice. I could live in genteel poverty and devote myself to study—or I could marry, rear a family, and pay the price of having to labor and scheme in commerce to support them. I chose to devote myself to Knowledge, my true love."

"And Art," Matt pointed out. "Couldn't you have made a living as a sculptor?"

"Oh, my hands have neither skill nor talent! I cannot paint or sculpt in the real world, Lord Wizard—or no better than a clumsy child can. It is only here, in a realm that can be governed by pure thought, that the glories I imagine can become real!"

"Sounds like your ideal habitat," Matt said, "provided you could leave it whenever you wanted to, for a little socializing. What did you do to get sent here in the first place?"

"Nothing." Arouetto smiled sadly. "I existed. That was enough."

Matt stared. "All you asked was to be left alone to study, and the king sent you here?"

"No, Rebozo did—or rather, the king's were the hands that sent me, but it was at Rebozo's urging. He told the king that I was a threat, though I cannot see why."

"I can," Matt said darkly. "Rebozo's power rests on the power of Satan, and you have the audacity to ignore it. If everybody else started thinking the way you do, people actually might start living morally, without fear of the Devil or faith in God, just because it was the right thing to do, just because life was better that way."

Arouetto's smile was sad again. "Come, my friend! Next you will have me believe that water flows uphill and winter is warm! I believe in the worth of humanity, but even I am not so foolish as to believe that most people will be good without some form of coercion!"

"Rebozo believes it, though," Matt said, "and anything that might encourage people to be good is going to win his instant animosity. As to the king, he's young enough to believe most of what his chancellor tells him."

"He will grow, though, and gain wisdom for himself," Arouetto said.

"Oh, yes," Matt said softly, remembering the conflict he had witnessed between chancellor and king. "You may be sure of it."

"He may then find my ideas not as threatening as his chancellor does." Oddly, Arouetto didn't seem all that eager about it.

Matt studied him closely a moment and guessed that his calmness was more a matter of willpower and discipline than of gut-level emotion; it spoke of the Stoicism of Marcus Aurelius. Also, now that he looked closely, he saw that the scholar wasn't really all that old; the bald head and the stooped shoulders were signs that, in this case, were misleading. His face was wrinkled, yes, but mostly with crow's-feet and laugh lines, along with some grooves in his forehead, and that prow of a nose made the whole face look leaner than it really was. Matt's revised guess for his age was mid-fifties, maybe sixty. Of course, in a medieval world, that *was* old. "Yes, I think the king would find your ideas interesting, even now," he said slowly. "In fact, I think he would find them vital—if he knew about them."

"There is the little problem of informing him, yes." The scholar sighed. "But why do you think he would find my studies so fascinating, Lord Wizard?"

"Because he's trying to convince himself that there's no Heaven or Hell," Matt said, "which means no God or Satan. In brief, he's trying to do away with religion."

"Then my ideas would *not* please him!" Arouetto said severely. "I believe most strongly in God, Lord Wizard—which no doubt had something to do with Rebozo's eagerness to be rid of me."

"But you also believe in humanity."

"I do, and see no conflict between the two. The churchmen teach that we are born in sin and are animal by nature. I cannot argue with our essential animality, but I will also affirm that we each hold within our souls a spark of the Divine. I have dedicated my life to discovering and revealing that innate goodness in man and woman which comes from God, and to developing all that is best in human nature."

"Ah! Then you believe that if you are a scholar, you have the obligation to teach!"

"Only if I am asked." Arouetto smiled. "And I have not been." He seemed relieved.

Matt was not. "Too bad there aren't any universities to confer the degree—you're definitely a Ph.D. No wonder Rebozo thought you were a threat."

"Yes—for if someone *had* asked me to teach, my students might have begun to think and question." Arouetto's eyes sparkled.

"But you're no threat at all to King Boncorro's overall plan—in fact, your ideas are just what he's aching for!"

"All the more reason to hide me away here, is it not? No, I am no threat to King Boncorro's goals—but I *am* a threat to the chancellor's plans for frustrating his Majesty's efforts, and corrupting the king himself into the bargain."

"Oh?" Matt's attention suddenly focused even more sharply on the scholar's words. "I only met the two of them briefly, you understand. You think the chancellor has a deliberate plan to stop Boncorro's chances of doing good?"

"Not just to stop him—to pervert all his efforts for the good of his people into ways to cause them suffering as great as any they have ever known. Nay, worse, for it will be a kind of agony of the spirit they have never encountered before, and are ill-prepared to endure!"

"That makes sense," Matt said slowly. It really did—the king having his own private in-house brothel, conferring status and legitimacy on prostitution; the organized campaign to seduce country girls into the business, and the men into crime—Matt realized that something that grew up that fast had to have been planned and encouraged. He wondered if Rebozo had agents leading the runaways south, instigating and twisting their revelry. "You mean Boncorro has a whole strategy mapped out for the enrichment of the commonwealth, but Rebozo has a strategy for corrupting it?"

"That is my guess—though I must confess I have no proof."

"Other than observation, generalization, and prediction, no. It's impossible to run a real laboratory experiment on people; you need field studies, and the field is pretty boggy." But Matt was galvanized, excited, and ebullient. "Your ideas really *are* what King Boncorro needs—something to temper his secularism with humanism, injecting values that might forestall the worst excesses Rebozo's trying to lead him into!"

"Only the worst," the scholar cautioned. "Humanism is not a religion, after all—though it is not opposed to religion, either."

Matt jumped up. "Let's go!"

Arouetto stared at him. "Go? Go where?"

"Why, back to Latruria, of course! You've got no business loafing around here when there's so much work for you at home!"

"But how are we to break out?" Arouetto asked, bewildered.

Matt shrugged it off with airy disregard. "With your brains and my magic, we should be able to find a way easily—but not if we don't try! Come on! Time for research! To the laboratory! Let's hit the books!"

Arouetto began to rise from his bench, his smile growing, his eyes kindling with excitement. It was too bad that the chimera chose just that moment to attack.

Chapter
Twenty-One

The chimera came flying over the wall of the house on short, stubby wings that could not possibly have borne its weight—after all, it was basically a winged lion with a dragon's tail. It dropped down at them like an eagle stooping, if eagles could roar loudly enough to shake a house.

Matt bellowed, "Duck!"

"No, a chimera!" Arouetto stood gazing up in wonder.

"I mean *get down*! Scholars are only supposed to be fascinated by *metaphorical* chimeras!" He hit Arouetto with a body block. They went flying, and a huge thud shook the ground while an angry roar shook the trees.

"But 'tis Classical!" Arouetto struggled to free himself. " 'Tis a monster from Greek legend, and I never dared to make one myself!"

Now that somebody had, of course, he was all eagerness to study it, and probably wouldn't remember why he hadn't made one himself until it bit his head off. He struggled valiantly, and Matt was amazed at the gaffer's strength. But he could feel hot breath on his legs, and the roar was echoing all about him as he rolled aside and shouted,

> "Like calculus degenerate,
> It don't want to integrate!
> His parents all refused to mate!
> Let all components separate!"

Teeth clashed shut, and a streak of pain slashed Matt's leg. He howled and rolled aside—just in time to see an eagle struggle loose from the chimera's back, while a small dragon disengaged itself from the monster's rear end, leaving a lion tail behind. The lion fell over, bellowing in pain, and the dragon bellowed, too, scorching the walls. The eagle was smarter—it screamed and flew away.

"We've only got a minute or two while they're disoriented!" Matt snapped. "Then we'll have two monsters to fight instead of one! Quick! Think up something to kill them!"

But Arouetto was out of commission. He was staring at the tableau in front of him, entranced.

Matt turned, brain racing, trying to think up a new cure—and discovered that lions and dragons seemed to be natural enemies.

Actually, first he discovered the fear of seeing a lion stalking toward him, pausing in its roaring only long enough to lick its chops. But the dragon saw, let out a blast like a steam whistle, and charged to get to the tasty morsel first.

They collided, of course.

Scaly shoulder slammed furry shoulder, and the lion turned on the dragon in instant fury, lashing out with a taloned paw and a bellow. But his claws rattled harmlessly off steely scales, and the dragon blasted him with high-octane halitosis. The lion howled in pain and fury and leaped.

Somehow, the big cat managed to land on the dragon's back. The reptile instantly dove to the ground and rolled, but the charred lion hopped loose, then jumped back in to dig its claws into the soft underbelly. The dragon screamed with agony and locked its jaws on the lion's neck, then started clawing him with *its* talons. Roaring and clawing, the two beasts rolled over and over, crushing marble benches and knocking over statuary.

"Wizard, stop them!" Arouetto cried. "They are hurting each other!"

"That's putting it mildly. Why me? You've had a lot more experience with this illusion stuff than I have!"

"Not with living creatures! Stop them! Annihilate them if you must, but end their pain!"

"Oh, *all* right," Matt grumbled. He took a good hard look at the bloody scene before him, then closed his eyes, envisioning that same scene, then adding a little touch he'd seen in his childhood . . .

Arouetto cried out in relief.

Matt opened his eyes and saw a yellow column poking down at an angle, with a rounded pink cylinder on the end that went back and forth across the struggling monsters. The first stroke eliminated the dragon's head and the lion's back; the second took off the top of the lion's head and the end of the dragon's tail. With each stroke, the pink cylinder removed more and more, not knocking them aside, but simply making them disappear. One last stroke took out the lion's feet and the dragon's spine, and they were gone. A last roar and steam blast seemed to echo in the distance, then faded away. Matt closed his eyes, imagining the yellow column fading away, too. Arouetto exclaimed in wonder, and Matt opened his eyes just in time to see the last vague outline dissipate. The giant characters "No. 2" lingered a moment longer, then they evaporated, too.

"Most amazing!" Arouetto breathed. "What was that mystical engine, Lord Wizard?"

"We call it an 'eraser' where I come from," Matt explained. "In this case, though, it was just a mental construct."

"Are not all these illusions?" Arouetto turned to him with a frown. "But who made the chimera?"

"Somebody who's out to get you." Matt never minded stating the obvious—after all, he had taught undergraduates.

"But who? I know all the sorcerers and wizards here, and we sorted out our differences long ago!"

Matt had a quick mental vision of that sorting out—the scholar's Greek warriors and Roman legions tearing apart the sorcerers' synthetic demons. He would have liked to have been on hand for that one. No, on second thought, maybe not—he had become too involved with the conflicts of this pocket universe as it was. "Well, if it's not one of the established residents, it must be somebody new in the neighborhood."

"But how would someone new know that I have an atrium? It is not obvious from the outside of the house."

"A point," Matt admitted, "and it raises a very nasty possibility."

"What is that?"

"Well, if it isn't somebody new, and it isn't somebody old, then it has to be somebody from outside this frame of reference."

"From the real world?" Arouetto stared. "But who?"

"Somebody who knows your weakness for anything Classical, and somebody who's used to keeping an eye on things, just in case one of you prisoners wants to make trouble. Add to that: somebody who has enough magical power to see into this pocket universe, and you have—"

"Rebozo!" Arouetto cried.

Matt nodded grimly. "Glad I didn't have to say it. If you came to the same conclusion, maybe it's not just my nasty, suspicious nature."

"I should think not! Once you state the evidence, the conclusion is obvious! But why would he seek to obliterate me now, when he has been content to keep me in obscurity thus . . . Of course! I must have become a greater threat!"

Matt nodded. "That would make sense, yes."

"But how?"

"Because there's suddenly a chance that you'll be able to break out of here."

"Why . . ." Arouetto's eyes glowed. "Of course! Because you are here with me!"

"Right." Matt nodded. "Neither one of us is all that much of a threat alone, but together, we're a time bomb!"

"A time bomb?" Arouetto frowned. "What is that?"

"I'll tell you when we have more time," Matt said. "Right now, I think we'd just better turn our attention to going back to the real world."

Arouetto turned to look at his villa sadly. "It will be regrettable, leaving this charming place."

"I don't mean to push you," Matt said. "If you want to stay—"

"No, no!" Arouetto turned back to him in alarm. "The company of real living people is far more important than this comfort. Of course, it would be pleasant to have both—but we never can, you know, Lord Wizard. One thing can only be gained at the price of another."

"Yes, I know," Matt said softly, "but you're wise enough to learn the price before you've bought it. I know a lot of people who get what they want, then discover what they've lost in the process—when it's too late to get it back."

"It seems to be a Law of Compensation." Arouetto gave him a conspiratorial smile. "And I am ready to yield this treasure, to gain my freedom."

"Maybe you'll win King Boncorro's favor," Matt said. "Maybe he'll build you a villa just like this, and you can commission sculptors to make these statues for real."

"That would be wonderful, of course," Arouetto sighed, "but no other sculptor could craft *these* statues, exactly as I have imagined them—for no other sculptor has my mind, and we cannot truly share and mingle our thoughts while we are alive, Lord Wizard. We must make do with the clumsy medium of words, written or spoken, and accept their imperfections."

"Again, compensation." Matt nodded. "Maybe we can figure out a way for you to come back and visit now and then."

"That would be pleasant." But Arouetto didn't seem to care that ardently. "Still, as I have said, one must make a choice in life, my friend—and I will choose living people over lifeless marble in an instant."

"Well, it might take a little longer than that," Matt cautioned. "My spells don't seem to have been working all that well in Latruria—in fact, I've been trying to hold down on the magic, and the reason I haven't been willing to admit it to myself is that it might not work as well as I'm used to."

"Certainly not," Arouetto said. "You are a wizard devoted to Right and Good; your magic is based on Faith."

Matt stared, taken aback by the scholar's instant understanding. Then he shook himself and protested, "But my spells worked before I believed in the power of religion in this universe!"

"You may have believed more than you know," Arouetto explained. "Besides, even if you did not knowingly believe very strongly in God, you did believe in Right and Goodness, and their power to ultimately triumph."

"Well, sure, *ultimately* . . ."

"Then, as I've said, your magic was based on Faith," Arouetto said with satisfaction. "But Latruria is a land steeped in cynicism, even in doubt, at least so far as the powers of Righteousness and Goodness are concerned. Therefore your magic was weakened."

Matt sighed. "That makes all too much sense. I wish my friend Saul were here—he's a natural skeptic, so the jaundiced views of the Latrurian people would only strengthen his magic."

"Is he a wizard, too?"

Matt felt a sudden gust of breeze, but answered, "Yes, though he even questions that."

"Who questions what?" said a brittle voice.

They spun, staring. Then a grin stretched wide across Matt's face, and he advanced with open arms. "Saul! What a sense of timing!"

After the glad greetings and the introductions, Matt had to try to explain to Arouetto why Saul wore a barbarian horseman's loose trousers and short tunic, why it was tucked into his pants instead of hanging over, and why he wore rider's boots when he didn't ride much.

"Inquisitive, isn't he?" Saul asked.

Matt shrugged. "He's a scholar." Then he tried to explain their predicament to his friend—and to Arouetto why Saul wore nothing but blue: light blue shirt and dark blue trousers. Matt did notice that the shirt bore a closer resemblance to homespun than to chambray, that the trousers were obviously monk's cloth instead of denim, and that their blue wasn't the real softness of indigo faded, but some local substitute. Still, he had to admit that Angelique had done a very creditable job of imitating blue jeans and chambray in a medieval setting. He was tempted to wonder why she had bothered—but then, he knew Saul.

Then they settled down to some serious plotting.

"Ortho the Frank knew you were in danger," Saul explained.

"Ortho? Why was *he* tuned in?"

"Mostly because Alisande has marched into Latruria with Ortho and a small army, to come and get you."

"A small army!" Matt cried, appalled. "Hey, no! *I* don't want to cause a war!"

"No, just to fight in ones that other people start," Saul said with sarcasm. "So she was already in Latruria and making pretty good speed toward Venarra, when Chancellor Rebozo, whoever he is, sent word to Alisande that you were no longer in Latruria."

"I'll just bet he did!" Matt fumed. "He hoped she'd get the idea that if I wasn't there, there was no point in marching farther south. She didn't just pack up and go home, did she?"

"Without you to bring back? No way! She sent word that she might as well pay a courtesy visit, as long as she had gone that far. Then she talked Sir Guy into calling for me."

"How'd you find me?"

"Ortho guessed that you must be in some sort of alternate magical pocket universe, and I thought of the physicists' idea that the higher dimensions are hidden inside the other three. So I went into a trance and fished around with my mind, trying to get outside the three-dimensional frame of reference—but I wasn't having any luck, until I heard your voice saying, 'I wish Saul were here.' I zeroed in on that."

"I'd like to say it wasn't necessary," Matt said, "but I'm afraid it was. Hate to have you pulling my chestnuts out of the fire again, Saul."

"Don't mention it—life always gets more interesting when you're around." Saul looked up at Arouetto, and Matt could almost see the chip settling onto his shoulder. "So you're a scholar, huh?"

"I am," Arouetto said, "though your friend seems to think the word 'student' is more apt to what I am. For myself, I see no differ-ence between the two."

"Older usage, yeah," Saul admitted. "Any particular reason why you don't call yourself a philosopher?"

"An excellent one—that I do not know enough, and am too poor in judgment." Arouetto's smile warmed. "It is Knowledge I love, Wizard Saul, not wisdom."

"Well, at least you know it—in contrast to a few philosophers I could name. And you're not a professor?"

Arouetto looked surprised. "What would I profess?"

"Whatever your major area of study is," Saul snapped.

"Greece and Reme? There is too much of them to know, for one man to have the audacity to profess his opinions about them!"

"Your humility does you credit," Saul grumbled, "but it's very frustrating when I'm trying to work up a good argument. Okay, Scholar Arouetto—if we want to get back to the real world, where do you think we should aim for? Merovence, so we're outside King Boncorro's jurisdiction?"

"Oh, no! We can do no good for Latruria unless we are in it!"

"Up to our necks," Saul griped, and Matt agreed. "If we *do* go back to Latruria, Rebozo will know it in a matter of minutes, and will hit us with everything he's got."

Saul's smile twisted. "I just love paradoxes. So what we need is someplace inside Latruria, that's outside Rebozo's powers. Neat, huh?"

"Very." Arouetto's eyes glowed again. "But as with any paradox, Wizard Saul, one can resolve it by stepping outside its terms—and there is one hill in Latruria that has held proof against even King Maledicto's miasma of evil, and has certainly held fast without King Boncorro's secular skepticism."

"Oh?" Saul looked up with foreboding. "What hill is that?"

"The Vatican."

"How did I know that was coming?" Saul sighed and looked up at Matt. "Think St. Peter's might be there, in this universe?"

"The largest cathedral in Europe?" asked Arouetto. "Be sure, it is!"

"Well, what the hey! I always have wanted to see the sights." Saul came to his feet. "Of course, I expect the Sistine Chapel hasn't been built yet, let alone decorated, but it's worth seeing anyway." He looked at Matt. "Who do we know in the Vatican?"

"Well," Arouetto said slowly, "there is Brother Thomas . . ."

Brother Thomas, it turned out, was an acquaintance of Arouetto's from their school days—and Matt got another shock when he found out that Arouetto was a deacon. He had attended the seminary because it was the only place devoted to any kind of learning, and the only one that had a good, though limited, library—excellent, so long as all you wanted to study was theology. When Arouetto realized how badly he wanted to study other subjects, he knew his calling was not for the priesthood.

Apparently, Brother Thomas had come to the same conclusion,

though for different reasons—Arouetto said he simply felt that he was not good enough for the job. In vain did his teachers explain to him that he did not have to be a saint, only a good man trying to be better and trying to serve his fellows. Brother Thomas remained adamant. His vocation was for the clergy, he agreed, but not for the priesthood—yet. Perhaps it would be, in God's own time. Until then, he would serve in whatever capacity his bishop wanted.

What his bishop wanted of him, it transpired, was to stay at the seminary as librarian, which was ideal from Brother Thomas' point of view, since it gave him the company of the books he dearly loved, and time to write the treatises about the problems that had been worrying him. He showed them to his teachers, and they exclaimed with delight—he had managed to come up with answers to the spiritual problems that had been perplexing them all, ever since merchants started bringing back alien ideas along with the spices of the Orient. He might not have been a priest, but he was a theologian—so the bishop transferred him to the cathedral library, where he remained happily filing and scribbling until the pope coopted him to run the Vatican library. Besides, that way the cardinals could keep a personal eye on the development of Brother Thomas' ideas; they weren't certain they liked the sound of some of his newer lines of thought.

Saul grinned. "Sounds like my kind of hombre."

Arouetto frowned. " 'Hombre'?"

"That's Iberian," Matt said quickly. "It means 'man.' " He turned to Saul. "So what do we do with this librarian, now that we've found him?"

"Think about him," Saul said simply. "Scholar Arouetto, can you show us what Brother Thomas looks like?"

The scholar closed his eyes, brow creasing in concentration, and a picture frame appeared next to him, with a canvas that gradually became clear, showing them a round face topped by a tonsure, a snub nose, small but kindly eyes, and a little mouth pursed in a smile. It was a gentle face, a tranquil face—just the kind of man who might start an intellectual earthquake.

Why did Matt have the feeling Brother Thomas was never coming out of the Vatican again?

"Theologian, huh?" Saul stared at the picture, brow knit. "He have anything to say about magic?"

Arouetto smiled. "It is one of the notions that has aroused consternation among the cardinals. Brother Thomas maintains that what we term 'magic' is really just the deft handling of unseen forces that surround us, but do not come from either Heaven or Hell—they simply arise from all living things. It is the life force, if you will. But the way of manipulating and concentrating that to affect objects and people, *that* is learned from God and His Saints, or the Devil and his minions. It is not the force that comes from God, but the knowledge."

Matt nodded. "Which explains why magic works in your universe but doesn't in ours—our life-forms don't give off that kind of energy."

"How is this?" Arouetto lifted his head like a hound striking a scent. "You come from another universe?"

"Yes, and we'll explain later," Saul said quickly. "Right now, we need to get out of *this* universe."

"But if that's magic, what's a miracle?" Matt cocked his head to the side. "Those happen in our universe, too."

"Ah!" Arouetto raised a forefinger. "Miracles *are* the work of God directly, or through His Saints—so says Brother Thomas. They are not a manipulation of natural forces, but an exercise of God's power itself."

"Meaning the One Who made the laws can break them when He wants to," Saul said with a sardonic smile. "Dealer wins all draws."

"Well, at least we're not trying for a new deal." Matt sighed. "We're just playing our cards better."

"I'll take three," Saul said. "Let's try to reach out to Brother Thomas, shall we? Use him as our anchor to pull ourselves out."

Arouetto frowned. "But how can you reach out to his universe from this one?"

"Who says we can't?" Saul countered. "Have you ever tried?"

"Why—no!" Arouetto said, startled. "I am no wizard, but only a poor scholar! Still, there are many sorcerers and wizards here—surely *they* have attempted it!"

Saul shrugged. "Maybe none of them had a confederate on the outside. From what I hear of sorcerers, none of them would help anybody else if he didn't have to, and definitely wouldn't want to increase the competition by bringing somebody back out of solitary. Wizards might not be outright people haters, but from what I've seen of them, they tend to be loners—lots of acquaintances, but not very many close friends."

"A few really good ones are all you need!" Matt protested.

Saul shot him one of his rare warm glances. "Hey, *I* know that, man—but most of the people I meet don't. They like to travel in packs: the bigger the better." He turned back to Arouetto. "So there's no proof any wizard or sorcerer *has* tried to get out, with a pull from the outside—and they certainly haven't ganged up trying. Here, you've got two experienced wizards, ready to work together, and a scholar who probably has more understanding of magic than he's willing to admit."

"Well . . . I *have* read the theories of Pythagoras," Arouetto admitted.

"Then you've got a book that didn't survive in our universe." Now it was Saul who tensed. "After this is all wrapped up, I want to see that text!"

"Why, surely, if my belongings have not all been vandalized. But how are we to proceed now?"

"Well, we know it's possible to reach in here from outside," Saul said, "because we know Rebozo did it, sending that chimera after you. In fact, he probably watches what goes on in here pretty closely, brewing up even bigger trouble, so we'd better get moving fast. If he can reach in, we can probably reach out. What would make Brother Thomas concentrate on you?"

Arouetto smiled. "Why, a picture of me with the inscription, 'Think of me!' "

"Of course," Saul said. "Pardon me while I feel dumb. Any time I'm getting too cocky, Matt, just tell me to come have a chat with this guy."

"Why, how is this?" Arouetto looked back and forth from one to the other with concern. "I do not mean offense!"

"Of course not," Saul said. "You just see the obvious that goes right past the two of us, 'cause we're busy looking for something complicated. Okay, Scholar Arouetto—think up a self-portrait with the inscription, and we two will get busy concentrating on a mental picture of Brother Thomas' face."

"Will that accomplish anything?" Arouetto asked doubtfully.

"Who knows? It's sure worth a try!"

"It is that." Arouetto shrugged. "Very well, then, here is my portrait." His brow furrowed with concentration, and a miniature appeared in a filigreed frame. It was a bit uglier than the real thing, but none the less recognizable. Underneath it was a small metal scroll engraved with the words, *Think of me.*

"Got it." Saul closed his eyes and grabbed Matt's hand. Matt squeezed back, closing his eyes and picturing Brother Thomas' face, then expanding the view to show him wearing a monk's robe and holding out a hand with the miniature in it. "Right hand."

"Right," Saul acknowledged.

Matt groped with his left hand, felt Arouetto catch it. "I have your hand, Lord Wizard!" the scholar said.

"Hold tight," Matt said between his teeth. "If anything happens, it'll happen fast."

Suddenly, he felt it, the way you feel someone's gaze on the back of your neck, only stronger, much stronger. It felt as if he had stepped out of the shade into a ray of noontime sun in summertime Nevada. From a distance he heard Saul say, "Got him! Now, Matt—'I'm Going Away,' past tense!"

Matt sang with him, not quite on the same pitch:

> "I've gone away
>> For to stay
>> A little while,
>> But I'm coming back,
>> Though I go ten thousand mile!"

The fabric of the universe seemed to wrench and tear about them. Reality rocked, and Matt clamped tight with both hands as his inner ear went crazy, registering a tilting and seesawing from side to side and back and forth. Dimly, he heard Arouetto cry out with alarm, and Saul cry out with elation. Himself, he just bit his lip and hoped for the best.

Then the world seemed to stabilize, a little at a time, until Matt finally realized that the rocking was going on in his stomach, not in the world around him. With trepidation, he opened his eyes . . .

And found himself in a small but spacious room with sunlight pouring in through open windows, the smell of flowers in the air, plain cream-colored plaster walls with the dark supporting beams showing, and a monk on a high stool, sitting at a higher desk, looking up at them in delight. Matt recognized Brother Thomas, not quite as noble-looking as Arouetto's picture of him—and in the monk's right hand was the miniature of Arouetto.

"Friend Arouetto!" Brother Thomas cried in a surprisingly deep voice. "What a joy to see you! It has been so long! But who are these wizardly companions of yours?"

Matt was just about to answer when the world darkened and he felt the room spinning again.

Chapter
Twenty-Two

All things considered, Matt was very relieved to see the same room around him when he came to. He'd had a bad moment when he thought Rebozo had magically pulled him away. He said as much, but Brother Thomas assured him, "No evil sorcery can touch you here. There is too much holiness about us, too many prayers filling the air." Then he frowned. "Of course, if you *wished* the powers of Evil to touch you, if even some part of you that you did not wish to acknowledge longed for that touch, you would breach our defenses."

"I don't think even my subconscious wants that," Matt said thickly. "It's seen a little too much of the results."

"Here, drink." The monk held a goblet near Matt's lips. "Gently, for 'tis brandy—but a sip or two will bring the color back to your cheeks."

Matt took a guarded sip, and heat exploded on his tongue, down his esophagus, and into his stomach. He exhaled, expecting to see fire, and found himself sitting upright. "Yes," he said hoarsely. "That'll straighten out a snake." He swallowed and said, "Nice brew."

"But perhaps a bit of water after it?" Brother Thomas smiled and held out another goblet. Matt took it, and the monk turned away to press the brandy on Saul, then Arouetto—both of whom, Matt was relieved to see, were looking pretty green around the gills themselves. The brandy straightened them up, of course, and Brother Thomas was right—it *did* bring the color back to their cheeks, though they needed the chaser, too.

"Didn't know you folks had brandy here," Saul said.

"We have a most talented monk in charge of our stillery," Brother Thomas explained.

"New invention, then." Saul nodded. "I'm sure it will catch on."

"Well, you seem to be somewhat restored." Brother Thomas beamed around at his collection of hulks beached on hardwood benches. "It is so good of you to visit a poor friar in his solitude! But tell me, to what do I owe the pleasure of this visit—especially when it is made in so unorthodox a manner?"

He was polite, but he was very curious—and very good at hearing them out, then asking questions that drew every last ounce of information from them. Finally he leaned back on his stool, resting against the desk, nodding in satisfaction that he had the whole story. "So! You have the audacity to set yourselves against the wickedness permitted by King Boncorro—or to seek to help him banish the wickedness that remains from the reign of King Maledicto, if you can first determine which is the case."

"I vote for leftovers," Matt said. "I've met Chancellor Rebozo."

"He has an unsavory reputation, yes," Brother Thomas agreed, "though most seem to think it is only because he toadies to the king and does whatever his Majesty commands, whether it be good or ill."

"He prefers ill," Matt averred, and Arouetto agreed. "Dismiss whatever reputation you have heard of his kindliness, Brother Thomas. He is a mean and cruel man, enjoying others' misery."

"You speak from your own experience?" Brother Thomas asked with interest.

"Yes," Matt and Arouetto said together.

The monk steepled his fingers together. "And what do you propose to do about it?"

Arouetto and Saul exchanged a blank look, but Matt said slowly, "The king is trying very hard to be a materialist and believe in nothing but the things he can see and taste and touch. The result is that he has made a very good beginning on transforming Latruria into a secular society."

Brother Thomas frowned. "But we have always had to contend with the secular aspects of life. The word only means 'worldly,' after all."

"Yes—but most people have looked beyond this world, to the next. King Boncorro is trying to convince himself, and his people, that this world is all there is."

Brother Thomas pursed his lips and whistled, gazing off into space.

"Yes," Matt said. "Taking it to a bit of an extreme, isn't he?"

"He is most surely! There is nothing wrong with seeking to cope with the trials and burdens of this world, mind you, nor to seek worldly pleasures, so long as you hurt no one else thereby—"

"You *sure* you're not a heretic?" Saul demanded.

"Quite sure." Brother Thomas grinned. "But the pope and his cardinals are not. Still, it is me you are asking, and it is I who shall answer. Christ told us to render unto Caesar that which is Caesar's, after all, which I interpret as meaning that we must pay some attention to worldly matters."

"Some." Matt held up a palm. "Not all."

"Not all, by any means. The Way of the World is cruel, with the stronger feeding upon the weaker, even grinding the weaker into the dust. We speak of slavery; we speak of toadying to those of higher rank and bullying those of lower; we speak of seeking to squeeze every last ounce of pleasure out of this life, with no concern for who may be hurt in the process. No, the secular life, with no spiritual values to balance it, will surely lead to evil. And this is the course on which King Boncorro has set every soul in his kingdom!"

"So far, yes," Matt agreed. "But if we can interest him in some sort of moral principles, maybe we can balance that downward trend and pull it up to a level."

"And how shall you manage that? He will have nothing to do with religion!"

"No," Matt said, "but he *is* interested in the old learning, in the writings of the Greeks and Remans."

"Is he truly?" Brother Thomas said slowly, turning to look at Arouetto.

The scholar held up both palms to fend him off. "Do not seek to saddle me with him, I pray! My faith is in God first, yes, but in humankind second! Would you have this secular king become a humanist?"

"Yes," Brother Thomas said, the fire of zeal lighting his eye. "It will bring him morality of a sort; it will bring him ethical principles!"

"But I am not a teacher!"

"Only because you haven't been asked," Matt pointed out.

"King Boncorro will not ask me to teach him!"

"Want to bet?"

"*I'll* bet," Saul said. "I'll bet that this Chancellor Rebozo won't let Arouetto within a mile of the king!"

"He must indeed have some protection." Brother Thomas' keen gaze seemed to sink right into Matt's brain.

"Saul and I might be enough protection, between us," Matt admitted, "but Saul's a secular humanist himself, and I have more than my share of spiritual weaknesses. Wouldn't we need some kind of shielding?"

Brother Thomas sighed. "All we can offer is prayer, but I speak ahead of myself. I cannot decide on so weighty a matter. You must speak to the Holy Father and let him judge your wisdom or folly."

"The pope?" Matt stared.

"Even so. I shall arrange an audience."

"Well, there's only the three of us," Matt said, "and that's not much of a house—but if you can give us a chance, maybe we can persuade him."

The only problem was, he wasn't sure what he was going to be trying to persuade the pope to do.

"Let you leave the Vatican?" The pope smiled. "To be sure! You may leave whenever you wish! But how shall you pass through the lines of the condottieri who surround us?"

"Condottieri?" Matt turned to Brother Thomas. "You didn't tell us about this."

The monk waved the objection away. "Surely a minor detail, for a wizard of your prowess."

"Maybe not," Saul said, glowering. "Who are these bandits, and how many of them are there?"

"Several thousand," the pope sighed, "and they have celebrated the third anniversary of their surrounding of our hill."

"Three years in place?" Saul looked up, almost indignantly. "How come they haven't all died of dysentery and cholera?"

"Oh, they live well," Brother Thomas told him. "Their days may be filled with drill and other military exercises, but their nights are wild with revelry. The king keeps them well-supplied with wine and women and money for gambling. They have settled down to stay, Lord Wizard. We speak not of a city of tents, mind you—they have built themselves wooden barracks, even houses for the officers. Their captains have captured the palaces of noblemen!"

"Captains, plural?" Saul demanded. "This isn't just one band, then?"

"Nay," said Brother Thomas. "It is eight bands, allied and agreed as to who has jurisdiction over which sector. In truth, they have taken the city of Reme and become its virtual government."

"So it's not just a campaign against you? You're simply the only hill that's been able to hold out?"

"Yes," said the pope, "though our endurance is certainly not due to our handful of valiant Swiss guardsmen. I think the mercenary captains are in awe of us—either that, or our prayers are answered more strongly than even I would expect."

"Or," Saul said slowly, "they have more to gain by leaving you be than by capturing you."

The pope turned to him, frowning. "How could that be?"

"Let's just say, purely hypothetically, you understand, that the bandits *did* take the Vatican," Saul said. "What would King Boncorro do then?"

The pope stood immobile as the consequences added up in his brain—but it was Brother Thomas who spoke. "He could not allow them to keep the ancient capital of the empire, could he?"

"Definitely not," Saul said. "Too much prestige in it—not to mention a central location, the Tiber for a supply line, and all the surrounding farmland to feed them. They would start raiding the other cities—and there's every chance they'd manage to take Latruria away from King Boncorro. After all, these guys aren't simple forest bandits, are they?"

"Not at all," Brother Thomas said, thin-lipped. "They are mercenary armies, seeking a living while they are unemployed."

"What makes you so sure they're unemployed?"

The other four men stared at Saul, astounded.

"Yes, of course," Matt said slowly. "King Boncorro couldn't just leave them at loose ends, could he? He'd have them raiding all over the peninsula, wreaking chaos—and undermining the prosperity he's trying to build. Better to pay them to stay out of the way."

"Wouldn't work," Saul said firmly. " 'Once you have paid the Danegeld, you never get rid of the Dane.' "

"Dane?" The pope looked from one to the other, puzzled.

"The Vikings who raided England," Matt explained. "One of the kings tried to pay them off—and it worked for a few months, sometimes a year. But sooner or later they came back to demand more."

"However," Saul said, "if you didn't just pay them to stay away, but hired them to do a definite job, they might stay occupied and permanently out of the way."

"You are saying that the king hired them to lock us in, but never to take us?"

"No, I'm saying he told them to conquer you, but the captains figured out fast that once they took the Vatican, the paychecks would stop—so they came up with a plausible story about not being able to march past the foot of your slope, and settled down to starve you out."

"But we have wells and water, and they have not attempted to keep the barges from selling us food!"

"Well, can they help it if they don't have a navy?" Saul asked.

"Meantime, the king pays them well to live in luxury. They're happy, he's happy—and you're penned up where you can't interfere with his plans."

"It is possible, it is very possible," the pope muttered, shaking his head. "I would not have thought him to be so devious."

Saul shrugged. "Okay, so maybe he just told his chancellor to find a way to keep the mercenaries out of the way and peaceful, and Rebozo decided it was worth sacrificing Reme, to make sure you guys couldn't bust up his plans. Would the king really worry about it?"

"Nay." The pope's lips thinned. "In fact, I can see that he might applaud the notion. But how are we to be rid of them?"

"Do you *want* to be?" Saul challenged.

"Of course!" the pope snapped. "There is no chance of doing God's work, of preaching the Gospel and administering the sacraments, if we are kept as virtual prisoners here!"

"But you have priests out in the countryside to do that work," Saul objected, "priests in secret, priests in hiding, but no less effective for all that. I've even run into one man who claims that nothing spreads a religion so much as persecution."

"I will allow that it tempers us and makes those of us who cling to the Faith crystalline in our belief," the pope said, "but 'spread'?"

"So it's the man in the field who does the real work, as always," Saul pointed out. "What do they need to be in touch with the bureaucrats at headquarters for?"

The pope's eyes narrowed. "I do not think I like you, Wizard Saul."

"Join the club," Saul said with a sardonic smile. "You've got plenty of company. But I notice you haven't answered the question."

"The valiant clergy must be in contact with us for the same reason that a body needs a head!" the pope snapped. "Without our direction, without our inspiration, their faith would falter, they would succumb to fear and to temptations of the flesh! Most serious of all, the usurper has set up a puppet pope in the north, at that little town just below the Alps. The imposter claims to be the true pope!"

"Which you are, of course," Saul said, poker-faced.

"Of course I am! The cardinals elected me, and stayed here with me, save for the handful who fled to do Boncorro's bidding! Oh, the people cry that it is a sign of his tolerance, of his allowing the faithful to practice their Faith again—but we know better, for we have heard this puppet pope's edicts! He teaches that each bishop can interpret the Scriptures for himself without the restriction of the papacy! He teaches that adultery is permissible, if it is done far from home! He teaches that the people need only heed the law of the king, but never the law of the Church!"

"He does kind of sound like a paid voice," Matt said to Saul.

"Yeah, well, it wasn't quite that clear back home," Saul growled. "And we haven't heard his side of the story."

The pope turned a black gaze on the Wizard of Sarcasm. "Must you question everything that is said? Have you no faith of any kind?"

"Yes!" Saul snapped. "I have faith in the ideas that have withstood every test I could put them to! I question everything, and only accept the ideas that have sound answers!"

"Even then, you're ready to revise your opinion on new evidence," Matt pointed out.

"Yeah, well, I admitted that the atrocity stories about the Phoenician religion were true, didn't I?"

"Only when the archaeologists dug up that graveyard of incinerated bodies," Matt retorted.

"Indeed!" The pope looked interested. "You will hearken to Truth, then!"

"Why, yes," Saul shot back. "Do you have any to tell me?"

The pope's face darkened again, and Arouetto interrupted quickly. "The condottieri have sealed off the Vatican. That, at least, is true."

The pope nodded. "And the Church needs the Holy See, just as the Empire of Reme needed its emperor."

"Whoa!" Matt held up a hand. "I thought it had turned into a real republic, with the Etruscans, the Latini, and the Carthaginians all equal partners."

Saul looked up with keen interest. "You know something I don't know?"

"Yes, and I'll fill you in later. When did they hire an emperor, your Holiness?"

"Why, when they had conquered so much territory, and so many peoples, that the senate could not wait for the tedious exchange of messages with the provinces that would decide their policies," the pope answered, frowning. "When decisions needed to be made more quickly than debate would allow. Do you not know of this?"

"We haven't had access to the books."

"Lamentable!" The pope shook his head. "Know, then, that it was Julius Caesar who was first able to find common ground between the views of all three powers, and who was able to make policies that satisfied them all—or persuade them to be satisfied."

"Here, too, huh?" Saul nodded. "He always was as much a politician as a general."

"Or just as *good* a politician," Matt qualified.

"He also had an excellent sense for commerce," the pope told them. "His trade policies ruled the empire till its closing days."

"Well, that's new," Saul admitted. "Did the Praetorian Guard still get so much of the real power?"

"The . . . Guard?" The pope frowned. "What were they?"

"Caesar's bodyguard," Matt explained. "Actually, it was Augustus who really built them up, after what had happened to his uncle."

"What *did* happen to his uncle?"

Matt stared, then said carefully, "The way I heard it, Caesar was assassinated."

"Assassinated? Never! He died in bed, aged but still keen of mind, and honored by all!"

Matt stared, and Saul muttered, *"Et tu, Brute."*

"Brutus?" The pope looked up. "Aye, he led the Latini in acclaiming Augustus the legitimate heir—who proved just as adroit a diplomat as his uncle. What need would he have had for a bodyguard? The people loved him, the patricians loved him! Oh, there are tales of madmen striking at him in the streets—but the mob bore them down ere they could come near him! The whole city was his bodyguard!"

Saul turned to Matt. "You mind explaining?"

"Change the foundation, you get a different shape of house," Matt explained. "Details at eleven." He turned back to the pope. "So the senate really did choose the emperor, right down to the last days of the empire?"

"They did indeed, and there were always many Caesars to choose from."

"*Real* Caesars?" Saul demanded. "Not just adopted Claudians? He didn't divorce his first wife and marry Livia?"

"Never! He maintained staunchly that divorce was the bane of the patricians, and did all he could to discourage it!"

"So his children were really *his* children," Matt said slowly, "and the empire was ruled by a line of diplomats, not a series of sadistic madmen. How about Caligula?"

The pope gave him a blank look, but Arouetto said, "He was a scion of the Claudians—mad, as the Lord Wizard says. When his incest with his sister was discovered, he was sent to the frontier, then executed for commanding a century of legionnaires to charge a thousand Germans. They were slain to a man, though they took five hundred Germans with them."

"So." Matt steepled his fingers. "The Claudians never took power, and the Etruscans and Carthaginians kept an informal system of checks and balances operating, so the emperor never really was a total despot. Power didn't corrupt the office?"

"Well, somewhat," Arouetto admitted, "but never more than it corrupts any bailiff or reeve."

"No absolute power, so no absolute corruption." Matt nodded. "Come to that, how many countries did the empire actually have to conquer, and how many joined to get better trade advantages?"

"Shrewdly guessed, for one who claims not to have read the books," the pope said with a frown, but Arouetto smiled. "I doubt not it was a shrewd guess indeed—and I have but to confirm the answer. Yes, Julius Caesar was as clever in commerce as in battle, as I've said, and invented a score of advantages for other nations to federate with Reme. The army conquered only those nations intent on stealing Reme's trade—pirates' nests and bandits' roosts—and those intent on overthrowing Reme herself, or raiding her provinces; it was for that reason we conquered the Germanies."

"Conquered the Germanies?" Matt stared. "On the other side of the Rhine?"

"Even so."

"Just when did the empire fall?" Saul demanded.

"The federated nations had almost all broken away by the year of Our Lord 653," Arouetto said, "but it was not until 704, when the last of the Caesars had died, that the Visigoths attacked Reme herself. The Ostrogoths marched up behind them and made short work of them, so Reme was not sacked—but an Ostrogoth declared himself to be emperor. No federated nation would obey a man who was not a Caesar, not even a Latrurian, so we may say that is the date at which the empire fell."

Matt frowned. "But Hardishane established *his* empire only a hundred years later!"

Arouetto nodded. "He rose up among the ruins of the empire, as it were, and forged an empire anew."

"That certainly minimized the Dark Ages." Saul was looking dazzled. "How did the Caesars keep the proletariat from tearing Reme apart?"

"Why, by conscripting them into the army and navy," Arouetto replied.

"Didn't the patricians object?" Matt asked. "What did they do for clients?"

"Oh, there were always a few old soldiers who wished to return to Reme to raise their families, rather than settling down in the provinces they had defended."

"But the sons of the senators?" Matt asked. "How did Caesar prevent them from hanging around Reme and getting into trouble?"

Saul gave a bark of laughter. "Who do you think were the officers?"

Arouetto nodded. "Even so—and the sons of the plebians became centurions, if they did not wish to go on trading voyages."

"Yeah." Saul smiled sourly. "The merchants did as much to spread the empire as the soldiers, didn't they?'

"Oh, more! For first the merchants would begin trading with a country and let them see the benefits of Reman civilization—"

"Which means they got them hooked on Reman goods and gave them a glimpse of central heating and public baths," Matt interpreted.

Saul nodded. "And filled the teenagers' heads with dazzling visions of the wonders of Reme, Carthage, and the cities of the Levant. *Sure* they'd want to join the empire—especially since the emperor always sent in a legion to protect his merchants. Right?"

Arouetto frowned. "Are you *sure* you have not read the books?"

"Your Holiness!" A monk broke in, the white showing all around his eyes. "The condottieri attack!"

"To the chapel, quickly!" the pope cried, then turned to his guests. "Come with us, for every prayer is needed, to beseech the Saints' protection!"

Matt had a vision of an invisible wall of prayer surrounding the Vatican. He could see Saul working himself up to a scathing reply and was just about to try to stop him when the monk burst out, "There are sorcerers with them, your Holiness! They have already thrown fireballs at the Holy City! The Saints protected us, and the fireballs fell back among the condottieri—but Heaven knows what they will try next!"

"Heaven does know, and will forestall them, Brother Athenius," the pope reassured him, then to his guests, "Follow us!"

They hurried after him, Matt catching up and saying, "With all respect, your Holiness, it might be a bit more practical for Wizard Saul and myself to stay here and fight magic with magic."

The pope screeched to a halt and stared. "But there will be danger!"

"We're used to it," Saul snapped, and Matt shrugged. "There will be danger even in the cathedral, your Holiness. We have taken such risks before."

"Then I shall accept your kind offer, and gratefully! But at least climb to the top of St. Peter's steeple! You can see all of the enemy from there, and the power of prayer may assist you!"

"The power of prayer!" Saul grumbled as they climbed the steeple. "What good is *that* going to be?"

"More than you know, here," Matt said. They came out into a small cupola above the belfry and looked out over the city of Reme. For a few moments both men stood speechless. Then Saul said, "Looks just like Rome to me, man. I can see the Colosseum, and the Forum, or what's left of it."

"No Trevi Fountain yet," Matt noted, "but it looks like the Aqueduct is still working."

"Give the bandits time, they'll get to it." Saul shivered. "Never thought I'd see the Eternal City in the Middle Ages!"

"Never thought I'd be standing on top of St. Peter's." Matt looked down a bit and saw a troop of horsemen riding up the slope toward the cathedral. "No wall, not even a fence! This place is wide open! What's been keeping them out?"

"If you dare say 'the power of prayer . . .' "

Matt shrugged. "Why should I say it? Just try a verse that stops them, and see what happens."

Saul grinned. "Why not?

> "Whoopi-ti-yi-yo! Get along, little horsies!
> It's your misfortune, and none of my own!
> Whoopi-ti-yi-yo, get along, little horsies!
> You know that you all long to be safe back home!"

He broke off, staring. "What the hey is *that?*"

Matt had felt it, too—a sudden surge of energy that left him almost giddy with a feeling of power, as if he could pick up the world and use it for a racquetball. "What do you *think* it is?"

As one, the horses turned and started back down the hill. The horsemen swore and yanked at the reins, and horses tossed their heads and whinnied protest, but they kept on going—and not just the ones on the road, either. As far and wide as they could see, a countercurrent struck the ranks of the condottieri cavalry. The horses had all turned and started back.

Saul ran over to the other side of the cupola and stared down. "They're doing it over here, too!"

"Never knew 'Whoopi-ti-yi-yo' qualified as magic words," Matt said conversationally.

Saul turned to glare at him. "I hate it when you're right."

"Only this time. Look! The sorcerers are fighting back!"

"If you can call this fighting," Saul grumbled, but he came to look. There was a blue glow in the middle of the condottieri army, and greenish smoke trailed up. The horses suddenly answered to the bit, turning and heading back uphill again.

"So. They know they've got some resistance." Saul nodded. "Why do I get the feeling we're not even needed here?"

"Maybe because those fireballs curved back on the army that threw them," Matt said. "On the other hand, those riders are halfway to the cathedral, and no one's stopping them. Do you suppose the Saints are waiting for *us* to do the job?"

"You mean we shouldn't have volunteered?"

"No, I mean that Heaven helps those who help themselves."

Saul grunted. "Those condottieri are helping themselves. They're all set to help themselves to everything that's not nailed down."

"So we have to help the clergy in a way they haven't been able to do," Matt summarized, "although it does seem kind of strange that they don't have even one clerical wizard on hand."

"In corporate headquarters?" Saul challenged. "All they'd have here are bureaucrats!"

"You might have a point. Okay, what do we do to push the bandits back out of here?"

"Well," Saul said slowly, "they're presumably all working for Evil, and I've heard a lot about the Aroma of Sanctity . . ."

With a soft burping sound, something exploded in the center of the cupola.

Chapter
Twenty-Three

Greasy smoke poured outward and upward, enveloping the whole top of the steeple.

"Gas attack!" Saul managed before he broke off into a bout of coughing that racked his lungs. He stumbled to the side and leaned over the railing, trying to get away from the smoke—but it followed him.

Matt stumbled toward the opposite railing, and the smoke tried to follow him, but there was just enough of a breeze to blow it back. A few tendrils did reach him, and the stench was only the precursor—he could feel his innards heaving. He suddenly realized that a person could actually die just from a bad smell—if it was vile enough . . .

He stuck his head over the rail as far as he could and chanted,

> "So blow, ye winds, heigh-ho!
> A-roving let it go!
> We'll smell no more of this septic sore,
> So blow it all away!

> "To the olfactory membrane
> Of the one who sent this pain,
> Stink bomb, return to your sender! Burn
> His nose, and not our *nez*!"

He wasn't sure if throwing a French word in there would work, but *nez* did rhyme with "away," at least in its native pronunciation. But work it did; the smoke boiled backward as if it were a genie returning to its lamp, then disappeared with a soft crunching sound. There was only a charred spot in the center of the cupola floor, to show where it had been . . .

And Saul, hanging over the railing, groaning in reverse as he tried to hold his stomach down.

Matt called,

> "Let upheavals pass!
>   One Bromo in your gas-
>   -trointestinal tract
>   Will settle your stomach back!"

Saul straightened up, looking surprised, then turned to Matt with a sigh of relief. "Never thought I'd be glad to hear that jingle."

"Singing commercials have to rank as one of the curses of civilization," Matt agreed, "but they work—presumably increasing sales in our home universe, and settling stomachs in this one."

"Funny, they had just the opposite effect back home," Saul said. He turned to look out over the condottieri army with a very vengeful look. "Chemical warfare. Full-scale."

"I can't say no," Matt sighed, "since they did it to us. After all, *ours* won't be lethal."

"I've smelled enough incense during my time to testify to that," Saul agreed, "though I will say St. Basil's nearly smoked me out of my apartment, the one time I tried it."

"Never trust anything that needs charcoal to keep it going," Matt agreed, "but we're out in the open, so the smoke shouldn't matter—and under the circumstances, I think St. Basil's is what the doctor ordered."

Saul snorted. "*What* doctor?"

"The Doctor of Divinity."

"Wish we could feed them back their own medicine," Saul growled. "Sweets to the sweet, after all."

Matt was watching a small upheaval in the center of the army, right below the main avenue. "We just did, and it didn't do much. These boys are used to bad smells, and know how to damp them out."

"Where'd you get that from?"

"They're Satanists—they must be used to the smell of brimstone by now. Okay, St. Basil's incense, it is."

"What else, in the Vatican?" Saul said.

"O bandits bending under Evil's yoke,
   Feel the steady heat of flame, and taste
   Good strong thick stupefying incense smoke!
   Then flee, or die by slow degrees,
   In vapors wrapped, as if they clasped a crook!"

Smoke billowed up everywhere—from the roads right in front of the riders, all along the bottom of the hill, drifting out over the army. Matt could hear the hacking and coughing all the way up to the top of the dome—but the shrieks of agony and cries of disgust took him by surprise. "We're hurting them!" He raised his hands to start a counterspell, but felt Saul's hand on his shoulder. "What do you think they were planning to do to us? Don't worry, they'll get away from it very fast."

Sure enough, the whole army was on the move—away from the smoke. Half a dozen horses carrying robed figures burst out of the far side, riding hard.

"There go your sorcerers," Saul said. "Nothing fatal, worse luck."

"The rest of the army isn't hanging around, either," Matt said. "Somehow, though, I wouldn't call this a rout."

"No, not when they're just going home for the night, and home's only a few blocks away. I can almost hear some of those footmen saying, 'All in a day's work.' "

"Yeah, and talking about how the officers messed it up again," Matt agreed.

"Don't enlisted men always? Look at 'em go!"

They watched as the army boiled, moving steadily outward, away from the Vatican. Already, the leading edge was breaking up into units and going into long, low houses that had a very temporary look. Several of them were inside the Colosseum, which explained why the bandits were making it look like a crowd charging into a football stadium with only ten minutes left till game time.

There was a huffing and a wheezing, and Arouetto hauled himself into view.

"Arouetto!" Matt stepped over to catch his elbow, giving support. "What are you doing here? You're in no shape for that climb!"

"I had need to tell you," the scholar panted, "what you no doubt already know—the condottieri are in retreat! The pope sends his thanks!"

"He's welcome," Saul said, "but I think maybe we'd better stay up here for a while and make sure they don't try to rally again today."

"Why should they?" Matt shrugged. "They've put in their time, and they've got some partying coming up. We should come back tomorrow before sunrise, though."

"Still, Wizard Saul speaks with prudence." Arouetto found himself a seat on a pile of stone blocks. "We should wait."

"Then while we're here," Saul said, finding another block to sit on, "I'd just like to double-check that history of Reme the pope gave us. You'll pardon me, scholar, but I'm just automatically suspicious of history as told by a clergyman. Was the pope's thumbnail history of the empire true?"

"So far as it went, yes," Arouetto said slowly, "though he did not mention Caesar Decembris, who converted to Christianity and led most of the empire with him, by his example—"

"Only 'most'?"

"Aye, he did not insist on converting those who did not wish it. That is why there were so many pagans left for Hardishane to convert. And, of course, there is a great deal that he did not tell you, about what happened after the empire fell."

"Sounds more like a slow slide than a fall," Saul said sourly, "but I'll take what I can get. Let's start with Hardishane. What was going on in the rest of the world while he was rebuilding the Western empire? Ever hear of a prophet named Mohammed?"

"Of course," Arouetto said, seeming surprised that they would think he had not. "He arose in Arabia during the last days of the empire, and preached a message from a holy book he wrote himself. It spread among the desert tribes, then became a fire that swept through Asia and North Africa, uniting their peoples in a new belief."

"Only the Near East and North Africa?" Matt asked. "They never got into Spain—I mean, Ibile?"

"Oh, they tried." Arouetto smiled. "But Reme would not allow it, and later the Gothic folk who had learned Latrurian civilization and military ways united behind a hero they called 'the Lord.' "

"El Cid," Saul murmured.

"Are those their words for it? They united behind him and drove the Moorish folk back whenever they sought to invade."

"That explains why the Moorish influence is so much less than it is in our universe," Matt said to Saul, but the Witch Doctor was already asking, "Did the Moslems set up their own empire?"

"Aye. United in their new religion, they were the first of the southern provinces to break away from the Latrurian empire. Within years, they had founded one of their own."

"But it was the missionaries who managed the conquest, not the generals?"

"At first, yes. But once Reme fell, the Moslems proclaimed a holy war and conquered what they could—though Heaven knows they had enough already! They battered at the gates of Byzantium itself, but were beaten back. Then, under the conqueror's sons, they settled down to the wise and enlightened rule of their own Arabian empire."

"Which hit its peak about the same time Hardishane welded Europe together into a new empire?"

"Aye." Arouetto frowned. "You really must tell me how you can come from another world that is so like this one, and yet so different!"

"When there's time, when there's time," Matt soothed. "Sounds as if you don't exactly disapprove of the Moslems."

"How can I?" Arouetto sighed. "How can I, when they esteem learning and the arts, and it is they who have preserved so many of the Greek and Latin books I so prize?"

"That doesn't exactly endear you to the Church, does it?"

"I do my best to be discreet," Arouetto admitted.

"After all," Saul said sourly, "the Latrurian empire may have tolerated all religions, but after Reme fell, the Church didn't have to be so tolerant, did it?"

"Under Hardishane, the Christian missionaries accomplished great deeds," Arouetto said evasively.

Matt shuddered at the thought of conversion by the sword and hoped Hardishane's monks hadn't been quite so brutal—but he didn't ask.

Saul did. "But it was just a matter of good example? It wasn't forced?"

"Rarely." But Arouetto wouldn't meet his gaze. "I will own, though, that some of the conversions may have had more to do with gaining status and wealth than with true faith."

"Of course—if you want to climb to the top, you have to be the same religion as the guys who're already up there," Saul said with a wry smile. "Still, it's not *exactly* coercion. But once nearly everybody was Christian, that seed of corruption took root and flowered, didn't it?"

"A rather noxious flower," Arouetto admitted. "In truth, it did—and yielded a harvest of intolerance. Then the Emperor of Byzantium—so he styled himself, though his empire had shrunk to the size of a kingdom—began to fear a new breed of Moslems who had come out of the East, the Turks, and called on Hardishane's heirs to join them in recapturing the Holy Land from the Infidels . . ."

"The Crusades." Saul's gaze was riveted to Arouetto.

"So they are called. We must admit, in all charity, that they did keep the Turks from overrunning Europe; they still have not taken Byzantium."

"Oh," Matt said. "You don't think too highly of the Crusaders?"

Arouetto sighed. "Some acted out of true religious fervor, but most went on Crusade for reasons of their own—greed for booty, or the lust for power, carving out a kingdom of their own in the East. Hardishane's grandsons fell to squabbling over the spoils, and Christian kingdom was pitted against Christian kingdom. Evil was thus given a door through which to enter, and did—and one by one the Christian kingdoms were subverted or seduced to the rule of the sorcerer-kings under the dominion of Evil."

"Such as Boncorro's grandfather." Matt turned to look out over the condottieri. "Or did he usurp from a usurper who—hey!"

"Horses?" Saul came to his feet, following Matt's gaze. "I thought this army was supposed to stay off duty till morning!"

"Do the condottieri march again?" Arouetto was on his feet, face pale.

"They do," Matt said. "Apparently they're really getting serious about this—and we're the reason why." He turned to Saul. "Maybe we should just get out of here, quick as we can."

Saul shook his head. "That won't stop them now. Up till now, they've only been putting up a token effort to justify their pay and keep the pope hemmed in—but now that they're making a real push, why not go on and finish the job, whether we're there or not?"

"If we take off running, maybe they'll follow us."

"The whole army?" Saul shook his head. "Not unless we can get to another fortress before their pursuit band catches us."

Arouetto gasped. "How can we defend ourselves?"

"By bringing in the guys who got me into this in the first place." Saul fished a bauble out of his shirt and pressed a nubbin on its side. "Witch Doctor to Black Knight! Come in, Sir Guy! Come in, and come on! I got your wizard out of stir for you—now come get us out of the crunch!"

The whole army drew to a halt as Sir Guy pulled the amulet out of his armor. "Black Knight to Witch Doctor. I hear you, Wizard Saul. In what manner of difficulty do you find yourself?"

"We're surrounded by an army," Saul said, "and it's not enough to break through and escape—we have to get rid of them! Any ideas, Sir Guy?"

"Many, but they require my being with you. What did you have in mind?"

"An aerial assault," Matt's voice said, and Alisande's heart leaped. He was alive and well, then, and in this world—he must be, to speak through that magical device! And there was nothing in his voice to suggest any hurt or weakness.

"Where is he?" she asked.

"Where are you?" Sir Guy asked.

"In the Vatican," Saul answered.

"Surely they must be well-protected there!" Alisande cried with relief.

"Surely the Holy Father's power must protect you," Sir Guy said.

"Other way around, actually. They were content to keep him penned in, until we showed up—but now they're out to break through. We think they have orders to come and get us."

"Majesty," said Sir Guy, "I am loath to leave you, but I believe it is vital to their welfare that Stegoman and I fly to their aid."

Alisande felt a chill at the thought of being without the support of the Black Knight and the dragon, but she felt a greater chill at the thought of losing her husband. "Go, then," she said.

"Great One, will you come?" Sir Guy asked.

"Aye," the dragon rumbled. "I could wish Matthew had not been so great a fool as to go wandering without me in the first place!"

"Wisdom and forethought are not always numbered among his virtues." Sir Guy turned back to the amulet. "We will fly to Reme and stoop upon the enemy, Wizard Saul. We shall hail you through this amulet when we are in sight of the city."

"Thanks, guys! Talk again when you're near! Over and out!"

"Tell Alisande I love her," Matt's voice called; in fact, he didn't quite finish the last word before the spell ceased.

"Your Majesty, I regret that we must leave you." Sir Guy bowed in the saddle before dismounting his charger.

"Needs must, Sir Guy. Needs must." And Alisande knew she needs must hold back the tears that suddenly welled up, tears of joy to hear Matthew's dear voice saying he loved her. How silly she was! She had never been so subject to womanly weaknesses before. Well, rarely . . .

But he was alive! And she was going to find him! "If you are in Venarra when we come there, Sir Guy, we shall stop. If you are not, we shall ride on to Reme."

"Would you and all your army could go there as quickly as we!" Sir

Guy sighed. "Since you cannot, though, Stegoman and I shall have to suffice. I pray you care well for my steed."

"Be assured that we shall," Alisande told him. "Go release the wizards!"

"Black Knight to Witch Doctor." Sir Guy's voice sounded awkward and stilted as it came through the amulet.

"At last!" The sweat stood on Matt's brow. The power coming to him through the clergy who were praying in the cathedral thrummed through him as if he were a high-voltage cable, but it drained from him as quickly as it came, as he recited the same verses over and over again, manufacturing more robots to replace the ones smashed by the condottieri's maces and catapults, and short-circuited by their iron crossbow bolts. It had given them a nasty surprise when they had seen a squadron of metal men come clanking out to block their way, and the retreat had been a real delight to watch. It had taken them a whole half hour to regroup and work themselves up to march again— but once begun, they found that the robots were vulnerable after all, though not very. A score of dead foot soldiers and six dead horsemen testified to the effectiveness of the automatons; it had taken that many deaths before the bandits had learned to stay back and lob in missiles. Since Matt's robot barricade kept being renewed, the bandits probably didn't know how effective their own strikes were. Matt just hoped they wore down before he did.

It would have to be soon. Even with the well of spiritual energy from the chapel to draw on, the sheer energy of the struggle was sapping him, not to mention the guilt of seeing all those dead bodies. He tried consoling himself by remembering how much suffering those men had probably caused as they looted and pillaged, but that reminded him that they had died without confession, dragged down by the weight of all their sins. He kept fighting doggedly.

Behind him, Saul blocked the other two main avenues with Roman legionnaires—suggested by Arouetto—and howling barbarian Visigoths. The 'ghosts' had sent the condotierri running at first, but they had plucked up their courage and marched back again, assuring themselves that ghosts couldn't hurt them. The first dozen casualties had convinced them otherwise, and they had retired to work out a new battle plan. Now they were content to stand back and shoot arrows—probably not trusting the pavement, since the roadway surfaces had all turned shiny black. Matt suspected their sorcerers hadn't figured out why.

He wished them luck—Marco Polo hadn't published, in this universe.

"They're still sending commandoes in through the back streets," Saul reported.

"Still?" Matt was beyond surprise. "I thought those debugging programs you invented were running them down."

"They are, each one shaped like the Hound of the Baskervilles. I'm surprised the captains can still find anybody brave enough to face them."

"The hound? I thought you started with wolves."

"I did, but I have to keep changing them, or they'll work up their nerve to face them. I'm going to try yetis next."

"Good idea. Me, I'm thinking of switching to tanks."

"Hey, no fair using gunpowder! You got any idea how much havoc you could create if these guys get to thinking about things that go boom in the night?"

"I know, that's all that stops me. I'm thinking of a giant crossbow instead of a cannon."

Behind him, he heard the squawk of a tinny voice coming through Saul's amulet.

"Yeah, Sir Guy!" Saul said, relief in every syllable. "You can see them? Great! Just strafe their ranks—you know, dive on them with all Stegoman's flame, then back up and dive again . . . No, the diving will scare them a lot more than just flying over burning everybody; they'll run faster if they think they stand a chance of escape. Besides, that'll make it harder for the sorcerers to hit you with fireballs or something . . . What? Stegoman says the fireballs would make a nice light snack? Well, tell him we'll feed him high-grade charcoal as soon as this is over!"

Matt felt relief make him weak inside, but pulled himself together. "Okay. Now we pull out all the stops, right?"

"You got it," Saul agreed. "As soon as we see him dive, sing out!"

Matt glanced back and forth from the northern sky to his robotic roadblocks on the south and west. He saw the dot growing bigger, saw it develop wings, saw it angle downward toward the condottieri . . .

"Now!" Saul cried, and together they chanted,

> "Double, double toil and trouble!
> Pavement burn and roadways buckle!
> Hollow stomach, dread and fear—
> Bandits, panic, drop your gear!
> Run and flee the fiery rubble!
> Double, double toil and trouble!"

The main roads exploded into flame, fire that roared downward onto the bandit army just as Stegoman's torch shot out to sear the first battalion. A massive howl of fear rose up, and the condottieri turned as a man, fleeing back down toward the barracks. But the dragon dove again, and the vanguard kept on running, past the barracks and toward the city limits.

"Get ready to counter their sorcerers!" Matt snapped.

"I'm ready," Saul said, "but I don't think they'll be doing anything for a while. They were all clustered together, and Sir Guy must have seen them. They were Stegoman's first target."

"They'll recover." Matt hoped he was wrong. "Anyway, even if they do all run, we'll have a lot of repair work to do."

"Look," Saul argued, "we can wait till tomorrow to fix the roads."

"I suppose so," Matt sighed. "Thus is it proved that coal does not make a good surface for traffic. You don't suppose this could happen to the tar in blacktop streets, do you?"

"If you had a dragon's torch to get it started? Could be. Remind me to go back to New York and try the experiment sometime."

"No, I think not." Matt stared out. "I can't believe it—they're still running! Their new slum at the foot of the hill looks to be all cleaned out! I just hope they get all the people evacuated in time."

"Look, we can kill the flames before they get that far."

"I know, but Stegoman is lining up to dive-bomb headquarters. How're they doing on your side?"

"Oh, just fine," said Saul. "Nobody's hitting the four minute mile yet, but I think some of them are doing very well, considering the light armor they're wearing."

"Have they passed their personal slum yet?"

"The last ones are just going through right now. I think we'd better call Stegoman back before the sorcerers regroup and find an anti-dragon spell."

Saul fingered the amulet. "So how are we going to keep them moving?"

"By conjuring up your random group of legionnaires, or my odd number of robots—and, of course, the occasional fire geyser right behind them. Keep your hounds roaming the city, too. I know it's wearing, but I think we can get the last of them out of here by nightfall."

This time it was a formal audience, and the pope was wearing his robes of state with the cardinals gathered behind him, glorious red behind dazzling white. Saul was very patient—he managed to keep it down to mere fidgeting through the ritual and the singing. Matt and

Sir Guy were the only ones to kneel to receive the pope's personal blessing, though—Saul the skeptic and cynic had his limits. Besides, the religion he had dropped out of was Protestant. Nonetheless, the Holy Father insisted on turning to bless him, too.

Later, in his solar, he told them, "I regret that I have no worldly power to give you in thanks."

"That's all right—the Church is better off that way," Saul said, and the pope cast him a quick, suspicious glance.

Matt said quickly, "Your blessing has already increased the power of our magic, your Holiness—I can feel it. Maybe it will be enough to cut through the magical inertia that seems to pervade Latruria—we can't have you folks always there as our ammo dump, you know."

The pope frowned. "I know not what an 'ammo dump' is, but we shall pray for you perpetually."

"I need it if anyone does," Matt sighed, and Saul developed whooping cough. Matt talked fast to cover him up. "Besides, we more or less brought this on ourselves—I'm sure the king wouldn't have told the condottieri to get serious about taking the Vatican if we hadn't been here."

"It is not the sort of policy I have come to expect from Boncorro," the pope admitted. "I was even surprised that he hemmed me in so tightly, when he had ceased his persecution of the priests and the faithful. I had supposed he felt the need to make a show of opposing me, since his grandfather had—but this . . ."

"I have my doubts that the king himself is behind it all," Matt told him. "After all, his chancellor is a bona fide sorcerer and servant of Evil, and everybody would assume any order he gave came from the king."

"But would not the king be angered when he learned of it?"

"Sure, but all information goes through the chancellor's hands. He can keep any info he wants from the king—unless Boncorro has been wise enough to set up his own spy network, separate from his chancellor's."

"They say he trusts the Lord Chancellor as much as he trusts any man," the pope said slowly.

"But that's not saying much, is it? Okay, I'll admit he probably does have his own spies, checking up on the chancellor—but they can't be everywhere at once." He rose. "Speaking of spies, I think we'd better take our leave, now—before the king's agents can track us."

"Go, and with my blessing." But the pope frowned. "This King Boncorro may not be a force for Evil, Lord Wizard, but he is also not a force for Good, and he cannot balance between them; simply by failing to do good, he advances the cause of Evil. Can you not help me in overthrowing him? He is the grandson of a usurper, after all."

"And what alternative can you offer?" Matt said. He wondered why Sir Guy glanced at Arouetto and away, but didn't mention it. "Getting rid of a neutral king isn't too smart, if the only available replacement is definitely evil. If you don't mind, Holy Father, I think it would be better to try to subvert King Boncorro and sway him toward the side of the angels than to try to assassinate him."

"I had not meant to murder him—only to dethrone him!"

"It doesn't work that way." Matt shook his head. "Kick a king off his throne, and he'll come back with an army—and if you beat him again, he'll just come back again. Again and again—until you finally kill him anyway. No, your Holiness, we would be much better advised to make the best of Boncorro—or try to make him the best."

"You have given me your advice," the pope said slowly, "and I shall now give you mine—for your own best interests, not that of the Church. It is this: leave Latruria."

"Good of you, I'm sure," Matt said, "but you know we can't."

"We are sworn to a vocation, too, your Holiness," Sir Guy said gently. "We cannot turn back unless we are beaten."

The pope sighed. "Well, I have given you my best rede, though I cannot say I regret your ignoring it."

As they were going out of the papal palace, Matt said to Arouetto, "How come he didn't include you in the blessing? Or the advice, for that matter."

"His Holiness does not completely trust me," Arouetto answered with a small smile. "He has not said it, but I believe he sees me as a threat."

"But can't say why, huh?" Saul asked. "If he could, he'd clap you in irons."

"Or a monk's cell, I suppose," Arouetto agreed. "Not that I would mind a life sentence to a library."

"Yes you would," Matt said, "if the only art and music around you were religious."

"There are worse fates," Arouetto replied. "Still, you are right—I would prefer to remain free, able to contemplate the beauties of Classical art and the works of my inspired contemporaries."

A handful of Swiss guards marched up and stamped to a halt, leading four well-groomed horses. The leader saluted the companions with his halberd and said, "His Holiness insists that you accept at least this much of a gift from him."

Sir Guy grinned. "This we will take, and gladly! Thank his Holiness for us!

"Yes, thanks indeed." Matt turned to the dragon, who lay waiting by the wall. "You don't mind, do you, Stegoman?"

"Mind?" the dragon snorted. "It is I who shall thank his Holiness most of all!"

Chapter
Twenty-Four

"You are free, then," Sir Guy said as they rode out of the Vatican and into Reme proper, "and so is the pope. But what progress have you made?"

"Well," Matt said, "we have Arouetto."

The scholar smiled sadly. "The Lord Wizard took me from my prison, because he seems to think I can reform the young king."

"Makes sense," Matt said. "Why else would the chancellor have locked you up in his special dungeon?"

"Why," said Sir Guy, "because he is the last legitimate heir to the throne of Latruria."

Matt, Saul, and Stegoman swung about to stare at the scholar, but all he did was glare ferociously at Sir Guy. The Black Knight only kicked his heels wide sides and said, "Deny it if you can."

"Would that I could," the scholar growled, "for it has been a dozen generations since my family ruled!"

"Hold on!" Matt held up a hand. "Maledicto wasn't *that* old!"

"No, but he was the usurper of a usurper of a usurper," Sir Guy explained, "or rather, of three families of usurpers. I would call them dynasties if they had lasted more than a few generations each—but they did not."

"Three centuries is a long time to say a bloodline's preserved," Matt said dubiously.

"Six centuries, rather," Sir Guy said, "for Scholar Arouetto's right comes from an ancestor who was the last emperor of the Latrurian empire."

Saul nodded slowly, gaze still on Arouetto. "No wonder you're interested in the Classics!"

"How could you know all this?" Arouetto demanded.

Sir Guy shrugged. "It is one of the things I know by right of birth."

"His family has been tracking the genealogies of the kings of Europe for several centuries." Matt didn't feel the need to explain that Sir Guy was the last lineal descendant of Emperor Hardishane. "You have your field of expertise, he has his. His career is trying to restore legitimate lines to the thrones of this continent—and just incidentally return their countries to devotion to Right and God."

"I can see that might entail such knowledge," Arouetto allowed. "But it is useless in my case, friend. I have no wish to rule, nor had my father nor my grandfather. We only wished to be left in peace, to pursue our studies."

Sir Guy made no reply, but his eyes glittered as he watched Arouetto.

The scholar sighed. "You may as well say it—the blood of the Caesars has grown thin. Well, perhaps it has, my friend—or perhaps my idea of worthy pursuits differs from that of my ancestors. Try to open your mind enough to imagine that my work might be as important as Julius Caesar's, in its way."

Sir Guy turned his face away quickly—probably to hide a look of infinite sadness, for to him, no work was so important as that of government—but Matt said, "There is something to what he says, Sir Guy. He has developed new standards for deciding what's right and wrong—but most of his conclusions are right in line with the Bible's. He just has a high opinion of a few things the Book doesn't mention, that's all—and there's a chance King Boncorro might embrace his ideas, though he scorns religion."

Sir Guy turned back to him slowly. "Do you mean that he might yet save the country that is his weal?"

"He might," Matt said, "by saving the king who governs it."

Sir Guy turned to Arouetto, looking him up and down as if he were seeing the scholar in a whole new light.

"Surely you do not mean that you have but to walk into the king's castle with this scholar," Stegoman rumbled, "and all will be mended!"

"Hey, even *I'm* not that stupid. Sure, we have to get him to the king, but even after that, it will take a while." Matt turned back to contemplate Arouetto. "But how are we going to get you in there without getting you killed?"

They were all silent for a while, thinking up ways and means. Finally Saul said, "Camouflage?"

Matt turned to him, puzzled. "What did you have in mind?"

"Safety in numbers," Saul explained. "If you could find a dozen more scholars and poets, maybe you could smuggle Arouetto in with the rest of them—provided the king would let them in, of course."

"I think he just might," Matt said slowly, "and that reminds me about a young friend of mine. I magicked him and his girlfriend out of Boncorro's castle, but I haven't had a chance to check and make sure they landed okay."

"How did this discussion of a college of scholars bring them to mind?" Stegoman rumbled.

"Because the kid's a poet, but he doesn't realize it," Matt said. "He thinks the only career worth having is knighthood."

"Well, the lad has a point," Sir Guy allowed, "though it is pleasant to be able to craft a verse when you are done hacking up the enemy."

"Must men always be thus?" Arouetto sighed.

" 'Must,' I don't know," Matt said, "but they always *will*. It has something to do with testosterone and the survival of the fittest."

Arouetto smiled sadly. "By that measure, I am not the fittest."

"Apparently not," Saul said, "since you've decided against reproducing. Your father seemed to know what he was doing, though."

"He was a poet and scholar," Arouetto said slowly, "but even he was exasperated at my mildness. Perhaps I chose more rightly than I knew, when I chose the celibate life."

"And perhaps the evolution you'll contribute to is cultural instead of physical," Matt said, annoyed. "You never know—you may have more intellectual descendants than I will have biological. For example, I'd love to hear you tell your basic ideas to Pascal, this young friend of mine, and see what they do to him."

"Pray Heaven they will not turn him from knighthood!" Sir Guy cried.

"I don't know—the kid is only the son of a squire, and he's that just because his grandfather was a wizard." Matt turned to Saul. "I really would like to check on him. I don't suppose your telecommunication amulet works without a mate at the other end?"

Saul shook his head. "Sorry. You'll have to settle for a crystal ball."

Matt sighed. "I don't happen to have one. Scholar Arouetto, you wouldn't happen to have a bottle of ink on you, would you?"

"No," the scholar said slowly, "but I have managed with powdered charcoal when I've had to."

Matt stared at him for a moment, then nodded. "Right. Why didn't I realize? Excuse me, folks—I have to go pick up sticks."

It only took a few charred sticks, scraped into a puddle of water in a depression on top of a boulder, to darken the fluid enough so that it was almost a mirror, but one that seemed to have some depth. Arouetto looked on with interest—he had rarely had the chance to watch wizards at work—and Sir Guy looked on with distrust. Stegoman took a nap.

"Okay," Saul said, "we're all ready. Now, how do you turn it on?"

"Add a verse, of course."

"Is it by nature adverse, then?" Arouetto asked, concerned.

"Some of the sociologists think so." Matt stared into the ink pool and intoned,

> "Mesmerizing pool of vision,
> Drawing from us all volition,
> Show us Pascal, at a distance!
> Show us, glow us, all entrance!
> Far-sight, far-see, well envision!
> Distant see-er—tele-vision!"

"I wouldn't tell anybody, not that," Saul muttered under his breath, but he was watching the pool, too.

The darkness seemed to lighten, *did* lighten, glowing from the center outward—and Matt saw a group of young men and women sitting around a table with a pitcher of wine in the middle. They were talking earnestly, which was amazing, considering that they were all wearing peasant working smocks, with the dust of fieldwork on them. Now and then someone threw back his head in silent laughter.

One of them was Pascal.

Flaminia sat beside him, and the two of them were doing most of the occasional laughing, and a lot of wide-eyed listening. Now and then one of them ventured a remark, and the others took it up earnestly.

"Your young friend seems to have landed on his feet," Saul commented.

"He certainly seems to like it well enough," Matt admitted. "At least I don't have to worry about yanking him out of trouble." He looked up at Arouetto. "But I would like to have him talk to you."

"Can we not go where he is?" the scholar demanded.

Matt scowled down at the pool. "I hate to use that much magic at one time. We have to remember that the king is still on the watch for us, with possibly not the nicest of intentions. Let's not make it *too* easy for him to zero in on us."

"Perhaps magic is not necessary." Arouetto pointed at the ink pool. "Can you not show us more of their surroundings? There might be some famous landmark among them."

"Well, I can try," Matt said dubiously, but he muttered a few words, something having to do with zooming out, and the figures grew smaller and smaller in the center, until they could see a hill high behind them, with a castle of reddish rock on its top, a castle with tall, spidery towers that surely could not have been held up just by piling one stone block on another—and a central keep surrounded by scaffolding, where some of the upper arrow slots had been widened to real windows, where glass winked in the late afternoon sun.

"It is the king's castle!" Arouetto's eyes glowed with success. "The king's castle, and we regard its western face, but from somewhat south! See how he is remaking its keep into a light-filled, gracious palace!" He looked up at Matt. "You did not send your young friends very far outside Venarra, did you, Lord Wizard?"

Matt swallowed thickly and said, "No, I guess I didn't, Arouetto. I'll admit there wasn't much time, but I guess I could have been a bit more specific than *that*."

"Lucky the king doesn't seem to think they're very important." Saul looked up at Matt. "Okay, now we know where they are—but how do we get there?"

Matt turned to Stegoman. After a minute the dragon opened one eye. "I could swear I can feel the pressure of thy thoughts, Wizard."

"You may be a psychic saurian," Matt answered. "Say, Stegoman, how do you feel about night flights?"

"How far is Venarra from Reme?" Matt called against the wind.

"Only fifty miles, as the dragon flies!" Sir Guy called back.

"Then we are nearly there," the huge voice rumbled beneath them. "Hold tightly to one another, small folk, and Sir Guy, hold tightly to my neck! Where is this grove, scholar?"

"West by southwest of the castle!" Matt called. "Right, Signor Arouetto?"

"Even so!" the scholar called back.

"How close to it?" Stegoman demanded.

"Perhaps half a mile—certainly outside the city wall!"

"Just land behind a grove big enough to give you cover," Matt advised.

"Then I shall!" Stegoman banked to the right, curving around and spiraling down. Matt risked a quick glance back at Saul; he was grinning with delight, the wind whipping his long hair behind him. Between them, Arouetto was pale and tight-lipped, but game, not complaining. Matt turned back to watch the rest of Stegoman's approach. He didn't know how the dragon was managing to find his way without even moonlight, but he wasn't about to ask.

There was a jolt as Stegoman's feet touched the ground, but Matt had felt worse jolts in a jet. The dragon ran a little way, which was worse than the jouncing of the thermals, but he cupped his wings to help slow himself down, and in a few minutes was sagging to the ground. "Off, I prithee! Thou art a heavy load!"

"I regret that I had to wear armor, good beast, but I could not risk being without it," Sir Guy said, hopping off. Matt leaped down in time to catch Arouetto, and Saul slid off the dragon's back grinning like a Cheshire cat. "Anytime you want to go for a spin, Stegoman, just let me know!"

"I will be delighted," the dragon huffed, "if there is only the one, or at most the two, of you."

"Sorry you had to carry so many." Matt came around to the dragon's front, resting a hand on his friend's head.

"Needs must," the dragon replied. "Let me rest, Matthew, while you seek this friend of yours."

"Well, I don't really expect them to be up *this* late." Matt turned to his companions. "Would you stay and keep Stegoman company, Sir Guy? The rest of us need to scout the territory, so we'll know where we're going come daybreak."

"I need no guardian!" the dragon exclaimed indignantly.

"Surely not!" Sir Guy sounded just as indignant as Stegoman. "But we would be poor friends indeed if we accepted your labor on our behalf, then went off to leave you! Nay, friend, I will stay with you."

"Well, so long as you know it is not necessary," Stegoman grumped. "What of the horses, Sir Guy?"

"I doubt not they have gone back to the Vatican, and the pope will keep them for us, as Matthew asked in his note . . ."

Their voices dwindled under the susurrus of the leaves as Matt pushed his way into the grove with Arouetto and Saul. "They should be in this direction."

"Should be? They are!" Saul halted, pointing ahead. "Listen!"

Matt stopped and heard a high, clear tenor voice with the rippling of a lute beneath it. He couldn't make out the words, but somehow the tone of it left no doubt that the young man was singing the praises of his lady.

"What have we got here, a bunch of college students?" Saul demanded.

"Not a college, perhaps, for they are not even clergy, let alone cardinals," Arouetto said, eyes glowing, "but certainly students. I recognize the earnestness of debate without rancor, with singing in the midst of it—though I've never seen such outside the walls of a seminary, and never with lasses among them." He turned to Matt. "You did well to send your young friends here."

Matt shook his head. "Pure blind chance . . . Wait a minute! Maybe not! I was trying to cut through the inertia of Latruria, so I sang the first Latin song that came to mind!"

"*Gaudeamus Igitur?*" Saul looked up, startled. "The very first college drinking song?"

" 'Let us therefore rejoice,' " Arouetto translated. "I should like to hear the rest of that, Lord Wizard."

"Don't worry, I'm sure you will!"

"If that's the case," Saul said, "I'm not surprised they're still up. Midnight's a little early for a bunch of students to be going to bed."

"Yes, I remember." Arouetto's smile fairly glowed in the dark. "Still, they look to be farmers. Even with the boundless energy of youth, I would have thought they would have lapsed into the sleep of exhaustion ere now."

"I'll bet they only farm from sunup until mid-morning," Matt said, "then sleep till mid-afternoon, and farm until dark."

"That is but half a day!"

"No, it's probably eight hours. They just sleep during the heat of the day, that's all."

"Assuming that they sleep," Saul said.

"Lacking evidence to the contrary . . ." Matt sighed.

Arouetto pushed forward. "Let us go nearer! I would hear their song!"

They started forward again, but something huge and furry stepped out to block their path, and a deep voice rumbled, "Well met, Wizard!"

Saul fell back with a curse, and Arouetto with a gasp—but Matt grinned. "Manny! How did you find me?"

"I did not," the manticore told him, "and since I could not, I found Pascal instead. But he has no money, and has put off the problem by promising the farmers all about that you will pay for my meat when you come."

"Talk about faith! But yeah, I broke out of prison, and I'll give him a few ducats to settle up. Anybody trying to pick on him?"

"No, worse luck," Manny sighed, "for I would not have felt bound by my promise to you if there had been an assassin to munch. His life seems to be tranquil enough when you are not about, Wizard."

"He's not the first one to feel that way," Matt said. "Well, let us have a chat with him, Manny. Stay low."

"As you wish, Wizard," Finally, the huge double grin flashed. "It is good to see you again."

"Hey, you, too." Matt raised a hand to pat the tawny wall. "Go hide now, okay?"

"Go well." Manny disappeared into the darkness and shrubbery.

There were a few moments of silence. Then Arouetto asked, in a trembling voice, "Was that a *manticore*?"

"Sure was," Matt confirmed. "Knew I couldn't fool you."

"Man, you have some of the *oddest* friends!" Saul expostulated.

"You should know, Saul. Well, let's meet my latest acquaintances and find out what their song is."

"Their" turned out to be right, because half a dozen voices joined in on the chorus. As they came out of the trees, the words of the last verse became clear. Sure enough, it was promising everlasting love and joy, if only the damsel would come away with the singer— and there he was, seated at a table in the open air, lit by a few candles inside cut-off bottles and gazing into the eyes of his beloved: Pascal; and the woman who was staring back at him adoringly was Flaminia.

Matt stopped still in astonishment.

"Which is your young friend, Lord Wizard?" Arouetto asked.

"The one who was singing," Matt said. "I didn't know he could."

Arouetto turned and looked, then smiled. "Love can lift a man to accomplish miracles, Lord Wizard."

"Miracles is right! As far as I knew, he was tone-deaf!'

"Guess you didn't know him as well as you thought," Saul said.

"No, I guess not. And he let *me* carry the whole burden of the minstrel routine!" Matt strode ahead, caught between relief to see his two young friends so happy and well, and anger at Pascal for holding out on him.

Pascal kissed Flaminia, and the other youngsters cheered. The lovers didn't even notice—they took their time and were just breaking off when one of the other young men noticed Matt. The youth looked up, alert and ready to defend, but open and provisionally affable. "Good evening, friend. Why have you come?"

Pascal looked up, then leaped to his feet. "Friend Matthew!" He jumped up to clasp Matt by the shoulders. "I rejoice to see you well! I will own that I had some concern for you, alone there in the town."

"And I was a little worried about *you*," Matt said, clapping him on the shoulder, "but I see you came out okay. How'd you connect with these people?"

"Why, I found myself in the middle of their fields, and they were kind enough to take us in."

"Small enough kindness, when we needed extra hands," a towheaded young man said, and the redheaded young woman next to him added, "For one with a voice like that, we can easily find room!"

"I thank you, friends," Pascal said, "but I hope that I do my share in the fields, too."

"Oh, without question!" said a burly young man whose blond hair contrasted oddly with his deep suntan, "and you have a bond with the land. Indeed, you seem to know as much about the raising of a crop as I do."

"Thank you, Escribo." Pascal smiled. "I am a squire's son, after all, and have known this work all my life."

Matt noticed that he didn't say he had actually *done* the work. "Your crops seem to be doing well, though."

"They do." Escribo nodded. "And with luck, we will reap well for our first harvest."

"First?" Matt looked around. "This is your first year, then?"

"It is," Escribo said. "The king lowered the taxes, and my father used the money to buy land from those who wished to work in Venarra. For five years he has bought more land and given employment to the landless youth of the district—but this spring they all chose to go into Venarra for work. My father nearly despaired, for he could never have worked so much land by himself—so I left my work at the inn in Venarra and came back to help him. But even together, we could see we would never be able to till so many acres—so I called in my friends, who had spent many hours in the inn but never had more than a few days' work at a time, and they came out to help us."

"We are city-bred, though," said another of the girls, "and know nothing of the land."

"You are apt pupils," said Escribo, and everyone laughed. Matt realized it was some sort of inside joke, but even as he was deciding not to ask, Arouetto said, "Whose words had you studied before, then?"

"Why, those of the courtiers who took rooms at our inn," said Escribo, "for it is the finest in Venarra, and noblemen lodged there with their families, until King Boncorro could make room for them in the castle. That is why there was so frequently a week's extra work for a dozen other younglings."

"And why they were always hanging around, waiting for more." Matt nodded.

"So you overheard the noblemen talking of poetry?"

"More often their tutors, lecturing their sons over wine," Escribo answered. "We began to find their talk fascinating, and tried our hands at it. But there were also the painters and sculptors that the king had brought to beautify his castle, and the builders of the new palace he is raising, and merchants coming to sell goods to the court, with tales of the wonders of the Moslem cities."

"And the merchants had picked up some of the knowledge of the Moslem scholars?"

"Even some of the books," a dark-haired young man said. "They allowed us to read a chapter or two while they dined."

"But none of us have the gift of verse that our new friend has." Escribo turned to Pascal. "And he says he has had no training in it!"

"I have not." Pascal blushed. "And you are kind, but I have little skill."

"Perhaps you are too modest," Arouetto said. "Let us hear your verses."

"Why, you did," Escribo said, "even as you came up."

"You sing your own words, then? Excellent! But we did not hear the beginning of it."

"He sings of other things besides love," a black-haired young man said. "Tell him of the work in the fields, Pascal."

"Oh, no, good Lelio!" Pascal cried, alarmed. "To a few good friends, aye, but to a stranger . . ."

"You are too modest." Flaminia slid up against him, resting her head against his chest. "Let the words flow, Pascal, that I may be swept away on their tide."

Pascal looked down at her in surprise, then smiled and said, "Well, for you, then, dear Flaminia, but not for him."

"Let him eavesdrop," she said. Pascal sighed and began to sing.

Matt stood in a daze, listening to the syllables cascade from Pascal's lips. They tinkled and swirled about him, dazzling and bearing him along in their flow, but somehow never lodging long enough for him to extract any meaning from them.

Then it was over, and Matt caught his breath. The boy was fantastically talented! But the sense of the words had eluded him; the only coherent thought that stayed behind was that this song wouldn't work much in the way of magic, for it had only been describing the land and the work and Pascal's state of mind, and would make no change except to bring back the good feeling he had gained from the land. Good feelings? Exultation!

"You have a gift like that," he said, "and you wanted to waste your time chasing a knighthood?"

Pascal's face darkened; he lowered his gaze as his friends broke out in a chorus of protest. When they had quieted, he raised his gaze to Matt and said, "These are only idle amusements, Matthew—a wonderful pleasure in themselves, but surely only for filling the idle hour, never for a life's work."

The chorus of protest struck again, but this time Arouetto's voice joined it, and went on when the others had quieted. "The souls of all men need rest and nourishment, young man, aye, and uplifting, too! If you are gifted in that, you may do more good than a whole company of knights!"

Pascal stared, astonished, but so did Escribo. He turned to Arouetto and demanded, "How can he, when it is all loveliness and no meaning?"

"Aye," Lelio seconded. "Our friend Pascal makes the most lovely strains of sound in the world, but how can he enlighten men when the meaning slips from our grasp even as we listen?"

He smiled at Arouetto as he said it, but it was a challenge, with resentment against the intruder behind it. The scholar only smiled down at him, though, and said, "Have you never heard that a poem should not mean, but be?"

Lelio stared—and so, for that matter, did the other young folks. Pascal finally broke the spell to protest, "But it *does* have meaning! It speaks of the way I felt as I labored, of the insight I gained suddenly, of the union between myself and the earth and Flaminia and us all!"

"It does, most surely," Arouetto agreed, "and if we sit down and read through those words, we can extract that meaning and state it clearly and concisely—but it is far better to experience the poem as a sensory delight, and absorb the meaning in the process."

"But might we not then be persuaded of a principle we would never approve, in clear and sober judgment?" a plump girl asked.

"Well asked, Berylla!" Lelio seconded.

"You might indeed," Arouetto told her. "*That* is why you should analyze the poem before you have heard it too many times—but do not deprive yourself of the pleasure of hearing it without weighing it at least once, and better, several times."

"Who are you?" Lelio asked.

"Lelio!" Berylla cried, shocked.

"No, it must be asked!" Lelio insisted. He leaned forward, frowning up at Arouetto. "For the same reason you have just told us to analyze a poem, we must know whose words we hear, that we may judge the rightness of any one idea of yours within the context of your whole philosophy. Who are you?"

"I am no philosopher, but only a poor scholar. My name is Arouetto."

The circle of young folk froze, staring. Then Berylla stammered. "Not—Not the Arouetto who has translated Ovid and Virgil for us?"

"Not the Arouetto whose *Story of Reme* is the talk of all the tutors?"

"Not the Arouetto whose *Geography* is the boon companion of every merchant?"

"I must admit my culpability." But there was a gleam of amusement and triumph in Arouetto's eye.

"A chair for the scholar!" Lelio leaped up, offering his own, while Escribo ran to fetch another.

"Wine for the scholar!" Berylla filled a goblet and set it in front of him.

"Anything the scholar wants," said another girl, with a deep soulful look.

"Why, I want what any scholar wants," Arouetto sighed, "the company of keen minds and their questions, filled with the enthusiasm of youth."

"Oh, that you shall have in plenty!" another young man assured him. "Is it true that you read Greek, but have not yet translated Homer?"

"I have not yet had that audacity," Arouetto confirmed.

"But you must! For if you do not, how shall we ever read those epics, which are fabled to be so excellent?"

"I cannot yet truly appreciate the spirit of the Athenians," Arouetto protested.

"But at least you *can* appreciate it—and we cannot, who have never read any book written by the Greeks!"

"What of Pythagoras?" Escribo pushed the extra chair over to Lelio and sat down in his own. "Can you explain why he was both mathematician and musician?"

"Ah! That, young man . . . What *is* your name?"

"Escribo, sir!"

"Escribo, Pythagoras was, above and beyond all else, a mystic, who sought nothing less than to understand the whole of the universe and the nature of human existence! Music and mathematics alike were means to understanding this whole, that is all."

"Music, a means to understanding the universe?" Flaminia leaned forward, staring. "How can that be?"

Arouetto began to tell them.

Saul sidled up to Matt and asked, "How's it feel to be the Forgotten Man?"

"A little deflating," Matt confessed, "but under the circumstances, I don't mind at all."

"Oh? Why not?"

"Because I think I've found just the thing to wangle a way into King Boncorro's favor."

Saul glanced at the seminar in surprise, then back at Matt. "Just don't suck them into anything that's going to go sour, okay?"

"No," Matt said slowly, "I don't think there's too much chance of that."

They watched and listened with delight and fond memories, until finally Pascal sat bolt-upright and cried, "My Heavens, the hour! And we must hoe tomorrow!"

"Let the weeds grow," Escribo told him. "One day will not hurt the crops so very much—but we may never again have such a chance to hear a true scholar speak!"

"We must not keep him if he grows weary," Berylla cautioned.

"Weary, when so many good-hearted young folk are pouring energy into me? Never!" Arouetto smiled. "I shall talk as long as you, my young friends!"

"The professor's ego trip," Saul sighed. "Hooks 'em every time."

"Even so, there are a lot worse ways of boosting your ego," Matt reminded him. "Besides, it only works on *real* teachers."

"And just what do you think you're going to do with them?"

"Crash the seminar, of course." Matt glanced at the stars and made a quick guess at the time. "Even so, I think *I* had better turn in—I'm going to need my energy tomorrow." He waited for a lull in the conversation, then called out, "Escribo! Mind if I lie down in your barn?"

"Barn?" The young man started up, looking guilty. "No, my friend! You must have a proper bed!"

"Tomorrow night," Matt told him. "Right now, I wouldn't dream of busting up the conference—and hay will make a fine bed, better than most I've had lately." He turned to the scholar. "Good night, Arouetto. Next time, charge tuition."

Chapter
Twenty-Five

"Look, I gave you a day to rest up," Matt said, "and I warned you we would have to leave around noon. Can I help it if you stayed up all night talking again?"

"But when I have been alone so many years," Arouetto groaned, "young and eager minds are so hard to resist!"

"I understand, and I wish more of my professors had thought that way. But now we have another prospective student for you to talk to."

"And who is that?"

"The king. Okay, Saul, grab his other hand. Ready? Chant!"

They had worked this out before they told Arouetto—decided they needed to make the most dramatic entrance possible, and worked out the verse that would do it. They stood in the center of the farmyard, calling out,

> "Stouthearted men, which fondly here admire
> Fair sounding discourse, studious delight,
> Transported to the throne room bright
> Of King Boncorro, where courtiers aspire
> To curry favor, and claw their way up higher!"

Nothing happened. Well, actually, for a moment they felt a terrific straining around them, a feeling of being caught in the center of a whirlpool made of two forces pulling and pushing against one another and trying to stretch them out of shape in the process—but the whirlpool suddenly seemed to snap back against them, rocking them all.

"What was that?" Arouetto gasped.

"That was our transportation spell, crashing headlong into King Boncorro's protective spell," Matt said. "Blast! He's too strong! Even the two of us together couldn't break through!"

"Well," Saul said, eyeing Stegoman, "we do have another means of transport that's *almost* as dramatic."

"More so, in its way." Matt turned to his old friend with a sigh. "Sorry to have to ask you again, Stegoman—but would you mind terribly much flying into the jaws of mortal danger again?"

As they circled around the castle, Arouetto reached over Matt's shoulder to point. "What troop of glittering cavalry is that?"

"Queen Alisande!" Matt yelped. "That's no army—that's my wife!"

"Think we ought to wait for her to catch up?" Saul called.

Matt thought about it while Stegoman swept through another quarter turn, coming closer. Below him, people in the courtyard began to scream and point, or run, according to their taste.

"No," Matt said, "let's go on in. A little more surprise won't hurt."

Five miles away Ortho the Frank pointed at the wheeling form and cried, "Your Majesty! 'Tis the dragon Stegoman!"

Alisande looked up, surprised, then cried, "Surely it is he! But why does he not come to us?"

"He goes to the king's castle instead, your Majesty! There must be a most strenuous reason!"

"Matthew in danger!" Alisande's hand fell to her sword, then windmilled up to signal to her army. "Ride, men of mine! Your master is endangered! Ride, and bring down that fell keep if we must!"

The army shouted behind her and kicked their horses into a canter.

Matt and Saul muttered quick ricochet spells, and the crossbow bolts and spears fell clattering to the parapet as Stegoman glided over. People shrieked and scrambled out of the way as he lowered down toward the courtyard; the effect was of a big circle opening in the daily traffic, and Stegoman came to rest in it. Then he lifted his head and roared, letting out a blast of flame. "Take my master to the king! And woe until him who tries to smite me!"

Matt slid down and turned to ease the scholar to the ground as Saul and Sir Guy helped lower him, then leaped down beside them.

"Stay here," Matt told Stegoman, "unless there's danger. If there is, take off and circle until we come out."

"Gladly." Stegoman glared about him, paying special attention to any of the guards who seemed to be trying to pluck up nerve. "Which of these churls would seek to hinder *me*?"

"Sorcerers," Matt answered, "though I suspect the main one is going to be too busy to worry about a bat wing in his bailey. Still, let's make it tougher for him." He began to march around Stegoman, chanting,

> "Weave a circle 'round him thrice!
> Whoever nears him, shrink with dread!
> For he on anthracite hath fed,
> And been drunk on spirits of petrol twice!"

"Rather more than twice," Stegoman said, "if 'spirits of petrol' refers to mine own flame. It is unkind of you, Matthew, to remind me of my unsavory past."

"Sorry, old saurhead," Matt apologized, "but I'm more concerned with reminding any potential attackers than you."

"Well, I will suffer it," Stegoman sighed, "and so will they, if they seek to meddle." He glared around him again. "Be about your business, now, so that we may leave soonest."

"Gotcha. Good luck." Matt turned away toward the door of the keep.

Saul caught up, with Arouetto in tow and Sir Guy as rear guard. "Think anybody will get in our way?"

"Somehow," Matt said, "I doubt it." He turned toward the door to the keep, to test his theory.

The guards at the door wavered, then crossed their pikes, though not with much precision.

"His Majesty wanted to know when I escaped from the prison to which he sent me," Matt said as he came up. "He would not appreciate having me stopped."

He didn't even miss a step. The guards wavered, but Sir Guy barked, "Stand aside!" Foot soldiers obeyed knights; that was all there was to it. They yanked their pikes aside and shoved the door open. Matt went right on in, with Arouetto and Saul close behind him.

They marched into the throne room and found it packed with courtiers as usual—but they were just pulling back as a footman madly fought his way through to the throne. Matt stopped just inside the doors, waiting until the servant had managed to clear the last of the courtiers and was running up on the dais; then Matt called, "Don't bother telling him we're coming. It's old news."

The footman spun about, staring in horror.

Matt started down the aisle, calling out, "You did want to know when I escaped, didn't you, your Majesty?"

King Boncorro stared in surprise—but Chancellor Rebozo, behind him, turned pale, looking as if he had seen a ghost, pointing a trembling hand at them.

King Boncorro gave Matt a smile of amusement that threatened to turn into a wolfish grin. "Indeed I did, Lord Wizard! You seem to be more powerful than I had thought! But how did you manage it?"

"I got out with a little help from my friends." Matt nodded at Saul and Sir Guy.

Rebozo cried, "Who is that with you?"

Matt ostensibly ignored him. "Your Majesty, this is Saul, the Witch Doctor, and this—"

"The scholar Arouetto!" Suddenly, Rebozo had gone from shock to rage. His staff snapped down to point at the scholar, and he began to chant in the arcane tongue.

"No, Rebozo," Boncorro said—but for once the chancellor ignored him, perhaps did not even hear him; he just kept chanting, his voice rising with menace.

King Boncorro flashed him a look of irritation. "I said, enough!" He raised an open hand, palm toward Rebozo, and snapped out a short sentence that sort of rhymed, in a language Matt didn't recognize— but Rebozo rocked as if he had been struck with a body blow. "I appreciate your attempts to protect me," said the king, "but I wish more information before we send this scholar back to his refuge."

Matt stared, shaken. He already had some idea of Rebozo's power— and for the king to be able to counter it so easily meant he had far more power than Matt would have thought possible in so young a man.

It made it worse that Saul was looking very interested. "I didn't catch any names in that couplet, Matt—no evil ones, and no holy ones, either."

"There were none," Arouetto assured him.

Saul shot him a keen glance. "You know that language."

"Both of them."

"Well, scholar!" Boncorro turned to him. "It is long since I have seen you—and I cannot say it is unpleasant. How is it you have chosen to grace us with your presence?"

Arouetto spread his hands. "Your Majesty, the residence you have afforded me is luxurious, but it is also lonely."

"So you have come for companionship? But how did you manage to leave?" Boncorro turned to Matt. "That was, I take it, your doing?"

"Yes, your Majesty. He struck me as just the sort of person you would enjoy having around your court."

Rebozo started forward in panic—and jarred to a halt, as something unseen stopped him. The whites showed all around his eyes.

"I must admit that I have enjoyed his conversation in the past," King Boncorro said, "but Rebozo advised me that his ideas would undermine my rule, and I believed him. Indeed, I find no reason to question my chancellor's advice, even now."

"I do, your Majesty," Matt said. "In fact, this scholar's thoughts are moving toward the same goal as your own."

There was no outward change in Boncorro's face or body, but somehow Matt felt the impact of a great deal more interest. "Is he truly!"

"Yes." Saul spoke up unexpectedly. "He's looking at the potential of human beings by themselves, your Majesty. He hasn't said much about magic yet, but he did get into that the other night, discussing the theories of Pythagoras."

"A heretic and blasphemer!" Rebozo burst out. "Pythagoras? The prime misleader of all human minds! Majesty, do not listen to them! They will lead you to your doom!"

" 'Heretic'? 'Blasphemer'?" Boncorro turned a skeptical eye toward his chancellor. "Odd words, from one who acknowledges Satan as his master."

"Even to Satan he would be an infidel! He disregards the supernatural persons, while he pursues supernatural power! He—"

"Indeed! This Pythagoras seems to have investigated exactly the questions that I, too, pursue! Why have you never told me of him before, Rebozo?"

The chancellor turned ashen again. "Why . . . because . . . because . . ."

"Because it might sidetrack you from the Hell-bound trajectory he has plotted for you, of course," Saul said sourly. "Even I can see that, and I've never met either of you before!"

"Has he really?" King Boncorro turned to him with a stare that would have made an elephant nervous—but Saul only glared back at him. "Come off it, your Majesty! You know that everyone you meet is trying to lead you toward their own goals, for their own purposes!"

The whole throne room was dreadfully quiet.

"Why, yes, I do know that," Boncorro said easily. "It includes yourself, of course."

"Of course," Saul said with his sardonic smile.

They locked gazes for more than a minute, as the silence stretched thin. Finally, Boncorro stirred and said, "It is refreshing to speak with an honest man."

"Diogenes would have approved of him," Arouetto said.

The gimlet gaze switched to him. "Who was Diogenes?"

"Majesty, no!" Rebozo cried in agony.

King Boncorro shot him a glare. "Would you keep me from learning, then? Yes, because it might weaken your influence over me! I grow weary of this, Rebozo."

The chancellor stared at him, and there was a flash of irritation in his face—or arrogance, even—but it faded instantly, into strain and trembling.

King Boncorro held him in the focus of his glare a few seconds longer, then turned back to Matt. "Is this what you sought to accomplish by bringing your friends, Lord Wizard?"

"Frankly, no," Matt said slowly, "though I did think you and Saul would find you have a lot in common, at least intellectually."

"Then why did you bring them?"

"To issue you a challenge," Matt answered. "I challenge you to come and watch the scholar Arouetto talk with a group of young scholars for only one evening."

The throne room was silent again, but Boncorro's brow was wrinkled in study now, not in threat. Then Rebozo moaned, and Boncorro said, "I see what you would gain thereby—you hope to interest me so much that I will turn to Arouetto's teaching, and away from Rebozo's. But why should this concern you?"

"Because," Matt said, "what happens in Latruria influences my people in Merovence—and whose counsel you listen to affects how your Latrurian folk will affect my Merovencians."

"So you fear that, if I follow Rebozo's line of thought, my people will subvert yours," Boncorro said. "But I have no concern over what happens to your people—only to my own, and that only because their welfare affects mine. Why should I accept this challenge of yours?"

"Because," Matt said, "what you learn might enhance the welfare of both your people and yourself."

King Boncorro stared at him again. All the courtiers held their breath and waited, sensing that their own destinies hung in the balance.

Finally, Boncorro said, "There may be some substance in what you say—be quiet, Rebozo! But I require more evidence than your opinion alone."

Matt's stomach thought about sinking. "What kind of evidence did your Majesty have in mind?"

"Some sign of your intentions," Boncorro said, "some sign of the validity of your ideas. I will give *you* a challenge, Lord Wizard—to answer two specific questions that Rebozo has been unable to answer to my satisfaction."

"What questions are those?" the chancellor cried.

The king held up his index finger. "One: who killed my father, and why?" He raised his middle finger beside it. "And two: who killed my grandfather—and why?"

"But I have answered both!" the chancellor cried. "It was the groom Accerese who slew your father! And it was the bandits who killed your grandfather!"

Boncorro seemed not to hear him, only gazed at Matt.

"Of course," Matt said slowly, "I would have to find you the answers to both questions in such a fashion that you were satisfied that I had found the truth."

"You would."

"Don't bite," Saul said beside him. "He's dealing from a stacked deck."

"Yes, but I've got an ace up my sleeve." Matt took a deep breath and said, "Very well, your Majesty. I accept your challenge."

"No!" Rebozo cried, and Boncorro snapped, "Be still, Rebozo! If there is no validity to what he says, he will fail. How long will you need to find your answer, Lord Wizard?"

"About half an hour." Matt pushed back his sleeves. "Starting right now." He held out his hands, fingers spread to look impressive, and chanted,

> "When we are frozen up within, and quite
> The phantom of ourselves,
> To hear the world applaud the hollow ghost
> Which blames the living man."

He took a deep breath, then went from Arnold to original,

> "What goes around, comes around—all debts get paid,
> If not in cold cash, then in shame and in pain.
> A life for a life, and a save for a savior—
> Spiro, arise! Come pay back your favor!"

"You need not compel," said a sepulchral voice, "I was more than willing to aid you; you had only to ask."

There he was, floating in midair, twice as large as life—Spiro the ghost, barely visible in the dim light of the throne room. The courtiers drew back with cries of horror. On the dais, Rebozo stared, trembling; his moan turned to a very soft keening.

Matt breathed a sigh of relief. "Sorry, oldster. I didn't know what kind of morass you were going to have to wade through to get here."

"Well, there was a net of spells that needed parting," Spiro admitted. "What would you have me do, Lord Wizard? Oh, yes, I know who you really are, now! Even in Purgatory the dead know far more than they did in life!"

Someone moaned in the crowd, and several others took it up.

"Thanks, friend," Matt said, aware of the effect.

"Ghost!" There was urgency in King Boncorro's voice. "How is it you are in Purgatory, but not in fire?"

The ghost turned slowly to regard the king with hollow eyes. "I owe you no answers."

"Then do it for charity, I beseech you! I have great need of spiritual answers! Tell me, I pray!"

"Nooo," Rebozo moaned. "No, no, no . . ."

"Well, I shall," Spiro said, relenting. "An act of charity will aid me greatly now. Know, King, that I was not wicked enough to need the worst of tortures to cleanse my soul enough for Heaven. I dwell in a desert, baking under the heat of a blazing sun by day, and freezing at night. I do not complain; I deserved far worse."

"Thank you," Boncorro whispered, wide-eyed.

"You are welcome." The ghost turned back to Matt. "What do you require, Wizard?"

"I need to speak to two ghosts," Matt said. "One of them is probably in Hell, or, just possibly, Purgatory. The other is probably in Heaven; we think he was a martyr."

"I cannot make my voice reach to Heaven," said the ghost, "but I shall seek throughout Purgatory, and can call down to Hell. What is the name of the depraved soul?"

Matt took a deep breath. "King Maledicto of Latruria!"

The courtiers gasped. Rebozo's keening tapered off into shocked silence.

But Spiro gave Matt a hard smile. "He is in Purgatory; I have seen him in its most abysmal depths. I shall summon him for you."

Matt realized that King Maledicto had been older than he had thought—a lot older.

"You do not summon a king!" Boncorro cried.

"Worldly rank means nothing here," the ghost retorted, "only the goodness of the soul. Maledicto, come!"

And the king's ghost was there, smaller than Spiro's, no longer malevolent, face contorted in agony. "What would you have of me, squire?" he gasped.

"A debt to the living, and to Heaven, King-that-was!" Spiro turned to Matt. "Ask!"

"Who killed you?" Matt demanded, the hairs standing up on the back of his neck. "Who killed you, and why?"

"Why? Because I repented and sought to confess!" Maledicto's tortured eyes lit with triumph. "And through the brave defense of two knights who held off my slayer, I succeeded! They are not here; I think they have gone to Heaven, with the monk who shrived me!"

"But how is this?" King Boncorro cried. "You, who slew and tortured so many! You, who caused so much agony through your devotion to Evil! How could you have come to repent?"

"Who speaks?" The king's ghost turned. "Ah! My grandson, alive after all! I rejoice to see you living and well! Take care of your soul! Do not follow me!"

"I will not!" Boncorro assured him, seeming to regain strength by that renunciation. "Why did you repent?"

"My son's death cut the heart out of me," the ghost answered, "and your disappearance took what little spirit remained, for I saw there would be nothing left to show I had ever lived. Indeed, if I had known you lived, I might have rallied and reformed, for you were hope for the future—but without you, tomorrow was already in ashes. There was, of a sudden, no purpose in my life, for even pleasure had palled. After ten years of meditating on that matter, and nerving myself for the death I knew would follow, I repented and went to a confessor secretly. As soon as I began to confess, the Devil knew, as I had been sure he would, and sent a masked sorcerer on a fiery monster to kill me—but thanks to the intervention of my two stalwart knights, the only two of my court who I was sure were secretly religious, I managed to be shriven first—so the sorcerer slew not only me, but also the priest who had given me absolution."

"But who was the sorcerer?" Boncorro demanded.

"I know not," King Maledicto sighed. "He was masked, and my soul is not yet risen enough to know more than it did in life." Suddenly, the flames billowed up higher around him. He cried out in pain, then called, "I must go, I cannot stay longer! Bless you, my grandson! Turn to God, and to Good!"

Rebozo cried out in pain at the name of the Lord, and so did many of the courtiers. The flames billowed up about the ghost, and when they died down and faded, he was gone.

"That is all that I can do myself," Spiro's ghost told them. "As I have said, my words cannot reach to Heaven—but there is one among you whose voice can."

Boncorro stared in shock.

"Who?" Matt asked, eyeing Rebozo nervously.

"Him!" Spiro's finger lanced out at Arouetto. "His life has not been blameless, but nearly so—his only real vice has been in failing to see enough of the wickedness that is in humankind, and in not seeking out his fellow people, to do good for them! He has helped those who have come to him, but has not sought them out. Withal, his soul is still solidly good, and bound for Heaven!"

"So that is why you wished him gone." King Boncorro fixed Rebozo with a glare that held not only conviction, but also sentence. Matt glanced at the chancellor. The man was wild-eyed and trembling. Matt braced himself for trouble—a man in that state might do anything, and this was a sorcerer.

"Pray, scholar!" Spiro enjoined. "Pray that the soul of Prince Casudo may appear! The time is right, the moment crucial! If Heaven hears your prayer, the martyr may come!"

Trembling, Arouetto bowed his head over his folded hands and murmured something in Latin.

Light burst through the throne room, banishing Spiro's ghost. It faded, pulling in on itself—and a shining specter floated there before them, three times their height. It was the form of a man in his thirties, bearded and lithe, with a look of exultation in his eyes.

"Father!" King Boncorro cried, and Rebozo sank keening to his knees.

The ghost turned and looked down; then its face softened into lines of doting. "My son! How my heart swells with joy to see you grown, and not fully corrupted! Oh, forgive me for having left you lorn!"

"I did, I did long ago!" Boncorro cried. "It was not your doing, after all! But I cannot forgive your murderer, or forgive God for taking you from me!"

"Ah." Prince Casudo's face saddened. "But you must not blame God, my son. You must blame it on me, for I wanted to die."

"You . . . *wanted* to leave me?" King Boncorro's voice was a hiss; his eyes stared wide.

"Oh, no, not that, never!" The ghost's hands came up as if to embrace, to hold. "But I did wish to die, for I was racked with a temptation that I knew must be my downfall!"

"Temptation?" Boncorro stared. "*You?*"

"Oh, yes! Do not think, my son, that simply because I had resisted so many temptations already, that I did not suffer them!"

"But what kind of temptation could have swayed so saintly a man?"

"The temptations of a beautiful serving maid," Prince Casudo sighed, "brought to this court by Chancellor Rebozo, and somehow preserved from my father's clutches. Sweet she was, though no virgin, and with a face and form that would have distracted a stone! And I was no stone, my son, oh, no—but she was of too low a station for a prince to marry . . ."

"You loved a woman other than my mother?" Boncorro's face was almost white.

"Love? Ah, no, to my shame, little enough of love was there, but a great deal of lust, an ocean of lust, crashing in on the beach of my celibacy all at once, in a tidal wave! Do not think too harshly of me, I pray—remember that I had been eight years without a wife, that the chambermaid was very attractive and flirtatious, that I found myself tempted to the point of succumbing—and that I knew myself well enough to know that if I fell, I would try to justify the deed, to find some excuse for it, to persuade myself that the sin was right and good, so that I could maintain the liaison even though I could not marry her! Those excuses would have led me little by little to em-brace the Devil's blasphemies, until, believing I was damned, I would have declared myself a servant of Satan, who would then have given the throne into my hand—and rather than saving Latruria, I would have taken the kingdom with me to damnation. Nay, I resisted the beckoning of her gazes and swayings, I refused the unspoken invita-tion in her eyes, I resisted the spoken invitations that came after, but my blood pounded so furiously in my veins that I knew I could not hold out forever! I besieged the gates of Heaven with my prayers, that the Lord would remove this temptation from me! I reminded myself time and again that God would not send me a trial too great for me to bear! But at last I pled with the Lord that, if he would not remove the temptress from me nor purge the lust from my heart, that he would take me home to the safety of Heaven! This was my sin, to ask to be removed from the strife of life! It is my fault, and none of the Lord's, if He heard me and granted my prayer by relaxing His protection so that the assassin's knife delivered me from my own weakness!"

"Weakness indeed!" Boncorro cried. "It was given to you to care for a kingdom, and to care for a son who would one day also care for that kingdom! How *dare* you desert me so! How dare you desert your kingdom!"

"But I never did, never truly!" the ghost pleaded. "Oh, aye, I quit this life, and could not be with you in the flesh, nor hold you when you were racked with grief nor counsel you in your confusion—but I was always with you as closely as I could be, ever hovering near to strengthen your mind and soothe your heart! Oh, I have not preserved you completely from Satan's wiles—but if your heart was in turmoil and you felt a sudden calmness, that was me, channeling God's grace to you! If you dreamed a nightmare, racked with confusion and fear, and I appeared to banish the monsters and show you magical wonders—that was more than a dream, it was I in the spirit! If you were tempted to hate, tempted to revenge, and a cool impulse stayed your hand and calmed you, that impulse was mine! I have never truly deserted you, my son, but have always been with you, in your heart and in your mind and, as much as I could, in your soul, strengthening you against temptation and counseling you against the sins of lust. It was I, it was always I, and I shall always be there to guide you and to give you solace, if you do not truly forsake the Lord God!"

Boncorro sat, staring at the ghost, as the color slowly came back into his face. Then, finally, his form relaxed and a single tear flowed from his eye. "God bless you, my father! I forgive you again, for in your place, I could have done no less, to save my kingdom—and my son, for I can only imagine the nightmare my life would have become if you had declared for Evil!"

"But can you forgive God?" the ghost whispered.

Silence answered him, a silence that held the whole throne room and stretched on and on as young King Boncorro stared up at him, a boy no longer, but a man in the fullness of his strength—of body, of mind, and of will.

Then at last he spoke, and his voice was low. "Yes, I can—but only because it has just dawned on me, through your talk, and . . . was that you, moving in my heart just now, to open it to grace?"

The ghost did not answer, but his eyes shone.

"It comes dimly to me," Boncorro went on, "that God may have worked for the best of us all—that my own orphaning has certainly made me the man that I am today, and that God may have wanted that, for His own reasons—but perhaps also for the welfare of the people of Latruria."

Behind him, Rebozo winced.

"I can begin to forgive Him, at least," Boncorro went on, "though I may need to understand a great deal more of His plan before I can seek to make amends. Tell me more, that it may make greater sense to me! Why were you murdered?"

"You have guessed it, and guessed aright," the ghost told him. "As soon as my murderer realized that I intended to turn to God, to turn my whole country to God if I gained the throne, he bent all efforts to assuring that I would not do so. Assassins began to appear about me—"

"The groom Accerese?"

"No, not he! Never he! The poor man only found my body—he did not wield the knife! Nay, he dwells here in glory among the Saints—for the small sins of his life were redeemed by the pain of his death, and his cleaving unto God until the last!"

"So much for your tortures, Rebozo," Boncorro said, not even looking over his shoulder at the crumpled man who winced and whimpered at every mention of the Deity's name. "But God protected you, my father?"

"He did," the ghost said, "but I also exercised unceasing vigilance, ever wary, and foiled many an attacker myself, by an adroit move and the blocking of a blow. One learns such things, growing up in a court filled with intrigue."

"Yes," Boncorro said softly, "one does."

"It is even so for you, my son. When your chancellor realized you, too, intended to be a reformer, he set the assassins on your trail—but you proved too wary for him, aye, and your magic too powerful."

Now Boncorro did swivel about to glare at Rebozo, who snapped upright, hands raised to fend him off. "Your Majesty, no! I will admit that I did set the hounds at first, but when I saw you would not turn religious, I was reassured and called them off! I bent my efforts thenceforth to corrupting you, only showing you the ways of ecstasy, the pleasures of power and debauchery and revelry!"

"And you made good progress, did you not?" Boncorro's gaze was steely.

"Yes, until this Merovencian spell caster came!" Rebozo cried. "It would not have been necessary to seek your death!"

"No, not at all," Boncorro said grimly. "I listened to you; yes, I yielded to temptation and gathered a harem of wenches! I condoned prostitution and its coercing of women into degradation! Oh, you did well for your master, Rebozo, but I begin to see that he was not me!" He turned back to the ghost. "Who killed you, my father?"

"No, my son!" The ghost held up his hands in supplication. "I would not have you seek revenge! That path leads to Hell!"

Boncorro stared up at him for a minute, eyes narrowed. Then he said, "Your rebuke is wise—I shall not revenge!" But he squared his shoulders, raising his chin with an air of authority his father had never shown. "But I am the king, as you never were, and I must render justice, as you never did! Tell me, for the sake of that justice—who murdered my grandfather? Who murdered you?"

"How could he know who slew your grandfather?" Rebozo cried, trembling. "He was dead!"

"Dead, but in Heaven—and though the Saints may not know everything, they know a great deal more than the living. Is it not true, my father? Do you not know, and that without a shadow of doubt, who killed Grandfather?"

"I do," Casudo's ghost admitted. "It was the same man who murdered me. He slew me when I proved to be incorruptible, not knowing that a week longer would have seen my fall from grace; he killed King Maledicto when he found him confessing his sins, then instantly became the loudest mourner of all."

"Who was it, then?" Boncorro's voice was steel, and it was no longer a son speaking to a father, but one young man speaking to another.

"Alas!" the ghost cried. "It was the single man most trusted by your grandfather and yourself—"

"You lie, foul phantom!" Rebozo screamed, leveling his staff.

"It was the Lord Chancellor Rebozo!" the ghost cried.

Chapter
Twenty-Six

Rebozo screamed a cursing verse in the archaic language, and the staff spat green fire. "Die, foul phantom! Get thee hence!"

Prince Casudo only folded his arms across his breast, closing his eyes and tilting his head back in prayer as the flames wrapped about him.

But King Boncorro glared at the chancellor, his lips moving, unheard in the midst of Rebozo's maniacal screams of hatred—and a giant snake coiled up from the floor to wrap Rebozo in its coils. Rebozo stared at the flat wedge head, only a foot from his face, and screamed in horror before the snake's coils choked off his breath. His staff fell clattering to the floor, and the green fire stopped, showing Prince Casudo's form still there, shining more brightly than ever.

King Boncorro rose from his throne, eyes narrowed under lowering brows, and stalked toward the chancellor, slipping a stiletto from his belt.

"No, your Majesty!" Rebozo rasped with the last shreds of breath. "This phantom is not real! It is only a phantasm made by the scholar Arouetto!"

"How great a fool do you think me?" King Boncorro glanced at the snake. "Loosen enough to give him a taste of breath! He shall die by my knife, not your coils." Then, to Rebozo again, "He is no wizard, but only a scholar—and has nothing to gain!"

"He has the Knowledge! If he knows the way, he can do the deed! And he has everything to gain, for he is the true and legitimate heir to the throne of Latruria."

Boncorro froze. Then he whipped about, glaring at Arouetto. "Is this true?"

"Be sure it is true." Sir Guy stepped forward, his hand on his sword, just a step from interposing himself between Arouetto and the young king. "He is the last descendant of the last Caesar."

"But I do not wish to rule!" Arouetto protested. "I have no taste for court life and less for intrigue! I abdicate, here and now, where all may hear me, in favor of King Boncorro, for his reign may cure the ills of Latruria! I wish only to be left to my books in peace!"

"I have heard it," Sir Guy said, "and I will abide by it. He is no longer the heir. The throne is yours."

Boncorro scowled down at them for a very long minute. Then he said, "I thank you, scholar. I shall keep the throne—but you may not have your life of peace, for I require your services and your advice. Rebozo has betrayed me three times over. He shall die for that. You shall be my new chancellor." Then he turned, raising his knife to execute the sentence.

"No, my son!" cried the ghost. "Do not send him to Hell! Let him confess his sins, let him repent!"

Boncorro hesitated, the dagger poised. "It is foolish to loose a snake to strike at your heel, my father."

"Do not loose him! Find him a priest this very day, let him confess, then behead him and burn his body! But do not burden your soul with his damnation!"

"This is not prudent," Boncorro said.

"The way of virtue is frequently imprudent, but always wise! Do this for me, my son—though I know I do not deserve it of you!"

"You deserve it ten times over." Boncorro sheathed his knife. "Your desertion does not outweigh ten years of love and care of a very small child. He shall have his chance for Heaven." He gestured, shouting a quick verse, and the snake dwindled, turning into iron, and clanking hard about Rebozo's wrists and ankles as fetters and chains.

But Rebozo had been given the respite he had needed to recover. With one quick motion he stooped and caught up his staff, crying, "Now, all my old henchmen! Strike, or know your doom! Smite this princeling, or die at the stake!" Then he shouted an unintelligible phrase, snapping the staff out toward Boncorro—and the snake reappeared, coiling up about the king.

Sir Guy shouted, "Havoc!" and sprang up on the dais, his sword whirling toward the serpent's head. Boncorro saw him and ignored the reptile, gesturing and shouting his own rhyme . . .

But his shout was answered by fifty others, as courtiers stepped forward, slipping wands from their sleeves and chanting verses in the archaic language—even as a fiery monster appeared between Rebozo and the king, blasting Boncorro with its fire as the traitor leaped astride the creature his magic had called. But flame met a thousand glinting points that rushed toward Rebozo, and caught the monster instead. It screamed with rage, thrashing in pain, but leaped at the king . . .

And a score of other monsters, lamias, gorgons, and nightmares of horn and sting and teeth, screamed in delight and converged on Matt and his friends, while another score rushed toward Boncorro.

Saul spread his hands, shouting,

> "Où sont les neiges d'antan?
> Les laissez-les faire ces monstres
> Devienent froids, gelés et durs!"

Matt shouted out,

> "Into the cradle, endlessly rocking,
> Go the horrible creatures immediately flocking!
> Bars o'er those cradles are instantly locking!"

Half of the monsters slowed, halted, and stood frozen; the others shrank down, their shrieks of dismay rising up the scale as cradles appeared behind them. They fell backward and in; iron grids clashed shut over the tops of the cradles, holding them in.

But other sorcerers were shouting other verses, and fires sprang up all about them. The ceiling rained knives and swords, the floor sprouted vipers and scorpions. Matt and Saul spun about and about, trying to quell one horror after another, yanking out verses in a very eclectic blend of classic poetry and TV commercials. Cans of insecticide appeared about them, sprinkling death on the vermin; fire extinguishers sprang into existence to combat the flames; giant steel umbrellas sent the cutlery cascading. But they were on the defensive, scarcely managing to keep up; the sorcerers definitely had the initiative.

On the dais, Boncorro was whirling, shouting verses in old tongues and new, sweat running down his face as he countered one nightmare form after another. He made his floor turn from mire back into solid stone, and set up dozens of shields and swords to parry and fence those weapons that Rebozo brought into existence.

Meanwhile, Sir Guy was manfully battering at Rebozo's steed, taking its blasts of fire on a shield that magically dispersed the creature's flames instead of conducting them. Sir Guy was singed and cut in three places on his face, but the monster was bleeding flame from a dozen, screaming in rage and frustration, for the knight danced about it, never in one place long enough to bite—and, worse, he was singing!

> *"Ran! Tan! Terre et ciel!*
> *Terre et ciel, et sang vermeil!*
> *Ran! Tan! Terre et ciel!*
> *Bois le vin gaulois!"*

It was magic all his own, warrior's magic, and the courtiers who weren't wizards paused in their pressing back toward the doorways, heads coming up, wide-eyed.

Matt took his cue.

> *"Allons, enfants de la patrie!*
> *Le jour de gloire est arrivé!*
> *Contre nous de la tyrannie!*
> *L'étandard sanglant est levé!*
> *L'étandard sanglant est levé!*
> *Entendez-vous, dans la campagne,*
> *Mugir, ces féroces soldats,*
> *Qui vienent jusque dans nos bras!*
> *Egorgez nos fils, nos compagnes!*
> *Aux armes, mes citoyens!*
> *Formez vos bataillons!*
> *Marchons, marchons, quand le sang impur*
> *Abreuve nos sillons!"*

It wasn't their language, but the words worked anyway, and the zeal imparted by the song. With a massive shout, the courtiers turned on the sorcerers, who turned to blast *them* . . .

A maddened yowl broke from the archway, and the manticore sprang in, fur bristling. It flew into the sorcerers, double jaws closing on one after another and tossing them aside. The remaining sorcerers screamed with fear and shrank back—but, unfortunately, so did the rest of the courtiers.

Then a massed shout thundered from the archway, overriding the noise from within, and a hundred knights strode into the throne room, swords mincing the sorcerers' monsters and cutting a way through to the sorcerers themselves. Behind them a golden-haired fury strode, a golden circlet about her helmet, shouting in rage, "Slay the foul fiends who would imperil my love! Rally to the Lord Wizard, to the Witch Doctor, and to the Black Knight!"

Behind her, Stegoman's huge head shot in through the door. A dozen sorcerers shouted and sprang to block his way, wands swirling, but the dragon roared in fury, and the sorcerers howled and fell, rolling in flames. Unarmed courtiers sprang aside, and the dragon charged toward the dais as hundreds of men-at-arms came running into the throne room to strike the sorcerers down.

Rebozo's monster saw Stegoman and sprang to meet him with a howl like a siren. The dragon roared in answer, and flame blasted flame. But behind them King Boncorro, undistracted now, turned on his traitorous chancellor and wove an unseen net in the air as he sang. Rebozo shouted in alarm, flourishing his staff and shrieking a verse—but before he could finish it, ruddy flames blasted up about him, freezing him in agony, and for one brief instant a dark horned form seemed to loom behind him before the flames abruptly ceased, leaving only a pile of ashes.

The fiery monster disappeared at the same instant, leaving only a fading shriek behind it—and every sorcerer in the hall screamed in pain, back arching, and fell rolling to the floor in agony.

Sir Guy lowered his sword, panting, and told the king, "Well struck, Your Majesty!"

"But I did not," Boncorro panted, staring at the heap of ashes with widened eyes. "My spell only inspired the agony of my traitorous courtiers! The flame that took him, that was not mine!"

"Even so," Sir Guy said grimly. "When the queen's army burst in, the end was clear, and the Devil gave his old punishment for failure."

"Queen Alisande?" Boncorro looked up and saw the blond avenging angel wrapped in the arms of the Lord Wizard, who broke off murmuring endearments long enough to say, "You know, there's something to be said for an army."

"Yes, and I thank your Majesty for its use." King Boncorro looked up at the ghost, who stood staring down at the carnage, aghast. "Mercy to so depraved a soul as that is unwise."

"No," the spirit muttered, shaking its head in denial. "It is always right, always! And a king must always do what is right!"

But Boncorro shook his head. "I think that there are times when a king must do what is prudent instead—and you must forgive me, my father, but on this Earth, I am called to be a king, not a saint."

Matt and King Boncorro lingered unobtrusively in the doorway of the twenty-by-twenty studio, watching the sculptor at work in the light from the wide northern windows. After a little while, Matt moved onward, beckoning to the king, who nodded and followed. When they were away from the door, Boncorro said, low-voiced, "His progress is amazing! And you say Arouetto has given him only a very little criticism and suggestion this past fortnight?"

"Only a little," Matt confirmed, "but the kid paid attention. He respects Arouetto, you see."

"Even though our scholar admits he is no sculptor?"

"No—*because* he admits he is no sculptor. But he does claim to be a connoisseur, and no one disputes it. At least, not twice—though whether that's because they're dazzled by his arguments, or just don't want to sit through another hour of his explaining the merits of various paintings and statues, I don't know."

At another doorway, they paused to watch several painters at work; at a third to watch a string quartet practicing; and a fourth time to watch singers rehearsing an opera. As they went on, Matt said, "Arouetto even has hopes of persuading the actors from the marketplace to try performing a script one of his students is writing. It will take some doing, convincing them to memorize lines instead of making it up from a scenario as they go along, but I think he might manage it."

"He is a most persuasive man," Boncorro admitted.

"He is," Matt agreed. "I'm amazed that he manages to stop persuading when he's teaching . . . here."

They paused in another doorway to see Arouetto sitting in a circle with the young men and women from Escribo's farm, discussing an issue with great earnestness.

"But there is as much sense in seeing the world as divided into male and female principles, as in seeing it divided into Good and Evil!" Escribo maintained.

"Nonsense!" cried Lelio. "There is good in the world, and there is evil! Our teacher's recent victory is reason enough to believe that!"

"No one denies it," Berylla replied. "It is a question of which is greater, that is all."

Lelio stared. "Do you say that the female principle can be greater than Good?"

"No—that it can exist *within* the principle of Good!" She turned to Arouetto. "Could that not be valid?"

"Perhaps," Arouetto said, "if you remember that, in the Far Eastern dualism, Good proceeds from male and female existing in balance, and Evil springs from one or the other being too prominent."

"Evil being a lack of balance, and Good being balance?" One of the girls looked up sharply. "That has a familiar ring! The Greeks?"

Arouetto nodded, visibly restraining his glee. "Flaminia, you seem to remember the quotation."

" 'Moderation in all things,' " Flaminia said, eyes wide in sudden understanding, "including moderation!"

"That is it," Arouetto said. "But tell me, could there be any connection between that principle and the motto, 'Know thyself'?"

"Far more than a motto, teacher!" another youth objected.

"It is indeed." Arouetto's eyes shone. "But how do *you* see that, Arno?"

As Arno began to answer, Pascal's head suddenly snapped up, his eyes widening in amazement. He thrust himself to his feet and strode off to a writing desk in a corner, where he began to scribble furiously.

"Thus the poet gains inspiration," Boncorro murmured, shaking his head in wonder. "This is something I can never truly understand, Lord Wizard!"

"That's all right, your Majesty—for all their talk about it, none of them can really understand the ordering of a state." Matt turned away, beckoning Boncorro out of earshot. "A few other scholars have already begun to hear of this villa and have come to talk and teach—in just two weeks! One is teaching rhetoric, another is teaching logic, and a third is teaching mathematics and music."

"An odd combination."

"No, he's the Pythagorean in the bunch. I'm trying to get him to tell me about Pythagoras' ideas about magic, but he claims the mystic master didn't believe in the stuff—he just taught how the world worked and the parts interacted."

"But if you understand that, you can work out ways to make wonders happen!"

"He doesn't realize that, fortunately. The man's a genius, but I don't think he has very good judgment." He glanced back at Arouetto. "I don't think your new chancellor is doing a very good job in government."

"He has already tried to resign, but I persuaded him to be chancellor only of this new center of study. He is ambitious; he hopes to build a community of scholars who will, together, pursue all human knowledge."

"Is he going to call it a 'university'?"

"If you mention the word, I am sure he will adopt it. Still, he is generous in his advice, when I ask it—and I have begun to select other men to do the work of the state. But I shall never again give any one man such broad powers as I entrusted to Rebozo—so Arouetto shall keep the title of chancellor, and I shall develop others for the men who do the work of government."

"Wise policy. You have very *good* judgment, your Majesty."

"I appreciate the praise, Lord Wizard." But Matt could see the young king brace himself against flattery.

"Well, I'm glad you accepted my challenge and watched Arouetto teach, at least—and even gladder that you seized upon the idea of bringing them all into the castle without my having to mention it."

"Which, I am sure, you would have—but there was so much value evident in the idea, that even I could not blind myself to it." Boncorro smiled. "Already, the noblemen have begun to take artists into their households, and their wives have begun to invite scholars to their social gatherings. There is a positive stampede to catch a tame poet!"

"Which means there will be a lot of charlatans showing up, very fast. Might I encourage your Majesty to test very thoroughly anyone claiming to be cultured?"

"Wise advice." Boncorro didn't say he had already thought of it— he only said, "I must become as much a connoisseur as Arouetto— but I think the becoming will be a joy, and an excellent means to rest and refresh my spirit after a day of intrigue and striving."

"There *is* something to be said for night school," Matt admitted. "Uh, I've, uh, taken the liberty of strolling through the marketplace in my minstrel's costume, and out into the suburbs . . ."

"Spying again, Lord Wizard?"

"Yes, but for *you* this time."

"And for Queen Alisande, of course."

"Well, of *course*! And already I'm hearing peasants singing arias while they work, and seeing people really beginning to look at all those pieces of statues left over from the Caesars. People are even beginning to debate what is Right and Virtuous on the street corners. Of course, one of those corners is in the red-light district . . ."

"But even there, the discussion should render some improvement in the way they treat one another." Boncorro nodded. "I can no longer deny it, Lord Wizard—my actions have been aimed at making people good, for my father was good, and that is the quality I will always admire secondmost."

"Second? May I ask what the first is?"

"Strength," said the king. "Survival. But come, Lord Wizard—we will be late in meeting the pope's ambassador."

Matt exchanged glad greetings with Brother Thomas, then introduced him to the king, and right away the whole meeting had a much less formal tone. Before they could even mention any matters of state or the purpose of the visit, Matt told Boncorro, "Brother Thomas is studying the notion that magical power is not good or evil in itself, and doesn't come from either God or Satan—that only the knowledge of how to use it comes from Good or Evil, and makes the magic what it is."

"Really!" said Boncorro with keen interest.

"Ah—well, yes, but I may not speak of that, your Majesty," Brother Thomas said uncomfortably. "The pope has not given me leave and is not sure that what I say can be correct."

"Correct?" Boncorro gave him a hard smile. "But surely, just between two men who pursue knowledge, we may speak of it! It is not as if you were going to preach it from the rooftops! Now tell me, if magic does not come from God, what are miracles?"

"Oh, something else altogether!" Brother Thomas fell without even realizing it, and the two of them were off into an hour's conversation that had overtones of argument, but undertones of keen enjoyment. They finally got around to mentioning the pope's objectives over dinner.

"His Holiness sends his thanks for freeing himself and his clergy, your Majesty, and allowing them to preach openly, without fear of persecution."

"It is my pleasure." Boncorro smiled. "And quite possible, now that most of the leading sorcerers in the land have revealed themselves in trying to aid Rebozo, and have been dealt with. Tell his Holiness that I am pleased by his attentions."

"I shall," said Brother Thomas. "He hopes that you will return this visit of courtesy and come to the Vatican to visit him."

The room was silent. Finally, the king spoke. "I thank his Holiness, but I fear that matters of state are too demanding at this time. I will send *my* ambassador, however."

"Ah," Brother Thomas said with regret. "You are still shy of religion, then?"

"Let us say that I am not yet ready to become an ardent Catholic, Brother Thomas—but I have begun to see a great deal of merit in many of your Church's views and am beginning to think God may exist after all. However, I will invite his Holiness to appoint a chaplain to my court—provided he is yourself."

"Your Majesty!" Brother Thomas said, dazed. "I am not worthy! I am not even a priest!"

"Then perhaps you had better be ordained," King Boncorro said shortly. "Now, good friar—you were saying that mathematics is, in essence, only a language for describing how the universe works. Might it not, then, be a means of effecting magic?"

And they were off again, with Brother Thomas explaining that trying to understand the universe was one more way of trying to understand its Creator, and that mathematics, therefore, could be another route to God.

Matt leaned over to Saul and said, "Maybe we ought to introduce the printing press. After all, we want this learning to reach the masses, don't we?"

"Maybe we shouldn't," Saul retorted. "Bring in the printing press, and your university will degenerate into 'publish or perish.' "

Their last day began with an impressive ceremony in the throne room, at which Boncorro knighted Pascal. Then, while he was still dazed, he declared the poet and Flaminia to be man and wife. Dazzled even more, the poet left the king's presence to begin his honeymoon.

Then they all went out of the castle into the bailey, where Alisande's knights stood bridled and ready, and Stegoman huffed beside Sir Guy, impatient to be off.

But Manny lay purring, watching Pascal and Flaminia move toward the entrance tunnel. He rose to his feet. "I must follow where his spell leads me, Wizard."

"Well, somebody's got to keep him out of trouble. His Majesty has sent word through all his reeves that any farmer who sells you a cow can just bill his Majesty. But don't stuff yourself, okay?"

"I shall be circumspect," the manticore promised. "Farewell, Wizard! Summon me at need!" He bounded off after the young couple, who were too busy gazing into one another's eyes to notice him.

Matt had to admit he wasn't entirely sorry to part company with the manticore. All those teeth made him nervous.

Then he turned and felt the fire of instant jealousy. King Boncorro was paying entirely too much attention to his sister monarch—and the attentions were anything but brotherly.

His eye gleamed as he bowed to the young queen, her habergeon again lashed behind her saddle, standing demurely clad in a gown that nonetheless should have been classified as a diplomatic weapon. Boncorro kissed her hand, and may be excused if he lingered, for she was very beautiful.

May be. Matt had to remind himself that the king wasn't really making advances—but his blood boiled anyway.

"I regret that you could not accept my invitation to stay longer, your Majesty," King Boncorro said.

"I am honored, your Majesty." Alisande gave the handsome young man a roguish smile, making Matt's blood boil. "But I must needs tend my own kingdom, and I have been absent too long."

"Ah, well!" Boncorro sighed. "Perhaps I might return this visit?"

"We will always be glad to welcome yourself and your knights at our court, your Majesty—my husband and I together."

A flash of irritation crossed Boncorro's features, but he took it in good part, turning to Matt and saying, "I suppose I should count it a compliment, Lord Wizard, that you have never allowed me more than a minute's conversation alone with your enchanting wife."

"A compliment . . . ? Oh! Yes. Of course. Definitely," Matt said.

"Well, I must despair of the opportunity, then," Boncorro sighed, "for I would not wish the early death of the Lord Wizard, when he has aided me so vastly—even though that may not have been his intention."

"A live ally is always worth more than a dead rival," Sir Guy pointed out.

"True, true," Boncorro admitted. "But if you should have a daughter, your Majesty, and if she is as beautiful as yourself, I will pray for an introduction."

"For your son, perhaps, your Majesty." Alisande dimpled. "But first I must see to an heir."

"Well, we're working on it," Matt reminded her.

"No," said Alisande, looking directly into his eyes. "*I* am. Your part is done."

"What do you mean?" Matt frowned, and the jealousy boiled over. "What is this? One look at a handsome king, and I'm suddenly redundant? I mean, I know he's—"

Sir Guy coughed. "Lord Wizard," he said, "I think her Majesty's meaning has escaped you."

"What do you mean? She was saying my part in it was—" Matt broke off as realization hit him, and stared at Alisande.

She smiled, as much with relief as with joy.

"Oh, darling!" Matt gathered her to him. "Why didn't you *tell* me?"

ABOUT THE AUTHOR

Christopher Stasheff spent his early childhood in Mount Vernon, New York, but spent the rest of his formative years in Ann Arbor, Michigan. He has always had difficulty distinguishing fantasy from reality and has tried to compromise by teaching college. When teaching proved too real, he gave it up in favor of writing full time.

He tends to pre-script his life, but can't understand why other people never get their lines right.